SHAWN SAMUELSON HENRY

MADE IN MAINE

A NOVEL

MADE IN MAINE

SHAWN SAMUELSON HENRY

Woodhall Press | Norwalk, CT

Woodhall Press, 81 Old Saugatuck Road, Norwalk, CT 06855
WoodhallPress.com

Cover design: Asha Hossain
Layout artist: LJ Mucci

Library of Congress Cataloging-in-Publication Data available

ISBN 978-1-954907-80-5 (paper: alk paper)
ISBN 978-1-954907-81-2 (electronic)

First Edition
Distributed by Independent Publishers Group
(800) 888-4741

Printed in the United States of America

For all who feel lonely or ashamed or unlovable because of how you look, where you live, whom you love, or who you are.

You are valuable.
You are worthy.
You matter.

1
LUNA

When I look in the mirror and turn my head sideways, the monster disappears. I almost look normal. Like you can actually notice the sea-glass green of my eye, the freckles on my cheek, the straight line of my nose, the delicate curve of my ear. Like you're not totally distracted by the other half of my face—the one that would be too gross and scary to be made into a kid's Halloween mask. Like I could walk into a restaurant and no one would notice. Like I wouldn't get the heads whipping around, pretending they hadn't just done a major double take and then totally lost their appetite. Or the parents shushing their little kids when they ask what happened to my face. Keeping my head turned, I grab my brush and sing "Be Our Guest" softly so Temmie won't hear me, as if I am swirling about with the dishes on stage. Leaping and twirling and dipping and swooping. And the

Broadway theater is packed full of people who adore me, are in awe of me, even a little bit in love with the magical, talented, gorgeous Belle.

Then I swivel my head and look in the mirror full on. And I'm back to being the Beast. My mic becomes a brush again, which I use to pull as much hair over the right side of my face as I can. But all my hair can't cover a birthmark the size of Texas and the color of ripe plums.

I don't go to restaurants. All the musicals I've seen are on a screen at home. I only go to school because I have to. So I always wear a hoodie, even when it's 80 degrees. The good news is that I live in northern Maine, where it's hardly ever 80 degrees.

Sometimes—actually, most of the time—I feel like my mere presence offends people. Like having to look at me is some sort of punishment. I'll either make them sick or my face will haunt their nightmares. But here's the thing: I don't blame them at all. People naturally want to look at things that are pretty and symmetrical. And it's honestly difficult to take in my face without feeling fear or revulsion.

I've read that ugly babies are only attractive in their doting mothers' eyes. I guess I went way beyond ugly. Beyond revolting. To horrifying.

Because even my mother couldn't stand the disgusting sight of me. That's why she gave me away right after I was born.

2

HUNTER

When I was a kid, I thought my dad was the coolest person in the whole world. He'd come home from his job at the mill and yell, "Hunter? What time is it?" And I knew the answer because there was only one answer. "I . . . t's Hoops Time!" And we'd go outside and play basketball, no matter how hot or cold it was, no matter if it was dark or if we both were hungry. Only when it was pouring rain or snow would Dad allow us to play inside, using a Nerf ball and net.

Then we'd make dinner, together. My job was to choose two plates from our mismatched collection and make one contribution to the meal. I'd carefully cut cucumbers or stir cocoa powder into milk or add blueberries to pancakes, and Dad would always say that my part of the meal was definitely the most delicious.

And then he'd read to me. About Michael Jordan. Or LeBron James. Or Steph Curry. And right before bed, he'd ask me to tell him a story about something that happened in my day. While I talked, he drew a picture of a scene from my story, and we'd tape it to my bedroom wall. Me sledding down Oak Hill. Me making twenty free throws in a row. Me holding our neighbor's lamb. It was like an art gallery of my life.

Then the mill closed. And slowly things in our town went to shit. At first it was subtle. Like a foreclosing here, a pickup for sale there. Then I noticed more kids like me showing up early for free breakfast at school, saying they couldn't sleep or they were sick of their mother's oatmeal. More people were hunting for food, both out in the woods and in dumpsters behind the two restaurants in town. And cars were in the bar parking lot all day long, not just at night. And I know this sounds cruel, but I heard a lot of people got rid of their pets. I didn't ask how. I didn't want to know.

When the mill closed, so did my dad.

Everything changed. I still play basketball, but never at home. And now I hate it when my dad comes to my games, because he's usually drunk. He yelled at the ref so much at one game that he was ejected. I don't want to remember, but it's like tattooed on my brain. "You been calling 'em for the other side all night long but nothing for our side! Goddamned nothing! Our kids are getting slammed, and you ain't calling nothing. You blind or something, ref? Well, open your damn eyes and look at my hand. You see this?"

Watching him stumble out, still giving the finger to the ref, was probably the worst moment of my life. *Jesus, Dad, what are you doing? Do you get how humiliating this is? For me? For you?* I wanted to tell him to stop but I was paralyzed, like when you can't move in a nightmare. So I just stood on the court, holding the ball, with sweat pouring down my face. Everyone was mesmerized by the drama, like it was some kind of horror movie.

But then Conor Cooper put his hand on my shoulder and said, "Geez, sorry, dude."

I punched him in the mouth.

Coach benched me for the rest of the game.

I sat there with my head down and wanted to disappear. I could feel the stares and the pity and even the mean laughter smothering me. How could I face my teammates after this? My girlfriend? Everyone in the stands watching me and my dad go apeshit? Coop?

Coop's my best friend. I don't know what came over me. I mean, he was just trying to be nice. So why the hell did I hit him?

I guess I'm as much of a jerk as my dad.

3
LUNA

I dance.

When I am dancing, I can forget. That my face is so gross, that I have no friends, that my mother hated me, that I don't really have like a future. Everything drops away and I am muscles and bone, sinew and strength. Music fills my body from the tips of my toes, where I am *en pointe*, all the way to the ends of my fingers. The music lifts my entire being and we become one, lofty and ethereal. I feel like a raptor gliding on an air current. Up and up and up. Where my body is free, where I am faceless, where I am happy.

This morning my aunt makes me eggs for breakfast. Usually I grab a granola bar and eat it on the way to school, but today is different. She pushes aside a pile of bills and ads to make room for my plate on the kitchen table and then plunks heavily in the wooden chair across from me. My aunt never sits down in the morning. Something's up.

Temmie is my mother's oldest sister, who took me in when my mother threw me away. She was already forty when my mother got pregnant with me. Their other two siblings were married with kids of their own and lived down by the coast. Temmie was working as an international flight attendant, but she quit and took a job at the mill when she adopted me. She called herself "Aunt Emmie," but I guess her oldest nephew shortened that to "Temmie." She's been Temmie for so long that most people have forgotten her real name. Now she's fifty-seven and her knees ache, especially when it's cold. That's most of the year. When she talks about traveling in Japan and Finland and Brazil, I wonder if she wishes she'd never stopped flying. Never adopted me. She could be, I don't know, looking at paintings in the Louvre or something on a day off; instead she's sitting in a farmhouse kitchen feeding her niece who looks like the messed-up offspring of Frankenstein's monster.

"Luna, I'm going to give it to you straight." Temmie doesn't waste time on small talk. She's honest and blunt, which sometimes gets her in trouble, but she doesn't care.

I take a bite of egg and swallow. "Ohh-kay?"

"The severance money the mill owners gave us is running out."

I put my fork down. Talking about money always makes my stomach hurt.

"I've been looking for work, but no one is much interested in hiring a middle-aged woman who can't walk very well. And everyone from the mill is in the same leaky boat. If we're careful, we can live off my airline pension. It's not much, but we'll get by. And the chickens and the gardens help. But we're going to have to cut out dance lessons."

I get it. I really do. It's so expensive to raise a kid, and she never planned to have one. But I can't help the tears that fill my eyes. I blink quickly, but my eyes pool up again, and I feel so stupid and ungrateful. The dance studio is the only place I go where I don't try to hide. The other three girls in my level have known me forever and are used to my face. Temmie told me that the dance instructor fled from an abusive relationship in New York and was kind of hiding out in our teeny town in Maine. Which may be why the studio feels so safe, like the instructor truly gets me. But cutting out dance? It feels like she's cutting off my oxygen. I know that sounds melodramatic, and I hate myself for being so selfish. But now what? What on earth will I do instead? I should get a job, but if no one is hiring a gimpy fifty-seven-year-old woman, they sure won't hire someone who looks like me.

I just nod and swipe at my face.

"Okay, then. Finish up those eggs and get ready for school." With a groan Temmie stands, pats my head with a sad smile, and limps out to feed the chickens. Without turning around, she mutters, "I'm sorry, kiddo." Softly, but I hear it.

I scrape my eggs into the compost bucket.

I don't even bother brushing my hair before shoving my head into my hoodie. Whatever.

4
HUNTER

I stop at Molly's on the way to school for a cinnamon roll. I already had a protein shake this morning, but there wasn't much other food around and I'm starving. And I'm really tired of school breakfasts. Sometimes Dad just kind of forgets about grocery shopping. Or that's what he says. That he forgot. The truth is he hates using his SNAP card in public. Like it makes him weak or something, using government assistance. So when he does shop, he goes right before the store closes, when there's no one else in there. I can tell he's embarrassed, the way he avoids looking at the cashier and kind of hunches over to shove the card into the reader. It sucks, losing your job and feeling so helpless. But he's not alone, even though he seems to think he is. I mean, most of my friends use SNAP cards. But my dad would rather hunt. If he doesn't get anything, I go hungry. I try to eat a lot at lunch in case there's no dinner at home. It's not great—the cafeteria food, I mean—but I don't care. I need the calories to get through practice.

The bells attached to the door jingle when I yank it open. I stand for a minute before going to the counter, just taking in the warmth and the aroma of coffee and cinnamon and hazelnut. Molly's is like the town center; I'm not surprised to see so many people already hanging out there, even though it's only 7:30. A few people I know nod or wave.

Teo comes running up to me with a huge grin on his face. I love this kid. I grab him and lift him up above my head, like I always do, and he laughs.

"Whaddya say-o, Teo?" I say as I bring him down and swing him up again. "You gonna have a good day-o, Teo?"

When I lower him again, he pats his tummy and says, "Mayo."

"You like to eat mayo, Teo?" It's our little routine, one we do every time we meet. It's dumb, I know, but he loves it. Or at least I think he does, 'cause he always laughs.

Teo waits until I've got my cinnamon roll, then he grabs my hand and drags me over to his table, where his mom is sitting. She has her hands wrapped around her mug. She gives me a like grateful smile. "How are you, Hunter?"

"Hey, Miz Callahan. I'm okay, thanks. Cold." I rub my hands together. They are still red even though I kept them in my pockets on my walk here. "You doing all right?"

Ms. Callahan nods. "We're fine. Someone decided to get up at five this morning and work on his drum solo." She smiles at Teo and rubs his head.

I've heard the story about how Teo and Bridget Callahan became a family. Teo is the biological son of one of the migrant workers who came several summers ago to pick blueberries. When the workers left to go south, Teo was placed on Ms. Callahan's back porch in a blueberry crate. He was only a few days old. A scrap of paper was tucked into the blanket he was wrapped in: "*Por favor ama a mi hijo. Ensenale sobre dios.*" (Please love my son. Teach him about God.)

It's little wonder she picked Ms. Callahan. She is seriously the kindest person I've ever met. She refused to bring the baby to Child Protective Services. Said he was a sign from God. I guess a lot of people were worried and warned her that he would need tons of special attention because of his Down syndrome, but nothing could change her mind. Five years later, she's obviously doing a great job, 'cause everybody knows Teo. And everybody loves him.

I give Teo one last high five and crouch down so our eyes are the same level. "Hey, Teo, buddy, I have to go to school. But the next time I see you, I want to hear some drumming, okay? Okay-o, Teo?" I stand up, and Teo puts both arms around my knees and squeezes. It's kind of stupid, but somehow I feel like I really matter. And it's a little five-year-old kid hugging my bony knees that does it. I don't feel like this much anymore. Sometimes I do with Emma, my girlfriend, I guess. Or when I'm nailing every shot on the court. Or when Coop and I are hanging out with the guys. But today Teo's hug puts this weird lump in my throat.

Because I wish my dad still made me feel the same way.

5
LUNA

Temmie isn't home when I come in after school. I'm used to going right from school to the studio, so it feels weird to be here in the middle of the afternoon. My whole body aches from holding in tears all day. More than just not getting to dance anymore is the painful realization that I am basically no one without it.

I can't sit still, so I plunge into a frenzy of work. I clean out the ashes from the woodstove and bring them to the compost pile by the garden. Just as I am dumping them, a gust of wind spews them back in my face. They stick in my hair and cover my jacket. I bring armloads of wood into the house and stack it next to the stove. And get a monster splinter in my thumb. Then the chickens are in my way and I stumble over one. And just as I've sorted through all the papers on the kitchen table, Temmie opens the door and the blast of cold air wrecks all my work. I burst into tears.

"Everything's going wrong!" I sob. Temmie wraps her arms around me and doesn't say a word.

Finally she lets go. "I see a little elf has been hard at work in here. Is that lentil soup I smell?"

"It's probably burned."

"One of those days, huh?" Temmie takes off her jacket and sits at the table. "Well, you've just made mine. Thanks for the soup and wood and the fire, honey. And I have a little something that just might make your day brighter."

Dinner has always been her storytelling time. No phones or screens of any kind are allowed during the meal. When I was little, Temmie entertained me with stories about the many faraway places she'd been. Usually the tales were true, but sometimes she made them up. The ones I remember best were about an imaginary little girl named Penelope. Penelope was delightfully naughty, but she was brave and sly and clever, never mean. Once Penelope hid in a toy store overnight and rearranged everything. She lined up all the dolls and stuffed animals in a parade up and down the aisles and built massive houses using game boxes as bricks. Another time, Penelope called a bakery, disguised her voice as the mother of a mean girl at school, and ordered gigantic cakes to be delivered to the homes of the mean girl's victims. "Put it on my bill," she told the baker. Penelope defended the downtrodden and defeated the bullies. I secretly wanted to be Penelope.

Temmie sprinkles some cheese on the soup and tastes it. "This," she says. "Is." She eats another spoonful and closes her eyes. "Amazing."

I take a small bite. It's not bad. Definitely not amazing, but Temmie senses how crappy my day's been.

"I went to the church today," she begins, "to visit Pastor Mark." She saws a slice off the end of the sunflower seed loaf she made yesterday and spreads butter on it. "For some help."

I stop chewing and stare at her. Temmie doesn't ask for help from anyone. Ever.

"He was out shoveling the parking lot. Good thing he's young and strong. Carol Pugh—you know, his assistant—let me wait in his office until he finished. He was surprised to see me when he came in, kept apologizing for keeping me waiting. I got right to the point and told him I needed some assistance. He hadn't even sat down before he was offering me cards to Hannaford's and Sunoco from his discretionary fund. Such a kind man. I told him not to be ridiculous. I don't want the church's money. Other people in this community are hungrier than we are."

Okay, I am seriously confused. Does she want spiritual help? Someone to pray for her?

She takes another bite as if to prove we aren't going hungry. I wait.

"Honey, I know how important dance is. I don't want you to stop just because I can't afford your lessons anymore. So I was trying to think of a safe place where you could dance in private. And the church sanctuary is what I came up with."

This is about me? My throat closes and I put my spoon down.

"Pastor Mark gets it. Said something about being emotionally and spiritually fed is as important as being physically nourished. He thought about it for less than ten seconds before deciding that you could dance in the sanctuary in the afternoons anytime between 3:15 and 6:45. Except Thursdays. That's the day the Free Room is open, and lots of people are coming and going. You know, to drop off donations or take what they need. There are a few meetings in the evenings, but they don't start until seven o'clock."

The black cloud that choked me all day starts to lift. I feel my posture changing, my shoulders rising.

"You will, of course, pay for your time. We Lemieuxs don't take charity."

She stirs her soup and doesn't look at me. "Pastor Mark said you could help out with the youngest Sunday school class. It's only about six or seven kiddos on a good day. They're between three and five years old. Mabel Frye has been working with the littles for decades. But she's getting old and doesn't have the energy she used to."

In public? With other people? No!

Temmie picks her head up and shrugs off my alarm. "I told him you'd start this Sunday."

6
HUNTER

Emma is complaining that since basketball started, we never hang out anymore. She doesn't really get how busy I am, between practice and school and working for my aunt. And, honestly, trying to manage stuff at home. Since Dad started seriously drinking, he doesn't take care of the house like he used to. I grew up with the mantra "Ridley Proud." That meant that if my room wasn't neat, I couldn't play until I'd cleaned it to meet the Ridley Proud standard. Our home and yard were immaculate, Ridley Proud. There were never dishes in the sink, laundry not folded and put away, or jackets not hung on the pegs in the mudroom. No clutter anywhere. My performance in basketball was Ridley Proud. And my schoolwork had to be done with Ridley Proud in mind. Always.

But though Dad still demands the Ridley Proud standard in everything, now he's not doing stuff like mopping or laundry. So I do, and it takes a lot of time. And he insists that I keep up my grades, even though the idea of going to college is kind of a joke at this point. We could never afford it.

My aunt, Gretchen, who never had a partner or children, pays me to help her out, like cut tree limbs or put on snow tires or caulk her shower. Sometimes it's little stuff, like changing lightbulbs or cleaning her rugs. She can easily change lightbulbs and clean rugs herself, but she knows I need the money. We don't discuss it—I don't know, maybe out of pride or something—but I'm glad I can help her, and she's glad she can give me a little spending money.

So anyway, here I am, at Molly's again before school, planning to spend that money on Emma. Who, by the way, has way more money than I do and doesn't need me to pay for her. But I like doing things for her. I told her that the only free time I had this week was before school.

"You want me to get up an hour early to go to Molly's with you?"

"Um, yeah?"

"Oh, my God. Why can't we hang out at night?"

"I already told you; I don't have time."

"Whatever. You know, Hunter, other guys hit on me all the time at parties. I could so easily be with any of them, and they would make me a priority."

She knows this will piss me off. I wonder how true it is? I know she parties a lot. She's in the like most popular group in the sophomore class. Suddenly, I feel so tired. "I'll be at Molly's at 6:45, Emma. Text me if you can't make it."

Of course she's late. It's close to seven o'clock, and I haven't heard from her. Two men are sitting at the table next to mine, discussing the economy in Edgewater. It seems like that's all anyone talks about since the mill closed a year ago.

"You hear about Portland?"

"Nope."

"Some dude donated one hundred million dollars to start up a new tech hub."

"You kidding?"

"Dead serious. And geez, it yanks my chain just thinking about that. I mean, Portland doesn't need it like we do. Why couldn't we be given that kind of dough? You don't have to have a city or a port to be a damn tech hub."

"I know. I don't know how we're gonna survive much longer. Those settlement payments are about gone. Know anything about plans for the mill building?"

"I heard talk about some Japanese company buying and refurbishing it. But someone else said it was too expensive to bring it all up to the new environmental codes. It'll take some doing to clean up the toxins in the ground and in the river."

"So the mill just sits there, like a big ugly constant reminder of when life was good."

Just then, Emma slides into the chair across from me. She is wearing a thick pink sweater under her puffy white jacket, and her lip gloss matches it perfectly. Her hair is all like flowy and her cheeks are bright red. She looks like she just stepped out of a Paris photo shoot or something. Not like she trudged through the snow on a bitter cold morning in Maine. Even her Uggs look new, not covered with salt and dirty snow like my boots.

I fall immediately under her spell. "God, you look fantastic!"

She laughs and bends over to kiss me with those shiny lips. Waves of peppermint and vanilla and desire wash over me. I wish we were someplace where I could do more than kiss her.

We order hot chocolate and cinnamon rolls from Samantha, who started working here after the mill closed. She's bubbly and chatty, totally unlike the owner, Molly, who's kind of crabby all the time. I get it, though, 'cause she's trying to make it in this shit economy too. I've overheard her grumbling about people ordering plain coffee, not "them fancy latte drinks," and then lingering for hours, just talking. People want to be together in their misery; maybe slowly sharing one small cup of coffee is the only way they can do it. Anyway, Samantha talks to everyone. And she's usually cheerful. Today she chats with an older man while she heats our cinnamon rolls.

"You got your wood all stacked? And your snow tires on? Supposed to be a doozy coming on Wednesday!"

The man's eyes light up in the way only a native Northerner's do in anticipation of a big snowstorm. "Yep, I sure do," he says. "And we finished canning the last of the turnips and pumpkins. 'Bout all set to hibernate. The almanac says it's going to be a long winter." Sparks of static electricity crackle when he pulls his hat off.

Samantha brings us our rolls. We dig in. Actually, *I* dig in. Emma carefully cuts a tiny piece and dips it in the cream cheese frosting pooled on the top. She licks her fork slowly, staring right at me like she's trying to seduce me. It works.

"Sooo," she says, deliberately running her tongue over her lips in a slow, sexy circle, "what's going on?"

I am totally distracted by her tongue. "You know you're driving me wild, right?" I shift in my chair.

"Huh. I guess that's your problem, isn't it?" She puckers her lips, gives me a pouty air kiss, and licks the fork again. "We could make that problem go away. Let's ditch and go back to my house. My parents are at work."

"I can't. I have a test in history. And if we miss any school, we can't go to practice."

She rolls her eyes. "I bet if I invited Logan, he would come." She smiles and dips her finger in the frosting. She places it on her tongue and wraps her lips around it. "In both senses of the word."

I need to change the subject. I hate it when she talks about other guys. "Did you, um, did you finish your math homework?"

"Math homework? Really? God, Hunter, you are so boring! No, I didn't do it. I'll just accidentally bump into Carter, maybe give him a little cleavage fix, and ask him if I can check my answers with his. It always works."

I've inhaled my entire roll. She pushes hers away after eating only a third of it.

"Can I—I mean, are you finished with that?"

"Yeah. That whole thing is probably a thousand calories."

"So can I have it?"

She makes a face. "Uh, I guess? I mean, if you feel okay eating off someone else's plate."

It doesn't bother me because I'm hungry. Emma checks her phone. "Did you see my post from yesterday? It's the picture of you and me from the other night after Coop dropped us off. You look so hot."

I didn't. I don't really keep up with social media the way she does. Honestly, she's kind of obsessed with it. She scrolls for a while, giving me the rundown of who's hooking up, whose hair is weird in their post, who looks fat, who isn't talking to someone because they're in a fight, and on and on. I can't keep track of it all. I really don't care about this stuff like she does. Finally, she puts her phone down. "Are you ready for the game tomorrow?"

"I hope so. Are you coming?"

"Of course I'll be there! You better play well. Like really well. I've got a rep to keep up."

"And what," I tease, "will happen if I don't play well?"

She stands up and puts on her jacket. "Then you may be in the market for a new girlfriend."

I laugh as I follow her out of Molly's, but I'm not sure she's completely kidding. And that makes me feel crappy.

7
LUNA

So now I'm working at church. At 9:30 on Sunday mornings. I don't mind getting up early because I don't stay up late on Saturday nights. I have basically zero social life, unless you count hanging with Temmie and the chickens.

I have to admit I was terrified the first Sunday. Temmie kept bugging me about eating breakfast, but I couldn't swallow, and my stomach was in knots. I mean, I'm really bad with new people because I know my face scares them. It's hard to carry on a conversation with someone who is looking at you in horror. Or not looking at you at all. So even though Temmie said I couldn't wear my hoodie to the church, I stuffed it in the bag I brought and put it on after she dropped me off.

There were six kids there, four girls and two boys. One of the little boys was in overalls; the other wore the smallest pair of jeans I've ever seen. Two of the girls had plastic barrettes in their silky hair.

One wore a sweater with a smiling snowman the front. They were all seated on teeny chairs at a table, playing with a wooden Noah's ark. Mrs. Frye, in a bright blue pullover and gray wool pants, sat at the table with them, murmuring as they chattered away. I stood in the doorway and watched, dreading the moment I had to enter. Because I was going to shatter this sweet tableau and probably freak them out.

I took a deep breath and slipped in. And yep, they all stared.

"Who is that?" The girl with the blonde ponytail pointed at me with the tiger she held in her hand.

Mrs. Frye smiled. "Oh, hello, dear!" She motioned for me to sit at the table. I did, my face burning with shame. "Children, this is Miss Luna. She's going to be here every week to play with you."

And then it came. I knew it would, 'cause little kids don't know better. But it still hurt. My face was so hot that I could feel it throbbing, like my heart was beating in my cheeks.

"What's on your face?" They all got up from their seats, ignoring Mrs. Frye's telling them to sit down, and crowded around me. "Is that jelly?"

"You should wash your face!"

I could feel the tears shoving their way to my ducts like pigs at the trough at feeding time. *God! This is exactly why I don't go out in public.*

Two of the girls grabbed my fingers. "Come on! This is where we wash our hands." They dragged me to the sink. *This is mortifying. I'm leaving. I hate this, I hate this, I hate this. My presence is unbearable, even here. But I need this job. If I leave, I can't dance. Oh, God.* I grabbed a paper towel, wet it, and scrubbed my birthmark. The kids watched, their eyes round with curiosity.

"Oops! It won't come off! Um, let's see. Maybe I should try to wash off my nose. What do you think?"

They looked at each other. *Wash off her nose?* I rubbed the paper towel over my nose. "Oh, no! It won't come off either! Should I try to scrub off my ears?"

The children started laughing. "Now do your mouth!"

"Now your eyes!"

"And your hair!"

Their giggles filled the room. Even Mrs. Frye was beaming.

When we decided that I was clean and none of my facial parts could come off, we all went back to playing with the ark. And then, bizarrely, I didn't think about my face because the kids wanted so much of my attention. Mrs. Frye got up to prepare the snack, so it was just me and those little, earnest people.

"Miss Luna, watch me! I can crash the boat and all the animals fall off!"

"Rosie, you're not s'posed to crash the boat."

"Miss Luna, can I crash the boat?"

I wasn't used to be an authority figure. For anything. "Um, well, maybe there's a terrible storm in the ocean. Let's hear the wind." I waved arms back and forth and blew out loudly; soon the children followed.

"Okay, now the rain's falling!" I waved my arms up and down. *Whoosh! Whoosh!* We all made it rain.

"And now," I shouted, "thunder!" We pounded on the table.

"Oh, no, the ark is falling over in this huge storm!" We tipped it over, scattering the animals.

"Miss Luna, why's there only one elephant? There's two giraffes."

"And two everything!"

"That's 'cause Joey lost it."

"No I didn't!"

"What if it doesn't know how to swim?"

"Oh, that would be so bad!"

"It would be drownded!"

"Can elephants swim, Miss Luna?"

"I wonder if the other elephant," I said tactfully, "is in the back of the boat where all the food is stored? Maybe that's why we can't see it."

It was fun. Like really, truly fun. I hadn't let my guard down like that for anyone before. One little boy, Teo, seemed different from the rest of the kids. Not only did his bright brown eyes, shaped like almonds, indicate Down's, but his mocha latte–colored skin stood out among the pale white skin of the rest of the children. And his black curls and deep dimples just added to his irresistible cuteness. Teo insisted on holding onto my elbow for the entire class. Every time I looked at him, he grinned at me. It made me smile. A lot. More than I had since, well, ever.

And suddenly the hour was up and reality returned. I hid in the supply closet, supposedly to put away the juice and crackers and toys while the parents came to pick up their kids. I overheard Mrs. Frye greeting them, talking about the Bible story we'd discussed, asking about their farms or whatever.

And then. I swear I'm not making this up.

One of the kids said, "Mommy, Miss Luna is soooo funny!" Another chimed in, "Yeah. And she's so pretty."

They're just little kids who don't know anything.

But I stood there in the supply closet with an enormous lump in my throat and tears streaming down my face.

So this is what it feels like to be accepted.

8
HUNTER

Every year on the first Saturday in December, the Moose and Loon hunting lodge opens its doors to the entire town for a huge party. The hunting season is over. The people who come up from Boston to rough it for a few days in the wilderness—maybe shoot their fancy guns at a moose or deer or bear, drink a lot, and brag about everything in their perfect lives—have gone back to their multimillion-dollar Back Bay brownstones. We call them the Citiots. Nate made that up; it's short for "city-idiots."

The owners of the lodge, PJ and Patsy Cutter, live somewhere out west and are only here during hunting season, October and November. They make enough money in two months to pay for the lodge's upkeep and taxes all year. Dad told me that Patsy Cutter's grandfather, the original owner, left it in his will that the lodge and the surrounding six thousand acres of land had to be kept in the family. The party is the Cutters' way of thanking the townspeople for tolerating the obnoxious hunting guests who flood the town with their self-entitled demands.

The theme is the same every year: "Darkness Falls upon Us." And it's so frickin' dark and cold now that everyone needs like one celebration together before the winter sends people into their houses until spring. Obviously, I'm a kid, so I'm out a ton—going to school, going to practice, hanging with friends. But there are some adults who barely leave home in winter, especially if they're unemployed or super old or sick. I don't blame them. Going out means putting on like three layers. And a hat and gloves and boots. And then the car windows need to be scraped. And the driveway needs to be shoveled. And the roads are covered with packed snow and ice, even after the plows have come through, so driving can be pretty hairy.

Anyway, back to the party. Okay, this may sound stupid, because it's just a community gathering, but it's awesome. It starts in the afternoon, when they open the indoor pool to the children. It's a huge deal, because that pool is the only one in Edgewater. Patsy Cutter's grandmother suffered from cerebral palsy, so her husband, Patsy's grandfather, installed the pool so she could swim laps every day. It's probably twenty-five yards long, with a diving board at the deep end. The kids, though, stay in the shallow end, where they can stand. There used to be talk of putting in a public outdoor pool on some property next to the mill, but when the mill closed, so did that idea. A few people go to the pond on Oak Hill, but the bottom is muddy and gross, and the mosquitoes and blackflies are insane. So hardly anyone in our town swims. Not many people even know how. But the kids love splashing around in that pool at the lodge once a year.

While the kids are playing with beach balls and squirt guns, half of the adults sit on the deck in shorts and T-shirts and just absorb the warmth of the pool room. The other half of the town bundles up to watch the snow volleyball game between the Unders and the Overs.

Definitely my favorite event, it's for the guys in the town—those under twenty-one versus those over. I've heard women protesting, like why can't they play too, but the women's competition comes after dinner. It's ridiculously sexist, but I guess no one changes it because it's an Edgewater tradition. Like it's almost sacred because they've done it so long the same way. Anyway, the game is played no matter the weather, and it is a Big Deal. Seriously, people place bets (no money, just beer) and talk about the game for months afterward. And the winners get big-time bragging rights.

Coop and I are stoked because we were asked to be on the Unders team this year. Our first time ever. It sounds dumb, but it's kind of a huge honor to be asked. When I was a kid, my dad played on the Overs. They won every time he was on the team. The year the mill closed, he only played for like five minutes. There was a dispute about whether a ball was in or out, and he couldn't let it go. He shoved this old dude who was the line judge, and the town cop had to restrain him. It sucked. He was already drunk, and it was only five o'clock in the afternoon. He's not allowed to play anymore.

I hate what drinking has done to my dad. After that basketball game—the one where he was ejected—I was pissed. Coop dropped me off at home, where I found my dad sitting on the couch watching TV. I grabbed a bottle of vodka from the cupboard and poured it down the sink. I was on the second one when he noticed what I was doing. I've only seen him move faster when he was juking me on the basketball court. "What the hell?" he roared. He grabbed my arm, reaching for the bottle. "Don't you dare dump that! I worked hard for that!"

I held the bottle up higher. "Yeah, and I worked hard to win the game tonight! I spent most of it on the bench." The tears were pouring down my face. "Because of you!"

"You don't know what it's like, Hunter. Just give me the damn bottle."

"You've got to stop this shit, Dad! It's ruining you!"

For someone so drunk, he was surprisingly strong. His punch landed in the middle of my stomach, sending me spiraling backward. I crashed into the table. "Jesus, Dad! What the hell?"

He was crying now too. "Just fucking give it to me!"

I whirled around and opened my fingers. The bottle smashed on the floor.

He shoved me, hard. I fell over the chair and landed on the glass. A shard sliced my palm open. When Dad saw the blood spurting out, he snapped out of his crazed trance. "Shit, Hunter! I didn't mean to. I'm sorry! Let me fix that."

He carefully washed and wrapped my hand and swept up the mess, apologizing over and over for getting drunk, for ruining the game, for hitting me. It reminded me of when I was a little kid and my old dad was back.

But even after he promised me he'd stop drinking, he didn't. I mean, he did for a while. Then I found beer in the refrigerator. He had the decency to look a little guilty when I called him on it, but he said beer is harmless, that he'd quit the hard stuff. But you can get wasted on beer, too. And he did. So nothing really changed. Actually, that shitty night did change something: our relationship. Like we weren't as free with each other. That easiness and trust we'd always had was replaced by this weird wariness. It sucks.

God, I miss him so much.

So, anyway, before I got way sidetracked, I was describing the Lodge Party. When the volleyball game is over, people head inside to warm up before dinner. Most people get duded up. Not like city fancy, but clean jeans and a shirt with buttons. Some of the women put on makeup. The men take off their caps and comb their hair. The lodge staff keeps the doors to the dining room closed until the last minute. Then it's weird, like we're at church or something, 'cause everyone gets all quiet. When it's totally silent, the double doors open, and the scene is out of a movie. The dining room is fully decked out in pine boughs and candles. Probably a major fire hazard, but it's seriously beautiful.

After dinner, which is always amazing, the women's contest begins. It's called "Desserting the Dark." Molly's chocolate zucchini cake usually wins, but the competition is always fierce. Bridget Callahan's cranberry apple pie is my favorite, with Carol Pugh's blueberry ice cream a close second.

The last event, the talent show, happens after everyone is stuffed. It doesn't matter if you're a kid just learning to tell jokes or an expert on the ukulele, everyone in it gets wild applause. Edgewater's garage band, Not Wicked Good, ends the show with the same ten songs they always play, and everyone dances.

Then the darkness falls. And for some people, it feels like it stays forever.

9
LUNA

I am starting to change into my dance clothes in the little room next to the sanctuary when I hear voices coming through the heating vent. They startle me; I'm used to the church being silent.

"Mark? Are you free? Bridget Callahan wants to see you." I recognize the voice of Pastor Mark's assistant, Mrs. Pugh. She's been really nice to me, like Temmie says she is to everyone.

"Sure. Send her in."

I yank off my jeans in a hurry. I don't want to hear a conversation not meant for my ears, especially between a pastor and a parishioner.

"Good to see you, Bridget. Have a seat. And how are you, little buddy?"

I hear a child's voice, but I can't make out the words. Then the woman, Bridget, I guess, laughs. "Teo is very proud of himself. He now wears big boy underwear!"

I freeze. I know Teo. He's that sweet little kid from Sunday school. I've never met his mother.

I hear Teo. "Bathroom?"

Pastor Mark tells them that Teo can use the bathroom next to his office. I pull on my leggings and sit to tie my dance shoes. I hear Teo's mom again.

"These little steps are so big. We've been potty training for months now. Anyway, I don't mean to bother you. I just wanted to ask about someone who is helping in Sunday school. Teo calls her 'Loon.' Do you know who I'm talking about?"

I feel my face turn hot. *Whoa. That's me.*

Pastor Mark sounds anxious. "Yes. That's Luna Lemieux, Temmie's niece. Does there . . . does there seem to be a problem?" *Even the pastor, someone who's not supposed to judge, assumes the worst when it involves me?*

"Oh, no! Just the opposite, actually. Teo talks about her all the time. I guess I just wanted to thank her. But I've never seen her."

"That doesn't surprise me. From what Mabel says, she's fantastic with the kids, but she doesn't talk with the parents. She's, um, a bit self-conscious. If you want to leave her a note, I'll be sure she gets it."

I bolt, my shoes still untied. I can't stand to hear another word. Two adults are in there talking about me, and it's weird and incredibly uncomfortable. I feel so exposed—so like *noticed*. And I hate that. My heart doesn't stop pounding until I am well into the beginning of my routine. The music and the movement eventually calm me. I close my eyes and let my body go. *This is why I'm helping in Sunday school. This is why I exist.*

And then I sense that I'm not alone. I open my eyes and there's Teo, bouncing up and down in time to the beat. He smiles at me and claps his hands. I keep my eyes open and bounce with him, then we slide and twirl and jump and laugh. For several minutes it's just me and Teo and music and dance. It feels magical.

And then I realize that his mom probably doesn't know where he is, that she's probably looking for him in the bathroom. So I stop, throw my hoodie back on, and lead Teo out into the hall. Pastor Mark is there with a woman wearing a black parka. With her dark brown hair in a messy bun, she reminds me of my dance instructor, though she's shorter and wider. She doesn't appear worried at all.

"I'm sorry! I shouldn't have . . . I mean, I . . . we got caught up in the music before I realized you must be looking for him!"

Teo holds onto my hand tightly and beams. "My Loon."

Pastor Mark introduces us. Ms. Callahan's smile is warm, genuine. "It is so good to meet you, Luna. Teo raves about you. And oh, my, you dance beautifully."

They saw? Oh, my God. "I . . . um, thank you. Teo is . . . um, he's . . . such a . . ." I find myself floundering. Like I can't articulate what he means to me. I feel like a complete idiot. The heat flares in my face. "I mean . . . I . . . I've got to go."

Ms. Callahan just smiles again. "Thank you."

Teo hugs my legs. "Bye, Loon!"

I pat his head. "Bye, Teo. And it was . . . it was um, nice to meet you. Um, Ms. Callahan." *God, I am so bad at talking with anyone over five. Get me out of here.*

I flee.

10

HUNTER

My ringtone yanks me out of a sexy dream about Emma. *Seriously? It's 6:22. On a Saturday!* Saturday is the one day I get to sleep in, 'cause Dad usually makes me get up and go to church on Sunday. It's my aunt. She's a mess.

"Hunter? I'm sorry to wake you, honey, but I need help with Raven. He's been vomiting all night, and now he's too weak to stand up. I've got to take him to the vet, but I can't lift him by myself."

I throw on my jeans and a sweatshirt and go downstairs. Dad's at the stove, fully dressed, frying eggs. "You get your days mixed up? It's not Sunday."

I pour a glass of milk and grab a granola bar while I tell Dad about Gretchen's black Lab.

"I can drop you over there on my way. Leaving in five." Dad works every Saturday at the town dump, where he's paid by the hour to sort recyclables. It's dirty work, and he comes home stinking and exhausted, but it's money that we desperately need.

Gretchen can barely drive, she's so worried about Raven. I get it. He's all she has. No kids, no partner. She keeps turning to look in the back seat at us. Raven's head is in my lap; my hand is on his back. I'm talking to him and stroking his fur. The vet's place is way out of town on a working farm. Gretchen drives as fast as the icy roads allow, which still feels too slow. She screeches to a halt right in front of the office, which is a big building near the barn. I carry Raven over my shoulder.

Shep, the vet, is waiting in the office. He's tall and thin with a reddish beard. He leads us back to the examining room, where I gently lay Raven on the table.

Shep keeps his eyes on Raven as he asks Gretchen questions. He moves his large hands over the dog's throat and chest and stomach. "Eaten anything strange?"

Gretchen is shaking. "I don't think so. Outside, he's only on-leash. When it's this cold, I keep him in the house and garage, so he couldn't have raided someone's garbage."

"Any worms or blood in the vomit?"

I start to feel nauseous.

"No."

"Excessive urination?"

"No."

"Any chance he could have ingested antifreeze?"

Gretchen's gasp makes me jerk my head away from Raven. Her face is like totally white. "Oh, my God! I spilled a little in the garage when I was putting it in my tank yesterday. I was going to wipe it up and then I got a call and totally forgot about it. Is he . . . is it . . . it's poisonous, isn't it?"

Shep's voice remains low and steady. "How much spilled?"

Gretchen looks like she's about to faint. Shep looks at me and jerks his head a little, pointing to the chair. I help her sit. "Um, not much. One big drop. Like a tablespoon, maybe? Oh, I am so careless! I—"

Shep cuts her off. "It happens. Especially in the winter. Good news is it wasn't much. Did the right thing coming here. I'll administer an antidote. Can you stick around? I'd like to watch him for the next hour or so."

Chairs line the wall in the reception area, so I guess it also serves as a waiting room. It's attached to a wide hall that leads to a huge, open room where the animals are kept. I remember wandering around in there, looking at the animals, when Gretchen and I brought Raven in to be neutered. Gretchen, who usually loves to talk, pulls out her phone and starts to do a crossword. Her knuckles are white as she clutches the phone.

The door opens and a woman comes in with a kid about my age. She's in a long fur coat and high-heeled boots. Her blonde hair is up in some fancy do and her makeup is perfect. Out of place, especially on a Saturday morning. I know most of the people in Edgewater, but I don't recognize her. She swishes up to the front counter and raps on it. No one comes. She looks at us and rolls her eyes. Then she turns to her kid and points him to a chair across from me. He looks at me as he's sitting. I feel like I've seen him before. Like a long time ago.

I smile. "Hey. 'Sup?"

He kind of looks right past me and says, "Dog."

He obviously doesn't know me well enough to mean "Dawg," so I assume he's here to pick up his dog. "Your dog sick? Or hurt?"

He just stares at the wall behind me. "Dog. Dog."

His mother explains. "Thaddeus is very excited by the prospect of getting a dog," she says. "We're here to ask the vet what kind he'd recommend. For a special . . . I mean, not . . . well, for support. A service dog." She seems both flustered and determined.

It's both her voice and the mention of his name that make me remember. I do know them. Well, kind of. When I was in fifth grade, Thaddeus was the new kid in our class. He didn't really talk to anyone. I remember he was obsessed with the gerbil we kept in the room, so much so that the teacher let him put his desk right next to the cage. That's all I remember about him. The gerbil. Oh, and the party.

His mom bought the old LeBlanc house and had the whole place renovated. Contractors with trucks that had logos from companies in Portland and Boston parked there for months. Most people fixed up their own places, so it was a pretty big deal to have this like dramatic makeover. Anyway, when it was finished, the whole class and their parents were invited to what his mom said was a party for the house.

It was bizarre. It felt like we were in a museum, not a house. I overheard someone say it was "too fuckin' fancy" for Edgewater. We all had to take off our shoes in this enormous mudroom that obviously had never seen a speck of mud. My friends and our parents were in jeans, but Thaddeus's mom wore a red dress with a slit up the side. And she carried around trays of appetizers that we didn't even recognize. She served the adults wine in glasses, not beer out of a cooler. We were encouraged to play with Thaddeus in his gigantic playroom, but he just sat in one corner with his back to us and worked on Legos. My friends and I played Ping-Pong and pop-a-shot, but because everything was brand new, we were kind of nervous, like we didn't want to break anything. Dad and I left as soon as we could without feeling like we were being rude. Soon after that, Thaddeus left our school. I hadn't seen him since. Until now.

"We have a dog too. I mean, my aunt does. He's sick, but he's going to be okay." I'm babbling. Nothing seems to register with Thaddeus. "Um, you still have that cool Ping-Pong table?"

His mother looks startled. "You know Thaddeus?"

"Not real— I mean, he was in our class in fifth grade. We went to your party."

Her smile fades. “Oh. It’s nice you remember.”

Thaddeus starts to rock back and forth. “Dog. Dog. Dog.”

Just then Shep comes in, drying his hands on a towel. He gives Gretchen a nod. “Doing fine. Just another half hour or so before you take him home.”

Gretchen stands up and gives Shep a cringeworthy hug, one I am sure he was not expecting. She’s just so relieved. Shep turns to Thaddeus’s mom. “Help you?”

“Hello, I’m Jessica Cloud. You’re the vet?”

Shep nods and rubs his beard.

“I’m here for a professional consultation. I will pay you for your time.”

Shep shakes his head. “About?”

“I need to know who raises the best service, slash, emotional support dogs in the country. There’s a facility in Ohio that is highly reputed. Another in eastern Oregon. Just wondering what you’d recommend. I need the best.”

Shep doesn’t say anything for a while. Then he looks up. “This for your son?”

Jessica nods. “His therapist in Boston recommended it.”

As soon as I hear the word “therapist,” I feel like I’m listening to stuff that’s private, none of my business. I get up. “I’m going to look at the dogs,” I tell Gretchen.

Shep interrupts Jessica and nods toward Thaddeus. “Take him with you.”

I look at Thaddeus. “Dogs?”

Thaddeus stands up. “Dog.”

We walk down the hall to the open room. This is not the recovery room; it’s more like an animal shelter. It houses animals that have been abandoned or “donated” to Shep. While he’s technically the town vet, he also serves as the keeper of the unwanted. He used to hire kids to help take care of them—walk them, feed them, stuff like that. But Gretchen told me she heard that since the mill closed, he’s been treating animals on a pay-what-you-can basis, and he's lost a ton of money. According to her, he couldn't afford to keep the kids, so he does it all himself now.

Rescue dogs are in four of the large cages against the wall. One is a graying golden retriever. Another looks like a labradoodle. Pacing back and forth in the third is a huge pit bull. We walk past them slowly. And then Thaddeus crouches in front of the fourth cage and says, "Dog." I peer past his shoulder into the cage, where a little bundle of matted gray fur is quivering. I can't begin to identify the breed. Probably a mix. It looks sick and emaciated.

Behind me I hear Jessica talking as she and Shep join us. "I would also like to know what you'd recommend for fencing. Should I invest in a full wooden fence over our seven acres? Or do an electric one? I've read that—"

Shep interrupts her. "Neither."

"Oh! Is there a new device that—"

"Nope."

"Well, then, what are you suggesting?"

"Well-trained, well-loved dogs don't need fences."

They stop behind me. Thaddeus hasn't moved. He stares into the cage. "Dog."

Jessica gasps. "Oh, no, honey! That's a, a mutt! It looks half dead. We're not getting a dog here."

I slip out of the way. Shep puts a hand on my shoulder. "I'll check on Raven in a minute." He turns back to watch Thaddeus. A few minutes pass in silence. "Looks like he's found his dog," he finally says. Softly. "She was left by the side of the road on the north slope of Oak Hill. Barely alive."

"But she hasn't been trained! Thaddeus needs one that—"

And then Thaddeus turns around. "My dog."

His mom sucks in her breath. "Did you . . . did you hear that?"

I look at her. There are tears running down her cheeks. "He just . . . he just put two words together! I know it seems like nothing, but he has verbal apraxia. He's never done that before! I'm . . ."

Shep gently leads me and Jessica out, leaving Thaddeus in front of the dog cage. "Bring Thaddeus here every day. He can get to know the dog, and she'll learn to trust him. And I can tell there's something of an animal whisperer in him. If he wants, he can help out with the other dogs. Feeding. Grooming. Walking. I'd love the help, but I can't pay him anything."

Jessica's eyes are still shiny with tears. "I . . . I didn't realize how much he needed a dog." She wipes away a tear with one finger, the way women do who don't want to smudge their mascara. "I guess we could try it? But it's not—"

Shep turns away before she can finish her sentence. "I'll see him here tomorrow. 'Bout noon."

He walks to the recovery room with me. Raven sees us and wags his tail, but he still looks sleepy. I carry him out to the car with Gretchen.

I feel like I just witnessed something strange. But good strange. And I'm like rooting for Thaddeus. I hope he gets that dog.

11
LUNA

This is the first year I've attended school in person. I hate it. I mean, I really hate it. School for someone like me is its own form of torture. Pluck a kid who's scary looking, who's never had to deal with a bunch of peers, who was isolated all the way until eleventh grade, and drop her in a regional high school in rural Maine where she knows basically no one, and, gee, just wonder how that goes. Temmie homeschooled me all through elementary school. She worked the late shift at the mill, so she could teach me in the mornings. When I was little and asked her why I didn't go to real school, she said that I couldn't because of my dance schedule. That I needed to finish early to get to the studio, that they wouldn't let me leave early if I went to the local elementary school. I took her at her word. And I loved home school. We read so many books and planted a garden and went skating on the pond when everyone else was in the big school. We listened to the soundtracks from Broadway shows on real vinyl records. And Temmie taught me geography through stories of the places she'd visited.

Now I understand that she was protecting the other kids from the monster. And me from their cruelty.

Temmie said she didn't know enough to teach me in middle school, so I did an online program. It wasn't much fun, but I got it over with quickly and then had tons of time to myself to read or dance or garden. I never really thought about changing my routine until Temmie brought it up last summer. I was out on the back porch, reading a novel and drinking lemonade. Temmie was wearing gardening gloves and had a trowel in one hand.

"So, kiddo, I just wanted to let you know that I've enrolled you in high school."

I was so into my book that I didn't really hear her. "Thanks, Temmie. You're really organized."

"I can take you or you can walk. It's only one point eight miles. I clocked it today."

I slowly picked my head up. "Wait, what? What's one point eight miles?"

"The school. Longfellow Regional High School."

"What are you talking about? I do school here."

She rubbed her sweaty forehead with her sleeve. "Not anymore, kiddo."

I was totally confused. "What? Why not?"

"Because, Luna, you've got to experience school. Real school. Classes with teachers. Labs. Games. Cafeteria lunches. Lockers. Gym class. Study hall. Being a part of something bigger than you and a screen."

"I don't want any of that! I learn perfectly well right here! Why on earth would I stop what's working?"

"Honey, your life with me is way too small. My fault, and I'm sorry. So you start the Tuesday after Labor Day. Actually, there's an orientation for new students on August 28. You'll have to register for classes next week." She opened the porch door and walked down the steps. I sat there, my book still opened in my lap, stunned.

"Temmie, wait! You can't just do that! You didn't even ask me!"

"You're right; I didn't ask you. And you're wrong; I did just do it."

I felt like I was sledding down a mountain, picking up momentum, totally out of control, and there was no way to stop.

I threw the book at the door. Hot tears of fury fell down my cheeks. "I am so not going to school! Have you not heard what people say when they see me?"

Temmie didn't even look at me. She just kept digging, methodically weeding. "They'll get used to you."

"I am a *fucking* freak! No one wants to be around me!"

I hardly ever swear. Not because I'm opposed to it, but it just seems redundant. Boring. But it still has an impact on Temmie. God, she had to know how this was going to ruin my life. How I would never be able to stand it.

She wasn't even fazed. "No need for profanity, Luna," she said calmly. Her lack of emotion infuriated me. "You're better than that. And you're not a freak."

Through the blur of my tears, I watched her toss weeds to the side, and I couldn't help but make the connection. "My own mother threw me away like those *fucking* weeds. And you say I'm not a freak? You're either blind or stupid!" I ran into the house and hid in my room for the rest of the day.

For weeks I argued and cried and rationalized and begged Temmie to change her mind. But she wouldn't budge.

So here I am, stuck at school. I've been here three months now, and it's as awful as I thought it would be. My seat is the same in every class. Front row, over to the far left. The teachers don't see me there because they're focused on the kids who are screwing around in the back. I never raise my hand. I rarely get called on. Hidden in my hoodie, I'm basically invisible. Which is exactly what I want. Except it's not, really. I just wish I had like one friend.

The days are excruciating, mostly because no one talks to me. Do you have any idea how long a school day is when you're just listening? Knowing that no one gives a rip if you're there or not? At lunchtime I escape to the library, where no food is allowed, but I can't sit alone in the caf and watch everyone else lead normal lives. I tried it the first day. I was waiting in line for a fish burger. A group of girls behind me were whispering and laughing.

"You ask her!"

"No, you ask her!"

"I don't want to go near her. What if she's contagious?"

"She'd make a great *before* picture."

"Before what?"

"You know, like a total makeover."

"They'd have to cut the side of her face off. No way makeup could cover that."

"She should at least try—like with heavy foundation. I mean, I'm kind of losing my appetite just looking at her."

"Maybe it's skin cancer."

"My grandma had skin cancer on her face, and it looked nothing like that."

"God, you guys are so immature! It's probably just some growth or something. Maybe a birthmark. Just drop it and keep moving. I'm hungry!"

"Oh, my God, can you imagine having a baby and it looked like that?"

I never got the burger. I ran out of the cafeteria and hid in the library. I wouldn't even talk to Temmie after dance. I just cried in my room.

Nobody else goes to the library during lunch, so it's me and old Mrs. Moss and rows of dusty books and lots of computers that no one uses anymore because everyone has a laptop. I read and sneak food from my backpack. It sounds like a scene made for Eeyore, but it's actually the only part of the school day that is slightly tolerable. My stomach unclenches and I can relax enough to eat. And pretend I am living in the worlds that lie in the pages of my book. Believe me, they are way better than the world I'm in here.

12
HUNTER

Mr. D seems pissed off this morning. Usually he jokes around with us a little before starting class, but not today. He's all business. "Let's go, guys. We need to finish this unit before Friday's test. Review Thursday. Open your laptops or notebooks and start jotting down the key ideas in today's lesson."

"Hey, Mr. D, you going to the Lodge Party?" Austin is known for being able to distract Mr. D by sending him off on tangents. Today Mr. D just stares at him.

"Jesus, what's his problem?" Austin mutters under his breath.

"Maybe he's not getting any," Josh whispers back.

I know it's coming. Because it's the same stupid joke every time we make fun of Mr. D. See, his full name is Ludovic Deboncoeur. If it's pronounced the French way, Ludo-veek Duh-bun-kur, it's not funny. But the butchered American pronunciation is more like Ludo-vick

Dee-bonk-her. So we made it Nudo-Prick He-Bonk-her. I know, I know; it's so dumb, but it cracks us up. And Austin delivers under his breath. "Nudoprick Hebonkher."

We try to stifle our laughter, but it slides out from behind our hands.

"That's enough!" Mr. D snaps.

To his credit, Mr. D is a really good teacher. He helps spice up the boring history textbook by telling stories. Like today he goes into this tale about the USS *Cyclops*, a US Navy ship that disappeared in 1918 somewhere in the Bermuda Triangle with more than three hundred men on board. Apparently there are lots of theories about what happened, but the ship has never been found.

Shea raises her hand. "Do you think a ship could disappear like that today?"

Mr. D doesn't answer directly, as usual. He always sends it back to us. "What do you think?"

For once, Austin is actually paying attention. "No way. With the tracking devices they have now?"

Others jump in. "Or radar?"

"Does that work anywhere? Or do you have to be within a couple hundred miles of shore?"

"It works in the middle of the ocean."

"We have GPS on our boat."

"For what? In case your little rowboat gets lost in the pond in your backyard?"

"No, you jerk! We take it down to Sebago Lake."

"That's nothing like the Bermuda Triangle."

"So? I bet ships all have GPS on them. So something like the *Cyclops* mystery couldn't happen today."

The bell rings before we finish. We pack up our stuff.

"Bro, you watchin' the volleyball game? Hunter and Coop are playing this year."

"Naw, gotta work."

"Seriously? You're always working."

"So? Better than sitting around polishing my gun just to go out and miss a buck about ten yards away!"

"Shut up! Is that what that asshole Andersen told you? He needs glasses, man. That buck was frickin' huge. And he was more like a hundred yards from me."

"At least I'm not counting on venison to feed me all winter. I can eat pizza at work."

"What if I told you that Mikayla was going to be at the party?"

"Then I may just find someone to cover my shift. Hot damn."

We're headed out the door when Mr. D calls to me. "Hunter? You going to make up your quiz?"

Crap. "Oh, that's right. I forgot."

The guys go on without me, and I return to my seat near the back of the room. Mr. D brings me a quiz I missed when I was out sick on Monday. I hate missing school, because it always takes so long to make up the work.

Mr. D sits at his desk, probably grading the same quiz that I'm taking. It's eerily quiet. I'm kind of getting into it; I know this material, and it's actually fun to write about it. Then I hear Mr. D. "Kiki? You good?"

I didn't even notice there was still someone else in the room. Kiki, our resident brainiac, is sitting at her desk with her head down. She stands up and glances at me. I immediately turn back to my quiz. But I can't help overhearing her.

"Um, Mr. D, I . . . I . . . I was just wondering if I could have an extension on the paper due tomorrow."

Kiki? Even I got it done over the weekend. I would feel a little superior, but I don't. Something bad must have happened. I don't know her well, but I do know that she aces everything, because Josh always sneaks a look at her grades when Mr. D returns our tests and papers.

She's really quiet, but when she talks, she sounds brilliant. Mr. D has said she'll make an excellent policy wonk someday. Whatever that is.

"Are you having trouble condensing your research?"

She bursts into tears. I can't help my head jerking up; it's like passing a car accident. Mr. D leaps to his feet and grabs the tissue box by the door. "You can have more time! I didn't mean—"

Kiki shakes her head. "It's not just the paper. It's everything. Last night I was at the laundromat until 11:30, doing the whole family's laundry. Our washing machine broke, and since Dad doesn't have a job anymore, we can't get a new one. Usually my mother does it, but she was canning applesauce all day and was too tired. I planned to write my paper at the laundromat until I realized they don't have Wi-Fi. I'm really sorry, Mr. D. I usually don't wait until the last minute." She plucks a tissue and blows her nose.

I put my head back down and try to focus.

"That's a heavy load," Mr. D says quietly. But I hear it. *This is so awkward! Should I excuse myself or stay put?*

"I just wish I could help more," she confesses. "Some of my friends have jobs, but no one's hiring now. I've looked. And when there is an opening, it usually goes to an adult who's out of work. And I don't hunt or fish, so I'm not bringing in any food. All I do is work in our vegetable garden. I picked four bushels of apples on my cousin's farm on Saturday. But I guess I just feel kind of useless . . ." Her voice trails off.

I had no idea. I mean, it's Kiki, who always seems so together. I should like talk to her, tell her a lot of us can relate. But maybe that would just embarrass her. *Damn the frickin' mill.*

There is silence for a minute. I start writing again. Then Mr. D speaks. "What are you hoping to do after you graduate next year?"

Kiki looks surprised—like, where did that question come from? "Um, I haven't really thought that far. Probably get a job, if anyone is hiring."

"Have you thought about going to college?"

"College? Oh, no! We could never afford that." She looks away from Mr. D. "I don't know; maybe I could take an online class or something."

"There are scholarships. Especially for people with your ability. I'll start researching. In the meantime, just hand in the paper when you finish. Don't worry about it."

Kiki rushes out after thanking Mr. D. When I finally finish the quiz and hand it in, Mr. D is sitting at his desk, just staring into space. With a really sad look on his face. It bums me out.

13
LUNA

Thursdays are the hardest days for me because I don't dance. This morning I'm already in a bad mood when I go downstairs. Temmie comments on the weather like I don't know that it's always cold and snowy around here now. I just grunt in response.

Then she hits me with it. "Hey, kiddo, I know the church is too busy for dancing today. You'll come with me to my knitting group."

She's serious? Knitting group? I'm not forty years old! "Uh, no thanks. I'll just come home and read or something."

"I don't want you here alone."

Why not? I spend all day alone. "I'll be fine."

Temmie is usually pretty chill, but she won't let this one go. She turns away from the stew she already has put in the slow cooker and heads up the stairs. "This one's non-negotiable. I'll see you here right after school."

Does she think I'm still six? What, is she worried I'm going to have a wild party? Do drugs? Off myself? God! Why on earth would I want to go to a knitting group with a bunch of women?

My mood hasn't lifted when I stomp into the house after school. Temmie is there, already in her coat, waiting for me. She hands me an apple and a granola bar. "You can bring your school stuff if you'd rather do homework there than hang out with us. Let's go."

The Edgewater Public Library is a big old wooden building that looks more like a house than a library. It's pretty—dark green shutters on weathered gray wood—but the shutters look like they could use a coat of paint.

The inside is filled with bookshelves of dark wood. There are reading lamps on tables that give the whole place a cozy vibe. Temmie leads me into the meeting room, which has a coatroom off to the side. Next to the coatroom is a small closed alcove that has one chair and a desk in it. It's open to the meeting room, but it's kind of hidden. I tell Temmie I need to do homework and that I'll sit right here. Temmie just nods her head, hangs up her coat, then carries her knitting bag into the meeting room. I plunk down in the chair and pull out my laptop. As I get set up to do chemistry problems, which I hate, I realize that I can see into the meeting room. But the way the chairs and couches are set up, the knitters can't see me. Perfect.

The meeting room is bright and airy. Huge windows line the west side so the afternoon sun is casting a warm glow over everything. The couches are obviously worn, but they look comfortable. Colorful pillows are everywhere. I feel less annoyed just by my proximity to this cheerfulness.

I really should get going on my chem, but I'm having fun people watching. The women greet each other warmly; they seem to be old friends. Temmie told me that it used to be a group of elderly women, but now that the mill has closed, it's expanded to include several younger women who are out of work. I look around the group. Despite the hugs and laughter, there is this weird sense of despair. Wrinkles line weather-beaten faces. Some of the women are gaunt, maybe from poverty. Too many cheap meals of ramen noodles have pushed others into obesity. The extra flesh looks uncomfortable; buttons and seams strain on clothes bought in a happier time. Red veins on a few noses indicate some seeking solace in a bottle. Probably cheap wine. And underlying the camaraderie and cheer is a haunted anxiety. The only thing that feels new is what is being created on the knitting needles. The room smells of slightly burned coffee, which an old woman in a wheelchair is serving along with gigantic frosted sugar cookies. My stomach rumbles. I hope Temmie grabs one for me.

A hush falls over the group when two women walk in. One is probably in her twenties or thirties; the other looks about forty. The younger one introduces her companion, who looks completely different from everyone else here. Her clothes are stylish and new, her jewelry expensive, her body lean and fit. I actually don't know if her clothes are new and her jewelry is expensive, but they look it.

"Hey, everybody, this is Jessica. I made her a latte at Molly's and convinced her to come to our group."

Jessica gives a little wave as the women murmur hellos. Jessica and the Molly's woman sit close to where I am.

Jessica looks uncomfortable, out of place. *Gee, I can relate.* "Samantha, you were sweet to invite me. But I didn't bring anything to do. I mean, all these women are knitting."

"Oh, you'll get put to work in a minute. Ruth'll ask you to serve refills, or Barbara will have you sort yarn."

Right on cue, a woman pipes up. "Hello, Jessica. I'm Ethel. Happy to have you. If you two girls aren't busy, would you mind balling these skeins for me?"

I settle into my chem homework to the rhythm of clicking knitting needles. I keep one ear on the stories and concerns and jokes flying around the cozy room.

"Who's going to the Lodge Party on Saturday?"

"I bet the whole town'll be there. Free food."

"Be nice to eat something besides spaghetti."

"I'll be there. With my Tupperware!"

"Ain't that the truth? Everyone's going to bring food home."

"You don't need to bring Tupperware. They have those fancy to-go containers. I still have mine from last year."

Near me, Samantha glances at Jessica. "You going?"

"I . . . no. I've actually never gone. It's not really my scene. Anyway, crowds make Thaddeus uncomfortable. He's my son. He's seventeen. Can't really navigate in public."

He's seventeen? Have I seen him at school? Someone else who can't deal? I kind of want to ask her about him, but there's no way I'm blowing my cover.

The general chatter continues. "I heard there's a new supermarket opening in January over on the east highway. Hannaford's, I think. 'Bout thirty miles from here. Wonder if they're hiring?"

"That'd be a bear of a commute in the winter. They don't always plow the access road."

"Speaking of food, Ethel, did Charlie bag himself a buck?"

"No, but our son got one. Charlie helped him field-dress and quarter it. We've got about a third of it in our freezer now. CJ kept a third and gave the other to a buddy of his. I get so tired of thinking of new ways to use venison, but I suppose I should be grateful we have meat."

"Oh, I'll give you my venison taco recipe. It's easy. Surprisingly good."

"Anyone hear anything about the mill building?"

The silence that falls feels heavy.

"Nope. Not a thing."

Jessica extracts herself from the yarn. "I'm so sorry, but I need to leave. I have to take a call with a client in Switzerland before they go to bed." She rises. "Thank you for the coffee and cookies. It was lovely to meet all of you. And your knitting is beautiful. Um, if you would consider selling a sweater, I would love to buy one!" She hurries out.

"Think we scared her off?"

"Nah."

"Do you think she was serious about buying a sweater?"

"That was insulting. We're not here to sell our work."

Samantha finishes winding a ball of pink yarn. "She was just complimenting your knitting."

"Well, that was an odd way of doing it."

Someone snorts. "That's her kind of folks. Life is easy when you're swimming in money."

"What do you think she'd pay for this?" A woman holds up a yellow sleeve. "Twenty bucks?"

"She'd be pretty chilly if that's all that's keeping her warm!"

Laughter fills the room. Then someone wails, "Barbara, what did I do wrong? This snowflake looks more like a baseball."

Barbara goes to the rescue, and Ethel refills coffee mugs.

I am oddly distracted. Usually I just tune out talking, like when we're given time in class to start our homework. But I guess I'm just nosy or something, because I keep listening.

"How's little Teo, Bridget?"

I jerk my head up and look. I didn't know Teo's mom was a part of this group. I spy her sitting in a beanbag chair, her legs curled up under her.

"Oh, he's great. Just great. I think, fingers crossed, that he's finally potty-trained. Very proud of himself too."

Samantha laughs. "He sure is! He showed me his Superman underwear the other day at Molly's. I think he used our bathroom three times!"

Bridget pauses in her knitting. "He's quite enamored with your niece, Temmie. They call her 'Miss Luna' at Sunday School, but he just says 'Loon.' 'My Loon.' So cute."

I freeze. They don't know I'm sitting right here. Temmie doesn't say anything.

Samantha does. "That's your niece? Miss Luna? Ohh! 'Cause the other day he stood in front of the display case at the counter and refused to move until Bridget bought a black-and-white cookie for her. He was so happy when he carried the little bag out. Kept saying, 'For my Loon.' God, he's such a sweetheart!"

Bridget laughs. "I'm not sure why he was so obsessed with those cookies," she muses. "He's never had one before. Honestly, it's too much sugar. But, oh, was he proud of his gift! He gave it to her on Sunday."

Temmie clears her throat. "Who's entering the Desserting the Dark competition?"

A bunch of women raise their hands. "No one can beat Molly," says Ethel, "but this year I'm trying a peach and blueberry crisp."

And the conversation turns to desserts, away from me. *Thank God.*

On the way home, I'm feeling wistful. Like I wish I had a group like that, where people are so easy with each other. It's like I'm missing something I've never had, something I've witnessed from the sidelines or seen in a book or movie. I long for someone to want to talk with me, confide in me, just hang out with me. That happens in my fantasy life.

In real life, I'm an island. The only people besides Temmie that I really talk to are in my little Sunday school class. *God, that is so pathetic!* But I actually like hanging out with the kids, who are so funny. Especially Teo. He always sits next to me. Sometimes he sticks his pudgy hand out and rubs my cheek. The birthmark side. Noooo way would I let anyone else come close to touching me, especially there, but for some weird reason, it's okay when he does it. Maybe because he's so gentle. Or because he's still so little and doesn't understand how ugly I am. Or because someday he's going to be as vulnerable to scorn and rejection as I am.

Sometimes I wish we lived in a city, where I wouldn't be such a freak show. I mean, I would still be a freak, but there would be other people with like crazy tattoos or blue hair or multiple piercings, and I'd blend in better.

"You get some homework done?" Temmie waves to a neighbor out shoveling as we drive past.

I ignore her question. Because I have one that's more pressing. "Why do you still live in this puny town after you've been all over the world? In huge cities? In progressive, international, cosmopolitan cities?"

Temmie doesn't take her eyes from the road. Doesn't ask how this is related to her question about my stupid homework. "Because this is home. I know it's not glamorous, but I know these people." She stops, and I think she's finished. And I'm not satisfied with the answer. Unlike a lot of people around here, she's left. She's experienced the whole world. She could *know* other people in more glamorous places.

But then she continues. "And they're the only people who remember your mother. Before she . . . well, before. When she could skate circles around everybody else on Ridgetop Pond. When she was the only one who dared to sled down Maple Mountain blindfolded. When she was the first one to skinny-dip in April and the last one in October. When she . . ."

I tune her out. Blah, blah, blah. I don't want to hear about my mother's daring exploits. I've heard them all before, and I hate them. If she was so brave, why did she throw me away?

Was I too hard to look at? Impossible to love? Would an ugly baby cramp her style or ruin her rep? Or did she finally meet her match, run into a challenge that even she, the charming daredevil, couldn't face?

14
HUNTER

A huge crowd is already gathered around the volleyball court when Dad drops me off. It's obvious that everybody here is as excited about the Lodge Party events as I am. Coach ended practice early so the team could watch me and Coop play.

I drop my bag by a makeshift bench someone has built out of hay bales. I sit to take off my boots and put on my sneakers. Coop hustles over and sits next to me. "I wonder who plowed the court?"

Most of the farmers with pickups have attachable snowplows; probably one of them did it for a six-pack. I look at the frozen grass, brown and matted. "That ground is gonna hurt when we fall."

Coop slugs me in the shoulder. "You wuss! Get used to it. Just remember, it's gonna hurt them worse."

We jog in place for a bit, do some stretches and jumping jacks, then join our teammates, who are warming up with a few balls. I hear someone shouting my name. I look out in the crowd and see Emma, bouncing up and down, holding a sign: "Hunt 'Em Dead!" I laugh and wave, and the whole group she's with starts chanting, "Hunter Ridley, hunt 'em dead!"

Coop grins. "Got your own personal fan club, huh?"

"Me?" I say. "Look over there!"

He does. And he spies the sign: "Colin on you, Cooper!"

And a new chant begins. "Colin on you, Coop, to win, win, win!"

It seems like everyone has a sign, young and old.

"They're Overs the Hill—Unders Rule"

"Give Up, UNDERStand?"

"Go Daddy!"

The last one sends a jolt through me. I remember cheering for my dad just like this little kid is. I wish Dad could still play. I scan the crowd; I don't see him. But it's so chaotic—people cheering, jumping up and down, passing flasks, doing the wave, getting on each other's shoulders—that I know I can easily miss him in the mass of hyped-up spectators.

The traditional blaring horn starts the game. And immediately we are laser-focused. Serve, receive, set, kill. The intensity grows as we realize, on both sides, that we are facing fierce competition. The Unders are more agile, the Overs more powerful.

I set up Coop, who spikes it past a burly Over. Our point. Coop and I high-five. The crowd on the Unders' side goes insane.

We are sweating, despite the cold, and strip down to T-shirts. The frenzy increases, all of us pummeling the ball in our desperation to win. For the Unders, it's about bragging rights, David beating Goliath, a major upset. For the Overs, it's a lot more. It's like a major release of pent-up frustration that goes way beyond the game. The guys who used to work at the mill want to earn back the respect and dignity and power they lost when it closed. I know it's just a game, and they're not getting their jobs back, but they really want to win.

At this. Because they lost, big time, at that. My aunt explained this to me when I was struggling with Dad, not understanding why he couldn't just stop drinking and be the dad he used to be.

With every successful spike, there is a flash of potency, what Gretchen calls an "existential justification." She said the only reason a serious rumble won't break out is the understanding that we are all in this together. If either side was playing against the mill owners and corporate administrators, then yeah, there would be serious fighting. And not just with verbal taunts. With fists. And worse.

Incredibly, the Unders win the first set. The Overs take the second, showing no mercy with the power of their shots. One guy on our team has his finger bent back so far from an Overs' slam that I think it's broken. Someone grabs duct tape from their truck and wraps the kid's fingers together before he comes back in.

And then, I swear I'm not making this up. It's like a cheesy Hollywood sports movie, neck-and-neck until the absolute final point. We have to win by two points, and it's tied at 21-all. They go up, 22–21. We even it at 22-all. It goes that way for point after agonizing point until it's 30-all. People in the crowd are screaming themselves hoarse. I glance at Emma, who has stripped off her jacket and is waving it around her head in excitement. The ball flies back and forth like a pendulum on hyperdrive; everyone both on the court and off is in this crazy trance. We go up 31-30, and the Unders' side goes wild. The six of us on the court form a huddle. Our captain has sweat pouring down his face, but you can see his breath when he speaks. "This is it, bros! I feel it. Get the ball to Hunter. High set. Hunter, they're leaving the middle open when they come up to the net. The back three are guarding the end line, playing too far back. Slip one in over the heads of the front line, a soft lob right to the middle."

We fist bump in agreement. The Overs serve. A hard shot. Our captain dives to receive it and taps it to Coop. Coop sets a long lob to me. I do exactly what our captain said. And it works. The ball lands on the ground behind the front line, and the place goes wild. My teammates dive on me and I am quickly at the bottom of a pile of insanely stoked guys. The pandemonium on our side rivals Fenway Park when the Red Sox won the World Series. The whole scene is so frickin' awesome.

We finally get up and are immediately swarmed by our friends. I grab Emma and throw her in the air, shrieking. I catch her, put her down, and then I do it again. She kisses me again and again. We are all laughing and screaming and pounding each other on the back.

Finally we join the horde of people heading inside. Coop runs up behind me and lifts me up. "We are the champions, we are the champions!" His rendition of Queen's quintessential victory song is terrible, but we all join in at the top of our lungs.

"Dinner or pool?" our captain shouts. We are covered with mud and still sweating, even though someone said the windchill had dropped to six above. So we race to the pool, strip down to our gym shorts, and jump in. Coop announces a cannonball contest. None of us can swim worth crap, but we can make gigantic splashes. Our contest draws another crowd, this time the little kids. They sit along the edge of the pool, cheering us on.

"Make it go higher!"

They scream when the water hits them.

"Higher!"

I see Teo and his mother on the deck, watching. He's wearing a little shark swimsuit and has bright orange water wings on his arms. "Hey-o, Teo," I call out, "this one's for you!" And then I let loose with the best cannonball yet, soaking the kids at the edge.

"Do it again!"

"Again, again!"

So we do. Over and over. It's like pure joy, this night. Cannonballs. Kids. Volleyball. Beating the Overs. Pure, total fun.

The guys finally quit because someone calls that dinner is ready. We grab towels and dry off. Then I see Teo, crying. His mother gets up and sort of hesitates, then she walks across the deck. She smiles apologetically. "A bit of a meltdown. Congratulations, Hunter! I hear it was a fantastic game."

"Thanks a lot, Miz Callahan."

"I wish I'd seen it. But Teo was so excited by the prospect of the pool."

I look at Teo. He's still sobbing. "He okay?"

"Oh, he's fine. He just wanted to jump in and make a big splash like you. But he can't swim, and I would never let him in where he can't stand."

It's a no-brainer. I'll take him. "If you trust me, Miz Callahan, I'd be happy to catch him."

So while the other guys get dressed and take off for dinner, I get back in the pool. Teo climbs onto the low diving board. I tread water and wait. He walks to the end, claps his hands, and leaps off into my arms. He laughs and hits my shoulders in raw excitement as I swim him to the ladder. Three more times before his mother says that everyone's hungry and it's time to eat. We stand on the deck, the water dripping in puddles at our feet.

I bend over and high-five Teo. "Say-o, Teo, you are now the Cannonball King!"

We high-five again, then Teo pulls on my arm so I'll bend over again. He wraps his short little arms around my neck. When he lets go, I tousle his black curls with my towel.

I didn't think this day could get any better. But it just did.

15

LUNA

Every year, out of politeness, Temmie asks me if I want to go to the Lodge Party. It's so stupid because she already knows the answer. I wouldn't be caught dead out in public around so many people. And who would I hang out with? Her?

Temmie, on the other hand, loves the whole thing because it's a tradition from her childhood. She knows almost everyone in Edgewater; either she grew up with them or worked with them at the mill. The party is a chance to catch up with lots of people before everyone goes into hibernation.

So today is no different. I'm planning to watch a new thriller that just came out on Netflix. And make something fun for my dinner, like a grilled peanut butter and raspberry jam sandwich. I won't even open my backpack, though I confess I am tempted to get a jump on my homework so I won't have to do it all on Sunday. But

Temmie throws a wrench in my plans late in the afternoon. "I need help bringing this platter of cream puffs to the dessert competition."

I look up from my phone, kind of disoriented. "What?"

"I need you to carry my dessert into the lodge. I'm afraid I'll slip and fall going down the hill. We'll leave in about an hour."

I'm confused. "But I'm not going to the party. I've never gone."

"Well, tonight will be your first time then, huh?"

"Temmie, I'm not going. Can't you ask one of your friends to help you?"

"Most of them will already be there. They're not going to want to climb the hill to the field where everyone parks. Not in this weather."

I see my quiet evening slipping away like a rogue helium balloon. "Temmie, please! I really, really don't want to go! You know how awful it is for me."

Temmie turns from where she is putting final flourishes on the chocolate icing. I have to admit that her cream puffs look amazing. To my surprise, she quickly wipes away a tear. "It won't necessarily be awful, Luna. If you hate it, we can leave."

She's crying over this? God! Why can't I just stay home?

But I know she needs help. And I know how much she loves this party. "Fine. I'll help you bring them in. But I'm not staying. I'll wait in the car and watch my movie."

It's not a victory for either of us. "Bundle up then" is all she says.

We shove a huge log in the woodstove so the house will be warm when we come home. I grab a thick sleeping bag and several blankets for the car. Temmie hands me a portable heater, one that runs on batteries. It reminds me of a hot water bottle, but one that never cools off. "You're going to need this."

I've never seen so many cars in one place in Edgewater. I didn't realize, even though Temmie has said it, that, yes, everyone goes to this party. We park on the hill. Temmie pulls her hat down low, and I put on a full face mask. That's one good thing about this bitter cold;

no one will think it's weird that I have a ski mask on. We head down the hill, our boots sliding a little in the snow. By the time we get to the lodge, the cream puffs have probably frozen. I follow Temmie through a crowd of people who are raving about the volleyball game. We enter the lodge kitchen from the back; only competitors are allowed. I place the tray on an enormous counter next to a bunch of other delectable-looking desserts, and then we are shepherded out by the contest organizers. Someone calls out. "Temmie? Is that you? I didn't recognize you at first. Must be a new hat."

I need to get out of here. "So that's all? You're good?"

Temmie nods.

"Have fun! I'll be in the car." I start to leave.

Temmie grabs my hand. "Honey, if you get cold, either come in or turn on the car and run the heater."

I jog back up the hill. By the time I reach our car, I'm hot. It's really quiet up here, even peaceful. No cloud cover and just a sliver of moon enhance the brilliance of the stars. I admit it to myself: *You'd never see a sky like this in one of those cosmopolitan centers.*

I make a cocoon in my seat with the blankets and sleeping bag and heater. It's so warm that I open the window an inch. I'm about half an hour into the movie, totally absorbed, when a voice outside the car makes me jump. I pause the movie, my heart pounding. I see a man leaning against the pickup truck parked next to me.

"I said, they're something, huh?" He gestures to the sky with a bottle in his gloved hand. "The stars. Putting on quite a show tonight."

At first I think he's talking to me. Then I see another guy walking toward him. He stops and stands in silence, looking up. Then he speaks.

"You're Hunter's dad, right? I'm Ludovic Deboncoeur, his history teacher. Hunter played quite a game tonight."

Mr. D? Oh, God. I hope he can't see me! I shrink down low in the seat. I can still see them, but I think I'm hidden from view.

"He did all right."

"Are you looking forward to the basketball season?"

"Yup."

"Hunter's a real team player. You should be proud."

"Yup."

Mr. D is like stamping his feet and rubbing his hands. I bet he was at the game, watching the kids from my class. That's dedication. I wish I had the courage to tell him that.

"So, are you going to the dinner?"

Hunter's dad holds up his bottle. "Got my dinner right here." He takes a swig and wipes his mouth on the back of his glove. "You got a wife, Mr. D?"

"Uh, no. No, I don't."

"That's good. Then you won't be hurt."

Mr. D doesn't say anything for a second. Then he clears his throat. "Um, did your wife hurt you?"

"She died. In childbirth. Like it was the fuckin' 1800s! And the clinic in this lousy town couldn't do anything for her. Time we got to a real hospital, it was too late. Excessive bleeding. They called it maternal mortality. I called it breaking my fuckin' heart."

"Oh, I am so sorry. I didn't know."

He takes another long drink. "But I didn't really have time to, you know, process it. Because of Hunter. Taking care of him was my whole world. And working at the mill was okay because it was all for Hunter."

He's slurring his words. How long has he been drinking? I don't think he was here when I came back up, but then I wasn't really paying attention to the other cars. He finishes the bottle and throws it in the back of the truck, where it clangs. "But now he's almost an adult. Doesn't need me anymore. Got his friends. And I got nothin'. No kid. No job. No wife. That's why I'm so pissed at the damn doctors who couldn't save her."

"You still have Hunter," Mr. D says, "and he needs you."

"Naw. He likes his coach. I just embarrass him. I'd be better off dead."

"Let me get you down to the dinner." Mr. D takes his arm.

Hunter's dad jerks it away. "I told you I don't need any dinner."

Mr. D is insistent. He takes his arm again. "Then you can just rest somewhere. Maybe sleep it off a bit."

I pray he doesn't get slugged in the face. They take off, and I watch them stumble down the hill before disappearing.

My little nest doesn't feel cozy anymore. I ache. *Why is life so hard?*

16
HUNTER

Best. Night. Ever. We were starving after the game and cannonball contest, so we chowed down at dinner. And then I think I ate like three desserts. They were insane. And the talent show. Oh, my God, the talent show! A month ago Coop and I dared Nate and Josh to enter because they were singing in the locker room after practice and they sucked. Big time. Hah! Joke's on us. They did a cover of Lil Nas X's "Old Town Road," and they had the whole place rocking with them. They were seriously amazing. Coop and I will never admit that, and now we have to bring them breakfast for a week. But geez. Who knew?

Everyone's going to Josh's to keep the night going. His family hosts the after-party every year. A huge bonfire, rides on the snowmobile, sledding on the hill. Some kids will do the polar bear challenge and jump in the pond if they can crack the ice. His parents will have a ton of food. And beer. For the adults, but I'm sure kids will sneak in six-packs. Whatever. It gets kind of old.

I want to go, mainly because the sledding hill is insane, but I'm worried about my dad. I haven't seen him since he dropped me off before the game.

Coop punches my arm. "Come on, dude. Let's go. I'll drive you."

"Nah, I'm good. I gotta get up early tomorrow."

"Seriously? Jesus, you can sleep when you're old. Just come with—" He looks up in alarm.

A bunch of men are running toward us in a panic. They stop. "Have you guys seen Teo?"

"What? No. I mean, I was in the pool with him a couple hours ago. But—"

"No, he's only been gone for like twenty minutes. From the dining room. His mother let him leave to use the bathroom, and he never came back. We've checked all the restrooms on this level, and people are already upstairs and outside looking. If you see him, let us know. We're afraid he's been taken."

Taken? Teo? What the hell?

I turn to Coop. "We gotta help. I love that kid. I don't know where he'd . . . maybe we should go back and check the pool?"

"No point. They always lock it before dinner." Coop laughs. "Remember when we tried to bust in one year? And that cop caught us? You almost wet your pants you were so scared!"

"Shut up! That's the fastest I've ever seen your ass run!"

"We should try to break in again. I bet we could this time."

"We're not breaking in, you idiot. We need to find Teo."

Coop shrugs. "Okay, you wuss. Then fine. We can at least start by the pool. But it's gonna be locked."

We jog down the long hall and leave the main building. The corridor leading to the pool is dimly lit. We turn the last corner and see the pool door wide open. The lights are still on.

Coop stops. "Whoa. This place is supposed to be locked and dark."

The men's restroom door is open. This is getting weirder. We walk in. "Teo? Teo?" My voice echoes in the emptiness. I spy something blue on the floor in front of the sinks. I pick it up. A tiny pair of jeans. Was Teo wearing jeans? I only saw him in his swimsuit.

Coop sees the pants and explodes. "Oh, my God. If a fuckin' pedophile did him in here, I'll kill him. I'm not kidding. I will fuckin' kill the perv."

My heart is slamming against my chest. Could some sicko really assault that awesome little kid? I won't let myself believe it. We check the stalls. Empty. We run out on the pool deck, yelling. "Teo? *Teo!*"

"Hunter?"

I whip around. It's my dad, walking slowly in the shadows by the deep end of the pool, rubbing his eyes. He looks like shit. "What's going on? What's with all that noise?"

"Dad? What are you doing in here?"

He wipes his mouth with his shirtsleeve. "I . . . I'm not sure. What are you—?"

I cut him off. "We're looking for Teo."

"Who?" He runs his hands over his forehead. "Jesus. Wait a minute. Let me get my boots. I'll help."

He heads back to the dark corner. I still don't know why he's here. I hear a crash. And then a groan. "Hunter? Little help?"

We find him lying on the concrete. The lounge chair he was sitting in, I guess to put on his boots, has flipped over. Coop and I grab his hands and pull him up. The smell hits us like a tsunami. He reeks of booze. *Was he passed out in here? Did he even see the game? The one frickin' year I get to play, and he couldn't be bothered to watch?* I turn away in disgust.

And that's when I see him.

At the bottom of the deep end. Under the diving board.

A tiny body.

17
LUNA

I am numb.

Why him?

In one month, that little boy slipped into my heart.

And now he's gone.

Missing him hurts. Like no pain I've ever felt before. And I hate myself for thinking this because it's not about me, but it feels like a punishment. Like I let my guard down, let someone in, let myself care too much, and boom, he's gone. *I don't deserve love.*

I actually ask to go to the funeral. Though I can tell Temmie is surprised by how her eyebrows go up, she just nods. We arrive at the church early, but it's already packed. We join the cluster of people standing in the back. For once my face doesn't generate stares and whispers because everyone is in like a zombie state. Complete silence.

Tons of tears. Desperate hugs. I cower against the wall. I don't want anyone trying to hug me. Not that they would, anyway.

The organist starts playing, and four men walk in carrying the smallest casket you could imagine. One of the pallbearers is actually a high school kid. I recognize him from my history class. Hunter, I think. When Teo's mom follows, you can hear people gasp. It's as if she's an old woman. Utterly broken. I only met her once, that day at church, but she looks like she's aged twenty years since then. Her hair is pulled back in a tight knot and her face is deathly pale except under her eyes, where dark circles make her look like she's been in a fight. She's gaunt and bent over, like she's wearing a heavy backpack. She walks haltingly, as if each step sends shooting pains through her whole body.

After some music and prayer, Pastor Mark steps up to the pulpit. He shuffles some papers then gathers them up and stuffs them into a drawer or something under the lectern. I get it. I bet he wrote and rewrote and tore up and threw away and is still at a loss. What can he possibly say to make sense of this tragedy?

Pastor Mark doesn't talk about how hard it is for him to lead a funeral for a child, like I was afraid he would. Because it's not about his challenge, it's about Teo. And us.

"Teo Callahan was a gift from God," he says. "Every child is. But Teo was a literal gift, to his mother, Bridget, and to this entire community. His birth parents somehow knew that Bridget would love him, that we would all cherish him. We did. This place is packed because we did." He pauses.

"Teo thrived here. He was the embodiment of happiness. And the pure love that radiated from him did not discriminate or judge. He brought joy to every single person who knew him." I see people wiping their tears and nodding their heads.

"Some of you have come to me in despair, wondering why God chose to take Teo. God did not will this. He is weeping along with all of us. This was a tragic accident with no one to blame. Through his tears, God welcomes our beloved Teo home." Tissues are passed down the pews. I've never seen so many people crying. Men and women and kids. Temmie digs in her purse and pulls out a tissue. She hands it to me. I didn't even realize I was crying too.

Pastor Mark's voice wavers. "I imagine that Teo is charming a host of heaven-dwellers, just as he beguiled all of us. The stories you've shared about our five-year-old Teo all feature a common thread: He brought joy and peace. It was as if he had an otherworldly sensitivity to those who struggled with pain or loneliness or anxiety.

"Are we sad? Terribly. Will we miss Teo? Desperately. Will our grief overwhelm us? Probably." There is a long moment of silence before he continues.

"It may offer little comfort now, but know that Teo is with us. Forever. Though his time was cut short, his heart and spirit remain. In the songs we sing, the hot chocolate we sip, the snow we shovel, the wildflowers we pick. When kindness wins over criticism. When acceptance beats exclusion. When delight replaces cynicism.

"We are a changed people in the wake of knowing Teo Callahan. We are better for his having been a part of us. And from the love and many kindnesses I saw you bestow upon that special little boy, he was better for having been a part of you."

Pastor Mark wraps us in a blanket with his words.

For the first time since I heard about Teo, I feel as if I can breathe. The excruciating tightness in my chest is gone.

But it's replaced with an aching sadness.

18
HUNTER

Emma comes up to me just as I'm entering the cafeteria, all breathless and wide-eyed. "Have you heard the rumors?"

I smile indulgently, like a grandfather would to a toddler. I'm sure she's got the latest on who got caught with someone else's girlfriend, who skipped math class to smoke weed in the woods, who got a tattoo on their butt.

She doesn't smile back. "This is serious, Hunter."

She drags me out of the caf and down the hall. I'm annoyed because I'm hungry. Really hungry. "What the hell, Em?"

People are streaming by on their way to lunch. The hall is loud with the banging of locker doors and kids laughing and yelling. Emma almost has to shout for me to hear her. "People are saying that your dad was there. You know, when Teo drowned."

"That's the rumor?"

She nods, her eyebrows furrowed in concern.

"Well, he was. Obviously. You know that. Remember? I told you he was sleeping in that back corner where the lounge chairs are stored. I'm pretty sure that's public knowledge." I pause. "So how is that a rumor?"

She puffs up with self-importance, the way she always does when she has dirt on someone. "Oh, my God, it's so bad. Get this. They're saying that he could have saved Teo. That he just watched him drown."

"*What?*"

She nods again. "That's what I've heard. From multiple sources. It's all over social media."

"*He was sleeping!*" Fury fills me. "I don't know who the fuck would spread that shit, but it's not true. I was there. You know that! Jesus, Em, I told you exactly what happened! Of all people, you should be stopping such a stupid rumor, telling them it's bullshit. My God!"

Emma raises her hands. "God, Hunter, don't shoot the messenger! I'm just letting you know."

"This is exactly why I hate social media! And what, people can't accept an accident for what it was? *An accident*? Without trying to pin the blame on someone?" My voice is shaking. "And you honestly think my dad wouldn't do everything he could to save a little kid?"

"I know your dad is a good guy," Emma protests. "But I also know he drinks. And, you know."

"Last time I checked," I say bitterly, "drinking wasn't a crime. And he wasn't the only one who was drunk that night."

Suddenly I notice that it's become eerily quiet. A bunch of people have stopped to watch this drama unfold. I whirl around and storm down the hall, away from the caf and its boiling pot of vicious rumors.

I sneak into the theater and go backstage. When I was in ninth grade, I worked as a grip, someone who changes the props between scenes. I only did it because I had a huge crush on a girl in the musical, but it was fun. And so different from the basketball world I knew. Anyway, I know I can hide here.

Huge, wracking sobs come as I huddle next to the dusty velvet curtain. *I hate this, I hate this, I hate this.*

Because even though technically the rumor is false, it's based in truth.

But it's not Dad's fault, it's mine.

I assume that someone left the door open because they knew Dad was still in there, passed out on the deck. Otherwise they would have shut the door. And Teo wouldn't have been able to go in there. To do cannonballs. *God!*

The one damn day of the year when there was something for Dad to do besides get plastered.

But I guess being part of a community celebration and seeing his own son play wasn't enough.

That means I'm not enough.

And because of that, Teo's dead.

19
LUNA

Today when Temmie insists that I come to her knitting group, I don't put up a fight. I'm sick of being on my own, and if hiding and eavesdropping on a bunch of women is my only option not to be, I'll take it.

I sit at the desk in the alcove again. When I peek into the meeting room, I notice that the women are in the spots they were last week and the two weeks before that. I guess it's just like us in the classroom, all creatures of habit. Samantha, the barista from Molly's, and Jessica, the new woman, are again sitting closest to me.

"You missed the last couple weeks. You been okay?" I can see why Samantha is, according to Temmie, such a popular fixture at Molly's. She sounds like she really cares, isn't just making small talk.

"I was in Switzerland. My client likes me to be there in person a couple of times a year. My parents came to stay with Thaddeus, so it's like a working vacation for me."

"Sounds divine," says Samantha.

"It is. And it's not only refreshing to be in a whirlwind of work, off a screen and face-to-face with my client, but honestly, it was a relief to be in a place not stained by perpetual sadness." She pauses. "Oh! That sounded terrible. I didn't mean that Edgewater—" Her face is bright red.

Samantha interrupts. "No need to apologize. It is a sad place right now. Between the horrible weather and the mill closing, and then Teo drowning on the one day that's usually a happy oasis in the bleakness. I get it."

"I don't know Bridget at all. I mean, I just met her that first day I came here. I cannot begin to imagine her pain. If anything happened to Thaddeus, I think I would crumple up and die. He is my world, my whole raison d'être." She looks around the group. "Is she . . . ? Do you know how she's doing?"

Samantha shrugs. "I don't know. She's been keeping a low profile. I haven't seen her at Molly's, and she hasn't been back here since it happened. Last week Barbara reported that she'd called her. Bridget told her that she just needed time alone. You know, to process it." She turns to the group. "Has anyone heard from Bridget this week?"

"I took soup to her the other night. She's hurting."

"Someone told me there are lawyers swarming around like she's herring in a lobster trap."

"Why? It was an accident."

"Not the way they see it. They figure she could sue the owners of the Moose and Loon for negligence."

"That's ridiculous. Negligence on whose part? The pool was empty."

The conversation is ping-ponging rapidly around the room. Everyone has something to contribute.

"No, it wasn't. Jack Ridley was on the deck, sleeping it off."

"Why was he in there?"

"Who knows?"

"At least he wasn't her real child. You know, her own."

Did I just hear that correctly?

Temmie, who hasn't said anything, drops her knitting and whirls around. Her face is on fire. "*What* did you say?"

"You know what I mean. I can't imagine losing your own flesh and blood. And he was . . . *you know*."

"No, I don't know," Temmie spits. "He was a child of God. Who happened to have a different genetic makeup. A chromosomal disorder. And don't you ever, *ever* imply that an adopted child is not *real*."

I shrink back further into my seat. No one can see me, I know, but I just want to disappear. The silence is unbearable. Then I hear the same woman Temmie just attacked. Her voice is distinctive, low and raspy. Like she's had a lifelong love affair with cigarettes.

"Don't bite my head off, Temmie. Do you honestly believe that if he'd been a normal baby, he would have been left with Bridget?"

"Let's change the sub—" Rose starts to say, but the woman interrupts. "Look, I'm sorry about Bridget's loss, don't get me wrong. I'm just saying that it would be different if he were her real son. That's all." I peek back in. She's standing now, packing her bag. She walks to the coatroom and grabs her jacket. "I mean, look at your own niece. Don't you think your sister would have kept her if she had been normal?" With that she leaves.

The rest of the women sit in stunned silence. Temmie is furious. "She has no idea what she's talking about."

Murmurs of agreement and sympathy fill the space. I am, oddly, not nearly as upset as Temmie is. Or maybe I am, but I'm numb to it. Nothing new. Same old story. And, frankly, she's probably right. Me and Teo, the town's misfits. Rejected by our mothers.

"Don't worry about her, Temmie. She's an idiot."

The conversation returns to Teo.

"I saw Teo and Bridget at the dinner. He disappeared after the desserts."

"Well, there should have been a lifeguard there if the pool was open. And it was."

"Does Bridget blame herself?"

"Don't all mothers? I mean, when something bad happens?"

"Not her fault. I mean, what are you gonna do, keep your kid on a leash?"

"But why was he in the pool? I thought he was just going to the restroom."

"And why did the lifeguard leave? And why wasn't the pool door closed? That's where the lawsuit comes in."

Near me, Samantha sucks in her breath. She starts packing her knitting bag.

"Is Bridget going to sue?"

"No one knows. Barbara, did she say when she was coming back?"

Barbara smiles, like, gently. "Soon. She misses us."

"I wish we could do something." Everyone echoes this sentiment.

Samantha rises quickly. Her face is drained of color. She blurts out, "I . . . I need to go. I forgot I had a . . . a . . . dentist appointment. See you next week!"

She flees, wrapping a scarf around her neck as she runs out. Maybe I read too many mysteries, but the panic on her face tells another story. She's not going to the dentist.

20
HUNTER

I agreed to help Gretchen after practice today. It's Thursday, the one day the Free Room is open at the church. Dad wouldn't be caught dead in there, but Gretchen loves browsing. She rarely takes anything, says someone needs it more than she does. I think she's just curious. Today, though, she has a couch and a gigantic roll of heavy-duty plastic to donate. "I never liked that couch. It's just sitting in the spare bedroom, serving no purpose whatsoever. It's not uncomfortable; someone will love it. And I don't need to cover my windows with the plastic anymore since I got new insulation put in."

Dad thinks she should try to sell them.

"Oh, Jack, that's too much effort. I want to make someone's day with these."

She needs Dad's truck to carry the stuff over. She meets me at home, and we drive to her house. Rattling around in the cab are beer bottles. Gretchen kicks one out of the way and sighs. "He's hurting, Hunter. I'm so sorry you've had to be the grown-up in the house ever since he lost his job."

I don't want to get into a discussion about Dad and his drinking. It just reminds me of Teo. And of what a loser I am. So I just shrug and turn on the radio. Gretchen doesn't push it.

We load the couch and plastic roll into the bed of the pickup. Mrs. Pugh meets us at the donation entrance. "Oh, my, what a gorgeous sofa! And oh, all that insulation! Thank you so much! Do you need a receipt?"

"Oh, that's not necessary," my aunt says. "But I'm coming in to look around. Hunter will carry these things in."

Mrs. Pugh puts me to work hauling some other heavy items while Gretchen wanders. There are probably twenty-five people in the room, looking for stuff. I'm struck again by how many folks are struggling.

Mrs. Pugh's voice rises about the chatter. "Hunter, will you run to my office and grab a roll of masking tape? It's in my desk. Top drawer on the left."

On my way down the hall, someone goes flying past me. I recognize the curly hair; it's the barista from Molly's. Samantha. She beelines it to Pastor Mark's office.

And then I hear her. Sobbing. *Shit. I gotta get out of here.* I hurry to Mrs. Pugh's desk and yank open the drawer. No masking tape. I check the others. Nothing. I quickly glance at the shelves next to her desk when I hear my father's name. And I freeze.

"People are blaming Jack Ridley. But it's all my fault! My friends and I were the last ones on the deck just talking and telling stories. The lifeguard, just a kid, really, had to go to his other job at Hannaford's. So we promised him we'd turn off the lights and close the door when we left. Then some guy brought Jack in. He was wasted, needed a place to take a nap. When we wanted to go to dinner, he was totally passed out. We decided to leave him with the lights on and the door open so he'd be able to see to get out. We planned to check on him later to make sure he was okay before we went home." She takes a ragged breath. "So it was my fault! I left him there because I wanted to go have fun. I should have woken him up. I am the reason that little boy died. How on earth can I live with that?"

My legs buckle and I fall into Mrs. Pugh's chair. Pastor Mark's voice is quiet, but I can hear every word.

"You are carrying a heavy burden, Samantha," he says. "So in trying to be kind to Jack, give him space and time to sober up, you feel as if you created an opportunity for there to be an accident."

"Not just an opportunity," she cries; "it happened! I should've stayed with him. Then I would have seen Teo!"

"You may have. But it wasn't your intention to be unkind or thoughtless. By leaving the lights on and the door open, you were providing dignity and safety to Jack. It was an accident, Samantha, and there was not a smidgen of malice in your action. Our God is a forgiving God. What is more difficult, it seems, is for you to forgive yourself."

"I loved that little boy," she says in a voice so soft I can barely hear it. "And I admire Bridget. Knowing that I have ruined her life is killing me. I can't sleep. I can't eat. I'm a robot at work. And my boyfriend left more than a year ago. There's no one I can talk to. I mean, really talk. Like this."

"Would you consider talking with Bridget? Telling her exactly what you've told me?"

"She'll hate me."

"What Bridget needs right now is a friend."

I get up woodenly and leave Mrs. Pugh's desk. Without the tape. The grief and guilt are like dominoes. And they all started with me and Dad.

I'm tempted to tell the stupid rumor spreaders at school this little tidbit. That it was actually Samantha's fault the door was left open. That would shut them up about my dad.

But I won't. What's the frickin' point? Exactly; there isn't one. Teo's not coming back.

21
LUNA

Temmie makes me get up and go to Sunday school this morning. She ignores my tears. "You've taken two weeks off since he drowned. It's high time to go back."

"But I can't! That's where I met him!"

Temmie seems oddly unemotional. "A commitment is a commitment, Luna, and we Lemieuxs honor our commitments."

I tune out her analogy of ripping off a Band-Aid. I wish I could rip off the grief that is draped over me like a permanent witch's costume.

I'm fuming as I get in the car. I hate Temmie a little bit less when she doesn't comment on the hoodie I've thrown on, even though we're going to church. She tucks some tissues into the pocket before I stomp off.

The children swarm around me as soon as I walk in.

"Miss Luna's here!"

"Where were you? We missed you!"

They look like overinflated balloons, about to pop with importance.

"Teo's in heaven!" Their reporting is breathless. "He went swimming without his mommy and floated to heaven."

"But now he can swim in heaven. That's what my daddy says."

"You can't swim in heaven! You just fly around. In the sky."

"No, you bounce on the clouds!"

"Have you ever been to heaven, Miss Luna? Do you fly or bounce?"

I can't even.

But it doesn't matter, because they just want to talk.

"My daddy said you swim!"

"Yeah, you swim through the clouds. Like this!"

"No, you go like this!"

And then five little children are windmilling their arms, bouncing and jumping and twirling in circles around the room.

Mrs. Frye settles them down and tells a Bible story.

These children are cute. Earnest. Innocent.

How much longer will they remember Teo? Two weeks? A month? A year?

I miss him more than ever.

22
HUNTER

Practice is brutal. Coach is furious because we missed eleven of seventeen free throws in the game yesterday. So at the end of a tough practice, he lines us up behind the foul shot line. For every missed attempt, we do a cumulative suicide. Start at the baseline. To the foul line, touch, back. To mid-court, touch, back. To the opposite foul line, touch, back. To the end line, touch, back. All at full sprint. And Coach checks to make sure we touch each line. "You cheat? Repeat."

If one guy misses, we do one suicide. If four guys miss, we do one plus two plus three plus four. That's ten frickin' suicides. We are already exhausted and drenched, and the pressure is getting to us. And if we don't make at least 75 percent of them as a team, we start all over. By the third round, after we've run twenty-four suicides, the guys are pissed. At Coach. At each other. At themselves. No one talks when we are finally finished.

Coop and Josh and Nate are the last ones in the locker room with me. Josh puts a hat on his wet hair. "You guys want to come over? We can take The Beast out."

My whole body aches and my legs are like Jell-O. I kind of just want to go home. But there will be food at Josh's. I'll go. Coop and Nate text their parents. I don't bother. Dad's probably drunk and won't even notice I'm gone.

Josh's house is warm and busy. His little sisters are at the kitchen table, helping his dad make chocolate chip cookies. A huge pot of stew is on the stove. We fill bowls and pile into the dining room, where his mother is frowning at her computer. She smiles and takes off her glasses when she sees us.

"Hey, guys! You're late. Long practice?"

Coop pauses before digging in; the rest of us are too hungry. "Coach was in a mood," he says. "That's about as polite as I can be."

She grins. "Suicides?"

We nod.

"I remember those days. Our coach stood at the other end of the gym, and if even one person didn't actually touch the end line with her hand, he made the whole team do it again."

Josh's mother was good. Really good. And she can still shoot like she did when she was in high school. I think Josh is as sweet a shooter as he is because he hated losing to his mom when they played H-O-R-S-E in the driveway.

"Nate, how is your grandmother? I heard she slipped on the ice and fell?"

"She's okay, not great. Nothing broken, but she's kind of gun-shy now. About the ice, I mean. So she's living with us for the winter. In my room. I'm sleeping on a mat in the attic."

Josh's mother reaches out and rubs Nate's shoulder. "You're a good kid, Nate. That's not easy, being kicked out of your room."

"It's okay. At least it's insulated up there."

She moves on to Coop and talks music for a while then asks me about my girlfriend. Emma's father works with Josh's dad. It's the first time all day I've been, like, chill and relaxed. The fire is blazing in the woodstove, and laughter and little girl squeals are coming from the kitchen. And something else. Brown sugar. Butter. Chocolate. Josh gets up. "Anyone else want dessert?"

Sadie comes in carrying a plate stacked with cookies. Hannah follows with a pitcher of milk. They giggle as they watch us attack like turkey vultures.

The side door opens and Josh's brother enters, his eyelashes frosted. "Dude! Where have you been? I had to shovel out by the barn myself while you're sitting in here stuffing your face!" He stamps to shake off the snow and uses his teeth to pull off his gloves. He hangs his jacket on a hook and sits to take off his boots. Josh's mother sends him to the kitchen for stew.

Josh stands up. "We're gonna take The Beast for a spin. We'll be back soon."

"Be careful," warns his mom. "That thing makes me nervous."

His dad calls out from the kitchen. "Josh? Remember it thawed last week!"

We thank Josh's parents and sisters for the food, grab our jackets, and head out.

While Josh is getting The Beast from the garage, I feel my phone buzz. I take off my glove and dig into my pocket. I pull it out and at look at the screen. *Crap.*

"Dad. Hey."

"Hunter? Where the hell are you?" *Jesus. He's wasted.*

"At Josh's."

"I need some money. I'm thirsty."

I have money from Gretchen. She paid me a lot for the trip to the Free Room at church. Dad knows how generous she is to me.

"Where's your money, Dad?"

"Spent it."

"On what?"

"Not really your business, now, is it? But dammit, I'm due to win the Maine Lotto. Then we'll be sittin' pretty."

"Jesus, Dad! All of it?"

"You watch your mouth. And get home. I'm still thirsty."

I shove the phone back in my pocket. Josh has The Beast running. He glides it toward us, hops off, and calls out, "Who's first?"

Without saying a word, I run to the snowmobile and jump on. The lump in my throat feels as big as a basketball. *Will he ever stop drinking? Be the dad he was? The one I need now?* In a blind rage, I rev the motor and cut across his yard into the woods. Behind me Josh is yelling something about the pond, but the wind and the engine are too loud for me to hear him. And I don't care. Nothing really matters anymore. How can he possibly understand? When he has this home filled with warmth and laughter and I have this constant pressing weight of being the reason my dad drinks and Teo's dead?

I fly over the snow. Faster than I've ever gone. I head up the hill and race out onto the pond. The ice is uneven from where it melted during last week's thaw. The ruts send vibrations through my arms as I try to hang on. I circle the pond like it's the Indy 500, pushing The Beast to go faster. On my third lap I see the guys, waving their arms. Josh jumps in my path, yelling, "Stop! It's not safe!"

I swerve around him and keep going.

The cracking ice sounds like a gunshot. The Beast shakes. I'm headed right to the center, where the dark water shows like the gaping mouth of a monster. I hurtle toward the black.

And then I don't see ice or snow or black water. All I see is Teo's little body at the bottom of the pool. And my father stumbling toward me on the deck. And all those kids at school, fucking blaming my dad.

The jagged edge of an ice chunk catches on the left ski and the snowmobile lurches in the air. I try to save it, but the momentum throws me off and it slams on its side. My head smashes into the ice.

Why won't they let me sleep? Stop punching my shoulder! It's so peaceful here. I just want to sleep. Go away.

Josh is pummeling my arms, my face, my shoulders. "Wake up, you frickin' idiot!" I hear Coop screaming my name. I'm not sure where I am, but I have a wicked headache. Nate keeps repeating, "Oh, my God!"

Slowly I sit up. Nate and Coop grab my arms and start pulling. Josh is frantic, yelling about getting off the ice. He rights the snowmobile and drives it off. More gunshot noises follow as they drag me to the pond's edge, where Josh is waiting. "Get on!" he shouts.

Coop and Nate run behind us. Every bump feels like someone is beating the crap out of my head. Back at the garage, they help me off The Beast. I take three steps in the snow and fall to my knees. Waves of pain and nausea hit. I throw up until there's nothing left in my stomach. Just a steaming pile of puke on the snow.

Josh is *pissed*. "Jesus, Hunter. You ready to explain what the hell that was out there?"

I need to sleep.

"You stupid idiot! You knew the ice was cracking!"

I am so tired. Why won't he stop talking?

"Hunter?" Coop looks worried. "You okay?"

I can't take this. I want everything to go back. To when it was good. Slowly my head clears. Things stop spinning. I just feel empty. And like I've screwed up again.

I stand up slowly and mumble an apology. "I'm . . . nothing. Sorry about The Beast. I didn't mean to tip it."

Josh punches me in the chest. Hard. "I wasn't worried about the snowmobile, you fucking moron!"

23
LUNA

School continues to be a drag. English is okay because Mrs. Laurence makes us read a lot. Most kids complain about that, but I love it. Temmie calls reading her Great Escape. It is for me too. And I like math because there's always a clear right answer. History is pretty interesting. But the subjects themselves can't make up for the fact that the school days just creep by in painful isolation.

Today's history lesson focuses on the Great Depression, specifically the recovery attempts by the TVA and the WPA. Mr. D explains the National Recovery Administration's incentive payments to farmers and the institution of a minimum wage. Then he asks why the minimum wage is important. He usually tries to tie our life in with what we're studying. But today, when I quickly peek beyond my hood like a scared turtle, all I see are blank stares and bored yawns.

Mr. D stops talking. He stops pacing. This weird silence fills the room. Finally someone says, "You good, Mr. D?"

He shakes his head, slowly. And kind of angrily. "I would like you to tell me," he says, "what is going on. I want honesty. This history is interesting—fascinating, even—and I feel as if I am teaching at a zombie university. Is anybody hearing anything I'm saying?"

The silence returns. I expected a crude joke or laughter or someone saying, "Oh, we're paying attention, Mr. D!" But instead an uncomfortable heaviness reigns.

A soft voice breaks the quiet. "It's Teo." It startles me because it's the girl who sits right behind me. I don't think I've ever heard her speak in class without being called on.

"Teo? Ahh. I see. Thank you, Kiki." Mr. D looks around. "Can you say more?" I turn around and watch her. Kiki gives him a desperate look and shakes her head. But she's opened a floodgate of emotion. It rolls across the classroom like a wave at high tide. Suddenly everyone wants to talk.

"It's so unfair. He was so cute."

"I can't believe someone left the door open."

"What else can go wrong? It's like our town is cursed. The one day of the year that's supposed to be fun turns into a tragedy."

"I heard the Moose and Loon is gonna get sued."

"Yeah, they're in deep shit."

"Why? Like what's the point? A lawsuit can't bring him back."

"It wasn't their fault. They weren't even there."

"Yeah, but Hunter's dad was." I hear a few gasps.

"Well, what's Teo's mother going to do? She can't sue him. He doesn't have any money."

A boy named Coop, who talks a lot, stands up. "Shut up, you guys. You don't know what you're talking about. Leave his dad out of this."

Mr. D raises his hands. "Coop, sit down. And let's keep this civil, please."

For once, Mr. D doesn't try to control the discussion. He just listens. His face is red, and beads of sweat start forming on his forehead. I wonder if he knew Teo. Or maybe someone he loved died a similar death. And then I remember. He was there that night. With Hunter's dad. He's obviously upset, pacing back and forth behind his desk.

The talk continues. "I think we should do something in Teo's honor."

"Like what? Plant a frickin' tree? What's that gonna do?"

"Geez, don't jump down her throat! She didn't say plant a tree. She said do something."

"Something meaningful. Big. So we won't ever forget that sweet little kid."

"Big? Really? With what? All the money coming out of your ass?"

"God! You don't have to be so crude! We could like raise it."

"That's my point. We can't ask anyone around here for money. No one has any."

"That's not totally true. Some people do."

"Yeah, the mill owners. See them around here lately?"

"They're probably sailing in the Bahamas."

"Or skiing in the Alps."

Mr. D stops abruptly. "All right, guys; close your textbooks. Open your notebooks or laptops."

"This a pop quiz, Mr. D?"

"No. Definitely not." He looks around the room. "So this is what I am hearing. You are seriously affected by Teo's death. You want to do something meaningful to celebrate his life. And you don't have the money to do so." He pauses. Around me I get a strange sense of intense attention. Like everyone is super alert. "All right. So let's do it. We are officially dedicating our time in this class to figuring out what and where and who and when and how. Right now, start jotting down ideas. You've got five minutes to brainstorm."

"Wait, what?"

I see Coop put his head down and start to write. Then a few more kids do. The room is totally quiet. I'm not exactly sure what we're supposed to be doing, so I just sit there.

After like five minutes, Mr. D asks Kiki to be the class scribe at the whiteboard. "Okay, when Kiki is ready, start sharing these ideas. You don't need to raise your hand. Just shout out, but give her enough time to write. And I am serious. You need to be too. The only rule is this: No hating on anyone's idea. There will be an opportunity to evaluate each one in due time. Ready, Kiki?"

Kiki nods and takes the cap off the marker. She divides the board into two columns. She labels one "WHAT" and the other "HOW." For someone who is as quiet as I am, she is stepping way out of her comfort zone.

She clears her throat. "So the WHAT means what we want to buy or do for Teo. Or, I mean, his mom. Or like in his memory. And the HOW is how we can do that. Like raise money. Or whatever."

The WHAT column fills first.

Donate to the Down Syndrome Foundation
Build a fountain in the empty lot next to the post office
Plant a garden in that empty lot
Name a drink after him at Molly's
Frame a picture of him for his mother
Give money to help kids with special needs

The HOW is harder. Hardly anyone has an idea.

Bake sale
Car wash
Snow shoveling
Community yard sale

Kiki looks at Mr. D expectantly. He turns to the class. "What do you think?"

Hunter stands up, startling the kids on either side of his desk. He pushes his brown hair out of his eyes. His hands are shaking. "Can I . . . can I say something, Mr. D?"

Mr. D nods. "Of course, Hunter."

"That rumor about my dad? I know it's out there. And you've all heard it."

I don't know what he's talking about. Except for what I heard at the knitting group, that his dad was sleeping on the deck. That must be where Mr. D took him.

"I'm so sick of the crap that's going around. Yeah, he was there. But he was asleep and never saw Teo."

I wonder how Hunter knew Teo well enough to be a pallbearer?

"Anyway, these are all good ideas," he says, "and maybe we can do some of them. But that night, it was like, I don't know. I'd never seen Teo so excited. Like cannonballs were the coolest thing ever. And when he jumped off the diving board, he was crazy happy. Like how we felt when we won States last year. Or when you bag a huge buck. He was like in his element. And then—" His voice breaks. Nobody says anything. It feels like we're all holding our breath.

"So what I wish we could do," he continues, "is build a fucking pool. Sorry, Mr. D. Obviously, that's a bullshit dream. But maybe we could raise enough money to teach every kid in this town how to swim. So nobody else—"

His eyes fill and he quickly sits down. Everyone is staring at him. Coop rushes to distract them.

"Hey, maybe we could use the lodge pool, like pay them to have it open beyond hunting season. Maybe all year round. And we could hire instructors, and it could be like an after-school activity. Or a summer thing?"

Other kids chime in, more enthusiastic than they've ever been in history class. "That would provide a bunch of jobs!"

"Yeah, swim instructors, lifeguards, pool maintenance guys—"

"Why just guys? Girls can maintain the pool too!"

"Whatever. You know what I mean."

"Someone look it up. What do lifeguards make per hour?"

"And what about swim instructors? How many kids are in this town? How many would we need?"

Kiki grabs the reins. "So we need to figure out a ton of numbers. But before we do, let's look at the HOW column."

The excitement fizzles out. Coop sighs. "No hating on the ideas, I know. But these aren't gonna get us the money we need."

Kiki agrees. "And anyway, we can't raise the money from people here. No one has it. Even for something like a big yard sale. If the mill were still open, we could do it. But we can't ask people to donate or buy extra stuff now. Not everyone has even the few bucks we used to spend on cupcakes at a bake sale."

People start brainstorming again. "Maybe we could open a GoFundMe page? In Teo's honor?"

"Yeah, maybe. But there are so many of those out there, and it seems like a lot of them are scams. I think we should try to earn it."

"Those charity websites are hit-or-miss. Too unreliable."

"We should still try."

Mr. D jumps in. "We obviously cannot make any decisions today. But you've raised some interesting issues and ideas. We're going to learn some economics in this class, along with history. I want you to think about this for the next twenty-four hours. Just say we decided that the best way to honor Teo's memory is to teach all the kids in Edgewater how to swim. Come to class tomorrow with your ideas in the following four categories: HOW, WHERE, WHEN, and WHO."

As we're packing up our stuff, the room is buzzing with excitement. Like people are really into this. I'm not paying attention as I try to cram my laptop into my backpack, and a bag of grapes falls out and onto the floor. Grapes roll under the desks and chairs. I want to just run out, but I get on my hands and knees to chase the runaways. *Sooo embarrassing.*

As I reach to collect them, I hear someone approach Mr. D's desk. "Just to let you know, this is a stupid waste of time. You're spending our class time to figure out a way to honor a kid's memory, someone a lot of us didn't even know!" I don't recognize his voice. Not that I'd know him anyway. He sounds furious.

"Like how did we all get roped into this? You'll be hearing from my dad." He storms out before Mr. D can say anything. I stuff the grapes into my pack and race out.

Thinking about the discussion in our history class distracts me for the rest of the day. Like I'm really glad we are maybe going to do something. I love Hunter's idea, though it feels way too ambitious. It will probably just die, like everything does in this town.

I'm changing for dance and once again overhear someone in Pastor Mark's office. I'm hurrying to get out of there when I recognize Ms. Callahan's voice. Hating myself, I stand still and listen. *Who have I become?*

"It sounds like today's a hard one for you, Bridget." Pastor Mark's voice is full of sympathy. "It doesn't help that the wind chill is twelve below and a blizzard is predicted for the weekend."

She sighs. "Maine winters are what they are. Look, Mark, I was raised Catholic. Confession was something we did every week. Even if we had nothing to confess, we'd make up something just for the absolution." She pauses. "I need to confess, and I know that's not the same in this church."

"If it would help you, I am happy to listen to a confession," he says solemnly. "But I won't issue penance."

"This is what is really bothering me. Beyond the grief of missing my little son so much that my bones literally ache. Teo's birth parents, or mother, I'm not sure who, trusted me with their baby. And I blew it. I didn't protect him the way they trusted me to. The way any mother should protect her child."

My heart starts pounding. *Yeah, tell that to my mother.*

Pastor Mark's voice is strong and confident. "They chose you because they must have observed your kindness. It was not random, Bridget. And I saw you take care of that lucky little boy. He was loved, deeply. He knew it. Yes, his life was shorter than we all expected, but it was full and rich and happy. And his death was an *accident*."

There is silence for a long while. I don't dare move.

"You didn't knowingly or deliberately put your child in harm's way. In your letting him go to the restroom alone, you were acknowledging his newfound independence. That is exactly what aware and loving parents do. They give their children roots, and they give their children wings."

I hear Ms. Callahan blow her nose. "I don't know if I can ever forgive myself. And that's a pretty untenable way to exist. Under this constant cloud of guilt."

My heart aches listening to her.

"People keep asking me what I want to do in Teo's honor. Yes, I want to do something, but nothing feels quite right."

"You'll know what it is when it comes to you."

She blows her nose again. "And am I a horrible person for hating the platitudes that I hear over and over? Like 'God needed another angel' or 'Teo wouldn't have lived a long life anyway' or 'He's in a better place now.' I know people mean well, but those stupid, vapid, meaningless statements give me no comfort." She pauses. "I'm sorry. I know I shouldn't be so judgmental. Or ungrateful."

"Sometimes," Pastor Mark says, "those platitudes comfort the people who give them more than those who receive them. A lot of people are desperately searching for meaning in Teo's death."

Out of nowhere I hear the song "You are My Sunshine." "I kept that ringtone because Teo loved it," Ms. Callahan says. "We sang it together every night. Why is the high school calling me? I better take this. Thank you, Mark." The door clicks shut.

My dance session doesn't serve as the catharsis it usually does. Because I am thinking about how similar Teo and I are. Were. Both rejected by our mothers because of a . . . a . . . an abnormality. Both adopted by nice women. But even nice women can't protect us from everything. Or everybody.

24
HUNTER

Mr. D wants to see me after school. *Shit.* I know I did a half-assed job on the project last week. Even though Mr. D seems pretty chill, he is insanely obsessed with integrity. He's drilled that in since the beginning of the year. Integrity in thought and word and action. Like don't hand in a crappy paper or cheat on a test because you didn't make time to study. He holds himself to the same standard. He grades fairly and hands papers back on time with tons of comments written all over them. He also makes time to come to our games, art shows, plays, whatever. That's cool. He says he likes to see who we are outside the classroom because that helps him inside the classroom. So he's probably going to ask me to redo the project.

He's definitely not keeping me after school to congratulate me on the game last night. We stunk. Lost to a team we should have beaten easily. No one could connect on offense, and our defense sucked. We had like thirteen turnovers. Everyone thought we would be awesome this year because after winning States last winter, we only lost two seniors. But we have been out of sync all season. We've still won most of our games, but we're not clicking like we should be.

I show up in Mr. D's room at 3:10. He's in there talking with a girl in a hoodie. I know she's in our class, but I don't know her. She never talks.

Mr. D looks at me. "Shut the door, Hunter."

Shut the door? This is serious! What did I do?

I close it and sit at a desk. My leg starts jiggling up and down.

"What time is practice?"

"Uh, not until five o'clock. The girls have the gym now."

"Good. Then you have time. Luna dances later, so you are both free to do this right now."

Uh, what is he talking about?

"All right, here's the deal. I spoke with Teo's mom, Bridget Callahan, yesterday. I just wanted to make sure she was on board with our doing something meaningful to honor and remember Teo. I don't know, maybe it's too soon or something. But honestly? She didn't seem too enthused. She definitely did *not* want to come to our class. Again, she is in the throes of grief. I get it. But she asked if, by chance, the two of you were in my class. Last night she emailed me with the specific request for you, Luna, and you, Hunter, to explain our project to her. I'm asking you, on behalf of our class, to go over to her house this afternoon to talk with her. Find out if she'd be okay with the class's idea of teaching the town to swim."

My leg stops bouncing. I can do this. It's for Teo. And, indirectly, for his mom. I look over at Luna. If anything, she's shrunk since Mr. D stopped talking. Which is pretty hard to do, since she's already tiny. But she's brought her knees under her sweatshirt and wrapped her arms around them, and her head is totally hidden in her hoodie. No one says anything.

Mr. D picks up a pen and starts fiddling with it. He seems sort of nervous too. "She explained why she chose you two. It seems that you both had a real connection with Teo." He clears his throat. "Which makes this whole thing both easier and harder, huh?"

25
LUNA

Hunter and I walk near the middle of the road to Ms. Callahan's house. I feel as if we are walking a gauntlet, and it's not just because of the towering snowbanks on either side. It's freezing out, but my face is burning. There is absolutely no way in the universe I would ever dream of doing something like this.

But I have to. For Teo.

I don't have any friends, so I have no idea how to talk to Hunter. So I don't. We walk for a long time before he speaks. He's like a foot and a half taller than I am, so he kind of bends over when he talks.

"How did you know Teo?" White puffs of steam punctuate each word that comes from his mouth.

"I didn't, really. I mean, not well. I only met him like six weeks ago. I kind of help with his Sunday school class."

He nods. The snow crunches under our boots. I glance at him and remember. "You were . . . um, one of the pallbearers."

"Yeah. Probably the worst day of my life."

"So, do you, like, know his mother?"

"Just as Teo's mom. I've never talked to her on her own, without Teo. She's got to be hurting, big time."

The rest of the way is silent. We arrive at her mailbox and head up the icy driveway. Smoke rises out of the chimney of her small white Cape Cod. Hunter knocks on the side door. It opens immediately. Teo's mom smiles sadly and asks us in. Her eyes are dark and like sunken in her face. She has a wool scarf wrapped around her neck even though she's inside. She looks even thinner than she was at the funeral.

"It's toasty in here," she says. The heat hits us like a wave as we remove our boots by the door. It feels like we've walked into a pizza oven. Hunter asks to use the bathroom. Ms. Callahan sends him upstairs. I take off my jacket, but I leave my hoodie pulled over my face. Within moments I am sweating.

"Ever since Teo died, I can't seem to get warm," Ms. Callahan says. "It's probably too hot for you." She sees me rubbing the sweat from my forehead. "Oh, honey, go ahead and take off your sweatshirt."

I panic. *What about my face?* But she looks so sad that I just do it. She stares. Like everyone does.

"Oh, my," she says. I wait for her to turn away in disgust. "You had a hoodie on when I met you in the church. Now I see. You look so much like your mother when she was your age. Your eyes! You've got her eyes. And her gorgeous cheekbones. And that beautiful hair! I remember being so jealous of her hair. All those natural blonde highlights."

No one has said anything like this to me before. Ever. "You . . . you knew my mom?"

"Oh, yes. Everyone knew your mom. She was hard to miss. Never met a stranger. She had more friends than you could count." She must see my eyes fill, because she quickly turns just as Hunter trudges down the stairs. "Here, come on in and have a seat. Can I get you something to eat? Drink? I have more food here than I can possibly get through in a month."

When I don't say anything, Hunter jumps in. "I would love a snack, Miz Callahan. Thank you. Anything you want to get rid of is fine."

She brings us a plate stacked with cookies and brownies and a pitcher of milk. "People have been so kind, dropping off soup and casseroles and baked goods, but honestly, the last thing I want is food. Please don't tell anyone I said that. But I would appreciate it if you would take some of this on your way out. Otherwise, it will go to waste."

Hunter has already eaten two cookies and is starting on his third. I nibble on a brownie, barely tasting it.

Ms. Callahan sits heavily in an armchair as if the mere act of living is exhausting. "So, Mr. Deboncoeur told me that your class has a project? To remember Teo?"

I look at Hunter. It was his idea; he should tell it. He does, between bites of cookie and gulps of milk. When he finishes, Ms. Callahan doesn't speak. The silence grows uncomfortable. *We've offended her. This was a terrible idea.*

"If . . . if this sounds like something you'd rather not have us do, that's . . . um, that's fine," Hunter stutters.

Tears run down Ms. Callahan's cheeks. She slowly pulls a tissue from the end table next to her. The lump in my throat makes it impossible to swallow. I put the brownie down and stare at my socks.

"I'm sorry," she says. "It's just still so raw." She blows her nose and looks at us both. "I don't know. It's a sweet idea, I guess, but . . . well, it feels unrealistic. I don't know how you could possibly fund it. If I had had life insurance on Teo, I would donate that. But in the happy chaos of becoming a parent when I never expected to, I just never got around to it."

Hunter rubs his eyes. I realize he's crying too. I barely know him, and he's crying in front of me. *This is so awkward! Should I say something? Or will that make it worse? I won't look at him.*

"Um, we . . . we had a few ideas for fundraising," I blurt. "But we haven't gotten too far with that. We were waiting to see what you thought."

"Tell me this." Ms. Callahan leans forward. "Is this like a class-only project? Or would it be open to the community? Several people have asked what they could do, and, frankly, I didn't think much of any of their ideas. But I like yours. Honestly. Much more practical than a rock garden."

It's not exactly clear what she is asking. "You mean would we accept help from the community at large?"

She nods. I look at Hunter. He's wiped his tears away. He shrugs. "I guess so."

"Okay, then I'm on board. Any questions I will direct to your teacher. And you two will be my liaisons, okay?"

I'm not sure what that means, but she's so earnest that I just nod. So does Hunter. We stand up and grab our jackets.

"Before you go, will you indulge me just for a couple of minutes?" Hunter and I sit back down. "Would you . . . I know this probably sounds strange . . . but would you please just talk about Teo? Like how he was with you? What he did? What he said? I sit here alone in my misery, and I want to hear stories about him. The few adults I have seen seem too scared to talk about him, as if the mere mention of his name will make me explode or something."

Hunter and I look at each other. I see his tears coming back, so I start. "Um, sure. You . . . you saw Teo dancing with me. In the sanctuary that day? Well, for the next couple of Sundays, Mrs. Frye and I added dance to our Sunday school class. We put on *VeggieTales* songs and let the kids dance. They loved it. Teo had amazing rhythm. He clapped his hands exactly to the beat. And one time," I pause. "It was his last time, actually. Mrs. Frye was sitting in her chair during dance time, and Teo looked at her and shook his head. He walked over, took her hand, and pulled her up. And made her dance!" I laugh a little, surprising myself. "I don't mean to be disrespectful, but it was so funny. I mean, she's old, and I don't think she's danced in years."

Ms. Callahan laughs too. "Oh, I wish I had seen that! I know exactly what you mean about Mrs. Frye. Bless her heart!"

She thinks for a minute. "He just loved music. Always had it on in the house. Now the quiet is so loud it hurts my ears."

"The first time I met Teo," says Hunter, "I was in line at Molly's. I'd ordered a turkey sandwich, and I forgot to ask for mayo on it. So I kind of shouted, 'With mayo!' Twice, because Molly had already started making it and I wanted to be sure she heard me. And then I felt something pulling on my pocket. I looked down, and there was this cute little person under a mass of curls. He said, 'Mayo!' And that started our little name game that we did every time we saw each other."

"I remember," says Ms. Callahan, "when you took him sledding. I was worried he'd get cold quickly, so I stayed and watched, but he hung in there with you and your friends for two hours! He was soaking wet when you brought him up to my car, but he was ecstatic. That was incredibly kind of you boys."

We sit for another fifteen minutes and remember Teo.

It's terrible and wonderful.

And all that time, I don't think about my hideous face at all. It's like I've slipped out of my body.

Down the road from Ms. Callahan's house, a car full of guys passes us. Music is blaring out the open windows. One guy leans out and pounds the side of the door. "Yo, Ridley! Whassup?"

They screech off, snow tires gripping the ice. About ten steps later, Hunter stops. Abruptly. He kind of ducks his head and barely looks at me. "Hey, uh, why don't you go ahead? I . . . I need to tell Miz Callahan something."

He turns around and heads back to her house. *He doesn't want to be seen with me.*

I get it. I really do.

But that doesn't make it hurt less.

26
HUNTER

Sitting there with Teo's mom, talking about Teo with her and Luna, is awful. I mean, it's fun to laugh about some of the stuff he did. But knowing he'll never get to dance or sing or do cannonballs or, hell, use the damn bathroom by himself again just sucks. And Jesus, his mom is a wreck. And I think I made it worse.

Because after Luna and I leave, I have to go back. To tell her the truth. She deserves that.

At the door I don't knock. I just barge in. It seems like she's expecting me, or she had been watching us walk down the driveway or something, because she isn't surprised.

"What's up, honey?" she asks.

I choke up and can barely talk. My throat is so thick that each word is its own agony. But she has to hear this. "It's . . . well . . . it's my fault. You know, why Teo drowned."

She takes my hand and leads me to a chair. I sit. She waits.

I can't even look at her. I stare at the bright rug of jungle animals covering the wide floorboards. "I should have explained to him that he couldn't go on the diving board alone. I don't think he understood that the water was so deep. And I kept calling him the Cannonball King, so of course he thought he could do it on his own. Oh, my God, I was so stupid!" I take a breath and it's shaky, like I'm a little kid having a temper tantrum.

I have to go on before I lose my courage. "And there's something else. My dad was on the pool deck. Passed out. And if he hadn't been so drunk, he wouldn't have been there, and the door would have been shut, so Teo wouldn't have gotten in."

There are tears pouring down her face. But there's more. She deserves to know the whole thing.

"See, if I was a better basketball player, or maybe got straight As, or was, I don't know, like more interesting or artistic or musical or whatever, my dad wouldn't drink so much. I think I . . . like . . . disappoint him." My chest hurts so much I can barely breathe. "Miz Callahan, I am so, so sorry. About Teo. I ruined his life. And yours too."

She wipes her face with a tissue. She pushes the box to me. "Oh, Hunter. Is that what you believe?"

I nod. I hate this. Her eyes are like pools of sadness.

"Well, I don't know your dad. And I obviously don't know what's behind his drinking. Sometimes there's a hole that people try to fill with alcohol. The problem is that often the more alcohol that's poured down that hole to fill it, the bigger the hole gets.

"But I do know, honey, that you are not the reason Teo drowned. It was a terrible accident. And I know your dad was there. And that you and your friend found Teo." She stops and gazes at the woodstove, where flames are dancing behind the mica doors. Then she turns back to me. "I also know how happy you made my son. That you would take time out of your evening with your friends to be in the pool with him says worlds about your character. Who you are. How big your heart is."

She takes a deep breath. "Blame doesn't help anyone feel better. I know I've spent a lot of time blaming myself for letting him out of that dining room on his own. But, honey, blame can just tear you up inside."

We sit in silence. I have to know. "How do you . . . how do you get up every day? And go on?"

She doesn't answer for a while. Finally she says, "There's a cardinal that comes to my bird feeder every morning. Keeping the feeder full is sometimes the only reason I get out of bed. Knowing that he's waiting for me. But I admit, Hunter, that there are many days when I climb right back under the covers after I've poured those sunflower seeds."

I think about my dad. *What was it like for him after my mother died?* "Do you . . . do you drink? To forget? Or escape? Or, I don't know, take the pain away?"

She looks out the window. The sun is already setting. "No, Hunter. I don't. My mother was an alcoholic, and I vowed I'd never touch the stuff after seeing how erratic and paranoid it seemed to make her. But more than that, I don't want to forget anything. About Teo. And I guess I think that maybe this pain is so intense because I loved him so much. Or at least that's what I tell myself when the hurting is unbearable."

I twist my tissue around my fingers. "Well, I've got to go to practice. Um, thanks. I mean, I just wanted you to know."

She stands up. "Thank you for trusting me, honey. And if . . . if you ever want to talk about your dad or Teo or basketball or anything, I'll listen." She stops for a second. "And I appreciate your class's thinking of Teo. I really do. Will you tell them that?"

I promise I will.

Then I leave in kind of a rush.

27
LUNA

I have a huge English paper due tomorrow, so I really don't want to go to the stupid knitting group today. But Temmie seems stressed out and isn't in the mood to argue. It's not worth it. I'll just work in my little cubicle.

I set up my laptop and start in. When I look up for a break, I see that Barbara is sitting next to Jessica, guiding her fingers as they grasp fat needles and thick yarn. "You're going to be a pro in no time, Jessica," Temmie says. "You've got our veteran star teaching you!"

Barbara winks at her. "You mean the oldest, don't you?" Temmie told me that, at eighty-eight, Barbara complains that her eyesight is failing and that she needs hearing aids, but she's still a whiz with yarn.

Samantha comes in and plops down next to Rose and Ethel.

"Oh, it feels so good to sit! Molly and I did a deep clean this morning. My hands are so dried out from the chemicals we used. Even with gloves." She pulls out her knitting.

Ethel smiles. "Oh, I feel you. My hands always crack in the winter. I even put lotion on them and wear gloves to bed." I know what she means. Temmie's fingertips get so cracked that they bleed. Something about the cold outside and the woodstove making the air inside so dry.

Ethel kindly catches Samantha up. "We were just talking about how we got our names," she says. "My father was madly in love with Ethel Merman, and he convinced my mother that I'd sing like a lark with that name. I think she was just exhausted by then, for I was the twelfth child." She laughs. "Of course I can't sing worth a hill of beans! I don't think my poor father ever forgave me for that."

Rose chimes in. "My parents were going to name me Hortense, for my maternal grandmother. But there was a pink rose bush in bloom right outside my parents' bedroom window. I was born at home, as most babies in Aroostook County were in those days. Those roses were so pretty and fragrant that they changed their minds." She sighs. "My grandmother told me in secret that she's eternally grateful for that rose bush. She despised her name. Just hated it!" She turns to Samantha. "What about you?"

"I was named after Samantha Smith. One of our famous Mainers. Do you remember reading about her? That informal child ambassador to Russia? Although then it was the Soviet Union."

"Oh, she was a darling little thing," Ethel says. "Cute as a button. Didn't she write a letter to some Soviet leader?"

"Yes. When she was ten years old, she wrote a letter to Yuri Andropov, essentially asking him not to start a nuclear war with the United States. Amazingly, he responded, and invited her to the Soviet Union!"

Rose adds, "Bless her heart. Then three years later she died in a plane crash. Such a sad story."

Samantha agrees. "I think I was one of many little girl babies around here named Samantha in the years right after her death. Kind of like the slew of babies named Diana after Princess Di's horrific car crash."

"Do you like your name?" Ethel asks.

"I do," Samantha says, "but I feel so pathetic in comparison. I mean, that little girl did more in her lifetime than I have in mine. And I've lived way longer!"

"You're an ambassador in your own right," Rose says quietly. "Jessica? What about—"

She's interrupted by the entrance of a large woman with a gray ponytail. It's like the very air changes when she comes in. Everyone stops knitting. "Well, look who's here! How are you, Polly?"

Immediately I am intrigued. Temmie has told me about Polly Gerard. She's a legend in this group, a sort of yarn sorceress. She's dyslexic and can't follow written instructions, so she creates her own sweater patterns. According to Temmie, they're always gorgeous. Apparently, everyone's been waiting to see her latest rendition.

"Hurry up, Polly! We've been so patient!"

She laughs and reaches into her red tote bag. "I'm calling this one 'Polly's Potpourri,' because I used a bunch of leftover yarn to make it." She pulls out the sweater and holds it up. It is a Henley-style pullover with a three-button opening at the neck. Blues and teals and whites immediately make me think of the ocean, where Temmie took me once when I was little. What looks like a cresting wave covers one shoulder; seagulls hover above the water on the other. It is breathtaking. Literally. No one utters a sound. Then Barbara breaks the collective silence. "Oh, Polly." She doesn't say another word. She doesn't need to.

Polly plunks into an armchair and laughs. "I had fun with this one," she says. "Good way to get rid of old yarn. But it's way too small for me. I'm getting fatter and fatter, and my knitting hasn't caught up with my eating. I don't know what I'm going to do with it."

"What about your daughter? She'd fit into it."

"Lizzie wouldn't be caught dead wearing something I made!"

"Would you . . . would you consider selling it?" Everyone turns. Jessica's face turns scarlet. "I . . . I hope I'm not offending you. I know you don't make these to sell. But I've never seen such a magnificent sweater, and it's totally original. I could spend every day of the next ten years learning to knit, and I'd still never be as proficient or creative as any of you. Would you at least think about it?"

Polly's fury turns her face as crimson as Jessica's. "I don't . . . I can't . . . I wouldn't think of . . ."

Even I, someone who is never really out in public or in conversation with a bunch of people, can understand that the offer is offensive. Unbelievably, Jessica plows on. "The material is worth what, a couple hundred dollars? And then the hours you put in. Probably thirty? Forty? Multiply those by what, fifty bucks an hour? And then because it's an original, add another five hundred."

Polly's burst of laughter sounds more like a ferocious bark. "Did you say *fifty* dollars an hour? Five zero? What planet do you come from?" She is shaking and has nowhere to put her outrage. "Oh, for God's sake, I can't do all that math! Just take it. At least someone will wear it."

Jessica is mortified. "Take it? No! I insist on paying you."

I am riveted. I've never witnessed a negotiation like this. I look at the other women, who seem as transfixed by this as I am. It's excruciating in its awkwardness. Jessica is from another world and clearly doesn't understand us. But she presses on, and, man, it's so painful.

Polly can barely contain her anger. She gives a fake laugh, one that contains zero humor. "Okay, then. I'll trade you. Take the sweater." She turns to the women and winks. "In exchange for getting rid of that dead tree in my front yard. I'll hire Judson's crew and send you the bill. Deal?"

Someone gasps. "That tree is enormous! It will cost a few grand to take it down!"

No way do people have that kind of money now. Not for a luxury like tree removal. They just pray that when it falls, it won't land on anyone's house or garage.

Jessica doesn't blink. In fact, she appears relieved. "Fantastic. Yes, it's a deal. Thank you so much!"

Polly looks flabbergasted, but she shakes Jessica's outstretched hand and then places the sweater in it. Right there, in the middle of the room, Jessica pulls it on over her head.

It is, in a word, stunning. The blue matches her eyes, and she's so tall and like willowy that it fits her perfectly.

Tension chokes the room.

Then someone claps. Someone else whistles. And Polly laughs again, this time with true levity. "You're a looker, that's for sure! Make my work look halfway decent."

Rose and Ethel and Samantha exchange relieved glances.

I return to my essay. My mind, however, is on that negotiation. Man, that was weird. And uncomfortable. I wonder if Jessica will ever come back to this group.

28
HUNTER

History class has amped way up. Mr. D decided that if we can cram all the formal history information into three classes, we can devote Thursdays and Fridays to our economics project. It means there is no time for screwing around in class. We used to have bets on who could get Mr. D off on a tangent, and we'd time him as he told a story. Austin, of course, always won. And often Mr. D would give us time in class to get a jump on our homework. But not now. He's all business, talking and writing at a crazy fast pace, like we're sprinting through the class. It's both exhausting and weirdly exhilarating.

Almost everyone is into it. The project, I mean. Like learning economics to justify the time we spend in class working on this swim lesson plan. But a few kids are not. Like *really* not. Pierce and his posse complain a lot, which is beginning to get on my nerves. He's all mad about the change. And why we're spending all this time on a kid he didn't even know. Today he's on a roll. "Mr. D," he says, "my dad wants to know why we're doing this extracurricular project that's not even related to history."

Mr. D turns from the whiteboard, where he's written "*Supply/Demand*" in large capital letters. "Pierce, if your father has an inquiry, he can email or call me. In the meantime, you can tell him that class has ramped into overdrive, that you are learning twice as much, because I believe in you guys." He turns back to the board to keep writing.

Pierce gives him the finger behind his back.

"What is your problem?" I mutter. I feel like I need to defend this, since Teo's death is on me and my dad.

"Shove it, Ridley," he whispers back.

I don't get it. His anger seems way out of proportion. "So you have to do a little more homework outside of class. Big whoop. Just trying to do something for the kids here."

"We wouldn't have to if your father weren't such a juicehead."

"Shut up," I whisper fiercely. "Just shut the hell up."

He smiles. I feel like I'm talking to the Grinch. The *before* Grinch.

Mr. D turns back to us. He grabs his phone and texts for a second. Then he rubs his hands. "Okay, guys, today's lesson is focused on a basic principle of economics. The law of supply and demand." He pauses. "By the way, I left the house so early this morning that I forgot to have breakfast. If you hear my stomach growling, that's—"

He's interrupted by a knock at the door. He sighs, looks at us in confusion, and opens it. Ms. Cox, who works in the main office, walks in carrying a box with a half dozen maple-glazed doughnuts. She must have just heated them in the microwave, because the aroma fills the classroom. She puts the box on Mr. D's desk. "Why, thank you, Ms. Cox," he says. "You know your pay. We agreed on these terms earlier."

Wait, he planned this?

He hands Ms. Cox a deli tissue from a box he pulls from a shelf behind his desk. She takes it, reaches into the box, and draws out a doughnut. "Oh, wow," she says. Slowly, dramatically, she brings it to her mouth and takes a bite. "This is amazing. It just melts in your mouth. Thank you, Mr. D!" She takes another bite, winks at him, and leaves the room.

Mr. D lifts the box lid. "So there are five doughnuts left. Since I paid for them, I'm going to save one for me." He pauses. "No, actually, I'm too hungry to wait. I gotta eat it now." Trying to mimic Ms. Cox's drama, he sinks his teeth into the doughnut. I look around. He's killing us, and he knows it. Everyone is salivating. He's like a field mouse surrounded by a bunch of hawks.

"Mr. D! Really?" A chorus of protests rebounds around the room.

Slowly, he finishes chewing. He takes a wipe from his desk and cleans his hands and mouth. Then he looks up. "Anyone want to buy one of these doughnuts?"

Immediately twelve of our hands shoot up. He nods. "Okay, so I paid five dollars for six. That's almost a dollar apiece. I had to pay Ms. Cox one doughnut for heating them in the faculty room and then bringing them to the classroom. Now, I kind of want to make a profit on this investment. So I am willing to sell these to the highest bidders, with the bidding starting at $1.25 each. Anyone?"

The twelve hands stay raised. "Hmm," he says. "It looks like we have a problem. Twelve people want four doughnuts. Should we cut each one in thirds?"

Josh shouts out. "No! I'll give you $1.50!"

And the bidding begins. Though the raises are slight, twenty-five cents at the most, each one feels monumental. My stomach is growling, but I drop out at $1.75. I'm not hungry enough to waste more than that on a doughnut. Finally, when only four students are left, the doughnuts sell for $2.40 apiece. The lucky four winners pay Mr. D their money, grab a doughnut, and eat. The rest of us watch them enviously.

Another knock sounds on the door. Ms. Cox reappears, carrying four larger boxes of doughnuts. *What on earth?*

"Oh, my. More doughnuts?" Mr. D's tone indicates that this is not a surprise.

She grins. "Molly must have been very pleased to see you this morning! Four dozen here!" She places the boxes on his desk and leaves again.

"Wait, what? There are four dozen more?" No one can quite figure out what is going on.

"Sure are," Mr. D says. "And I'm selling them. Let's start the bidding where we left off. Who's going to give me $2.40?"

We catch on quickly. No one speaks. "Okay, then. How about two dollars?" Again, silence. The price keeps dropping, and no one breaks. Finally, he sells them for twenty-five cents apiece. I buy two. They are amazing.

"So, wait, that isn't fair," protests Josh. "I paid almost ten times that for my doughnut!"

Mr. D draws a line graph on the whiteboard. "Ah, you are right. Therein lies the rule of supply and demand. When the supply was low, the demand was high. Twelve of you wanted what only four could have. And you wanted it badly enough to pay over market price. But when there was what we call a glut, or excessive supply, the demand dropped dramatically, along with the price. Everyone who wanted one got one or, in some cases, two or three, and there are still a dozen left. I can't sell them here; the market is saturated. So I've lost big time on my investment. But if I went next door and offered them for sale in Mr. Howell's class, I could sell them for a lot more than twenty-five cents and maybe recoup some of my losses." Heads are nodding. We get it.

Just then the door swings opens and Mr. Winslow barges in. He surveys the room. His eyes land on the remaining box of doughnuts. "Uh, what's going on?"

"Mr. Winslow, what would you pay for a doughnut?"

The principal ignores Josh's question and glares at Mr. D. "Ludovic, see me in my office at lunch." He storms out, slamming the door behind him.

Mr. D looks like he's just been scolded. "Okay, then. Let's get back to work. To our project. We agreed last time to call it the Teo Legacy Project, right?"

Near me, I hear Pierce let out a loud sigh of disgust. Mr. D ignores it. "Anyone come up with new ideas for fundraising?"

Gordon raises his hand. "This just came to me, you know, when you were trying to sell four dozen doughnuts. So we have this chest freezer in our garage. And it's stuffed full of blueberries. In gallon bags. Like probably sixty of 'em. My mom uses them to make jam, but we don't touch it. We're, well, not to be mean or anything, but we're just sick of it. We have it all the time. Like seriously, I would rather have toast with nothing on it than that jam." He pauses and looks around. I see several kids nodding their heads.

"But if we used the berries to make jam and sell it to people who don't have acres of wild blueberries in their backyards like almost everybody here does, we could probably make a killing. Like you did at first with the four doughnuts."

For a few seconds people think about his idea. "But wouldn't your mother be pissed if we took all her berries?" asks Coop. "I mean, picking those tiny things takes a lot of time."

Gordon hesitates. "Well, if she knew why we were using them, she'd be okay, I think. I mean, I could sweet-talk her, say that we really want her recipe because it's so delicious. Hell, she could even supervise us if we made it. And I'd tell her it would be going to a good cause. It may even be a relief to her. There's no way she's going to use all those berries. She kind of gets obsessed when she picks. Like she doesn't want to waste any."

It turns out that Gordon's mother is not the only one who freezes staggering numbers of blueberries. A lot of my classmates say their freezers are similarly stuffed. There will be some interesting negotiations at dinner tonight.

We spend the rest of the class figuring out all that is involved in making blueberry jam. Mr. D divides us into five groups. One will price bulk sugar, pectin, and canning jars; another will research laws about selling homemade goods. The third will try to find a commercial kitchen we can use, the fourth will research comparative products, and the last will investigate sales venues.

If this is even possible.

29
LUNA

I hate group projects.

But not for the reason that most kids hate group projects. Others hate them because the workload inevitably is uneven, or because no one can agree on what to do. I just don't want to work with people. Because that means they have to look at me. I don't want to be the cause of their ruined day.

I am mortified when Mr. D puts me in a group with Kiki, Coop, Pierce, and Hunter. I don't have anything against Kiki and Pierce and Coop because I don't know them. Obviously. Hunter's the only one I've had a real conversation with, and that was a disaster. He couldn't even walk back from Ms. Callahan's house with me.

Our group is supposed to research the laws about selling homemade products. Kiki immediately opens her notebook to a blank page. "I'll record everything we find out," she says.

Coop laughs. "Sweet! I love it when girls are in my group! They do all the work!"

I should tell him how sexist and ridiculous that comment is, but then he would look at me. So I remain silent, hidden in my hoodie.

Hunter punches Coop. "Shut up. This is not a normal project. You can loaf in your other classes, but this actually counts."

Coop rubs his arm and glares at Hunter. "Geez, bro, I was just kidding. I know it counts. I was there with you at the pool."

Pierce glances at me and Kiki and rolls his eyes. Then he does a double take. "Whoa. I've never noticed that," he says, pointing to my face. "Does it hurt?"

"Dude!" says Coop. But for once, I'm not offended. Because he doesn't say it meanly. It's more like he's genuinely curious.

"No," I say.

"Hey, Pierce, does *your* face hurt?" says Coop. "'Cause it's killing me!"

"Har. Har. Hilarious, Cooper." He turns back to me. "Seriously, you could probably get that thing removed. Like maybe with laser surgery."

This time it's Hunter who comes to my defense. "Jesus, Pierce, you have the sensitivity of a warthog. She's perfect the way she is. Move on."

I'm so embarrassed by the attention and disgust and support that I want to disappear. But I also don't want them to have the last word. Because it's my body, not public property. And as much as I hate it, it's the only one I have. "Actually, Pierce," I start to say. Hunter and Coop and Kiki look at me in surprise. "We have looked into laser removal. It won't work because the mark surrounds my eye. Too dangerous. And it's too expensive, anyway."

Pierce doesn't flinch. "Yeah, not worth risking your eyesight. And it's not like it's a handicap. I mean, you can still see and walk and think. Like you're actually lucky."

Lucky? Me? With this disfigurement that made my mother leave? But he has a point. And maybe I need to be called on it. It could be a lot more challenging.

Mr. D has given us permission to be on our phones because we all need to do research. I immediately put my head down and focus on the screen in my lap. It's quiet in the room; people are taking this seriously.

"Here's a site that I think is legit," declares Coop. "It's from a website called Forager. The subject is 'Maine's Cottage Food Law.'"

I've found the same website. But I don't say anything.

Coop mutters to himself as he scrolls. "Allowed venues, allowed foods, limitations, business, labeling. Yeah, this is all relevant. Should we just print the information from this site? Instead of writing it all down?"

Kiki shakes her head. "No, because we won't learn it that way. Let's at least get the highlights down to present to the class."

For the next twenty minutes, we glean as much information as we can from the website. It's pretty interesting. For a while, I forget that I'm not talking to anyone and join Coop and Hunter in calling out facts for Kiki to write down. Pierce stays on his phone and doesn't say anything.

To make blueberry jam to sell, we need to get a license, which we can get after the kitchen we use is inspected and approved by the Division of Quality Assurance & Regulations. No smoking or pets are allowed in that kitchen. If we choose to sell at a farmers' market, we need to obtain a Mobile Food Vendor license from the same division.

The label requirements are very specific. Our company name and address must be on the label, as well as the exact ingredients, in descending order of weight. Any allergens, such as nuts, soy, wheat, milk, or eggs, must be listed. When Temmie and I made blueberry jam last summer, we only used berries, sugar, lemon juice, and pectin. Not a lot of allergens there.

Pierce hasn't contributed anything. Kiki looks at him. "What did you find out?"

He shrugs. "Nothing."

"Well, what were you doing this whole time?"

"Nothing. Playing a game."

Kiki is pissed. "Um, why? Like this is a whole-class thing. You're supposed to be helping."

I am amazed at her bravery. I wouldn't be able to confront him like that.

"Not interested," he states flatly. "We're being railroaded into this. All for some kid I didn't even know."

Hunter sounds annoyed. "Luna knew Teo. He was in her Sunday school class. Maybe she can enlighten you."

"Really not interested," says Pierce. There's this weird anger emanating from him.

"Whatever, jerk," says Coop. We sit there for a second. It's painful, the tension.

Kiki breaks it. She smiles at me. "It's cool that you, you know, teach at church. The only thing I remember about my Sunday school was making a gigantic papier-mâché whale."

Coop's voice is softer than usual when he asks, "What was he like in Sunday school?"

I'm furious at Hunter for putting me on the spot, but this is for Teo's memory. And the more people who know about Teo, the more meaningful this project is going to be. And maybe Pierce will actually want to help.

So I tell them. About his dancing with me. Sitting next to me. Calling me "Loon." Buying me a cookie that looked like my face. Patting my disgusting birthmark. Getting Mrs. Frye to dance.

And I don't even mean to, but by the end, I'm crying.

And so are Kiki and Coop.

And Hunter.

And, bizarrely, Pierce. Who won't look at us and bolts out of there the second the bell rings.

30
HUNTER

Dad has invited Gretchen over tonight for his "famous Jacko-Tacos." I love it when he makes them, not only because they're really good, but it means it's like a festive night. Gretchen arrives early to hang out in the kitchen and talk as he cooks. When I get home from practice, the whole house smells like a Mexican restaurant. I walk in the kitchen and see Dad and Gretchen both bent over in laughter. It's the kind of infectious laughter that sets me off, even though I don't know what's so funny.

Gretchen wipes the tears from her cheeks. "Oh, my God, I haven't laughed that hard in months! Your dad and I were remembering a Halloween when we were teenagers. Long past the age of trick-or-treating. We were bored, you know, how kids get. So we decided to prank the neighbors, a crabby old couple."

"Mr. and Mrs. Mitchell," Dad says. "But we called them Mr. and Mrs. Witchell. He was a farmer, and she taught piano lessons."

"Anyway," says Gretchen, "we told them that afternoon that we'd heard on the news that a prisoner had escaped from the county jail. About eight miles from us."

Gretchen chimes in. "And we said he was described as extremely tall, wearing black, and was said to be armed and dangerous."

"I had this pair of stilts that I'd practiced with for weeks. Got pretty good at 'em too," Dad says. "So I wore my father's trench coat, a black hat, and these long pants. You know, to cover the stilts. And I walked over there."

Gretchen's eyes are bright with the retelling. "So he's slowly circling their house. The plan was that I would call them and say I'd spotted the escaped prisoner in the field right behind their house. You know, just to give them a scare. So I did."

Dad starts laughing again. "But what we didn't consider," he says, "was their dog. He came flying out of the house at me."

"I was watching from the house," says Gretchen. "Your dad jumped off those stilts so fast! But the pants got caught, and he fell over trying to get untangled."

"I was so scared! I couldn't get out of there fast enough," laughs Dad.

"He finally ripped the pants off and ran into our yard, wearing the coat and just his boxers. I'd never seen him in such a panic!"

"Oh, man. I never did go back for my stilts or Dad's pants and hat. I wonder what the Mitchells did with them."

"We're lucky it was just a dog and not a gun. And then," adds Gretchen, "Dad was looking for his hat for the Christmas Eve service. Mom said he'd gotten so forgetful that he'd probably left it somewhere. And we were too chicken to tell!"

"We had some good times, didn't we?" Dad gives Gretchen a warm smile.

"Tell Hunter about the time your art teacher confiscated your notebook—and it was full of caricatures of him."

"You remember that? Oh, I got in so much trouble. Dad and Mom grounded me for weeks, and I had to write an apology letter."

"And I swear they lectured you about respect every night for the rest of the year."

"I did get an A in art that year. For performance. But he gave me a D in behavior and attitude."

They entertain me for a solid two hours. I love it. When dinner is over at last, and every dish is cleaned and put away, Gretchen asks us if we'll go to the vet with her. Dad shakes his head. "I got some work to do," he says. "I'll be back later."

I'm disappointed. I want this night—the laughter, the three of us, the stories—to go on and on. "Really, Dad? Can't you come?"

He gives my neck and shoulders a little massage. "Not tonight. You help your aunt. Then get your homework done. I'll see you later."

On the ride to Shep's, I blurt it out. "Why did he have to ruin it? He's going to the bar, isn't he?"

"I honestly don't know what he's doing," she admits. "Maybe. But I thought he said he was doing some work?"

"Yeah, work on his liver, maybe," I mutter darkly. "We were having such a good time!"

"I guess," she says, "that's what we should focus on. The good times. When he's not distracted by alcohol. And this will pass, this season of unemployment. I mean, something's got to come into the mill building, get people working again. And you know that when he's busy, earning a wage, feeling empowered, he'll lay off the booze. He's a really good person, your dad. At his core."

I know he is. Maybe that's why I miss him so much.

At the vet I offer to run in and pick up Raven's medicine. Gretchen is happy to sit in the warmth of the car and wait. In the office there is a sign: "Lambing. In barn." I go back out to the car to tell Gretchen where I'm going and then head to the barn. A fancy white SUV is parked there, the motor running. Just as I pass by, the door opens. "Excuse me?"

I turn. It's that woman who was here when Raven was so sick. Thaddeus's mother. She seems anxious. "Do you work here?"

"No," I tell her. "I'm just picking up medicine. Shep left a note saying he's in the barn."

She gets out of the car. "I'm sorry. Now I remember you. We met here a while ago. You knew my son, Thaddeus, right? Please, call me Jessica. And you are . . . ?"

"Hunter. Hunter Ridley."

"I'm waiting for Thaddeus. He works here now. And he's usually finished much earlier than this. Would you . . . would you mind if I joined you? You're headed into the barn?"

"Sure."

"Thaddeus has a very set schedule; it upsets him if he doesn't follow it. That's why I'm worried. He should have been out by now."

I remember our class gerbil. "It's cool that he has a job here. He loves animals, doesn't he? He was really attached to Jeremy the Gerbil in Mrs. Eaton's room."

"You remember that?" Jessica sounds surprised.

We enter the barn, which is warm and smells of hay and wet wool and animal feces. I hear Shep's voice and a guttural cry coming from way back at the other end. We make our way past several pens filled with sheep. This barn is huge; I'm amazed at how much room there is in here. When we round the last corner, Jessica takes a sharp breath and covers her mouth with her hands.

There is Thaddeus, his arms covered in blood.

Next to him is a ewe, licking a newborn lamb. Shep crouches behind her, talking softly. Thaddeus repeats "Your baby, your baby, your baby" on loop. The ewe stops licking the lamb, who tries to stand on wobbly legs. Twice it falls, then it stands and nuzzles its mother, probably searching for milk. But the ewe butts it away. Her whole body convulses, and I hear Shep call to Thaddeus, “Gonna need you again. She’s too tiny. Can you slip your arm in to help her?”

I have to admit that I’m feeling sort of lightheaded. Thaddeus moves behind the ewe, his eyes laser-focused. I watch him pull a lamb from the womb of a heaving ewe. A wave of nausea hits me, I guess from all the blood. I am both grossed out and in total awe of him. I could never do that.

The mother breaks the amniotic sac and proceeds to lick the second lamb, then she allows both lambs to suck from her teats. Shep stands and stretches. He gives Thaddeus a clean towel and a gentle pat on the back. “That’s it for tonight. Nice work there, mate.” Thaddeus looks so happy. We hear him say to Shep, “Two babies. Two babies.”

I look over at Jessica to, like, congratulate her. Because that was seriously amazing, what her son just did. There are tears streaming down her face. I get it. We don’t say anything, just slip back out of the barn.

I remember that look, that same look, Dad used to have for me.

31

LUNA

Temmie told me once about an old movie about a group of American tourists taking a whirlwind trip through Europe. It was called *If it's Tuesday, This Must Be Belgium*. In direct contrast with the excitement of whipping around Europe, my life is pathetic. *If It's Thursday, This Must Be Hiding in the Library to Spy on the Women Knitting and Gossiping.* Wow. Best-selling film of all time! Standing room only! International sensation!

The talk is about the weather. And a bunch of people I don't know. And blah blah blah. Honestly, my math problems are more interesting.

I have finished twenty-three of the thirty I have to do when Jessica bursts into the room, breathless. "I know I'm late," she declares, "and I can't stay long. But I wanted to tell Polly and everyone what happened over the weekend."

I perk up. This should be entertaining.

She leaps right in. "One of my clients, who is filthy rich, flew me to Aspen for the weekend." Already I see it, the awkwardness that ricochets around the room. I doubt anyone here has been to Aspen. Heck, we can't afford to go to Sugarloaf or Sunday River. We can't afford to ski, period. But Jessica is oblivious and blunders on. "It feels like an unnecessary indulgence, I know, but relationships sealed on the ski slope and in the lodge afterward are important ones. Plus, I think this client is bored and needs someone with whom to 'be seen on the scene.'"

Polly gives a loud snort.

"So my client," continues Jessica, "is Cheri Reina. Bigwig in the fashion industry. Her line is eclectic, never the same thing two years in a row. She repped some huge lines in the past, made a name for herself, and set out on her own. And whatever she debuts sells out. Because people trust her style sense.

"I arrived on Friday evening. We did four runs down Buttermilk Mountain then had drinks and dinner at the Little Nell. Amazing truffle fries.

"So lots of people in the restaurant were already dressed in their fancy evening wear, but Cheri and I came directly from the mountain. When I took off my jacket, Cheri said, 'Oh, my God!'"

I look at the women. Most have stopped knitting to listen. Even Polly's scorn hasn't prevented her from paying attention.

"So I turned around to look behind me. I assumed it was another celebrity sighting, because we'd already spied three. But Cheri was staring at *me*. 'Where on earth did you get that sweater?' I told her that a woman in my town knit it. That I had traded her for it." She looks right at Polly.

"Cheri could not stop raving. Her exact words were 'It's gorgeous! I've never seen anything like it!' And then she asked me where she could order one. And I told her it was a one-of-a-kind special. That she couldn't just order it. And she responded, 'I'm Cheri Reina. I don't do *can't*. Of course I can. You just need to figure out how.'"

Jessica pauses for a second. I can't really read the room. I'll ask Temmie about this later. She has a much better sense of people than I do.

Jessica continues. "At first I just dismissed her spoiled-girl act. Then I asked her, 'Just curious. If you knew that you were getting an original, hand-knitted sweater from Maine, how much would you pay for it?' And she said, 'Oh, you know I don't like to talk about money. But if I did, I would say that the price is irrelevant. It's hard to be unique these days, so I would be willing to pay what that's worth. Like, I don't know, four, five, six grand.'"

Ethel drops her needle. Ruth claps her hands. Rose laughs out loud. And everyone looks at Polly, who just shakes her head.

"And before I left the restaurant, three other women asked me where I got my sweater. So I just wanted to let you know that, Polly. How much your work was appreciated."

She leaves in a rush, a client waiting, can't be late, good to see everyone, stay warm, take care.

The air has changed in here, but I don't know if it's for the better or not.

I have an idea.

32
HUNTER

Emma wants to hang out after my practice, so we meet at Molly's. In theory, we're supposed to be studying. At least that's what she agreed to when I said I had a ton of homework. She's already in a booth when I get there.

"Hey," she says as I drop my backpack on the bench. "You look cute. But your hair is still wet."

"I hurried to get here. I need food. You want anything?"

"Get me a mocha. A skinny. Two shots of vanilla."

Samantha is working. Knowing that she was on the pool deck with my passed-out dad makes me feel weird around her, even though she doesn't know I know. I give her my order quickly and pay.

Emma is kind of snippy. "I still can't believe you blew me off on Saturday. My parents were out of town too."

"I didn't blow you off. I told you I had that thing at Gordon's."

She starts scrolling through her phone. "Yeah, what was that again? Oh, my God, this is hilarious. Look at this video of Logan from Saturday. After like ten Jell-O shots. He can't even stand up."

I look. Whatever.

Emma senses my lack of enthusiasm. "What? It's funny!"

"Well, you asked about Gordon's. And then went straight to your phone."

"Oh, my God. You sound like my grandmother." She turns her phone over and puts it down. Dramatically. She cups her face with her hands and opens her eyes wide. "Do tell me about what you did at Gordon's."

I want to stay mad at her, but I like fall under her spell. I ignore her sarcasm and start in. "So we went over there to do kind of a trial run of the jam. You know, the blueberry jam we're gonna sell to make money for the Teo thing."

"You guys made it? I thought you'd have a professional or someone like Molly do it. In a commercial kitchen. I mean, aren't there laws about sanitation and stuff?"

"Yeah. Kiki had already had the health inspector out to approve Gordon's kitchen. It was spotless. And Kiki made sure we all wore hairnets and gloves, that the jars were sanitized according to code, that we kept a careful account of—"

"Wait!" Emma interrupts. "You in a hairnet? This I've got to see. Do you have pics?"

"No! Not every second of my life is documented like yours."

"Too bad. That would have been so funny. Anyway, who's paying for all this?"

"Gordon's parents fronted the money. For the sugar, pectin, jars, whatever. They both have jobs. We'll pay them back. And a lot of parents have offered their frozen berries as a donation, so that's awesome. Anyway, my job was to stir the jam while it was cooking. We got to taste it at the end. It was seriously good. And we made eighty pints!"

Emma is definitely not as excited about this as I am. So I just drop it. Samantha arrives with our food. I take a huge bite of my turkey sandwich. Emma's back on her phone.

The bell jingles and I see Mr. D walk in. He sits at a table near our booth, but since he's facing the other way, he doesn't see us. He pulls out a stack of papers and leaves them on the table. He heads to the counter to order. Samantha greets him and then this weird wave of, like, shock crosses her face. "You're the . . . the one who . . . that night . . ."

He stares at her. "Oh, my. You're right. I knew I knew you from somewhere, but it was so out of context. I . . . I am so sorry."

"No, I am! Because I didn't stay with him. Like you asked!"

"I should have stayed. Not dumped the responsibility on you. That wasn't fair."

They smile at each other, like, sadly. "The whole thing was such a tragedy," Samantha says. "I've talked to Pastor Mark. Who keeps insisting that it wasn't my fault."

"Oh, God, if anything, it's mine. I shouldn't have put him there," Mr. D says. And then I have a horrible sinking feeling. *They're talking about my dad. Mr. D was with him? Is this why we're doing the Teo Legacy Project? Because of his guilt?*

Emma doesn't witness the drama unfolding behind her. Her thumbs are flying on her phone. She laughs.

"Let's get out of here," I whisper.

"What? Why? We just got here," she says. She looks around. "Hey, isn't that your teacher? Mr. D?"

"Shut up!" I hiss. "I don't want him to see me!"

Emma's intrigued. "Why not? I thought you liked him."

"Because," I explain, "I just heard him saying something about that night. I think he brought my dad to the pool. And now he feels like shit about it."

"Oh, God. Hunter, you've got to stop obsessing about that night." She is dead serious. "I mean, you and I both know the truth. It was a shitty accident. That's all. Not your dad's fault. Period. Time to move on. And you guys are doing that project, right? Doesn't that make you feel better?"

It's probably the most logical thing I've ever heard her say. And I appreciate it. But I just can't explain the constant guilt I feel.

Emma has clearly moved on. "Do you think they're flirting? Mr. D and Samantha? I mean, they're both what, mid-thirties?"

I look at them and see them hugging. But, despite Emma's insinuation, it doesn't look flirty. It looks more sympathetic.

Mr. D sits down. The bell rings again and a young woman who clearly is a friend of Samantha's waltzes in. "Sam! You better have a cinnamon roll left for me!"

She passes Mr. D, who is already marking papers. He looks up briefly and nods. She reaches the counter and whispers to Samantha. It's loud enough so we can hear it. "Oh, my God! Yes, please! Who is that?"

Samantha laughs. "Nice to see you too, Megan!"

"I am serious! I've never seen him before! That bod is unbelievable. He looks like a swimmer—you know, narrow waist, broad shoulders. I just want to run my fingers through that hair. And that chiseled jaw?"

"You are terrible! Totally objectifying a human being."

"Okay, I'm sure he's smart and sensitive too. Do you know him? Will you introduce me?"

Emma is eating this up. "Wait, we can't leave. We've got to see how this plays out."

Samantha brings Megan over to Mr. D. "Pardon me, but someone would like to be introduced. This is my friend Megan."

Mr. D stands up and shakes her hand. "Ludovic. Nice to meet you."

"May I?" Megan asks, already pulling out a chair. She takes off her jacket and hangs it over the back. She's wearing green hospital scrubs.

"Um, sure. I was just grading some tests." Mr. D moves his chair around to make room for her. Now I can see his face. I scrunch down in the booth so he can't see me.

"You're a teacher? Ha!" She turns to Samantha, who is heading back to the counter. "I told you he was smart and sensitive!"

Mr. D's face turns red. Emma grins and whispers to me, "Dang, she's aggressive!"

Megan pulls in her chair and leans forward. "Have you ever done speed dating? It's like way old-fashioned. I mean it's much easier just to use a dating app and swipe right, but I did it last weekend in Portland."

Samantha brings food to a table of elderly men playing Rummikub. Megan goes on like she's getting paid per word. "You get three minutes with each person. Then you move on. So this one dude's bragging about being in a sled dog race up near the Canadian border. And he's going on and on, super ego-head. He never even asks me a question. When I finally manage to slip in a sentence, I go, 'Oh, isn't that a coincidence, because I raced the Iditarod last year in Alaska!' And he thinks I'm lying, so I go into detail about harnesses, the lead dog, mushing on the trail. Totally take the wind out of his sail."

Mr. D looks amused. "Have you? Raced the Iditarod?"

Megan bursts out laughing. "Are you kidding? I mean, look at me! But I never forgot that book we read in middle school. Jack London, I think. *The Call of the Wild*. I just elaborated on that."

Samantha brings her a warm cinnamon roll.

"Thank you!" She takes a bite, leans back, and sighs. "These are orgasmic." She offers a forkful to Mr. D, who quickly shakes his head. "Then another guy keeps going on about California, how he's looking for someone who has traveled. His arrogance is really annoying me, so I yawn and say, 'Well, I guess I've done a bit of traveling. I've backpacked through Peru and Mexico. Did some trekking in Poland, wandered around Norway, Sweden, and Denmark one summer.' That shuts him right up."

Samantha, who is standing by their table, calls her on it. "Megan, you've never been out of New England. You are such a liar!"

"No, I'm not. You've been to every one of those places too. He just didn't realize I was talking about towns in Maine!" Her laughter fills the shop. She focuses on Mr. D. "Okay, let's do it. Tell me five things about you, then ask me five things about me."

Mr. D seems confused. "Oh, I'm afraid there's nothing . . . I mean, I don't . . ."

"Oh, you're humble, too? On top of sensitive, intelligent, creative, and hot? Okay, you don't like to brag about yourself. Incredibly refreshing. Then I'll start. I'm twenty-eight, I've never married, I work intake at the clinic, I blast country music when I'm driving, and I love Shakespeare. Okay, your turn."

She talks so quickly I have trouble keeping up. *Is this how adults hook up?* Mr. D's expression has changed from amusement to alarm. "No, really, I—"

"So I'll ask you questions, then. You can't lie, even if it feels like you're bragging. Deal? Deal. Number one: Do you eat dessert?"

He looks confused.

"It's not a hard question! Just answer it!"

"I . . . I . . . um, yes, I eat dessert."

"Good. Although your BMI would say otherwise. Quite a specimen."

Emma kicks me under the table. "Can you believe she said that about your teacher? Ewww!"

Megan continues. Following this conversation feels like we're on a motorboat at full throttle. "Number two: What is your favorite dessert?"

"Look, this is fun, I suppose, but—" Mr. D is definitely not a gamer. At least not for this.

She cuts him off. "What is your favorite dessert?"

"Geez, I don't know. I'll say apple crisp."

"Number three: Warm or cold?"

"Wait, what? Warm or cold what?"

"Apple crisp!"

"Uh, warm, I guess."

"Excellent. Number four: With or without vanilla ice cream?"

"Definitely with."

"Number five: If you could go on an adventure anywhere in the United States, where would you go and what would you do?"

"Whoa. That's much harder than dessert. Um, I guess I'd like to go mountain biking in the Utah Canyonlands. What about you? What would you do?"

"I'd like to compete in the Iditarod in Alaska."

Mr. D laughs. "You know, I have a feeling you will someday. If this is your normal pace in life."

"*He's actually flirting back!*" Emma whispers. I'm not sure. I'm feeling a bit sorry for him. Like he's been ambushed.

Megan grins. "I don't waste time. Life is short. So you're coming to my apartment for apple crisp, warm, with vanilla ice cream, on Saturday night." She takes another bite of roll. "See what I did there?"

Mr. D laughs. "Wow. You're good. But I'm going to the basketball game on Saturday night. With some work colleagues. And I am so sorry, Megan, you're delightful, but I'm . . . I'm . . ."

"You already have a girlfriend?" She looks at his hand. "No ring. In my world, that means I still have a chance."

Mr. D wipes his forehead. Emma notices. "He's sweating! I cannot wait to post this! His students are going to die laughing!"

I whip around. "You took a video?"

She's still laughing. "Yeah. Got the whole thing. One sec . . . and . . . done. We'll see if he's actually at the game on Saturday. Or eating apple crisp in bed with the sled dog racer."

I feel violated. And pissed off. For him. His time out of school and his love life or whatever is none of our business. But she doesn't get that. Before I say something I regret, I mutter something about homework and pack my stuff. Emma's already getting responses to her post. I don't even think she notices when I leave.

33
LUNA

When I walk into history, Mr. D has already projected the top ten principles of economics onto the SmartScreen. He's pacing back and forth, obviously in a hurry to get started. It feels like we've doubled our learning in this class, which I guess is good, but sometimes it makes my brain hurt.

I overheard someone say that Mr. Winslow is on Mr. D's case about spending too much time on this project, so Mr. D has been on like a teaching rampage. He's almost manic, making sure we know absolutely everything about both history and economics. I wonder if he cares more about our learning it or about his reputation as a teacher? Or keeping Mr. Winslow off his back? Whatever. I don't care about his motivation. I'll memorize whatever I have to if it means we can still do the Teo project. What matters most is that we get the kids in this town swimming.

We get hung up on the last principle, the one about the trade-off between inflation and unemployment. It's a touchy subject because so many people around here are out of work.

A voice calls out. "Hey, Mr. D, I have a question."

I hear snickering. Which makes me mad, since Temmie is one of those who's unemployed. *It's not funny.*

"Yes, Pierce?"

"So let's use an example. Um, how 'bout apples? If the price of apples skyrocketed due to inflation, then would it be worth it to make, say, an *apple crisp*?"

A bunch of kids burst out laughing. I don't get it. Mr. D looks furious. "What's your question, Pierce?"

He can barely swallow his laughter. "Well, wouldn't it be more economical to sell the apples directly? 'Cause like wouldn't you lose money on them if you made them into a warm apple crisp with vanilla ice cream?"

Mr. D's face is red. Like really red. I think I understand Pierce's question, but I don't get why everyone is laughing. Mr. D fumbles for a second then composes himself. "If that is a question with true integrity, I'll answer it. If not, you're wasting my time. Yes, the raw material is usually cheaper than composites. Which is why it's far more economical to make your own baked goods than buy them at a bakery, which must charge a good deal more because, as we've already learned, their costs include labor, rent, utilities, advertising, equipment, inventory, permits, licenses, and so on. Anything else before we move on?"

"No, Mr. D," says Pierce. "You answered my question quite *crisply*. Thank you." There's another eruption of laughter.

Mr. D calls on Gordon to update those of us who weren't at his house on Saturday. Gordon says there are eighty pint jars of jam now sitting on his dining room table.

Kiki jumps in. "Everything was up to code. But we still have so much work to do before we can even think about selling them. One thing is we need to create a label. You know, to put on the jars. But before that, we have to seriously think about our brand."

I don't know Kiki well, obviously. I don't know anybody in the school well. But from working with her on this project, I am impressed. She's smart and organized and like forward thinking.

Mr. D looks around the room. "Pierce, why don't you come up here and be our scribe for the day."

I turn around and see Pierce shaking his head. The laughter is gone. "Why don't I? Why *don't* I? I'll tell you why I *don't*. Because this is a waste of my time. And everyone else's who thought we were in this class to learn history. So, no thank you; I won't be your stupid scribe."

The atmosphere totally changes. People look around, stunned. Coop jumps up. "I'll do it."

As he's walking up to the front, Mr. D says calmly, "Pierce, if you would prefer to spend this time getting a head start on your history homework, that's fine with me. And that goes for everyone else. I personally believe in the value of this legacy project, not only as a relevant and experiential economics lesson but also as a communal balm of sorts. But it is extracurricular, and I respect your decision not to participate."

Coop has already written "BRAND" on the whiteboard. He turns to Kiki. "Now what?"

"Well, like what's our name? Or are we even going to have one? We could just label them something like 'Maine Wild Blueberry Jam.' But that's boring. What do you guys think?"

"How about identifying the cause?" Gordon says. "Call it 'The Teo Legacy Project Jam'?"

Coop writes both suggestions. "I like having Teo's name right out there," says Shea. "It kind of like honors his memory."

"I agree," says Hunter. "Although we're going to be selling this at fairs and farmers' markets all over the state, right? I think people around here would definitely buy it because they know about Teo. But would people in Portland or Lewiston or Augusta?"

"Besides," Gordon says, "our point in selling it farther away is that people around here are not exactly flush with extra cash."

Kiki jumps in. "And our goal, if this takes off, is to maybe sell beyond Maine. Like on the internet. But we'd need a special license to do that. Shea, you were going to research that, right?"

Shea nods. "Yes, I'm so sorry! I don't have that info yet."

I notice a boy across the room raise his hand. I think his name is Eliot. If there's a male equivalent to me, Eliot is it. He hides like I do. And honestly, I've never heard him speak, so I'm shocked to see his hand up. Everyone else is just calling out freely. Coop notices him too. "Eliot?"

Immediately his face turns bright red. He looks down. "I maybe c-c-c-could make, make . . . could make a w-w-w-website."

No one says anything. I think we're all equally startled to hear him. His stuttering makes me anxious for him; I understand why he doesn't talk in class.

Mr. D steps in. "Eliot, that's exactly what we need. A tech person. If we get the license, then we could advertise the jam on the website. Fantastic. You guys are rocking and rolling. But we may be getting ahead of ourselves. We'd have to investigate packing and shipping options."

Kiki assigns that task to two girls. She asks Eliot to have a mock-up of a website in a week. "First, though," she says, "we need a name. And a logo. Our brand. Like are we cutesy or touristy or edgy or ironic? Are we appealing to grandparents or teenagers? Like why should someone buy our jam? The brand is everything. It's going to make or break us. Any more ideas?"

"I got it!" says Gordon. "How about 'Edge'? It's short, catchy, and way edgier than 'Edgewater.'"

People groan at the pun. But they like the name. A lot.

"That could be the name of our website too," says Coop. "And maybe that's where we could include the story of Teo. Eliot, would that be possible?"

Eliot shakes his head. He holds up his phone. "I l-l-looked up 'Edge.' That d-d-d-domain is already ta–ta-taken. B-b-by a literary ma-ma-magazine."

"Crap," says Coop. "That was good. Okay, then, how about this? *Made in Maine.* Just that. Simple. To the point. And it will sell both here and out of state."

Hunter nods. "Dude, that's actually not a bad idea. Quite surprising, since it came from you. That Maine thing holds more cachet the farther you get from here."

Coop bursts out laughing. "Ca-shay? What the hell does that mean? You sound like a frickin' dictionary."

I see the tops of Hunter's ears turn pink. "Shut up, moron. It means, like, prestige. Maybe you should read a book once in a while."

"Maybe you should talk like a human, not like the president of the nerd patrol."

I watch the two of them joke with each other and feel this weird stab of envy. I've never had a friendship like theirs. Or like anyone's, actually.

I look around. Most people are into this. Excited. Eliot is on his phone again. He raises his hand. "No one has a 'Ma-Ma-Made in Maine' do-domain. J-j-just 'Maine Ma-Ma-Made.'"

"Hey, I have an idea," shouts Pierce. Is he choosing to participate after all? "We could have a Maine maid come and clean our houses. And make us apple crisp."

This time no one laughs.

As everyone is filing out, Mr. D asks me and Hunter to stay behind for a minute.

"Ms. Callahan asked if the two of you would go over there this afternoon. She'd like an update on this project from you."

Hunter looks at me, anxiously. "Um, I can't. We have the early practice. Right after school."

And he'd have to be seen with me. No way is that going to happen again.

"I can go," I tell Mr. D.

Ms. Callahan's woodstove is roaring when I arrive; I can hear the logs hissing and crackling. A pot of homemade applesauce is cooling on the stove, making the whole kitchen smell like cinnamon.

"It's so cozy in here," I say, taking off my coat. The warmth extends beyond physical. A word we just learned in English class is fitting: "hygge."

Ms. Callahan sighs. "Cozy, yes. Way too quiet too." She ladles out a bowlful of applesauce and sets it in front of me. "Thanks for coming. I have something I want to give you for the project. But first tell me how it's coming along."

I do. The research. The jam. The name. She's the kind of listener who asks thoughtful questions and makes you feel as if you are the most important reporter on Earth. Like your story really matters.

"*Made in Maine.* I like it. Sort of a double entendre, you know? Something to ponder. What does it mean to be made in Maine? Like so many of us were?" She stares off into space. I wonder if she's thinking about Teo. She turns back to me and gives a little laugh. "You know, when you said, 'Made in Maine,' I thought for a moment you meant two words, not three: 'Maiden Maine.' Hah!"

She seems deep in thought. Finally she refocuses. "I love playing with words, don't you? But I won't take up too much more of your time. I have something for the project. It's a donation, not a loan. It's not much, but it will help with a few more jars or something. This was money I was just starting to save for Teo's care in case I died before he did."

She hands me an envelope full of cash. "Nobody uses cash anymore," she apologizes. "But I assume you don't have an account set up yet. This should tide you over until you do. I think it's just a bit over seven hundred dollars."

"I . . . I . . . Thank you, Ms. Callahan. So much."

"Oh, I almost forgot. The pool. I know someone in your class has reached out to the owners of the Moose and Loon to inquire about using it. But I wanted to let you know that PJ and Patsy have been so lovely to me throughout this whole thing. They feel terrible about Teo, even though they weren't here when it happened. Usually they stay for the party, their last hurrah of the season before returning to their home out west. But this year they had to get back to be with Patsy's mother. Pancreatic cancer. She died the same day Teo did. They're grieving too."

I didn't know this.

"I've been contacted by lawyers who believe I should sue PJ and Patsy. I refuse to go down that road. It wasn't their fault. I'm tired of division; I want to focus on bringing people together. That's why I'm so supportive of this project. Anyway, they are going to up their liability insurance. And they will pay for the facility maintenance for the months we are using the pool."

I think for a minute. "That means we need to raise enough money to cover the other costs for the pool. Like lifeguards and swim instructors. And maybe snow removal from the parking lot? Or is that under facility maintenance?"

"Hmm. Not sure about that. Have your classmates ask PJ. He's extremely well organized." She smiles at me. "It's a lot to consider, isn't it?" She stands up and clears my bowl. In the kitchen she gazes out at the snowy field behind her house. The sun is setting, making the snow kind of glow. "For me, this is the saddest time of day," she said. "My mother used to call this twilight hour 'the gloaming.' When you have children, it's such a busy hour. And when you don't . . ." Her voice fades away. That familiar ache lodges itself in my throat.

Suddenly she gasps. "What in heaven's name—?" She points. "The fence! Look!"

I join her at the window. A neat split-rail fence casts long shadows on the snow. "What's wrong?"

"It's fixed! It was missing rails, and, and, it was even falling over at the top of the hill. And now it looks beautiful. What . . .? Who . . .?" She looks at me in disbelief.

A warm feeling floods my body. People are taking care of her, and they're not doing it for praise.

34
HUNTER

Yesterday after practice I jogged to Ms. Callahan's, hoping to catch Luna there. I felt bad about not being able to go with her. About halfway there, I ran into Luna walking back.

"Hey! I guess I'm too late."

Luna gave me a weird look. And kept walking.

"Wait! I thought you might still be at Miz Callahan's. And I could help you, you know, fill her in." I caught up to her. For a tiny person, she has wheels. Like I was having to work to keep up.

She still didn't say anything. "Um, what did you guys talk about?"

She finally stopped. She seemed like mad at me. "I'll tell you in class tomorrow. I've got to go." She took off, practically running.

Whatever.

But today I'm still bothered. Like she must hate me or something. Why wouldn't she talk to me yesterday? I don't think I said anything wrong. I barely said anything at all.

I never see her hanging out with anyone, so I can't ask her friends what her deal is. And today I'm feeling crappy about a lot of stuff, like that stupid video of Mr. D, and an argument I had with Dad about doing the laundry, and never being able to be enough for Emma, and pulling a groin muscle so I have to sit out at practice. And most of all, I'm feeling so sad about Teo. I really need to talk with someone who was his friend.

I catch Luna just as she's heading into the library at lunchtime. "Hey, Luna! Are you . . . um, busy now?"

She gives me an odd look. Almost guilty, like I've caught her doing something bad. "I . . . I . . . no. I mean, yes. I'm going in here to read."

I want to ask if she'll have lunch with me in the cafeteria, but I don't push it. "Okay if I join you?"

She looks confused. "Um, yes? You mean you're reading too?"

"Yeah." I think quickly. "We began *The Crucible* in class yesterday. I thought maybe I'd reread the first act."

This is, without a doubt, the biggest line of cheese I've ever used. If Coop were here, he would bust out laughing. Reread something on my own? Seriously? But it's not a pickup line. I just want to talk to her.

She shrugs and heads to a table in the back that's mostly hidden behind a large bookcase. We pull books out of our packs and start to read. My eyes are running over the words, but I'm absorbing nothing. Mrs. Moss's desk is empty. She must be in the restroom or something. It's totally silent; I guess we have the place to ourselves. I'm just about to bring up Teo when I hear the rustling of a wrapper. I look up and see Luna chewing something.

I can't help myself. "You're eating? In the library?"

Her face turns bright red. "I . . . I . . ."

I laugh and whisper, "It's okay. I won't turn you in."

She reaches into the side pocket of her backpack and pulls out a granola bar. "Here."

I accept it because I'm starving. "Thanks." I take a huge bite. Almonds and coconut. Then I shake my head. "Contraband in the library. Who would have thought you were such a rebel?" I don't know why, but I think she can take a joke, like she's fun to tease. Maybe because she's so quiet and, I don't know, like humble. So different from Emma.

"You ate it. Now you're a co-conspirator." She can dish it right back.

"What else you got in that pocket of sin?" I should go to the cafeteria for a real meal. My stomach is growling.

She pulls out a bag of grapes, one of carrots, and some cheese crackers and hides them behind a large open binder that's serving as our screen. We continue to read, nibbling on her food. I'm so hungry that I want to down it all in three bites, but I restrain myself because it's not my food.

The door opens and Mr. D walks in, phone to his ear. We freeze and duck lower behind the binder. Mr. D looks around kind of anxiously, like he's worried Mrs. Moss is going to bust him. Talking on a phone in the library? He's a rebel too.

We don't mean to eavesdrop, but it's so quiet that we can hear everything he says. He sounds pissed.

"Yeah, I would have brought it up last night, but you were busy with the lambs. There's always something, isn't there?"

He raises his voice. "What do you mean, *what do I mean*? I mean something always comes up to prevent you from talking about *us*."

He listens and paces. "So yeah. Molly's. That woman? Totally mortifying. What? No! She didn't give me time to explain. And now, somehow, it's all over social media."

Luna and I look at each other in alarm. She raises her eyebrows. I shake my head.

"Yeah, that's me. The Original Chick Magnet. Whatever. It's actually not funny. Not anymore. I am so sick of hiding, Shep. And you won't talk about it!"

Shep? The vet? Oh, God, no. Please, no. This isn't our business. We shouldn't be hearing this!

"What do I want? What do I want?" His voice grows louder and angrier. "I want to stop pretending. I want to stop lying. I want women to stop flirting with me. I want a wedding. I want to be married to you, Shep! Jesus, I want to be out!"

And I'm not sure how it happens. But I notice Luna's hands are shaking. I reach over to cover them with mine, and I bump the binder. It crashes to the floor.

And Mr. D's eyes are huge and horrified as he races around the bookcase and sees us.

Before we can say anything, he turns and runs. He yanks open the swinging door just as Mrs. Moss is entering. She shrieks and pitches forward, smashing into Mr. D. Her cafeteria tray goes flying, lettuce and spaghetti spilling all over the floor.

"Oh, my goodness! I am so sorry!" Mr. D helps her up and retrieves her glasses, which are covered in marinara sauce.

Mrs. Moss is noticeably flustered. She straightens her skirt and brushes lettuce off her blazer. "Mr. Deboncoeur! Why are you in such a rush? You know running is not allowed in the library!"

"I know. I . . . I am so sorry. Here, let me clean this up. I'll just run to the restroom for paper towels. And I'll get you another meal. Are you hurt?"

"Oh, for Pete's sake, I'm fine. I'm a tough old bird. But I can't see without my glasses. Would you please clean them while you're in the restroom?" She sits at her desk and pulls out a mirror and a comb.

Mr. D bolts. I glance at Luna. Her eyebrows are furrowed, like in sympathy. She looks at me and puts her hands up in a gesture I interpret as "*Now what do we do?*"

I have no idea. "I guess just keep reading?" So we do.

Mr. D returns to the library and lays Mrs. Moss's now-sparkling glasses on her desk. He uses a huge wad of paper towels to clean up the mess. He leaves again and comes back with a new tray of food. Then he heads back to where we are still kind of paralyzed, staring at our books in a pretense of reading.

"Hey, guys. Um, you mind stopping by my room right after school?"

We just nod.

I am distracted all afternoon. Not because he's gay. But because twice now I've been like a voyeur of my teacher. Unlike Emma, I hate knowing things that other people want to keep private.

I get to Mr. D's door at 3:10. Luna's in the hall, waiting. "I didn't want to go in alone," she says.

Together we knock and walk in. Mr. D gets up and closes the door. He's sweating. This must be agonizing for him.

"Hey, thanks for coming, guys. I wanted to apologize for interrupting your studying at lunchtime. I . . . I . . . well, I guess it's obvious that I didn't know anyone was in there."

He grabs a tissue and wipes the back of his neck. "I suppose it's a bit of an elephant in the room at this point, but I'm curious if you . . . I mean, I wonder if you . . . um, just how much did you hear?"

Oh, my God; this is so painful for all of us. Surprisingly, it's Luna who speaks up. "Mr. D, it was really quiet in there. We heard everything."

Mr. D looks as stunned as I am, by both her boldness and her honesty. She's usually so shy.

I can't let her do this alone. "We didn't mean to be, like, hiding," I say. "We were just reading. Well, and eating. And we know we're not supposed to. So I guess we *were* sort of hiding."

Then Luna blows me away. "Mr. D, are you worried that we know you want to get married? And maybe your partner doesn't want to? Or is it . . . is it that we know you're gay?"

There's an awful, tense silence. *What would Coop say right now?*

"Or," I break in, "that Mrs. Moss caught you running in the library?"

It works. The image of that collision, the salad and spaghetti and glasses in airborne suspension, and poor Mrs. Moss's little body crashing into his, opens the floodgates. All three of us burst into that uncontrollable church laughter, the kind that should be stifled but absolutely can't be.

Finally, we stop. Mr. D wipes his eyes. "That was one of the most ludicrous things I've ever done. Absolutely ridiculous." He pauses, and the laughter drains from his face. "I know I haven't answered your question. And it deserves a response. And honestly, I'm not sure how to."

"Mr. D, I don't mean to be disrespectful," says Luna, "but being gay isn't a big deal to us. I mean, you're not super old, but it seems like in your generation, it was the kind of thing you had to hide."

"Yeah," I say, "like even for guys who maybe don't seem accepting or joke about it, everyone is actually open. I mean, you love who you love."

"We won't tell anyone," Luna assures him.

"But if you were out," I add, "it'd be cool with people. Or it should be. Because it's not going to change how we, you know, think of you or whatever."

He doesn't seem relieved like I thought. "Thank you for your honesty and support. I really appreciate it. But for now, I'm going to ask that you keep it a secret. And, um, please don't post this."

I'm kind of insulted that he thinks we would do that. But I don't blame him. That video Emma posted blew up around here. We promise we won't and leave quickly. As I shut the door behind us, I see Mr. D sitting at his desk, his head in his hands, in a posture of defeat.

35
LUNA

Pastor Mark slips into the sanctuary while I am dancing. He usually just leaves me alone, so something must be up. I stop. He kind of apologizes for interrupting and asks me to come by his office before I leave. The rest of my dancing is rough, like my timing is way off as the worry seeps in. *Has a parent complained? Does Mrs. Frye not like working with me?*

I quit early and head down the hall. Mrs. Pugh is on the phone when I walk in. She waves me on to his office.

Pastor Mark is staring out the window at the snow when I knock on his open door. "Come in, come in. You can leave the door open."

He motions toward a chair; I perch on the edge of it. He smiles kindly at me. "Right before you came in, I was thinking about snow. How it's both beautiful and menacing. Like the ocean. Or . . . or a mountain lion." He's still kind of dreamlike. "Or a glass of beer." He shakes his head and refocuses. "Sorry, Luna. Just trying to flesh out my sermon for Sunday. Please, relax. I have a quick question for you."

I breathe a tiny bit easier. I don't think I'm in trouble.

"But before I do, I wanted to thank you again for your work with the littles. I hear they adore you." He picks up a red stress ball and squeezes it. "And I could see how Teo just delighted in you. And how deeply you felt his death." He looks up from the ball. "How are you doing?"

I shrug. I don't mean to be rude, but when someone as kind as Pastor Mark asks me that, I can't lie. He waits. Unlike many adults, he doesn't feel the need to fill silences.

I think about what he said about beer and the ocean. "I kind of feel that way about Teo. That beautiful and dangerous thing." I gaze out at the snow. "I mean, not Teo, but what I felt about him. Or our, I don't know; I guess it was a friendship. It was really nice, and not having it anymore is awful."

He nods. "There's a huge risk in caring about someone. Love is both wonderful and indescribably painful."

We sit in silence for a few moments. Well, not total silence, because we hear Mrs. Pugh on the phone. "Oh, you are such a card," she laughs. "I needed that. Thank you for making my day!" I can't help but think that whoever she's talking to is having a brighter day because of her.

"I know you've got homework and other stuff to do," Pastor Mark says, "so I'll get to my point. Temmie was in today, dropping off something a neighbor wanted to donate to the Free Room. We got to talking, and I told her I was going to clear out Betty Orcutt's house on Friday afternoon. I don't know if you knew her? She was a longtime church member who died a couple weeks ago. Anyway, Temmie and Carol insisted that I not do it alone; even though it's a small house, it's pretty full."

I have no idea where he's going with this.

"Temmie offered her help. And here's where you come in. She also offered your help. But before accepting it, I wanted to ask you. It would mean that you wouldn't get to dance."

He's been so generous to me. Of course I'll help. But it kind of annoys me that Temmie would just volunteer me without my permission. Whatever.

"Sure," I say.

"Thank you so much. With the three of us working, it shouldn't take more than a couple of hours."

I am curious. "Is this . . . is this something pastors do normally? I mean, after someone dies?"

His laughter is so genuine that it makes me laugh too, even though my question is sincere. I mean, why is he the one to clear out the house?

"Your question is a great one. In fact, most of what I do in this job has little to do with preaching. Like shoveling the parking lot. Or visiting people in the hospital. Or conducting wellness checks on parishioners in their homes. Stuff no one teaches you in seminary."

"But that's so nice of you! I mean, I'm sure people appreciate your visiting them."

"Some do. And others toss out my offers of hope and solace along with yesterday's empties and losing lottery tickets. But I usually get put to work, maybe chopping wood or something, so I guess my visits are worthwhile.

"But to get back to your original question, Betty was a widow who had no children. She was ninety-seven and had outlived her siblings and cousins. Honestly, as far as I know, she was the last living member of her family. I visited her every Tuesday at lunchtime, mainly to see if she was okay. She was fiercely stubborn, refused to leave her home. And remarkably fit up until the end. She left her house to the church in her will. I'm not sure what we're going to do with it, but cleaning it out is the first step."

36
HUNTER

It's a teacher workday today, which means kids get the day off. A bunch of us agree to meet at Molly's in the morning to work on the Teo Legacy Project. Technically, the whole class is invited, but I know not everyone will be there. Pierce and his friends won't, and some of the quieter ones, like Luna and Eliot, won't either.

Kids arrive in noisy bunches. We grab the biggest table, which is soon covered with spreadsheets, graphs, even a business plan. Kiki has done an analysis of the competition. Shea developed a marketing strategy. Mr. D would be seriously proud. I mean, we're kids who knew nothing about economics last semester. And here we are, up early on a day off, on a freezing winter morning, actually applying what we've learned.

Kiki looks around. "Who's going to ask about a Teo drink?" It was one of our original ideas. Teo loved coming to Molly's. This should be easy, because it's not going to cost us anything.

"I think Josh should. He can talk his way into anything."

"Or out of anything."

"Yeah, like the speeding ticket he got last summer? He told the cop there was a family medical emergency!"

"What, his brother had a hangnail?"

"Shut up! My mother had a migraine. And she needed me home."

"Dude, a migraine is not a medical emergency!"

"Well, there would have been a medical emergency if I'd come home with a speeding ticket. I woulda gotten my ass whupped."

Josh goes up to the counter and asks Samantha if Molly is available. She tells him to wait. A few minutes later, Molly comes out, rubbing her hands on an apron covered with flour.

Josh gives her his trademark megawatt smile. "Hi, Molly, I'm Josh. What are you making?"

"Snickerdoodles. What do you need?"

"Oh, I love your snickerdoodles! They're even better than my father's, which is saying something, 'cause he's a great baker." *Ooh, he's good.*

"And—?"

Josh gets it. She's not into small talk. "Well, my friends and I are trying to do some stuff to honor Teo Callahan's memory. We know he really liked coming here. And he loved your hot chocolate. So we wondered if you would be willing to name a drink after him. Maybe something like Teo's Toasty Tonic?"

I don't hear anything. Josh's voice gets higher. "That was just a suggestion. Something we came up with. Of course you could choose the name yourself. Like if you wanted to do this."

Finally I hear Molly. She sounds exhausted. "Josh, I'm going to have to say no. I mean, it's a nice gesture, but there aren't enough drinks on the menu to honor everyone who dies in this town."

Josh murmurs something I don't catch. He heads back to the table with his head down.

Molly calls out, "And Josh? Please make sure you and your friends pick up after yourselves!"

Josh sits down. "It's a no-go."

"You mean the Mighty Josh with the Silver Tongue struck out?"

"No way!"

"Way," he says. "Sorry."

Despite all the kidding, Josh is bummed. Kiki changes the subject. "Hey, can anyone here draw?"

"Beth has cool handwriting."

"Carlos is a great artist."

"Yeah, but he's not here. And he hangs out with Pierce. I doubt he'd help us."

"You can't just assume that. Without asking, I mean."

"Yeah, I guess. But I doubt he's interested in helping."

"Anyone know what Pierce's problem is?"

"I think he hates Mr. D."

"Well, he could still help. We're doing this for the kids, not Mr. D."

"Whatever. He doesn't care about them anyway. He's outta here as soon as he graduates."

"Isn't he planning to enlist?"

"I thought he said something about joining the Marines."

"No, I think it's the Navy. Did you know that his dad was a SEAL?"

"Dang. That's impressive."

"Wait, I thought he owned the hardware store."

"Well, now he does. But he used to be in the Navy."

"I think I know who you mean. He has a mustache, right? I've seen him in the hardware store. That guy is ripped."

"He told me his dad wants him to be a SEAL."

"That may be why he's always working out."

Kiki finally butts in. "Hey, guys, let's focus here. We need an artist to design our logo."

Coop looks at me. "Hunter's dad is incredible. You should see the pictures he's done. All over Hunter's wall."

Kiki turns to me. "Do you think he'd do it?"

"Um, I can ask him. Like what exactly do we need?"

Kiki turns to the group. "What should we put on the label? Should it have blueberries? A lighthouse? A lobster? A moose?"

"Those are kind of overdone, you know? Plus, we don't even live near the coast, so lighthouses and lobsters don't make any sense."

"That's fair."

"How about a pool? Since the whole point of this is swimming."

"Or a life buoy?"

"I don't know. That feels too depressing."

Ideas keep coming. Pine trees. Sunrise. Cardinals. Mountains. Snow.

Nothing strikes us as perfect. We decide to table it for now. We gather up our papers and stuff and head out. Coop walks out with me. "I think," he says, "your dad might have some ideas. I mean, he's the artist."

I'm nervous about asking him. His mood swings have gotten crazy. But it's for the kids. I hear his voice in my head, the mantra he'd repeat when I was sick of practicing free throws. *Keep your eyes on the prize, son. Eyes on the prize.*

37
LUNA

On the way to the library, I share my idea with Temmie. She just listens. I am taken aback by her lack of enthusiasm. "Will you at least ask the group?"

"Can't promise that. I'll think about it."

"Well, what's wrong with the plan?"

"Let me just think about it." *Adults are infuriating. Why can't she just give me a straight answer?*

Today I don't bother with homework. I'm too upset by Temmie's indifference. I sit and fume and hear the same old boring discussion of the weather. *It's Maine. It's winter. Snow. Ice. Cold. Can we move on to something more interesting?*

In desperation I pull out my phone to watch dance videos. And then I sense a hush fall over the group. I look up and see Ms. Callahan taking off her coat. It's the first time she's been here since Teo drowned. Barbara goes right over and gives her a hug. Ms. Callahan carries a plate of what looks like blondies over to the coffee table. She notices everyone watching her.

"I have so many treats in my freezer, more than I can possibly eat. So let me provide the refreshments for the next four or five weeks, okay?"

Someone laughs. "Maybe you'll bring in something we made," she says wryly.

Ms. Callahan sits in a chair across from Samantha and Jessica. No one says anything; talking about the latest six inches of snow feels trivial and irrelevant. Finally, Ethel speaks. "Bridget, sweetie, we're so glad to see you. How are you doing?"

Ms. Callahan looks around at everyone. "I'm okay. Some days I actually notice the sun shining. Probably because they're so rare. But other days I'm so full of rage I just want to throw every plate and glass and dish I own against the wall."

"Have you? Smashed anything?"

"Oh, God, no," she says. "I couldn't afford to replace them. And the cleanup would take forever."

A soft wave of laughter sweeps over the group.

"You all have been so supportive," she says. "Thank you for your goodies and your notes and your calls. I really appreciated them, even though that probably wasn't apparent. I've kind of been a hermit."

I hear murmurs of understanding and empathy.

"But I wanted to come today to tell you about what the high school kids are doing." As Ms. Callahan talks about the Teo Legacy Project, she grows more and more animated. At the end of her impromptu presentation, she sighs. "It's going to take a shipload of money to make this happen, but the kids are so earnest in their spreadsheets and research and dreams."

Barbara voices what most of the women are probably thinking. "How can we help?"

I feel like a tethered racehorse. My leg is bouncing up and down. *Temmie! Now! Please!*

Temmie clears her throat. "They need a lot of money." *And? Go on!* She drops a needle and bends over to pick it up. *That's it? That's all you're going to say?*

But I guess she's not finished. "Luna had an idea. We can help by doing just what we're doing."

The women look confused. *Go on! Explain it!* She's driving me crazy.

Temmie looks at Jessica. "Jessica, if you were serious about people wanting sweaters handmade in Maine, then why don't we donate ours? To the cause, I mean. Sell them."

The women turn to each other, considering.

"We've never done anything like that before, but it's worth a try, I suppose."

"Oh, I could never make a sweater worth that much."

"I'd be terrified of messing up the whole time."

"Count me out. No way do I want that pressure."

"I think it would be fun!"

I hear Temmie's voice again. "Jessica? Is this realistic?"

Jessica is beaming. "I think it's a fantastic idea! I'll contact Cheri right away. She knows the market. We could make five, six thousand per sweater. How much do the kids need for the—"

"Hold on," says a gruff voice. It's Polly. "It feels a bit like prostitution."

Temmie is indignant. "It's charity, Polly. We're not keeping the money. And, my God, wouldn't it be neat to have something good come out of this tragedy?"

Polly thinks for a second. She looks directly at Ms. Callahan. "There's no way we could make that kind of money here. If it'll help our kids learn to swim, then prostitution be damned. All right, I'm in."

Barbara nods. "I am too. But I've always used a pattern. Polly, you're going to need to give us a lesson in free-form knitting. Oh my, learning a new skill at my age is something. Isn't this exciting?"

Other women jump on board. The buzz that follows energizes the group in a way I've never witnessed before from my hidden nook. Someone hands out paper for sketching designs. Rose thinks she'll try to replicate a blooming rose bush; Ethel wants to create a water lily montage. They decide that all the scenes should somehow incorporate Maine in traditional and unique ways. Someone chooses mud as a theme, and she's not being ironic. "It'll be a challenge. To make mud beautiful. Springtime in Maine."

Since she's sitting closest to me, I hear Samantha describe her design to Jessica. "Most of the sweater will be plain, a heather green. Around the cuffs of the sleeves and the neck will be twining blueberry branches on an ivory background. And the bottom will be a bit below the waist in front and longer in the back, to cover the butt. For both warmth and flattery. Like it?"

Jessica is clearly thrilled. It's like she belongs to the group now. "My contribution to the project," she announces, "since I can't knit worth beans, will be to pay for the materials. Where do you buy your yarn?"

"The only yarn store in town is Sheepishly Yours. On the verge of bankruptcy, I heard."

"Oh, we don't have to buy new yarn!" says a woman whose name I don't know. "Surely we can bring in our leftover yarn and share it."

Jessica insists. "Don't skimp. Get the best wool you can, and get plenty of it. I'll just keep a running tab at the store. Maybe if we buy enough, it will help keep the store solvent." She's on a roll. "And then I'll get help with sales and marketing. Probably have to hire an agent. We should have a website too. I know a great tech guy in Boston, who could—"

"*NO!*"

I jerk my head away from Jessica to see who interrupted. Tears are streaming down Ms. Callahan's face. She makes no effort to stop them. "I . . . I . . . I am beyond moved by your kindness," she chokes out. "That you all would drop your own projects and do this for

Teo—well, not for him, but for all the other kids—it's just amazing. And Jessica, your generosity is wonderful. Thank you, everyone."

She stops to wipe her cheeks with a tissue Barbara hands her. "But let's not hire a bunch of professionals. I mean, if we have to, then we will, but first let's see if we can find what we need in Edgewater. Starting with the kids in Ludovic Deboncoeur's class."

The snow is coming down in hard pellets; I can hear it pounding on the roof. I watch the women make their icy way down the sidewalk to Sheepishly Yours. Someone is pushing Ruth's wheelchair. The younger women are holding the arms of the older women so they don't fall. I can't wait to tell Mr. D and our class.

Thanks, Temmie, for thinking about it.

38
HUNTER

My pulled muscle still hurts, but I practice anyway. We only have a few games left in the regular season before the playoffs begin. Coach keeps us late, working on a new defense.

I'm ravenous when I get home. Dad pulls a tuna casserole out of the oven just as I walk in. "There's my boy," he greets me. "How was practice?"

He listens carefully as I describe the strategy Coach is teaching us. A modified zone with the point guard playing man-to-man.

"You just gotta watch down low," he cautions. "You're vulnerable to a backdoor layup. But I'm guessing you protect the top of the key better with this new one. It sounds like it'd work on teams who don't have strong three-point shooters. Otherwise, you gotta play man-to-man."

He's focused and clear-headed. I relax. The wariness that fills me every time I walk in the door disappears, and we laugh and talk for more than an hour. When we've exhausted basketball talk, I bring up the logo.

"You're asking me to design a logo? You sure you don't want one of your friends doing it?" he asks.

"You're the best artist around," I say. Proudly. "And it's not just our class working on this project. Like the whole community can be a part of it."

"Okay, then. I'll give it a stab."

For the next forty minutes, he messes around with ideas. His sketches are fantastic. He's like in the zone, concentrating in complete silence. At last he scoops up all the drawings but one and deposits them in our recycling bin. The remaining one he hands to me. "Here you go, bud. I hope this'll do."

It's haunting. A little boy is standing knee-deep in a pond. Beyond him are pine trees; behind them rise mountains. It's weird, because it makes me both happy and sad. Like the boy could be having a blast, splashing around, his family and friends right behind him. Or he could be lonely and scared. "Wow," I breathe. "Is this . . . is this Teo?"

He just gives me a sad smile and doesn't answer.

"Thanks so much, Dad."

When I go to bed, I'm full.

With more than tuna casserole.

39

LUNA

On this Friday afternoon I overhear slips of conversations about weekend plans. Skating, movies, keggers. *Gee, wouldn't people be jealous if they knew what I have planned? To clean out an old woman's house?*

Temmie picks me up after school. We meet Pastor Mark at the church and follow his Subaru way out of town to Mrs. Orcutt's house. I can't imagine living on my own this far out in the woods. Much less at ninety-seven. The driveway is unplowed; we barely make it up, even with our snow tires.

Pastor Mark leads us in. "It's chilly in here. I had the electricity shut off. No need to heat an empty house."

"What are you planning to do with it?" Temmie asks.

"Well, I don't know. Doreen Berwick, you know, of Berwick Realty over in Northriver, told me that if she could find a buyer, it would probably be just for the land. This house is in pretty poor condition. She thinks it'll just get torn down."

It's kind of creepy, going through the stuff of a dead person. Like, what if there's something in here that's private? Or embarrassing? Or needs context? I wouldn't want anyone going through my stuff after I died. I don't even like Temmie in my room now, and I honestly don't have anything to hide.

Temmie and Pastor Mark are all business. We start in the bedroom. Pastor Mark gives us instructions. "Just bag anything you think someone can use, as long as it's in decent condition. Carol will inspect and wash everything before she puts it in the Free Room."

Temmie takes charge. I can't decide if something is worth saving, so she does all the evaluating. I'm just grunt labor. The comforters are thick and fluffy; we'll save those. The sheets are too worn; they go in a throw-away pile. I toss three towels that are completely threadbare and then find a whole stack in the closet that look brand-new. Why didn't she use them?

Methodically, we go through closets and drawers, saving and discarding. We're not sure what to do with linen tablecloths and old record albums. "What do you think, Mark?"

He doesn't know. "Do people use linen tablecloths anymore? Carol's up on that stuff. Let me give her a quick call." He pulls out his phone and presses a button. And waits. "Or not. There's absolutely zero reception out here. Let's go ahead and save them. Carol can make the final decision at church."

The house is cold, but the activity of packing and lifting and hauling bags out to our cars keeps us warm. We finish the kitchen, bathroom, and bedroom. The living room will take more time because it's packed with furniture and books.

Temmie discovers an old record player. "Mark, this is an original Victrola! Someone's going to love this!" She wraps it carefully in a blanket from the bedroom and marks it with a "SAVE" tag.

A huge bookcase towers over us, reaching almost all the way to the vaulted ceiling. Pastor Mark rubs the back of his neck as he stares up at it. "Whew! I guess we'll toss most of the books, as they're falling apart. Looks like an old family bible on the top shelf. I wonder if it has records of births and deaths and marriages in it?" He stretches then looks out the window at the setting sun. "I didn't realize it had gotten so late! Look, I can finish up here. You've been a huge help; this would have taken me days by myself. Thank you so much."

I can tell by the way she's walking that Temmie's knees hurt. She needs to get home and put them up.

"How are you going to get the rest of this stuff out of here?" Temmie asks.

"Carol will get some folks with pickups to come out with me next week. For the furniture that's salvageable. For the other stuff, I'll ask Doreen. She'll know who does trash removal for something like this. You know, before she puts the house on the market."

"All right, Mark. We'll get going then. Happy to help again if you need us." She rubs my shoulders. "We're a decent team, eh?"

He smiles. "The best! Take good care, now. And thanks again."

Temmie groans getting into the car. "That's work for someone a lot younger," she says. "Let's get burgers at McDonald's. I can't face cooking."

I stare at her. Temmie *never* wastes money on junk food. She's more exhausted than I realized. "I can cook," I offer. "Or we can heat up the leftover quiche."

"Naw, let's splurge. No dishes this way. And I already made a dessert."

There's a long line at the drive-thru. Temmie has the news on as we sit idling in the warm car. I wonder why she bothers. *Corrupt politicians. Economy tanking. Another storm on the horizon. Unemployment high. Inflation higher. Homicide rate drops. Petty crime increases.* Seriously, there's nothing new.

I look in the window and see a bunch of kids, probably my age, sitting around a table. Laughing. Eating. Stealing someone's fries. Looking at each other's phones. Taking selfies. And I feel this aching fill my chest. *I will never be part of a group like that.*

Temmie sees me looking and reaches out to pat my arm. I yank it away and stare out my window. Away from the scene in there. She pays for our food, and we drive home in silence.

I drop my backpack on the bench in the kitchen. Temmie lays out the burgers and gets ketchup for the fries. "Hang up your jacket and hat, kiddo."

"Why do you always assume that I won't hang up my stuff?" My anger surprises even me.

Temmie gets a plastic bag and fills it with ice for her knees.

"I mean, I'm seventeen years old! You don't have to treat me like I'm seven!" I want to run up to my room and slam the door, but it's freezing on the second floor.

"If you want a drink, pour yourself some milk."

I stomp to the refrigerator and grab the jug. When I bang the glass on the counter, it shatters. I burst into tears.

Temmie doesn't say anything as she sweeps up the shards and dumps them in the trash barrel. She puts a box of tissues next to my place at the table. I've totally lost my appetite. The food smells like grease and is making me nauseous.

Temmie dips a fry into the ketchup. It looks like she's eating blood. "You gotta eat, kiddo."

"I'm not hungry."

"Not for food, right?"

She gets it. And I should be grateful, but I'm more embarrassed. "I'm like the biggest loser in the school! I can't even believe I'm jealous of kids hanging out in a stupid McDonald's! It's so—" I'm crying too hard to finish.

"You got to give them time, honey. To get to know you."

"They've had time! And believe me, it doesn't change anything!" I wrap my burger back up and pound it with my fist. Again and again. Smashing it. Ruining it. Hating myself for wasting Temmie's money and spoiling her night.

"Has someone gotten to know you?" Temmie asks softly.

"No! Well, sort of. A teeny bit." I do *not* want to talk about Hunter. But Temmie waits. "He's just a guy in my class. The one I went with to Teo's mom's house."

"And what happened?"

God, can we please just drop it?

I grab a tissue and wipe my eyes. Temmie's hand rests on the table next to her half-eaten burger. *When did she start getting those brown age spots?* I look at her face. There are deep wrinkles near her eyes, and her hair is streaked with gray. She deserves an explanation.

"He was nice when we were there. But he wouldn't be caught dead walking back with me. Like if anyone saw him, they would . . . they would . . . I don't know, wonder why he was with the freak."

Temmie nods slowly. "Has he ever talked to you in school?"

"Only when he has to. In class, I mean." Then I remember. "Oh, and once in the library. But that was just because no one else was around."

She's quiet for a while, like she's thinking. "You know that game we play? Please Explain?"

I nod. I love it. We often play it at dinner. One of us just blurts out a random statement, like "*He pays for his groceries with cash.* Please explain." Immediately the other person has to come up with an explanation:

He is buying stuff like junk food or alcohol that he doesn't want his wife to see on their credit card statement.

He's homeless, and he's taking the ones and change he was given on the street corner to buy food for his kids.

He believes that credit cards are the government's way of spying on citizens, so he refuses to use them.

Sometimes we create elaborate plotlines and backstories just from one prompt, making them funny or tragic or melodramatic.

"What's the purpose of that game, besides fun?" Temmie asks.

I don't answer. *I'm not stupid!* I obviously know what she's getting at: You don't always know someone's motivation.

But I'm pretty sure I know Hunter's. Just the thought of his rejection, his "You go on, I have to tell Miz Callahan something" upsets me again.

"Okay, Temmie," I say. "Let's play it. I'll go first. *Woman sees her hideous baby and throws her away*. Please explain."

Her head jerks up in shock. Immediately after I say it, I regret it. Temmie's been such a good mother to me. She doesn't deserve my snarkiness.

But I really want to know.

"Oh, Luna." There is so much compassion in her eyes that I just feel mean. "Is that what you think? That she threw you away?"

The tears start again. I just nod.

"Luna, your mother was . . . was . . . well, complicated. She was wild, which was hilarious and exciting, but that had a darker side. She was fiercely competitive. Had to win at everything. Be the best, the boldest, the most daring. And she loved danger. She fed on it."

I've heard all of this before. It doesn't help. So she could be the best at everything except raising her own disfigured baby?

"What I've never told you, honey," Temmie continues, "is this: Your mother was a drug addict."

Wait, what?

"She was the life of the party, the one who did beer funnels, who'd try any drug from pot to ecstasy to crack cocaine. It was heroin that knocked her over, that found a home in her brain and wouldn't let go. When heroin wasn't enough, she turned to fentanyl. And, my God, that stuff is crazy strong."

I know about the opioid crisis. But I didn't know any of this. And it infuriates me. *When the hell were you going to tell me this?*

Temmie senses my rage. She holds up her hand and looks away. Like she has to get this out before I say a thing. "When she found out she was pregnant with you, she quit. Cold turkey. It was, by far, the hardest thing she'd ever done. Watching her detox was just awful. I didn't think she could do it. But she was determined. For you. And I was so proud of her.

"She got a little job at Sheepishly Yours, where she was bored to death but gritted it out. She made little booties and hats and onesies for you while she sat in the store. She avoided her friends because they were still using. Partying a lot."

I can't wrap my head around this. *She did all of this for me? Then why—?*

"She loved you, honey. You should have seen the way she'd rub her little baby bump and talk to you. I actually was envious. She'd never been so devoted to anyone. And believe me, there were plenty of men who would have given anything to be the center of her world like you were."

This doesn't make any sense! You're lying. You must be lying. "What are you—" But Temmie won't be interrupted.

"But just a week after you were born, her friends threw her a party. She was exhausted. Totally sleep-deprived and lonely. She missed her friends. And she missed being the life of the party. When I warned her not to go, she essentially told me to mind my own business, that she'd be fine. I guess the temptation to use again was too powerful to resist. She brought you to me the day after, still high as a kite. Said she couldn't be the mother you needed. That I could. And I was already in love with you, so it was an easy decision."

Oh, now I get it. The same old rejection story. "So she loved me when I was inside her, but once she saw me, got to meet me, she dumped me."

"No, Luna. She loved you in and out of her."

"But she loved drugs more."

Tears fill Temmie's eyes. "Addicts don't love drugs, honey. They hate them. But they need them. The way you and I need air or water."

Temmie, do you think I'm stupid? You just said that she gave up drugs when she was pregnant! Obviously, I repulsed her, wasn't worth her sobriety. Returned because of defects. Full refund. No questions asked.

I am already sick of this conversation. I get up and throw my flattened burger in the compost bucket. I just want to get out of here. But I have to know.

"Then what happened?"

"I don't have the full story. Nobody here does. She told me that day, when she brought you here, that she had to escape because she was afraid of her dealer. She claimed some guy was driving her to Nashville. Going to try to make it in the music scene. A fresh start. I never heard from her again. I've been Googling her name for years, and nothing's ever turned up."

Such a load of bullshit. Her dealer? Yeah, right. She had to escape any connection with her monster baby.

"I miss her desperately, kiddo. She was my baby sister. I hope she's alive and clean and living a life of purpose. But honestly, I assume she's dead. Fentanyl shows no mercy."

Temmie removes the ice bag and lumbers to her feet. She limps over to the counter and slides the pan of blueberry buckle into the oven.

"I'll just warm this up for ten minutes. I have a feeling you'll be hungry."

I don't even try to answer. Dessert feels utterly disconnected to what she's just told me.

She sits back down. "While we're talking about this, and Luna, I know how painful it is, I have to confess something else. Well, not confess, really, but apologize. To you."

I just want to cover my ears and scream. She plows on. "When she gave me her baby, I wasn't ready to be a parent, not really. I didn't know anything. But I committed to taking care of you. That became my whole focus. You. Your well-being. Your safety. And I was so intent on protecting you from absolutely every perceived threat in the universe, I went too far. I never should have homeschooled you. It prevented you from interacting with kids your age, from making friends, from learning how to deal with your anxiety. And it was selfish. By essentially hiding you, I didn't have to share you with anyone. And the worst thing is that I made you feel like you needed to be hidden. Oh, honey, I am so sorry."

I love Temmie. I really do. But I think she's still protecting me from the truth. And that pisses me off. I ignore her pathetic apology. "I deserve honesty, Temmie. Weren't you really protecting everyone else from me? From having to look at my gross face?"

"I did you a terrible disservice. Do people look twice at you when they first meet you? Of course. It's human nature. But I haven't let enough people get to know you, to have a chance to look twice and then get beyond the birthmark and get into what makes you you."

The black cloud explodes in my heart. "Temmie, I'm sorry, but that whole story is such trash." I hear myself screaming in a way I never have before. "*Trash!* Just like me! I was trash to her! I don't believe she ever loved me! Or made little sweaters or booties or anything for me. How can a mother hate her baby so much that she *throws her away*?" I am sobbing. I wish I could rip my skin off and escape.

Just then there is a loud knock at the kitchen door. Temmie puts both hands on the table and pushes herself to her feet.

I flee.

From my room I hear Temmie, greeting people, ushering them in, seating them at the table. Then she calls up the stairs. "Luna? You have visitors."

Is this some kind of a sick joke? Visitors? Me?

The only person who has ever come to my house for me is a dancer whose mom sometimes gave me rides. When we could still afford lessons. I'm in no mood to see anyone. Doesn't whoever is there know that this is the town dump?

Temmie calls again. Her voice is insistent, almost urgent. *What the hell ever.* I wipe my face with my sleeve and stomp down.

And there sit Hunter Ridley and Colin Cooper, at my kitchen table, eating Temmie's blueberry buckle. *What on earth? How do they know where I live?*

Hunter stands when I walk in. "Luna, hey. Um, we were driving by, and I thought I'd give you, um, well, this."

He grabs a paper bag from the table and hands it to me. I am so confused. I'm still having trouble computing why Coop and Hunter are here. In my house.

I open the bag and pull out a box of coconut-almond granola bars. Hunter is grinning. He looks like a little kid giving a birthday present that he hopes you're going to love. And I can't help the little smile that I give him back. "Uh, thanks?"

Temmie puts a dish of buckle in front of me. "Eat this while it's hot. Anyone want vanilla ice cream on it?"

Coop has already finished his. "Oh, I would have! That was amazing." Temmie smiles, fills his dish again, and gets the ice cream. Coop digs in. "Thank you so much. Dang, this is seriously awesome."

Temmie gets a dish of buckle for herself and sits. "Okay, guys, tell me where you are with this Teo Legacy Project."

For the next half hour or so, we discuss the project, from swimming lessons to blueberry jam to supply-and-demand economics. I forget for a while that there are two guys from my class sitting at my kitchen table. And they came on their own; like, no one made them.

I even talk a little.

And it's fun.

But then they leave, and all I can think about is my druggie mother.

And how I wasn't enough.

40

HUNTER

This afternoon after practice I got the text. *4-3-2-1 CHALLENGE tonight. 8 pm. McD's drive-thru. Give word at pickup window.* Usually I love this night, but I'm not really in the mood for it today. It's weird, but I kind of feel like I'm growing out of it. Someone started this high school challenge night like twenty years ago, and it's become a regular thing in our town. Usually there are between fifteen and twenty teams. The Edgewater cops hate it. Every year it's on a different night so they don't know when it's going to happen. Basically, it's like a scavenger hunt, but it's crazy and dangerous and usually illegal.

The "4" means four people on a team; "3" means three challenges; "2" is two hours, and "1" is one car per team. A secret group of seniors announces the date and creates the challenges. Then the same group evaluates each team's results and announces the winners at midnight.

By text. Fourth place. Then third. Then second. Then first. The winners get wicked bragging rights and major street cred for months.

My team is me, Josh, Nate, and Coop. We've been together for this challenge since freshman year. Last year we came in third overall, which is impressive for tenth graders. We agree after practice that we'll meet at Josh's at 7:40. We'll use his truck for the night.

I don't want to go home, so Coop and I buy food at Hannaford's for dinner. Grocery store food is way cheaper than fast food, and sometimes it's almost as good. As we're standing in line, I see a display of granola bars and think of Luna. They're on sale, so I grab a box. I convince Coop to make a pit stop at her house, telling him that if we get there at dinner time, we might get more food.

It works. Her mother has some blueberry dessert that is incredible. And Luna actually talks a little. She reminds me of a colt that I watched Josh train one summer. Hesitant, skittish, afraid, but really powerful. And she's so different from most of the girls I know. Like she doesn't care that I'm like more than decent at basketball. She doesn't worry about stuff like popularity. Like even though she's shy, she believes in her own opinion. I could tell that from working with her on the Teo thing. And she's so quiet. Emma and her friends talk all the time, usually about nothing. Or not nothing, but it's stupid shit, like celebrity gossip. I wish Luna would talk more. I kind of want to know her better. You know, like as a friend. It's embarrassing to admit, 'cause it makes me feel like a jerk, but I never paid attention to her before. I mean, it wasn't until this project that I really even became aware of her. And she's been in my history class all year. *Am I that guy, the one who only notices hot girls? God, I hope not.*

It's so warm and, I don't know, safe, I guess, in Luna's kitchen that I don't really want to leave. But Josh and Nate are waiting.

There's a line at McDonald's when we turn into the drive-thru lane. We can't meet as a group of cars because the cops would figure it out. But they won't suspect kids in cars getting food. The rules are strict: No instructions will be given out until eight o'clock. By the time we get to order, it's already 8:08.

Josh leans out the driver's-side window. "Gimme a Quarter Pounder with cheese. And a large Coke." At the pickup window, a kid with bad acne hands him his drink. Josh grabs it. "Quite a *challenge* managing this line, huh?"

The kid gives a little smile and sticks a small piece of pink paper in the bag. "Good luck," he says. He's either part of the senior group or they've bribed him to be the distributor.

Josh peels out while Nate unfolds the paper. He reads the challenges:

> *1. Take a selfie with a farm animal. (Cats and dogs don't count.) All four members must be in the picture.*
>
> *2. Jump off Bowdoin's Bluff. One person on video. Three jumpers must be naked and jump together.*
>
> *3. Break into a house or business and steal something worth $50 or more. Video documentation of the whole process required. Item must be presented at finish.*

"Wait, what? Jesus, who thought of the third one? That's upping the game!" Josh is as surprised as I am.

Nate is all business. "Yeah, yeah, we're not wusses. We can kick ass this year. What do we do first? Find an open barn?"

"No," says Coop. "That's the easiest one. That will take about five minutes. Let's do the last one first, before the cops are tipped off. That's the only way we'll win."

"I may have to get gas," Josh warns. "It's a twenty-five-minute drive to Bowdoin's Bluff. Why the hell are they making us go so far out?"

"That's all part of the challenge," Nate says. "Gonna have to speed. And that access road probably isn't plowed."

I want to win as much as anyone. But breaking-and-entering and larceny? That's like way more than a misdemeanor. And it just feels wrong. "Dudes, I don't know about this. Like I'd be pissed if someone stole my crap just for a stupid game."

Coop, thank God, gets it. "Yeah. Me too."

Josh doesn't. "Oh, my God. Are you guys serious? Do you need to go home to Mommy and read a bedtime story?"

"Fuck you, Josh."

Josh realizes what he's said. "Oh. Sorry, Hunter. About your mother, I mean. But come on! This is one night. We're not, like, doing it as a regular thing. One time. You guys in or out?"

Coop looks at me. *We could bail. But that would leave them hanging. I'm not a quitter. But it's wrong. This is the last year I'm doing this shit.* I shrug. "Whatever."

"I think I know a place we could hit," Nate says. "Like a mile before my house. It may be deserted anyway. The walk doesn't get shoveled, and I've never seen a car there. And the cops don't ever go out there."

"Sounds good to me," Josh says, whipping the steering wheel around. "Once I'm past that huge farm, tell me where to turn."

We park half a mile from the house and hike through the woods. If we approach from the back, we have a better chance of not being seen.

Josh starts the video when we get close. The house is totally dark. The only sound we hear is our boots crunching in the snow. Coop and Nate creep up to the back door. Coop tries it, and to our surprise, it swings open. "Shit!" He grabs the handle and eases it shut.

"What are you waiting for?" Josh hisses. "Just go!"

Coop slips in. We wait. My heart is pounding. In about five seconds, he comes racing out. "Go! Run, run, *run!*"

We take off. Crashing through the branches, stumbling in the deep snow, all the way back to the truck. Everyone is heaving by the time we reach it. "What," pants Nate, "was that?"

Coop is bent, his hands on his knees. "You said it was empty, dumbass!"

"It's totally dark! I thought it was!"

"Well, I heard something. Someone."

"What? What they'd say? Did they have a gun?" Josh is both terrified and stoked. "Or maybe it was a ghost?"

Coop shakes his head. "Shut up, you idiot. I'm serious! I heard someone."

Nate is worried. "You think they saw you? I mean, could they ID you like in a lineup?" *Oh, my God. A lineup? What the hell are we doing?*

"I don't know. It was so frickin' dark in there."

"Shit. We are so screwed."

I can't get past the part about hearing someone. "What exactly did you hear? Like a TV on?"

Coop's breathing is still ragged. "No. It was definitely a real person. A male voice. And I only heard one word."

"What was it?"

"Help."

I can't believe this. "Someone said 'Help'? What the hell? What if they really need help? Why didn't you look?"

"Oh, so now you're pissed that I didn't stay and make some tea and play cards and maybe shovel the guy's driveway? Are you frickin' serious? I didn't see any of you pansies offer to go in. I didn't look because I didn't want to get caught! And you wouldn't have either, assholes."

Coop's right. We all would have taken off. But we have to go back. "Let's at least see if the guy really needs help."

Josh is getting in the truck. "No fuckin' way I'm going back."

Something won't let me leave. "We don't have to go in. We can just peek in the windows."

"Bro, just forget it. He's probably got a gun."

No one moves. I start walking back. I turn around and yell, "If you're not too chickenshit to be in the woods for fifteen more minutes, wait for me."

And that's enough. They jog to catch up. "What if," says Josh, "it's a total scam? Like they have a gun and just said 'Help' to get us back there? They're probably setting their sights on us right now, calling us a bunch of suckers."

We slow down near the house and sneak around to the front. There's a car in the driveway, with its trunk wide open. It's stuffed full of dark bags. "What the—?" Nate stops. "I've never seen that car here."

We creep around to the back and silently peer in. It's too dark to see anything. "Shit," says Coop. "What should we do?"

"I'm going in," I say. I pull my hat down low and my jacket collar up so only my eyes show. "Wait here."

I push the back door open just enough to slide in. It's almost as cold in here as it is outside. I take two steps in and listen. Nothing. I take my phone out and turn on the flashlight. If anyone's in here, the light will be on them and they won't be able to see me. The kitchen is empty. I tiptoe across the floor into what I think is the living room and shine my light.

And there I see it. A body, lying partway under a huge bookcase or something.

All my instincts tell me to run, but I can't. What if he's dead? What if he was murdered?

"Hello? Can you hear me?" My voice is shaking. A low moan comes from the body. I don't know if we should call the cops or try to help him ourselves. I know from watching *CSI* reruns that you're not supposed to disturb a crime scene. I run back outside. "There's a guy in here. Still alive. Help me!"

With our phone flashlights on, we can see enough to crawl around the bookcase. Josh tries to move it. "Jesus Christ! What's this thing made of? Lead?"

"Just a second. We've got to do it together. Ready? Lift on three. One, two, three!" The four of us pick it up and lower it to the floor away from the body. Josh shines his light on the guy's face and gasps.

It's Pastor Mark from Teo's funeral. What is he doing here? Does he rob houses at night?

I kneel by his head. "Are you okay?" His eyes are shut, but he's definitely breathing. I look at the guys. "Should we call 9-1-1?"

Coop tries. "No reception. Nate, you took that EMT course last year. Can you look at him?"

Nate, who seemed to be frozen in fear, jumps into action. "Someone turn on the frickin' lights."

Josh tries. Nothing. "The power's off."

"Then just shine your phones on him." Watching Nate switch into "medic mode" is awesome. He checks everything he can and figures that Pastor Mark is okay except for his left shoulder and arm. And a bump on the back of his head. And he's crazy cold.

"We've got to get him outta here. Fast. I think we can take him. Josh and Coop, go get the truck. Like run. Hunter and I will wrap him up and get him ready to move. As soon as we get reception, I'll call the emergency room at the clinic and let them know we're bringing him in. Go, move!"

I search for blankets. The bed has been stripped. The closets and drawers are empty. "Dude, there are no blankets or tablecloths or anything."

Nate yanks his hat off and puts it on Pastor Mark's head. "Gimme your jacket." As we are laying our coats over him, Pastor Mark's eyes open. "Thank you. Cold." They close again.

"I don't think he can sit up," says Nate. "Let's put the mattress in the truck bed. We can ride back there with him and kind of protect him with our bodies. Jesus, what is taking them so long?" We tug the mattress out of the bedroom and wait for Josh and Coop.

We spend the next few hours in the clinic ER's waiting room. Playing games on our phones, watching the TV that is set on some stupid home shopping channel, and arguing about college basketball. The later it gets, the less we talk. Only two other people come in. One has a huge cut on his leg, said his chainsaw nicked it a few hours ago and he can't stop the bleeding. I almost faint when I see all the blood. That's way more than a nick. The other is a woman who burned her arm loading her woodstove. I can't imagine dealing with trauma like this every night.

Coop is nervous. "How are we going to explain being in that house?"

"We spin it," Nate reassures him. "Listen up so we're all on the same page. This is our story: We were driving from my house to go out when I noticed the car's open trunk in that driveway and decided to investigate. That's all. Got it?"

Emma's been texting me all night. She's got the scoop on the 4-3-2-1 Challenge. In a string of texts with lots of capital letters and OMGs, she explains that no one won. Four teams got arrested for trespassing at Bowdoin's Bluff before word got out that the cops were onto it. The other teams quit to save their asses.

Josh is asleep when the doctor finally comes out. Nate punches him awake. The doctor smiles at us. "You guys were great to stick around. Mark has a broken arm and a fractured collarbone. We casted the arm; he has a sling for the collarbone. Those are the outward injuries. That bump on the back of his head caused a slight concussion, nothing to worry about. More painful than anything else, especially if he's a back sleeper. The more urgent concerns were dehydration and early stages of hypothermia. If you hadn't found him when you did, I'd be having a very different conversation with his loved ones. You kids are heroes."

He shakes our hands and thanks us. Profusely.

"Can we go in and see him?"

The doctor shakes his head. "He's sleeping now. I'm going to keep him here overnight. Standard concussion protocol. But I'm sure he'd appreciate seeing you in a few days. You said he's the pastor, right? Go visit him at church."

We turn to go. I am so tired. It feels like it was days ago that we were with Luna in her kitchen. The doctor calls to us as we are filing out.

"Hey, guys? You should be proud of yourselves. You saved a life tonight."

We high-five each other in relief. Nate is stoked. "He called us heroes! And that's coming from someone who does heroic stuff every day, so it means something."

I'm glad we could help. And I'm glad we saved his life. But the truth? We're like total frauds. We were there to rob the house. And that makes me feel like shit.

41

LUNA

Mrs. Pugh told Temmie about what happened to Pastor Mark after we left. I feel horrible, but Temmie reassures me that it wasn't our fault, that he will be okay. So I am surprised to hear his voice through the heating vent as I am changing in the church. Actually, I hear Mrs. Pugh's first. And she is ticked.

"And what, pray tell, are you doing here? You should be home in bed!"

"Good afternoon to you too, Carol." His voice sounds weaker than normal, but his humor is intact.

"And don't think that just because you got hurt and almost left us, you're excused! I would like to know what in God's name you thought you were doing, trying to move furniture all by yourself!"

"I wasn't . . . well, Temmie and Luna had just left. They were helping me. So I wasn't alone except for about five minutes. I was just trying to reach a Bible on the top shelf. I had to climb partway up the bookcase. And then the Bible was stuck. All I remember is tugging on it. Ridiculously clumsy of me."

She doesn't want to hear it. "There are plenty of people in this community who are ready and willing to help. God knows most of them are desperate to be needed. But you are just too stubborn to see that. Too stubborn or too stupid. So I've already sent a crew up to the Orcutt place to haul out the furniture. You are not going back there. And you have dinners coming to you for the next two weeks. People are begging to be of service."

"I don't need—"

I know it's none of my business and I should stop listening. But I've never witnessed this side of Mrs. Pugh. Fierce. Angry. "You don't know what you need, Mark. You're so busy giving and doing for everyone else that you've forgotten how to accept help. My father called that 'benevolent arrogance.' And may I ask how on earth you drove here with one arm in a cast?"

"I'm fine. It's not like I had to shift or anything!"

"Humph. And one of those boys who found you wants to meet with you. I told him to wait a few weeks, but you know kids these days, not a whit of patience. Even though you shouldn't be here, since you are, would you mind seeing him? This afternoon?"

"Of course." There is a long pause. I lace up my shoes. Then I hear his voice again. There is no humor in it this time. "Carol, what should I do for those kids?"

"Nothing."

"But they saved my life!"

"Exactly. There is nothing you can do but thank them."

"That's not enough."

"Oh, for the love of Santa Claus, just stop. We take care of each other in this town. We don't carry a scale around, weighing our debts.

Or a ledger, keeping track of who owes whom and how much. Of all people, you should know that. You've saved more lives than you realize."

I think about this conversation as I dance. How do you thank someone for saving your life? It's impossible, because there's nothing of equal value.

Temmie gave up her life to save mine. I imagine there are lots of days she regrets that.

42
HUNTER

I've had like a constant headache since the night of the Challenge. I leave practice early, something I never do, telling Coach I have a stomach bug. *Just add lying to the list.*

The other guys don't seem bothered like I am. If anything, it's the opposite. They're kind of soaking it up, our role as local heroes. They've told the story over and over. We were even featured on the feel-good part of the evening news on WNMT. I know that's just a Podunk regional TV station, but people made it into a big deal, seeing us on it. When people ask me about it, I change the subject. Emma acts like my agent and tells everyone I won't talk about it because I'm traumatized. I don't have the energy to explain my guilt to her. But someone needs to know the truth, so I come to the church to give it to him.

Mrs. Pugh is waiting for me at the church entrance. "You are so dear to visit," she says. "I wanted to thank you personally for saving our Mark."

God, this is so uncomfortable! What would she say if she knew? "Uh, yep. I mean, anyone would've."

She shows me into Pastor Mark's office. She leaves the door open but calls out, "I'll be in the copy room down the hall if you need me."

Pastor Mark looks pale and worn out. The cast on his arm is heavy and bulky. It rests in a thick black sling. I sit in one of the chairs in front of his desk. "Mrs. Pugh said I could see you today, but if you're too tired or in pain or something, I can leave."

He looks as uncomfortable as I feel. "No, no, I'm glad you're here. Thank you for coming."

"I wanted to, like, check on you. You know, see if you're okay."

"I . . . I . . ." He stops, and his face turns red. And I'm sweating. *Does he know the truth? Can he sense what a fraud I am?* There's this long, awkward silence. I can't even look at him.

Finally, he starts again. "Look, Hunter, I'm not sure how to say this. But you and your friends saved my life. If it weren't for your quick thinking and decisive action, I'd be dead. I want you to know how deeply grateful I am for you. For all of you."

I need to stop him. He needs to know. "Um, yeah, about that night—"

He looks at me like he is genuinely puzzled.

"Pastor Mark, I came here for two reasons. The first was to see how you were. But the second, the second, um . . ." I am burning up. I unzip my jacket and take off my hat. "See, no one knows I came here today. To see you. Like it's kind of a big story at school, and people think we're like so cool. And it's easy to start to believe that."

"I'd say that saving a life—in this case, rescuing an idiot—earns you some well-deserved bragging rights," he says.

He doesn't know. "No, see, that's the thing. Um, we . . . we lied. And I can't stand it anymore."

"Oh?" He leans back and waits. *This is so frickin' hard.*

"We said we were just out driving, like we were heading into town. To hang out or whatever. But we were . . . um, we were . . . well, that isn't the truth."

Pastor Mark reaches over and picks up a red stress ball with his good hand. He fidgets with it while I swallow again.

"The truth is, we were . . . we were . . . God! This is so hard! We were breaking into that house. To . . . to rob it."

The only sign of his surprise is the way his eyebrows shoot up. "Are you . . . are you and your friends using? Or dealing?"

"No! Well, this doesn't make it any better, but we were doing this stupid challenge thing. It's like a big competition. One of the tasks was that. To steal something. And we wanted to win."

We sit in this heaviness for what feels like forever. I guess he needs time to process this truth. I wish he would just yell at me. I can feel sweat dripping down my back into my boxers.

"Did you?"

"Did I what?"

"Win."

"Win? No! We spent the night in the ER."

He squeezes the ball. Over and over. "And now everyone thinks you're a hero."

"Yeah. And it sucks. Because it's not true."

He swivels in his chair and looks out the window. It's snowing again. "My parents would respectfully disagree," he says. He swivels back. "I won't condescend to you, Hunter. I get it. You were breaking the law, breaking the Seventh Commandment, and breaking your own moral code. All for a stupid game. For what? To be the big guy? To show your friends you're tough? For the thrills and cheap laughs in the halls on Monday morning?"

I feel like I'm going to throw up.

His fingers dig into the ball. And hold on. "So yeah, I see why you feel like a fraud. People think you're a hero, and you know you're a trespasser and a thief." He stands up and walks to the window, his back to me. "That's the hard truth."

He turns around. "But here's the other truth. You came back. I was pretty out of it when you guys showed up, but I remember your coming in. After the first one of you took off. I couldn't speak, but I could hear you. You could have grabbed something, left, and won the game. But you didn't. You stayed. And if you hadn't, I would have died.

"But it was more than that. You guys worked together, figured out a plan, immediately went into action. And then you stayed again. You didn't have to hang in the ER all night. But you did. And that, Hunter, that's character. Character. Grit and grace and character."

Tears are running down my cheeks.

"While I was lying there," he continues, "I prayed. Some people are saying that you guys showed up there and saved my life because I'm blessed. But to me that's drivel. Every one of us is blessed, simply by being. Even those who experience horrible misfortunes are blessed. I didn't pray to be saved; I prayed that this accident would provide meaning. I had no idea what that would be. Still figuring that out. And it sounds like you are too. And I thank God for the opportunity to continue to live and figure out what we're meant to be and do."

I was not expecting this—this like raw honesty. And it gets me thinking. *What am I meant to do? Who am I meant to be*?

We talk a little bit longer, but I can see he's fading. "Thank you for hearing me, Pastor Mark," I tell him. "And, um, inspiring me." I put my hat and coat back on. At the door I turn. "And for what it's worth, everyone is glad, really glad, you're okay."

On my way home, Emma texts. She's all worried about me 'cause Coop told her I was sick. I agree to meet her at Molly's for a quick snack. But first I stop at Miz Callahan's house. She's surprised to see me, but she invites me right in. As always, she prepares a plate of cookies and pours a glass of milk. "These are the last of the post-funeral treats from my freezer," she says. Cheerfully. Maybe too cheerfully.

"What was your favorite?" I ask, my mouth full of chocolate chip cookie.

"Oh, I don't know. I only ate a couple bites of the several dozen that people made. I'm sure they were delicious, but everything just tasted like sawdust." She shakes her head a little. "My favorite cookie of all time is a molasses ginger snap. Soft, chewy, and rolled in sugar. When they bake, they crinkle on top. My mother used to make them at Christmas."

She massages her forehead like she's trying to get out of that memory and back to the present. "So, Hunter, what can I do for you?"

"I just was passing by on my way to Molly's. I stopped to see Pastor Mark."

"How's he doing? I heard about that awful accident."

"He's okay, I guess."

"He's lucky to be alive. You and your buddies did an amazing thing."

I don't have the energy to tell her the whole story. So I just shrug. She must sense my discomfort. "Hey, I have to tell you about my knitting group. You can tell your class. Wait, they may already know. Apparently, it was Luna's idea. Has she said anything?"

"Luna? No. At least I haven't heard her." What I don't say is that Coop and I were just over at Luna's house on Challenge night. We were talking about the Teo Legacy Project, and she never said anything about an idea. *She must hate me.*

"We are joining the Teo Legacy Project! By knitting sweaters. Original, one-of-a-kind sweaters to sell."

As Miz Callahan describes the different designs and stuff, I can tell she is stoked. And I am too, because if this works, it would be serious bank for our project. And I like the fact that it's growing beyond our class. She shows me the beginning of her sweater. It's mostly black, but there are white columns in it. She says the white will be flecked with black.

"We're all giving titles to our sweaters," she explains. "If I can pull this off, if it looks anything like my design on paper, it's going to be called 'Birch Trees in Moonlight.'"

She asks me about developing a website to sell both the sweaters and the jam. I tell her about Eliot, our class IT guy. "And," I say, "my dad is designing the *Made in Maine* logo."

"I wonder," she says, "if we could use that logo too? Like if we could somehow get it onto material that we could sew into the backs of the sweaters? I love the idea of a cross-brand. And all of it to teach our children to feel at home and safe in the water."

I run all the way to Molly's. Even though I probably ate, like, five cookies, I feel a lot lighter than when I left practice an hour ago. And my headache is gone.

There's a crowd at Molly's, which surprises me. Then I remember that it's meat loaf night. It's the cheapest dinner she makes, and people love it. I spy Emma in a booth near the counter.

"Oh, my God," she whispers when I slip through the line. "They're all talking about you!"

I slide in next to her. Her eyes are bright with excitement. "Just listen for a minute. You're like famous!"

Our backs are to the people, but their voices drift over to us.

"There were a few of them, I heard."

"Yep, just a bunch of teenagers. Boys."

"You just never know, do you? I mean, what kids'll do."

"He's such a nice man, that Mark."

"He's a damn fool. A lucky damn fool."

"Heart of gold. He did my mother's funeral. Wonderful service."

"Why the hell was he trying to move a bookcase on his own?"

"You know him. Never backs away from a chore. He cuts my grass in the summer. Says it justifies his owning a lawnmower."

"Well, he ain't from here if he thinks working alone in the winter is smart."

"Did he think he could carry the bookcase by himself?"

"Kind of an idiot, ain't he? Take two men to move that. Way bigger men than him."

"How did that huge sucker fit in Betty Orcutt's house, anyway? Her little cottage looks so small from the road."

"Oh, it had a vaulted ceiling, you know."

"All her furniture's down at the church, if anyone wants it. In the Free Room."

"I love that place. I was looking for a space heater and found one there. In good condition."

"I got me a nice winter jacket there. Practically brand-new."

"Carol Pugh is a saint. You know she cleans everything before it goes in there?"

"What about those kids who found him, huh?"

Emma pokes me. "Can I tell them? That you're right here?"

"No!" *That's the last thing I want.*

"Why not? They'll want selfies with you!"

"*Jesus, drop it!*" She looks hurt, so I try to soften my tone. "They won't talk if they know we're listening. Maybe they'll say more."

They do.

"Yep, you never know. You think they're just into gangster rap and video games, and then they surprise you like this."

"I think the Lord sent those boys there that night. I mean, what are the chances?"

"They shouldn'ta moved him. Coulda had a spine injury."

"Well, thank God he didn't."

"Who's taking care of him?"

"No one. Carol told me he's back at work."

"Well, what can we do for him?"

"She's set up a dinner schedule. If you want to bring him one, call her."

I look at Emma. "We should make him a meal."

She bursts out laughing. "You? Bake something? Uh, no thank you."

"How hard could it be? Come on, let's do it together."

"Believe me, we can do other things together." She slowly undoes two buttons on her shirt. "Let someone else cook for him. You just stick to basketball. And, you know, other things you're good at." And she leans over and kisses me, like slowly and seductively, and I kind of forget about cooking.

43

LUNA

The Teo Legacy Project has made school a teeny bit more tolerable. Like I kind of look forward to history class when I know we're going to be focused on the project. The success of the first huge batch of jam, combined with the amazing support from the women in the library's knitting group, has gotten us rolling. Like really rolling.

Today Austin has a new idea. "We should try to get our jam in touristy places. Like L.L.Bean. How do we do that?"

Everyone looks at Kiki, who has become our resident expert on stuff like regulations.

"I'll tell you what I know," she says. "There are all these different regulations for selling jam. If you make it at home and sell it at craft fairs, that's one thing. But if it's more commercialized, like if we had it at Bean's, then it's more regulated. I guess that's obvious. And would we want it just at the store in Freeport or also in the catalog?"

Gordon jumps in. "I think the more places it's sold, the better. But if we got lucky and had it in the catalog, we'd have to massively increase our operation. Like up to thousands, right?"

"Yeah, people all over the country buy from Bean's. We'd have to make it in a certified commercial kitchen to sell it in stores. The quality control and inspection rules are much stricter."

Almost everyone is a part of this conversation. I don't contribute, but I'm listening. It feels discouraging as reality sets in.

"Shit. Where are we going to find a commercial kitchen? And how the hell would we pay for it? I mean, how many hundreds of jars of jam would it take to pay for just like one fancy stove?"

"Good question. And we don't have an unlimited supply of berries. At least not until they're ripe in the summer. We only have what's in people's freezers now."

"And are we talking long-term, like making this a regular production, or are we just trying to make enough to open the pool?"

"For now, for the Teo Legacy Project, I guess our goal is to make enough money to open the pool. One year."

"Yeah, but then what?"

"Well, maybe if we can do a year, someone else can take up these projects and continue them. They could be an ongoing thing."

"I like the idea of his legacy living on for years."

"So, back to the jam. How much are we going to charge for a jar?"

"I did comparison shopping. In Hannaford's it's like five to seven dollars for the equivalent. In fancy stores and online catalogs, it's closer to fifteen or twenty."

"Twenty bucks for a small jar of jam? Who pays that?"

"Well, that's what we have to figure out. Who are we selling to?"

"That goes back to our brand. Are we like lululemon or Walmart?"

"That's such a girl comparison."

"What's that supposed to mean?"

"You know, clothing."

"They sell more than clothing at Walmart."

"Yeah, but lululemon doesn't."

"Well, what would you use?"

"I don't know, maybe a Lambo or Bugatti versus a Chevy. Or Kia."

"Shut up! I drive a Chevy! And it's better than that hunk of junk you're cruising around in."

"Yeah, my grandmother's wheels are better than his."

"Guys! We are so off topic!"

"Yeah, guys! Don't diss my car."

"Uh, dudes? Can we focus here?"

"Miz Callahan told me that some woman in her group said that those sweaters could sell for thousands of dollars in places like Aspen. Like someone already offered her that."

"Wicked high end. But is *Made in Maine* only going to cater to rich people? I mean, is that our brand?"

"I don't know. I mean, I would love it if we could make a ton of money for the project, but it feels like, you know, too exclusive. No way could I buy a sweater for that much. Hell, I wouldn't even waste twenty bucks on a jar of jam."

"Even if I could buy a sweater for several grand, I wouldn't. But that's not the point. Someone will."

"I doubt Ms. Callahan would want it to be super exclusive. That's not who she is. That's not who we are."

"I wonder if our brand could be both."

"Both what?"

"Like both high end and affordable. Like the sweaters are definitely high end. But the jam would be lower end."

"Interesting. So to own a *Made in Maine* sweater is a huge deal, like way out of mortal reach, but most people could at least afford our jam."

"No matter the cost, our brand should be super high quality. In everything."

"And it's unique."

"And the charity factor."

"We have to figure out how to market this stuff. Just because someone said she knows someone who would buy a sweater, that doesn't get our brand out there."

"It will help if we have a great website."

"Yeah, but we need publicity first. Get the word out. Get people to go to our website."

"We should have WNMT feature it. You know, a feel-good story. People would eat that up."

"Yeah, like Coop and Hunter saving that minister."

"You guys were on TV?"

"Go to YouTube. I'm sure it's there."

"We could contact the station. But we have a long way to go before that. Like making the labels. Making more jam. Finishing the sweaters. Pricing everything. Getting our website up and running."

"*Shee-eet*. That's a crapload of work."

"No one watches TV anymore. We'd need to advertise on social media."

"Get an influencer to promote our brand."

"Yeah, like we've got a few of those in our back pocket."

I wonder if we've gotten in way over our heads, like this is some stupid fantasy that a bunch of idealistic and naive kids dreamed up.

44

HUNTER

I'm kind of avoiding the cafeteria this week because I don't want to talk about the whole Challenge night rescue thing. So I slip into the library, thinking maybe I can just hang with Luna. If she'll even let me sit with her.

She's not at the table behind the bookcase. Mrs. Moss sees me looking around. "Can I help you?"

"Oh, no thanks. Just looking for someone."

"They're all back in that study nook. Working on some science project." She points to the far end of the library, where there is a glassed-in room for group study and discussion. Is Luna back there? With other people?

I walk back to the room. Gigantic art projects completely cover the glass windows, so I can't see who's in there. I knock.

The door opens a crack. "What do you want?" Pierce looks both angry and guilty.

"Oh, hey. Just looking for Luna."

"She's not here. Goodbye." He shuts the door in my face. And it pisses me off. I knock again. Pierce opens the door again, this time with a grin. "Yes? May I help you?"

"Don't slam the door in my face, jerk."

To my complete surprise, instead of punching me, like I think he's going to, Pierce opens the door and pulls me in. His posse of guys sits around the table. A pile of brownies wrapped in foil are in the center, along with a bottle of Coke and plastic cups.

"What are you guys doing?"

"Can you keep a secret?"

"Uh, yeah. Those CBD?"

"Maybe. But that's not the secret."

"Uh, okay. What is?"

He grins. "Know what's on the other side of this wall?"

I shake my head. I have no sense of direction or architectural understanding.

"You'll figure it out. But you can't tell anyone. Ready? Nobody make a sound or we're busted. Okay, Knox, do your thing."

Knox stands on a chair, stretches his arms up to the ceiling tile, and carefully punches it open. He reaches in and pulls out a dusty sweatshirt. Immediately I hear voices. Grown-up voices.

"The teachers' room?" I whisper, incredulous.

Pierce laughs silently. "It's awesome, the stuff we hear!"

Knox climbs down. "Shut up!" he hisses.

Pierce pours cups of Coke and passes them to the guys.

The voices drift down. I recognize Mrs. Laurence's. "You're looking gleeful today, Ludo," she says. "What's up?"

Mr. D laughs. "You will not believe the night I had."

"Oh, good. I'm in the mood for a story!" That's Ms. Scott. Her voice is high-pitched and like fluttery.

"Wait for me!" someone calls out. I think it's Ms. Eberhardt. "I'm just nuking this cup of noodles."

We hear drinks and paper bags being opened. The ding of the microwave. A chair being pulled out. I'm torn between wanting to listen and knowing it's private. *Shit.* "Dudes," I whisper, "I gotta go."

Pierce grabs my arm. "No way, Ridley. You're committed now. You rat on us, you're dead."

"I'm not ratting," I protest. "I'm just leaving."

"Shut up!" Knox punches my arm. Hard.

"You butted in here. Not our fault. But you'll leave when I say you can leave." Pierce steels his eyes on mine. *What the hell?*

"Obviously I trust you," we hear Mr. D say. "I am over the moon ecstatic and dying to share this."

"Oh, my God, this sounds juicy," Ms. Eberhardt says.

"Spill it," demands Ms. Scott. "We're the four amigos. Who tell each other everything."

"Okay, but it can't leave here. So last night Shep and I had kind of a fight. I wanted to talk with him about school, about the project my juniors are doing, about us. I even made him his favorite dinner, chicken enchiladas. But he barely ate. And he wasn't following the conversation at all. Said he had work to do in the barn and just left. I was so angry. Like he can't take ten minutes to talk? And honestly, he's been weird all winter. Like really preoccupied and distant. I thought it was over. We were over.

"I was going to go to the girls' basketball game, but it was snowing so hard, and the roads weren't plowed. So I chopped a bunch of wood and finally went to bed around midnight. Alone."

Shit, shit, shit! We should not be listening to this!

"Wait, what? Mr. D and Shep? Like the vet?" Knox's eyes are round with surprise. "He's gay?"

I look around. The guys are covering their mouths, trying not to laugh. Pierce's fierce whisper sounds pissed. "Shut up, you idiots!"

There's a pause. Mrs. Laurence can't stand it. "Go on! You're killing us! Don't eat!"

Mr. D laughs. "Wait, let me take a bite. Okay, so I was fast asleep when I heard our dog, Willa, barking. Like insistently. She's never in the house; she's either outside or in the barn. But she was next to me, pulling the comforter with her teeth. I looked at the clock: 1:54. And Shep's side of the bed was still empty. Immediately I was wide awake. Like worried that something had happened to him. So I threw on my jacket and boots and followed her out to the barn."

"What was wrong?"

"Well, Willa kept barking; it was still pounding down snow, and my heart was racing. I realized I didn't have my phone and had no way of calling 9-1-1.

"So we got to the barn, which was totally silent and dark, and I was frantic. Where on earth was he? I started to the back, where the lambing usually happens, when I heard Shep. Who told me to stop."

"Was he hurt?"

"I couldn't tell! It was so dark in there. Of course I asked him if he was okay, but he just spoke to Willa. 'Good girl! You did it! Now *place*.'"

"What on earth?" I can tell the other teachers are hanging on his words, totally caught up in his story.

"Shep didn't say anything. What the hell? I mean, it was two in the morning! There was a faint light from way back of the barn, and my eyes slowly adjusted. I saw him walk past Willa, who was still panting. Next to her was a sheep, a mama with her newborn lamb. And old Moldy the mare next to them. Shep stopped and stood on the other side of Moldy. I asked him if he needed help with lambing, although the one time I tried, I fainted at the sight of all that blood."

"I could never do that," says Mrs. Laurence. "The mere sight of blood makes me—"

She's interrupted by Ms. Scott. "Shh! Let him finish!"

Mr. D is still chewing when he speaks again. "Sorry, but I am so hungry. Anyway, I was seriously concerned. Why was he just standing there? And why were sheep and a horse sharing a stall? It was a bizarre tableau, like one you'd see on a religious Christmas card."

He stops, probably to take a drink. The guys in here don't move, don't even look at each other. They're all staring at the ceiling, as if looking there will help them hear better.

"I've read about extreme fatigue causing temporary psychosis," Mr. D goes on. "So I tried to get him to come to the house. Then he held up his hand and went, 'We're a rebus.'"

"What?" Ms. Eberhardt bursts out. "That makes no sense!"

"I know," agrees Mr. D. "I was freaking out. Like I seriously thought he'd lost it. So he went, 'It's a secret message in pictures. Can you read us?' He looked so pleased with himself. And you guys know Shep. He's always stoic, barely ever smiles. So I decided to humor him and then make sure he slept. For a long time. I would turn off our alarms. I even planned to call in sick and take him to the doctor. So I said, 'Okay, Shep, I'll read the rebus.' In a voice meant for five-year-olds. "Um, dog, sheep, horse, man. Now let's go to the house.'

"But he wouldn't budge. Said something like I was close but not completely accurate. Told me to be more specific."

"This is crazy," says Ms. Scott. "What was he doing?"

"I had no idea. But I lost my patience. 'Whatever. Mutt, ewe, mare, dude. Nice little farm riddle. I can't believe you woke me up for that. I'm going back to bed.'

"I started to go back to the house when I heard him flick a switch. And suddenly the barn was glowing. Hundreds of tiny white Christmas lights, strung all over, flashed on. I just stood there staring. It was surreal. Then he said, 'I'll read it for you: Willa. Ewe. Mare-e. Me?'"

For a minute we don't hear anything. Then all three teachers start screaming. And it's a jumble of laughing and asking questions and congratulating him and more screaming.

"Oh, my God, this is the best!"

"More! I want more details! Then what?"

"So we were laughing and crying and hugging and, God, I felt like it was all a dream. He had been nervous for weeks, which explains why he'd been so aloof. And why he blew me off at dinner. And it took him way longer than he thought it would to put up all the lights. But it was so awesome. He'd thought of everything. He had music cued up, hot chocolate in a thermos, and heart-shaped cookies from Molly's." Mr. D sounds choked up. "If you had told me that it would be Shep who proposed, I would have said you were crazy. I'm still trying to process this. Hey, thanks for listening. I'm afraid I took up most of your lunch break."

"Oh, my God, Ludo, that is one of the most romantic proposals I've ever heard," sighs Ms. Scott.

"That totally made my day," agrees Ms. Eberhardt. "You are so lucky. He sounds amazing."

"And he's lucky too," says Mrs. Laurence. "That was beautiful. Are you . . . are you telling anyone else? Beyond our little lunch group?"

"No way. Not everyone's as open-minded as you three. It's not worth the hassle that would surely come up. And honestly, I don't want to make anyone uncomfortable."

"Oh, for God's sake, Ludo. It's the twenty-first century! No one cares."

"Still, I think I'll just keep it between us. Thanks, mates."

Knox slowly stuffs the sweatshirt back in and replaces the tile. "Oh, my God."

Pierce rubs his hands together. "I cannot believe we just heard that. That was probably the juiciest thing ever. Wait till this gets around."

"*No one says anything.*" There is so much anger and shame in me that I can barely speak. "That was not our business. I swear, if this gets out, I'll—"

"You'll what, Ridley? You're so full of shit. You can't stop us."

"Just respect his privacy, Pierce. What did he ever do to you?"

"Suck my dick, Ridley. And now you can't tell on us. Because you were here too."

45

LUNA

I am walking to church after school when I hear someone shout my name. I turn and see Hunter running down the sidewalk. His jacket is open, and his backpack is unzipped. Papers and books are spilling out of it. He looks like an ad for Marie Kondo. The *before* picture.

"Sorry, I know you're on your way to church. I just wondered if you can maybe come over to my house tonight. To, um, work on a project."

I am confused. "The Teo Project?"

"Yeah. Sort of."

"Isn't it something . . . I mean, can't we do it at school?"

"No, not really. It's okay if you can't. I mean . . ." He kind of drifts off.

He looks so sad, standing there. I don't have a ton of homework. "I guess so?"

He grins. "Your enthusiasm is overwhelming."

He gives me his address. Temmie will need to drive me. Still not sure why we can't do it in class.

On the way, she grills me. "The only thing I know about Jack Ridley is that he lost his wife when their son was born. But I don't know what Hunter is like. I mean, I only met him that one time, when they came over to bring you granola bars. What will you be doing? Will his father be home? Is this a party or a date? Who else is going to be there?"

I want to remind Temmie of her recent apology to me—the one about keeping me to herself and not letting me be out in the world, make friends, be normal. But I am too nervous about going to Hunter's house.

My answer to every one of her rapid-fire questions is "I don't know, I don't know, I don't know." You would think she'd applaud my honesty, but it just makes her more anxious. "You really don't know anything about this boy, do you?"

"Um, not true. I know he's in my history class. I know he was one of Teo's pallbearers. And he and I have gone to see Teo's mom. He plays basketball. He's funny. He really likes your blueberry buckle. And he rescued Pastor Mark. Besides, Temmie, it's not a date! We're just working on the project."

"Well, I don't understand why you can't work on this at school. Do you think I should stay?"

At first I'm mortified. I'm seventeen. I should be able to take care of myself. Then I think it would make me and Temmie more comfortable. "You can come in when you drop me. You know, to say hi and find out what time to pick me up. Then you should probably leave. If I need you, I'll text you."

She nods, but I can see the worry line pulsing in the middle of her forehead.

Coop and Hunter greet us at the front door. "Hey, Luna. Hey, Miz Lemieux." They usher us in, take our jackets, and lead us to the kitchen. Spread out on the counter are bags of flour and sugar, small boxes of baking powder and salt. A jar of molasses. Butter. Eggs. All the ingredients look brand-new.

Hunter explains. "Miz Callahan told me about her favorite cookie. I thought maybe you could help me make some? And then we can deliver them tomorrow after school."

"And I'm his chauffeur," announces Coop. "He doesn't really like me. He just uses me for my wheels. Today it was Hannaford's. When his daddy decides he can stop riding his tricycle and drive, he's gonna owe me sooo many rides!"

It must be a sore subject. Hunter looks embarrassed. "Maybe he knows you need as much practice as you can get."

Coop laughs. "Whatever. This summer we can put streamers on the handlebars to make your ride even cooler! Okay, I gotta get going. If I'm not home by seven o'clock, I'm gonna be in trooou-ble." He looks at his phone. "Actually, I'm fine. It's only 6:20. Ms. Lemieux, do you know how to play Castle?"

Temmie seems startled. "No, I . . . no."

Hunter glares at Coop. "Dude! Not everyone wants to play your stupid little card games. I swear, you're obsessed."

Coop ignores him. "I'll teach you. Just a couple games before I have to leave. While they make their cookies."

I am giggling to myself. He may have met his match. Temmie doesn't let anyone win; they have to earn it. She and Coop sit at the table. Coop explains the rules. Hunter and I look at the recipe he's found online. Soon we are measuring and mixing.

And it's easy, being here.

Coop takes the first two games. Then Temmie takes over. She wins three before Coop decides he has to get going. Temmie leaves with him. But first she and Hunter exchange phone numbers. "What time should I be back for Luna?"

"Is nine o'clock too late? I didn't realize the dough had to chill for an hour before we bake it. I don't really bake much. Or at all, really. I just wanted to do something for Miz Callahan."

Temmie assures him that nine o'clock is fine, and she slips out.

The counter is covered with flour and strewn with baking stuff. I start to clean up, but Hunter stops me. "We can do that later," he says. "Do you know the game they were playing? I need some tips. I swear, Coop beats me every time. He's getting way too cocky."

We play cards and talk. It sounds stupid, but this is the first time I've done something like this. Just hanging at a friend's house. We talk about the project and Mr. D. And basketball and dance. And movies and music.

"Your mom seems chill," he says. "That was nice of her to humor Coop."

"She's actually my aunt," I say. "But, yeah, she's cool."

I wait for him to ask. Why I live with my aunt and not my parents. But he doesn't. I change the subject.

"Where's your dad tonight?"

"Um, I'm not sure," he says. "He goes out a lot at night." He looks at me. "Do you know about my dad?"

I don't know what he means. "What, is he famous?"

"Hah! More like infamous. I mean, he's awesome when he's not drinking. But he's not the same at all when he is."

"Oh. I . . . oh."

"It turns him mean. And loud. I wish—"

"I am so sorry."

"I think when my mom died when I was born, he tried so hard to take care of me and be like two parents for me. And he was great. But when the mill closed, he kind of lost his direction."

"Does he have a job now?"

"Not really. He sometimes gets projects, like carpentry or manual labor, but nothing consistent."

"It's so depressing. Temmie worked at the mill too. And she doesn't have a job now."

"Does she drink?"

"No."

"That's good. It sucks."

"Has he ever tried to quit? I know there's an AA group that meets at church. I sometimes see them going in when I'm leaving."

"Yeah, no. You've got to admit you have a problem to do that."

Just then a blast of air hits us as the kitchen door bursts open. "Hunter? Emma?"

I turn around. He stares. "Whoa! You're not Emma!"

Hunter's face turns bright red. "Dad, this is Luna. A friend from school. Luna, my dad."

"What's this mess?" his dad asks. "And where did all this food come from?"

"We'll clean up, Dad," says Hunter. "We're making cookies. And I bought the ingredients. With my own money. Did you eat dinner?"

"I had a burger at the bar. How much longer are you going to be doing this? You've got to get to bed early. Big game tomorrow." He reaches in the refrigerator and takes out a beer. It's apparent that it's not his first.

"I got it, Dad."

Hunter is uneasy. He carefully wipes the counter. I fill the sink and start washing dishes. Mr. Ridley leans against the refrigerator. "So where's Emma? You two have a fight?"

"No, Dad. We're good."

"You got to hang onto her. Her family has money." He finishes the beer and takes out another. "So Luna is what? Some kind of charity case?"

I sense Hunter stiffen next to me. "Jesus, Dad! Are you kidding me?"

"Well, I mean, can't really blame me, right?"

"Luna is my friend, Dad. My friend! We're making cookies for Teo's mother. Remember Teo? The boy who drowned while you were passed out right next to him?"

Mr. Ridley freezes for a second. Then he's across the kitchen in a giant step. In one flashing movement, he lunges forward and slaps Hunter's face. Hard. "You watch your mouth, son. You know better." He storms out of the kitchen.

I am rigid, terrified. Hunter doesn't look at me. He furiously wipes the counter clean.

"I . . . I should go," I say quietly. "I'll text Temmie and start walking."

"No. We're both getting out of here. Just a second." He leaves the kitchen. I finish the dishes, shaking. Hunter returns, carrying his backpack. He snatches a piece of junk mail from the counter and scribbles a note on the back of it: *Gone to Coop's.*

Then he takes the cookie dough from the refrigerator, grabs the bag of sugar, and turns to me. "Come on. Get your jacket."

We flee from the house. I tell him we can text Temmie, but he doesn't want to. "If you don't mind, I need to cool off. It's only like three miles. Is it okay if we walk?"

"It will help the cookies chill, I guess." That makes him smile. Sort of.

He doesn't talk anymore until we are about halfway there. "Geez, Luna, I am so sorry. About all of that. What he said. What he did."

I don't say anything. I'm both embarrassed, reminded of my ugliness, and sorry for Hunter. I'm even sorry for his dad.

"The thing is, he hasn't always been like this. I don't know what to do anymore. Like I love him so much, but at times like this, when he's so drunk, I hate him."

We arrive at my house, both chilled from the cold and warmed from the walking. Temmie is surprised to see us.

"We decided to bake them here," I announce. I give her a warning look.

She doesn't ask. "Go right ahead. Just set the oven for 50 degrees less than it says. Otherwise they'll burn. I really should get that fixed someday." Temmie sits in the living room with a heating pad on her knee. The sounds of the old movie she's watching are oddly comforting.

We make the dough into little balls and roll them in sugar before putting them on the cookie sheet. The silence doesn't feel as tense as it did before. While the first batch bakes, I pull out a worn deck of cards and we continue to play Castle. Focusing on the game makes conversation less awkward. I win twice in a row. I can tell it bothers him. "What am I doing wrong? First Coop and now you."

"Maybe we're just brilliant," I say.

He rolls his eyes. But I can tell he appreciates my not treating him like a Ming vase. "Yeah, I don't think so."

"Seriously? You need to strategize better. Like don't play the power cards as soon as you get them. Save them for when you need them."

It works. I almost wish I hadn't told him, because he wins the next four games.

It's close to ten o'clock by the time we've finished baking the entire batch of cookies. They're really good. We make a plan to bring them to Teo's mom right after school tomorrow.

Hunter texts Coop, where he'll spend the night. Coop arrives quickly. "See what I mean? He just needs me for rides! Oh, my God, it smells so good in here! Dude, hook me up." I pile a stack of cookies on a paper plate and pour milk into a disposable cup. Temmie comes to the door as they are leaving. "Still sore about losing?" she teases.

"I'll be back," warns Coop. "Don't get too confident! And wow, these are amazing. Save me some for tomorrow!"

Hunter catches my eye. "Thanks," he whispers.

I stay up until midnight, finishing my homework and just thinking. About Hunter. And addiction. And how hard it is to be a single parent.

Like Temmie and Mr. Ridley.

And Ms. Callahan.

46
HUNTER

Gretchen's having me and Dad over for dinner tonight. She asked me to pick up a carton of soup and a loaf of rosemary bread from Molly's after practice. In front of me in line is a woman in hospital scrubs. I recognize her from her apple crisp plan with Mr. D. Margaret, I think. Or Martha? She's talking with Samantha, who is working behind the counter.

"He's *gay*?" Her voice rises above the general din of the late-afternoon coffee drinkers. "Are you kidding me?"

"Shhh! Megan! Be quiet!" *Megan,* that's right. I get the feeling that trying to stifle her is like raking leaves in a windstorm. A hush has suddenly fallen over the shop. I look around. No one is staring, but I know they're listening.

Megan is oblivious. She continues at the same decibel. "I should have known. God! Why are the hot and smart and thoughtful ones always gay? It's so unfair! Why didn't he tell us?"

Samantha smiles. "Knowing you, you didn't give him a chance."

Megan sighs. "Are you positive? How do you know?"

"Apparently he just got engaged. Some kids were in here yesterday talking about it."

Some kids? *Oh, my God, no. Pierce and his posse.*

Megan lowers her voice. "You know, maybe he tried. I didn't really give him a chance. I just assumed when he hesitated about coming to my house for dessert that he was with someone else. With boobs." She drums her red-polished nails on the counter. "What a bummer. For me, that is. Is the other guy hot?"

"I don't remember. I only met him once, when I took Arlo in for shots. I do remember that he was very gentle. And quiet."

"When's the wedding? Are they doing it here or going to some exotic island? Some fancy destination thing?"

"I don't know. I doubt it."

"Okay, my next mission is going to be getting an invitation to that wedding. Because he must have a bunch of friends, and they can't all be gay. You need to set up another meeting for the three of us. To talk about the Teo Legacy Project. Okay? Oh, I can tell him about my progress!"

"Do you have any news? From the clinic?"

"Yes! I met with the director the day after you and Ludovic (*sigh*) and I had coffee here. And I told her about the project and asked her very sweetly—you would have been so proud if you'd heard me—if she would be willing to donate staff and time for training a bunch of lifeguards in CPR, first aid, and AED—you know, automated external defibrillator—certification. And she was totally on board. Isn't that awesome?"

Yes. It is. But I am so pissed at Pierce that I can't think of anything else.

47
LUNA

"Luna," calls Temmie as she makes her way down the icy steps, "I need help in the knitting room. From you."

"What?" I am already in the car, which is frigid.

Temmie lumbers into the seat and puts her huge knitting bag in my lap. "I need you to wind these skeins into balls."

Really? "I thought they had machines to do that," I say darkly.

"Yup. They do. And when we all were buying our yarn, there was such a long wait for the machine, I decided you could do it for me."

I'm torn. I don't want to be seen in there, but I do want to see how the sweaters are coming along. And I can give a progress report to our class. "Okay. But I'm keeping my hoodie on, and we have to sit in the back."

There's a heightened sense of purpose in the community room. Even the women who are not making a sweater for the project are somehow involved, mostly as consultants or cheerleaders.

There are fifteen sweaters in the works. Five are intended for women, five for men, and five are unisex. Each one, like a painting, has a title. Since we don't know who will purchase them, the size is totally random. The faster knitters by default are making theirs at the larger end; those who are slower or more deliberate will make theirs smaller.

Jessica has given up learning how to knit and is serving coffee to everyone instead. Just as she brings a mug to Temmie, her phone rings. "Oh, it's Cheri. I need to get this. Cheri? Hi! You do? Wait, when? Hey, do you mind if I put you on speaker? I'm actually with the knitters right now. Okay, hang on a second."

She turns to the women. "This is lovely serendipity. Remember I told you about my client in Aspen who loved Polly's sweater? Cheri Reina? She is huge in the fashion industry, has connections with everyone. She's calling to check on our progress. I'm putting her on speaker so you can hear her." She pushes a button. "Okay, Cheri, you're on speaker. Where are you today?"

"I'm at a show in Taos. Just got eight inches of fresh powder, so I'm going to ski this evening after the expo. And hi, you wonderful knitting women!"

"Hi, Cheri!" Some of the older women lean forward, their hands cupping their ears. I doubt they can hear her.

"I've got to get back to the show, but I had a quick question for you. Do you think those sweaters could be finished by mid-March?"

"I don't know. They seem to be coming along." Jessica looks around. Some women are nodding their heads; others shake theirs. "Why? I mean, should they be?"

Cheri laughs. "Well, even though it sounds counterintuitive—like who even cares about the new line of winter clothes in the spring, when you're so sick of sweaters and scarves and boots, right—but that's when the shows are. For the next season, I mean."

"Why are they so early? Why don't the winter clothes get shown in the fall?"

"They have to be about six months ahead of when people are going to start buying. So if there's a lot of interest in a particular line or style, the manufacturers have time to ramp up production."

"Of course. That makes sense. But we're only going to have fifteen sweaters. Period. There's not going to be any ramping up production."

"I know. It's still important for you to get on the scene when everyone else is. Think about how you plan to present these. Since it's a tiny and limited edition, I would recommend a video."

"Okay. A video we can manage. But where is it going to be shown?"

"At auction. I have a couple contacts who owe me a favor. The auction is going to be the highlight of the Saturday-evening event at the major spring show in New York. It's the second week of April."

"So who's going to be bidding?"

"Believe me, if we market this well, they'll all be bidding. Not only because—if that one you were wearing in Aspen is any indication—the sweaters are amazing, but because the big houses will want to be known for selling only originals. One-of-a-kind merch barely exists anymore because it's too expensive. You'll see."

"So if a fashion house buys the sweaters at auction, do we get the money then? Or do we have to wait until they sell them?"

"We'll have to negotiate that. If we make it clear that it's for a charity, they'll probably give you the entire profit up front. They'll publicize that, which, frankly, will make them look good. Give them an edge in the highly competitive fashion world."

"Hmm. Intriguing. Okay, I'll crack the whip on these knitters and start thinking about a video. Thanks so much, Cheri!"

"Glad to help. I can't wait to buy one!"

Jessica beams as she looks around the room. "Can you believe this is actually happening? Your sweaters are going to be featured at Fashion Week in New York!"

I get a sense, looking around, that these women are both excited and intimidated by the prospect. It's Polly who articulates this. "Look, Jessica, we're not New Yorkers. And we wear sweaters to keep warm, not to be fashionable. So we are way out of our league here. Like we're being pulled behind some runaway horses."

Other women nod in agreement. Jessica looks lost.

Ms. Callahan rescues her. "Maybe it would be less daunting to simply think about how warm we're going to make someone. Or where and when they'll wear the sweater. Doing barn chores or going for a winter walk or . . . or . . . skiing in Aspen. The sweaters have their origin stories right here, with us. Their future lives are just in our imagination right now."

I love this. Temmie and I could have a field day imagining the future of the one she's making.

Ms. Callahan goes on. "When Luna, as a representative of her class, told me they'd decided on *Made in Maine* as their brand, my mind played a little word game and turned the three words into two: 'Maiden Maine.' And this project and these sweaters are in the infancy of their maiden voyages, starting in Maine and going who knows where."

"Jessica, Cheri mentioned a video display," says Ethel. "How are we going to display them?"

People pause in their knitting to ponder this.

"We could just lay them out on the couches in here. Or maybe hang them on a clothesline strung from that door over to that wall? After all, this is where they were created."

"That's an idea. We have to make sure, though, that both the front and back are shown. I guess that would be the job of whoever is filming it. For the video."

"Good point. Hmm. Well, let's think about catalogs. How are they done there?"

"It varies. Depends on the company."

"I think we should have people wearing them."

"It's going to have to be someone skinny. I'd never fit in mine."

Ms. Callahan stands up. "I've got it! We'll have a fashion show. But not the traditional runway kind. It will be filmed. Outside. In the snow. Where there's a sledding hill and a pond for skating. And you know who's going to model our sweaters? The kids who started this whole thing."

"Oh, Bridget. That's brilliant!"

"And there's something else," Ms. Callahan continues. "You're going to be in it too. If you want to be on film, fantastic. If you don't, then it will just be your voice. Giving the title of your sweater and sort of explaining the design."

Everyone turns to Jessica. She is beaming. "That is a hundred times better than what I had in mind," she confesses. "Honestly. I love it."

Ms. Callahan continues. "I'll organize the students. Let's set a date. A Saturday, with Sunday as a backup. In case it's snowing too hard on Saturday to film. If we're finished by mid-March like Cheri requested, that means maybe we could film on the first Saturday after the 15th." She pulls out her phone. "That's the . . . let's see . . . the 18th of March. In the afternoon. I'll ask the kids where the sledding and skating are best and let you know. We should carpool if we can. And Jessica, are there releases or something we'll need to sign? And ones for the kids?"

Jessica will procure them. Ethel will bring brownies. Barbara will make hot chocolate. Rose will set up a little table. Jojo will drive Ruth and Mabel. I feel as if I am watching a movie in fast motion as the plans develop.

Now everyone needs to finish their sweaters.

48

HUNTER

We are fired up for the game tonight, the last one of our regular season. We have to win in order to go on in the postseason playoffs. During the warm-up drills, I glance into the bleachers, which are already packed. No sign of my dad. *Gee, big surprise*. When I asked him if he was coming tonight, he said, "Ain't no welcome mat in that gym for me." I'm both pissed off and relieved that he's not here. Whatever.

I spy Emma sitting with a bunch of her friends. They don't see me looking because they're all on their phones. Two rows behind them is a familiar face, but it takes me a second to place it. Oh, my God, it's Ms. Callahan! What is she doing here? Adrenaline pumps through my body, and I sink four three-pointers in a row. Too bad it's just the pregame shootaround.

The game is intense. Nate, who is usually really reliable with his threes, is way off. He can't hit anything, so he stops shooting. The further behind we get, the more stupid mistakes we make. Like dribbling down and just heaving a three-point shot instead of setting up a play. I've never seen Coop more flustered. He loses the ball off the dribble twice in a row before Coach benches him. And we commit an unprecedented nine turnovers in the first half. We're down by thirteen at halftime.

We don't say anything as we wait to get chewed out by Coach in the locker room. But he's strangely quiet. He looks at each one of us without speaking. Finally he says, "Next week. After school. What are you going to be doing?"

We wait. No one is sure if he wants an answer. Or if we're just supposed to think about that.

"Because it looks to me like you want some time to yourselves. Maybe join the pond rats for a hockey game. Or get ahead on your assignments. Or spend an hour or two browsing in the library for some good books to read. That sound good, eh? Just go home, get a big snack, put your feet up, and relax? Have some *me* time?

"If that's where you'd rather be than in the gym for practice, keep doing what you're doing out there. Let them have the offensive rebounds. Take stupid shots when you're not set. Reach out instead of moving your damn feet to block their path. Telegraph those passes so they can intercept them. Show everyone in the damn bleachers that you're tired of playing and you'd rather be somewhere else."

He storms out. He's never been so sarcastic before.

I guess embarrassing us works. Or maybe our opponent has gotten cocky. We put our heads down and get to work. Methodically. In our huddle we make a pact to pass the ball at least twice before anyone shoots. Like we've done in practice over and over. Slowly we catch up, and then it's back and forth for the entire fourth quarter. We're exhausted trying to defend against this team, which is really good, but we refuse to quit. The crowd is screaming; we can barely hear Coach calling the plays. With seven seconds to go, and us down two, Nate is fouled on a layup, which he misses. The other coach calls time-out.

Coach puts his hands on Nate's shoulders. "You got this. Just like in practice. Easy does it." He turns to the rest of us. "If he makes 'em both, get back on defense. No press. Just don't let 'em get an easy bucket. And for God's sake, don't foul. If he misses the second shot, get the rebound. If they get it, foul right away. That's our only chance to get the ball back."

Nate is nervous. He bounces the ball about ten times at the foul line. First free throw slides right through. Nothing but net. The crowd goes crazy. The second shot takes a long bounce off the rim. I jump up to grab the rebound. I know I don't have time to set up a play, so I just throw it back up. It rolls around the rim and drops in. Now our fans are stomping on the bleachers in a wild frenzy.

Three seconds left. We race back on D. Their point guard, who has been sinking threes all night, dribbles up the court at a run. He shoots. Just as the ball leaves his hands, I leap up and swat it away. The buzzer goes off, and I am surrounded by my teammates, pounding my back and yelling. "You fuckin' genius! That was amazing! Dude! You're a frickin' maniac!"

Coach has a huge smile on his face. He punches my arm. "That's the way we do it!"

Everyone gathers in a huddle. Coach says, "I knew you had it in you. You were *men* in that half. *Men!* Men don't quit when they're down. I'm proud of you. Now go shake their hands. And I'll see every one of you at practice."

Josh's parents invite the guys on the team and all the parents over for a celebratory dinner. Coop says he'll drive me. His parents will meet us there. We shower and dress then head down the hall that leads to the parking lot. I'm hoping to maybe see Miz Callahan to thank her for coming. But she's gone. Emma, though, is waiting for me, surrounded by her friends.

"Hey, hotshot," she greets me. We kiss. Her eyes are like all shiny. I'm not sure if she's high or just really excited about the game. Her friends congratulate me.

"So, what are we doing tonight?" Emma slips her hand into my back pocket.

"Um, well, we're having a team dinner. At Josh's. Just the team."

"So how long is that gonna take?" Her hand is caressing my butt. Very distracting.

"I don't know."

"Well, can we get together later?" If she keeps this up, I'm not going to be able to walk.

"Maybe. I'll text you."

"Did you just say 'maybe'? What the hell, Hunter?" She yanks her hand out of my pants.

"What? I just don't know how long we'll be there. Come on, Emma, it's the last game of the regular season! The whole team is going."

"Whatever. *Maybe* I'll be available when you're finished. *Maybe* you'll get a little more of this." She wraps her arms around me, presses her breasts into me, and pulls me close. Then she grinds a little. *Oh, my God.* She feels my boner, grins, and lets me go. "Or *maybe* not. I *may be* busy." She and her friends run off, laughing. *She is so frickin' sexy.*

"You're so pussy whipped," says Coop. "Come on! I'm starving."

We get in his car and wait for a few minutes while it warms up. Coop keeps his eyes on the dashboard when he asks, "Your dad show up?"

"Naw."

"Shit."

"I guess."

He drives through town on the way to Josh's. As we're passing the bar, Coop slows down. "Hey, isn't that your dad's truck?"

I see it. Old. Rusted out. Bungee cords on the tailgate to hold it shut. *He's at the bar? On the night of my game?*

"Let's pick him up," Coop says. He whips the wheel around and turns into the parking lot. "All the parents are going."

Just then the bar door opens and two men walk out. One is Dad, obviously smashed. I don't recognize the other guy. They stop at Dad's truck and have some sort of argument. Finally the guy half shoves Dad into the passenger seat then climbs into the driver's side and takes off.

Coop doesn't say anything.

"I'm . . . I've got to . . . just go ahead." I get out of the car.

"What are you doing?" Coop sounds scared.

"Don't worry about it. Go to Josh's." I slam the door and walk across the icy parking lot. A huge guy is sitting on a stool at the entrance. I can tell he's jacked even though he's wearing a sweatshirt. He barely looks at me. "You got ID?" *A bouncer? Really? At this Podunk bar in Edgewater?* Then I remember hearing about a bust, teenagers being served. The bouncer is probably part of the bar's probation. Well, this guy's not going to stop me. I have to know if this is where my dad goes every night.

"Uh, no. I'm not drinking. I just need to ask someone something."

"Yeah, that's what they all say. Get outta here."

"It has to do with a potential lawsuit," says a deep voice next to me. Startled, I turn. It's Coop, faking his voice. "Prosecution of a DUI case."

"Oh, really?" The bouncer grins. "You're so full of shit. I'll give you three minutes for your effort."

It's crowded. People are sitting at the bar watching hockey on the big screen above the bartender. A bunch of twentysomethings are playing pool in the back room. A woman carrying a basket of fries squeezes past us. As she passes, Coop grabs a fry and pops it in his mouth.

"Hey! It's the kids from the game!" An old guy at the bar is pointing to us. Heads spin around, and then there's this weird like wave of clapping. For us. *What on earth?* I look at Coop. He shrugs, as confused as I am.

The bartender waves. "Come on over!" Men scoot over to make room for us, and they slap us on the back. The barkeep fills two glasses with ice and puts them on the bar. "What'll it be? Coke? Sprite? Root beer? Man, that game was unbelievable! We never thought you'd come back from the first half. And that block at the end? Swee-eet!"

"Wait, what? You had *our* game on in here?"

"Yep. Every Edgewater game. At least when Jack Ridley's here. He's your dad, right?"

"Um, yeah."

"There was quite an argument tonight. Some people wanted to watch the Duke versus North Carolina game. But no way. Jack wouldn't hear of it. He sat right there, like he does every time you guys play, and watched every second. He was dancing and screaming after your winning shot. And then that block . . . unbelievable!"

This is so far from what I expected. I need a minute to process it. I drink my Coke in stunned silence while Coop discusses the game, practically play by play, with the guys at the bar. Somehow a basket of fries appears, which he attacks. Everyone's laughing and shouting and giving us high fives. It's so weird and unexpected and awesome.

Coop finishes the fries. "Ready to go?"

But I'm not. I still haven't asked. "Just a sec." I turn back to the bartender. "So, just wondering. Does my dad come here every night?"

He nods. "If you guys are playing, he comes early to get his front-row seat. If not, he shows up about nine o'clock, practically frozen stiff. He's been out working. But he doesn't say where."

Working? He doesn't have a job.

"Who took him home tonight?"

"Oh, that's Finn. He owes me a few favors. He's in great shape; he'll just jog back after getting him home."

"Okay. Um, thanks. For the Coke. And the food. And, you know, taking care of my dad."

"Not a problem. We'll be rooting for you guys in the playoffs."

Back in the car, Coop is feeling it. "Those guys were awesome! Who knew anyone even watched WNMT? It's out of Northriver, right? Man, we were like frickin' celebrities in there!"

"Yeah. That was cool." I hate to ask, 'cause he's already gone out of his way. "Hey, do you mind just taking me home?"

I expect a protest. Like an "are you kidding me, we haven't even gone to the party, and you were the star of the game" kind of protest. But he gets it. And I know he won't say anything at the party. About my dad, I mean.

At home I find Dad on the couch. Passed out. I take off his boots and cover him with a blanket. And then I sit in the recliner next to him. I turn off my phone and just watch him sleep. At midnight I grab more blankets off our beds and pile them onto both of us. And that's where we spend the night. Together.

It's the closest I've felt to my dad in a long time.

49
LUNA

I'm heading to the library at lunchtime when Kiki calls to me in the hall. "Luna? Do you want to eat together?"

"Is there . . . are we meeting about the project?"

She smiles. "Well, we could talk about it, but it's not a meeting. I just wanted to, you know, hang out."

I'm so surprised that I don't answer for a few seconds. No one has ever asked. "I . . . guess?"

It's so loud in the cafeteria. I shrink into my hoodie and sort of blindly follow Kiki. We find an empty small table behind a large group of girls. "Sophomores," Kiki informs me. She rolls her eyes. "Just listen to their conversation for about a minute, and you'll get why." She points to her eyes.

"But first," she says, "let's eat. Are you a dancer? You carry yourself like one."

I do? I'm not used to people noticing me. "Yeah, I used to take lessons."

"Ballet? Jazz? Tap? Hip-hop?"

"A little of everything. Now I just kind of free-form. It's, I don't know, it's like my happy place, dancing."

"Where do you dance? Like in your room?"

"No, my room is tiny. I actually have this deal at church. Like I get to dance in the sanctuary after school in exchange for working with the littles at Sunday school."

"Oh, that's right," she says. "That's how you knew Teo."

"Yeah. What . . . what do you do? For fun?"

"Not much, really," she admits. "I mostly do homework and try to help around the house. Dad never found a job after the whole mill thing, so we can't afford to do much. I did teach myself to play the ukulele watching YouTube videos. I love to go out in our garden and play there. It's, like, really peaceful. And it's, like, the one time I don't feel stressed. It sounds like that's how you feel about dance."

"What kind of garden? My aunt and I have a vegetable one."

"Yeah, that's mostly what ours is too. The growing season is so short, but we can a lot of what we grow. Potatoes, beans, peppers, zucchini, tomatoes, cucumbers, stuff like that. Are you—"

Just then someone's loud indignation interrupts our conversation. It comes from the table next to ours. "He didn't text? Like all night?"

My back is to the sophomores. But Kiki can see them. "Now," she whispers. "Just listen. They're ridiculous."

"No! I sent him like thirty texts! I even called him, but it went right to voicemail."

"God, Emma, what are you gonna do?"

"If you dump Hunter, I get dibs. He's so hot!"

"Maybe he hooked up with someone at Josh's."

"It was only the team! And their parents."

"Well, what did he say today?"

"He wouldn't explain. Said he just decided to go home."

"Yeah, right. Face it, Emma, he's not that into you. Or he's got someone else and he's too chickenshit to admit it."

"He must. Like what, he can't answer texts from home? You're screwed, Emma."

"As if. I'm sick of his shit anyway. It's not like I would marry him. I mean, God, he doesn't even have a car. I was just using him for his bod. And like his status."

"So it's cancel time?"

"Not yet. I want to make him suffer first."

"You know, I've seen him around with that new girl. In the hoodie? You know, 'Half-moon Face'? You think they're doing it?"

"Oh, my God, be serious. I mean, have you seen her?"

The color drains out of Kiki's face. And it all flows into mine so that it must look like a full moon.

A blood moon.

I get up and run out of the cafeteria.

50

HUNTER

It takes me way over the allotted time to finish my English test. Mrs. Laurence is chill with me staying into lunch, though. She says she'd rather have us take our time thinking about the questions than rush through to finish in an hour.

I'm walking to the cafeteria when I see Luna running toward me, her head down. I stop. "Hey! Where are you headed?"

She looks up at me then quickly drops her head again and keeps running. In that brief second, I see her tears.

"Luna? What's wrong?" She's all the way down the hall and doesn't stop.

"Luna! Wait!" Kiki comes flying out of the cafeteria. She sees me and stops. "You should tell Emma that Luna has more brains and class than she ever will." She takes off running. "Luna!"

What the hell?

I jog to catch up with Kiki. "What are you talking about? What's wrong with Luna?"

She stops again, her eyes blazing. "I really doubt she wants to see you now. Go deal with your stupid, loser girlfriend."

I have no idea what has just happened, but I've never heard a mean word come from Kiki before.

I barge into the cafeteria. I desperately need to eat, but I have to find Emma first. She's sitting at a table with her friends.

"Emma, what is going on?"

She's on her phone and ignores me.

"*Emma!*" I try not to sound as angry as I am, because she loves the melodrama. She's probably filming me right now. She looks up, all innocent.

"Oh, it's the mighty Hunter! Be still, my beating heart and throbbing loins!"

Her sarcasm sends her friends into stupid giggles. "What's your deal, Emma?"

"I should ask you the same thing, Hunter." She is mad. Like really mad. "Sit down. *Now* you have time for me?"

"What are you . . . wait, are you *still* talking about that? I told you. I. Went. Home." I yank out a chair and sit.

She twirls a piece of hair around her finger. "You're not eating? You usually have about three servings of the crap they serve in here."

"What happened with Luna?"

Emma furrows her eyebrows. "Who?"

"Luna Lemieux. She's a junior. Did she . . . I mean, did you or one of your—?" I'm not sure what to ask.

Emma's still looking at me. "Luna Lemieux? I'm not sure I know her. What does she look like?" She smiles at her friends.

"I don't know; I mean, she's like tiny. Blondish light brown hair. And she wears a hoodie a lot."

"Hmm," Emma says. "That's not very descriptive. That could be a lot of girls in this school. Does she have . . . um, any *distinguishing characteristics*?"

Her friends burst out laughing, like they can't hold it in any longer. "Oh, my God, Emma! You are so bad!"

It hits me, hard. She knows exactly who Luna is. Why the hell is she stringing me along? What is Emma's problem with her? They don't have any classes or anything together.

"I don't know what kind of game you're playing, but I'm not amused. You know who she is. What happened?"

Emma stops smiling. "I don't know, Hunter. Why don't you tell me?"

"What?"

"Tell me what happened. The other night? When we were supposed to get together after Josh's party? And you decided to, quote, 'go home'? Like I'm gonna believe that."

Suddenly I am so tired. "Whatever, Emma. It's true. I went home. And turned off my phone. Sorry."

"You are such a dick, Hunter. Just man up and tell me the truth. You were with her, weren't you?"

"What? With her? With who?"

"Half-moon Face! Everybody's seen you with her! Just admit it!"

I stand up, furious. "*That's* what you call her? I . . . I can't believe . . . how do—?" I stare at her perfect face, one that used to drive me wild. One that I couldn't get enough of. And then I look at her friends, who've been watching this like it's frickin' Wimbledon. And yes, two have their phones out, filming the drama. "Does that make you feel cool? Beautiful? Popular? Mocking someone who is maybe not as cool or beautiful or popular as you?"

"Chill out, Hunter. We're just kidding. Having a little fun."

I shove in my chair. "Fun? It's not *fun*. It's mean. I'm done here." I look at her smirking face. "In fact, *we're* done. Don't text me."

"Don't worry," she shoots back. "I wouldn't waste my time. I can do way better than the kid of the town drunk. With a surprisingly small dick."

I storm out, the gasps and laughter loud behind me.

The dick comment doesn't hurt.

But the one about my dad does.

A lot.

I need to find Luna. I race into the library. No one there but Mrs. Moss, cutting into a piece of quiche. She smiles. "Boys are in the back room, as usual," she says. "This must be some science project!"

I start to leave, and then stop. I am as furious with Pierce as I am with Emma. I might as well confront him too.

Without knocking, I barge into the room. Pierce and his minions again, with more junk food and stupid smiles. Pierce doesn't seem fazed at all by my abrupt entry. "We knew you'd be back," he sneers. "Eavesdropping can be as addictive as gambling or heroin."

"I didn't come to eavesdrop, asshole," I say.

"Well, what do you want then?" He stands up to face me.

"You told, didn't you? About Mr. D?"

"It may have gotten out," he admits. But he doesn't seem at all ashamed.

"That was a *secret*!" I hiss. "None of your fucking business!" I want to hit him. Pierce reaches up and deliberately pulls the sweatshirt from the vent. Which means anything we say will be heard in the faculty room. My hands are balled into fists, and the sweat is dripping down my back. Pierce turns back to me and dramatically puts his finger to his lips.

"Ludo, I'm not sure what more we can say. We didn't tell anyone, certainly not the students." It's Ms. Scott.

Mr. D's voice is angry. "I thought I could trust you!"

Ms. Eberhardt sounds just as mad. "You *can* trust us, Ludo. I promise we didn't say anything. I have no idea how it got out. It may have been just a dumb rumor that grew. But we've been your loyal friends for—"

She's interrupted by a loud knock. Mr. Winslow's voice booms through the vent. "Hey, ladies, hate to interrupt this little klatch, but I need to speak with Ludovic. So if you don't mind finishing your lunch somewhere else?"

Pierce and his friends are riveted. I make a conscious decision to stay. I need to hear this, especially if Mr. D is in trouble because of Pierce's big mouth.

"You get that information about the state tests I sent you?" It sounds like Mr. Winslow pulls out a chair and sits down.

"Yes. I didn't acknowledge it because they're not until May. But yes, I got it. Thanks for sending it."

"Okay then."

There's this weird silence.

"Ludovic, what the hell are you thinking?"

"I . . . I'm sorry?"

"Did you not hear me? Or did you not understand me? I said, what the hell are you thinking?"

"Uh, I haven't given them a lot of thought yet. Again, we don't administer them until May. Pretty standard routine. Uh, you are talking about the tests, right?"

"For a smart guy, Ludovic, you can be pretty obtuse. No, I'm not talking about the damned tests."

"Then what—?"

"I'm talking about your flaming wedding!"

The guys in the room have to cover their mouths to stop from exploding in laughter. I can barely contain my rage.

"*I beg your pardon?*"

"Do you have any idea how many emails and phone calls I've gotten over this? Do you?"

"My wedding? Emails about my *wedding*?"

"Parents are up in arms! Why did you tell your students?"

"For the record," Mr. D says, his teeth clenched, "I never told my students about my engagement. I told three teachers. That's it."

"So it is true. Well, the students know. It doesn't really matter how, now, does it? The problem is that it's a distraction. And now the parents are on my back. They want to know what the hell we're teaching the kids, why you're flaunting your *alternative lifestyle* in front of impressionable teenagers, how the administration can possibly endorse such inappropriate behavior, and why you haven't been fired."

"Fired? For what?"

"Did you not just hear what I said?" Mr. Winslow thunders.

"What did I do wrong?"

"Your personal life doesn't belong in the classroom! Ever! That's basic, standard Teaching 101. Are you stupid? Or are you trying to prove something?"

We hear paper crinkling, like it's being balled up. "I told you, I never said anything about my engagement in the classroom."

"Doesn't matter. It's apparently common knowledge now."

"Mr. Winslow, are you saying that nothing about us as people outside of school should ever be in school?"

"Of course that's what I'm saying!"

"So, in your office. Those pictures of you and your wife. Your dog. Your sons. Vacation at the beach. Skiing at Sugarloaf. Even a trip to Disney World. All on display for anyone coming into your office to see. Those seem pretty personal to me."

"My office is not a classroom," he responds in a steely voice.

"Fair enough. So I have another question: Did you give the same lecture to Miss Michaud before she became Mrs. Laurence? Because I seem to remember her class giving her an engagement party. And you were in attendance, if I recollect correctly."

"That's different."

"Oh? How so?"

"Don't play coy, Ludovic. It's totally different. Mrs. Laurence is married to a *man.*"

"Yeah, and I will be too."

We hear the scrape of a chair.

Then the door slams.

Pierce slowly replaces the sweatshirt. I can't even look at any of them as I storm out.

51
LUNA

I just want to go home. I hide in the girls' locker room and call Temmie. The minute she answers, I start crying again.

"Oh, honey, what's wrong?" Her voice is hot chocolate and a thick comforter. Lilacs and sunshine and soft music. Her voice is *home.*

I choke out what happened in the cafeteria. "Can I please come home?"

There's a long silence. Then I hear Temmie blowing her nose. "No, kiddo. You need to stay." She quietly hangs up.

The betrayal feels like an arrow in my heart. *Et tu, Temmie*?

I walk blindly to my next class. And I don't hear a thing my science teacher says. Or anyone, actually, for the rest of the day. I desperately want to curl up in my bed and never go out again, but to get there I would have to see Temmie.

It's only muscle memory that guides my boots to the church after school. I put on loud hip-hop music and move with it, angrily at first, then with more controlled grace. I feel the shame leave my body, glugging out like an upside-down jug of maple syrup. My heart stops racing, and I can finally breathe again. And forget how furious I am with those sophomore girls, with Temmie, with my mother, with everyone.

When I stop, it all comes back.

They're not wrong. 'Half-moon Face' is actually a perfect description. *Will this define me for life? Will I always be a huge, ugly birthmark with a body attached? Is that all people see?*

I am drenched with sweat. I slowly wrap up in layers to walk home. When I push open the outside door, I am startled by two figures standing there.

Kiki. And Hunter.

"There you are! Hey! Can we walk home with you?" Kiki asks.

"Don't bother." I put my head down and start walking. Fast. They catch up and move to either side of me. I feel like a perp between two cops.

"It's not a bother," she says. She sounds kind, not condescending.

I glance at Hunter. "Don't you have practice?"

Hunter shifts his backpack. "Yeah. I mean, I did. We finished."

"Whatever. At least it's dark, so no one will see you with me."

"What is that supposed to mean?" Hunter sounds pissed.

"Like I don't want to ruin your rep." I pull the strings tighter on my hoodie. "If it's too dark, just follow the moonlight coming from my face."

Kiki inhales sharply and Hunter grabs my arm. He's gentle, but he pulls me to a stop. "Luna, I am so sorry. She's a bitch who doesn't care about anyone. Except herself."

"She's your girlfriend!"

"Not anymore. I didn't know how mean she was. I guess that makes me a jerk too."

"Whatever. You guys don't have to walk me home. I'd kind of rather be alone."

"I get that," Kiki says. "But I really have to pee. Do you mind if I use your bathroom?"

"And I'm not leaving you alone," says Hunter, "because I know how much that sucks."

I think about his father hitting him. *I'm not the only one who's suffering.* "Whatever."

The bitter cold forces us to move again.

"On the way to the church," Kiki's quiet voice breaks the silence, "we were having an argument about superpowers. I say being able to fly would protect you more than invisibility."

"Nope," says Hunter; "no one can see you if you're invisible." He thinks for a second. "Okay, that was really dumb. Obviously, right? But I mean like if people were shooting at you or chasing you. You could totally escape. But if you were just flying to escape, you'd still be a target."

"I disagree," Kiki shoots back. "If you could fly, then you could attack from above and behind. And there wouldn't be constraints like roads or buildings or rivers."

"If you were invisible, you wouldn't have to attack from behind! You could attack from like this far away!"

Their banter distracts me and helps ease the swollen lump in my throat. At my house, Coop is sitting in his car in the driveway. "Hey, what's up?" He gets out. "Took you guys long enough. I'm starving!"

Are they expecting to come in? I'm sure Temmie doesn't have enough food for five people! This is awkward. And, anyway, I'm not speaking to Temmie.

Coop hops out of his car. I'm trying to think how to tell them to leave when Temmie opens the door. "Come on in. Hang your jackets on these hooks and put your backpacks over there. Wash your hands then come help yourselves." *What?*

Temmie has a big salad and a towering stack of cornbread on the counter next to a steaming pot of chili. *What on earth?*

It's all Coop can do to wait until everyone has a full plate before digging in. "This is incredible, Ms. Lemieux," he says. "Too bad you can't play cards as well as you cook!"

"Best of five right after dinner," Temmie retorts. "I wouldn't advise bragging too early."

Coop takes another hunk of corn bread and looks at me and Kiki. "You guys coming to our game tomorrow night?"

Before I can say no, Kiki looks at me. "Yes. We are. My dad and I are picking you up at seven o'clock."

Coop starts talking about basketball and the team, and then he segues into childhood tales about Hunter. I don't want to let myself relax. To be a part of this. But they're so natural and easy here, like they hang here all the time. Despite the dark cloud that's above my head, I get sucked into the fun. We end up laughing so hard my stomach hurts.

Coop refills his chili bowl. "Remember when you were grounded in the summer before sixth grade? You weren't allowed to leave the house. And we biked over and snuck you out and spent all day at Gordon's. We were so hungry, but we couldn't go inside 'cause then you'd be caught. So we ate about five pounds of blueberries out in his field. When your dad got home, he saw your purple teeth. Man, he was pissed!"

Hunter laughs. "And I was totally sunburned! So busted! God, we were idiots. How did we think we could get away with that?"

After dinner and several rounds of Castle, Coop drives Hunter and Kiki home. Temmie and I clean up in silence. I'm not quite as mad at her as I was earlier. "Thank you."

"You're welcome, kiddo." She puts the dish towel on the refrigerator handle. "I'm sorry it was a hard day. Again, I take responsibility for keeping you to myself for way too long. I just made it tougher for you now. But, honey, you can't run away." She grabs the broom and starts sweeping. "Like I did. By trying to protect you from cruelty. But cruelty's just a horrible fact of life."

I get the dustpan and sweep up her pile.

"Your mother ran away too. Guess we share a coward gene. That's going to end with you. Running away doesn't help. You got to stay and deal with the hard stuff."

"How did . . . did you . . . did they—?"

"Hunter asked me. Those are nice kids, Luna."

52

HUNTER

Gretchen wrenched her back shoveling snow, so I am riding around with her doing a bunch of errands. Sitting doesn't hurt it, but carrying stuff does. Our last stop is at the feed store. I lug a 50-lb bag of dogfood to the car and throw it in the trunk.

"Thanks so much, honey." Gretchen is like really grateful. "Seeing the food reminds me. I have one more errand if you have the time. Do you mind running into the vet's office to pick up Raven's medicine?"

We head out to the vet. Gretchen stays in the car while I run in. Shep is talking to Thaddeus's mother. He raises his eyebrows at me when I come in, but I wave him off. I can wait.

Jessica hears me enter. "Hunter! It's good to see you."

"Um, yeah, hi, Jessica. Um, how's Thaddeus?"

"Thanks for asking. Really. He's doing well. He's working here a lot now, thanks to Shep. In fact, Shep is teaching him to shear sheep."

I know nothing about shearing sheep. Except that it's hard to do. "Wow! That's impressive."

"You here for Raven's medication?" Shep asks.

"Yes. Please."

"It's out back. If you don't mind, Jessica, I'm going to start mixing it. It takes about ten minutes in the centrifuge. I'll be right back." She smiles and waves him out.

"When is the season for sheep shearing?" I ask. "I assume it's in the spring or early summer when it's warmer?"

"That's what I would have thought too," Jessica says. "But I've done quite a bit of research. And I learned that shearing ewes before they give birth is actually better for both mama and baby. It's far cleaner; wool absorbs water, manure, mud, and birth fluids, all of which can promote the growth of pathogens." She laughs. "I sound like a farming textbook. But it's interesting, right? Oh, I also learned that shearing ewes midpregnancy increases lamb birth weights. Perhaps because the mamas eat more to stay warm and therefore give more nutrition to their babies. Lambs can find the teat more easily on shorn sheep, and the quality of the wool is higher if cut before the ewe gives birth. So he's already doing it, even though it's still so cold."

Shep returns. "It'll be ready shortly."

Jessica looks at Shep. "Hunter and I were just talking about shearing sheep," she explains. "I have a question. What do you do with the wool?"

"I just give it to a guy north of here. He comes every two weeks or so with his pickup."

"You don't sell it?"

"No. I probably should. Especially as our flock gets bigger and bigger."

"Interesting. That's a potential business opportunity. What does it take to make wool into yarn?"

"That's not in my bailiwick. But I know it's fairly involved. Cleaning, boiling, carding, spinning, dyeing. You need a lot of room. And the know-how." He looks away for a minute and then over to me. "You know, I've been thinking about that project. The one you kids are doing for Teo. And I was going to ask Ludo if he'd be interested in the wool. Like if he could find people to process it. Once those sweaters sell, people could knit their own from wool grown and processed in Maine."

Whoa! This could be awesome. Jessica claps her hands together. "That's exactly what I was thinking! The yarn would be authentic, made in Maine, but not nearly as expensive as a sweater. Would you be willing to sell the wool to us? What about that guy in the pickup? What does he do with the wool?"

"I'd probably have to give him first rights. I think he's been using it to make throw rugs. But he's a good guy and would be open to negotiating. And the way these sheep are reproducing, there's plenty of wool for the both of you. But again, it's quite an operation. Where would you process it? If you were doing this commercially, you'd need space. And equipment."

Jessica ponders this. "The only place I can think of is that huge, empty mill. Do you think if I hired that guy—what's his name, anyway?"

"Gustav. Gustav Olafsson."

"If I hired Gustav as a consultant, would he be willing to teach a bunch of former mill workers how to turn wool into yarn?"

"Uh, you're getting ahead of yourself. I can arrange for you to talk with Gustav. Sure. But as to refurbishing the mill? That's a can of worms. The toxins in that place are scary. You'd need major environmental rehab before occupying it, and even things like using the water would require serious research. I'd suggest meeting with the owners before even thinking about using it."

Jessica seems undeterred. "Please ask Gustav to contact me." She turns to me. "Would you be willing to sit in on a meeting with me and Gustav? And any of your friends who are doing the project?"

"I . . . sure."

She's on a roll. "And it just occurred to me: I have a client who's been itching for a new investment opportunity. Wants something new and different. And meaningful. This could be it!"

I get the feeling that Jessica is the kind of person who gets things done. She starts to leave and then turns back. "Oh, my goodness, I almost forgot. I understand that congratulations are in order! Thaddeus kept saying 'Shep wedding' the other night."

He smiles again. "Thank you. I'd be honored if you and Thaddeus could be there. It's going to be tiny. In the church. One o'clock on Monday, March 20. Intentionally on the vernal equinox. Very informal, intimate. And a little reception back here afterward."

Jessica leaves, a huge smile on her face. I look at Shep. "Um, yeah, congratulations. We, um, we really like Mr. D." My face is hot as I say it. Because Mr. D probably thinks that Luna and I blew his cover. That we're immature adolescents who lied and can't keep a secret.

Shep smiles. "Thanks, Hunter. I do too. And I'm proud of all you guys are doing to honor Teo." He gets Raven's medicine and I leave. Ashamed, even though I didn't tell. But I know who did, and I couldn't stop him.

53
LUNA

Saturdays are usually chill. After Temmie and I do a bunch of cleaning and laundry and filling the woodbin or whatever, the afternoons are mine. No obligations, nowhere to go. It sounds kind of geeky, but I love to just hang in the living room next to the woodstove and read. Novels. Sometimes Temmie joins me, and we trade books. And talk about them, like our own two-person book club. Lately, though, she's spent every free moment working on her sweater.

That's exactly what we're doing, snuggled under quilts with mugs of hot chocolate, when there's a knock at the door. Temmie and I look at each other, like I-am-so-cozy-right-now-so-will-you-please-answer-it? I know, given Temmie's knees, that it's easier for me to get up. I sigh, throw back the comforter, and answer the door.

It's Hunter. "Hey, Luna!"

"Um, hi?"

"My Aunt Gretchen and I were wondering if you and your aunt could join us. On a little hike."

"Um, now?"

"Yeah. Before it gets too dark. I mean, it's fine if you don't want to. Like we didn't give you any notice."

Temmie comes to the door. "We would love to join you, Hunter, as long as it's not too strenuous for a middle-aged woman with bum knees."

Really? She just decides for me? Like I'm a toddler with no voice of my own? Before I can protest, Hunter smiles. Like he's really happy. *Whatever.*

We bundle up and sit in the back seat of his aunt's Volkswagen. Surprisingly, given how small this town is, Temmie and Gretchen don't know each other. But they know a lot of people in common. Soon they are chatting away like old friends. Hunter and I don't really say anything. I wonder whose idea this was?

Gretchen looks in the rearview mirror at me and Temmie. "Have you two ever been to the CDG?"

I have no idea what's she's talking about. Temmie slowly shakes her head, like she's unsure. "I remember my little sister talking about going there," she says. "But I never did. And I don't remember what or where it was. Or what CDG stood for."

Hunter grins. "Car Demolition Garage."

Gretchen laughs. "Uh, no. Hunter's never been there either. I'm keeping it a secret."

Temmie guesses. "Chinese Dumpling Gourmet."

"Cave Diving Grotto." I love playing with words.

Temmie adds another. "Charles de Gaulle."

Hunter won't be outdone. "City Dump of Garbage."

Gretchen swats his arm. "Really, Hunter? I would take you and your friends to hike at the city dump? Okay, stop guessing. And tell Luna and Temmie about your conversation with Shep and Jessica the other day."

So Hunter tells us about the wool. He asks if I'll join him at the meeting with Gustav. With maybe a few other people from our class. It sounds intriguing.

"I'll ask Jessica to talk to the knitters about it," says Temmie. "Wouldn't it be neat to use yarn made from the wool of local sheep?"

Gretchen turns off the road into a tiny parking lot marked only with a crude wooden trailhead sign. "We're here. When we get close, I'm going to ask you to close your eyes. I promise it's safe; you won't fall off a cliff or anything."

We slowly climb the icy path. Temmie is tough; she doesn't complain at all, even though the trail is kind of steep. In about fifteen minutes, Gretchen stops. "Okay. Hold each other's hands and close your eyes. I'll take Hunter's hand." She leads us down a slight incline. I want to peek, but I don't.

"Okay. Open them. Ta-da!"

In front of us is what I can only describe as an ice castle. A massive, gleaming, towering ice castle. I've never seen anything like it. And, from the expressions of awe on their faces, neither have Temmie and Hunter.

Gretchen laughs. "It's something, isn't it? My father first showed it to me when I was a little girl. Your grandfather," she says to Hunter, "told me it was a castle just for princesses like me. It's called Chateau de Glace. In summer it's a huge waterfall. But hardly anyone knows about it because it's so tucked away, off the beaten path."

Hunter and I hike down into it. Temmie doesn't trust her knees, so she stays with Gretchen. Hunter laughs. "I keep thinking of that movie, *Frozen*."

He belts out two lines. "Let it go, let it go! Can't hold it back anymore! Let the storm rage on, the cold never bothered me anyway."

"Good thing you play basketball," I tease.

"Ouch! Just ouch!"

I wish I could spend an entire day here. Dancing.

By the time we get back to the trailhead, it's dark.

Gretchen turns to Temmie. "I told my brother that I was feeding Hunter tonight," she says. "Would you like to join us? It's just chicken and rice, nothing fancy. But we'd love the company."

Temmie looks at me. "Luna? What's your homework load like?"

It's Saturday night. What she's really asking is, do I want to eat with them? I appreciate it. "It's under control. I think I have time."

"Oh, good!" declares Gretchen. On the way back she points out what looks like an old shack. "In a month or so, the sap will start running. If you're up for it, we can come out here and watch them make maple syrup."

Ten minutes later, Hunter turns around. "Would you be up for walking the last mile with me, Luna?"

Um, what? "I guess?"

Gretchen pulls over. "His motive is obvious. If you walk slowly enough, dinner will be ready by the time you get to my house."

Hunter laughs. "You know me too well, Gretchen."

We get out, and Temmie and Gretchen drive on. Hunter immediately apologizes. "Sorry, that was weird. Of me, I mean. I just wanted to get you alone. Where our voices don't echo and our aunts can't hear us. To ask you about Mr. D."

We start walking. "What about him?"

"Did you hear that he's getting married?"

"He is? That's awesome!" Hunter doesn't say anything. "Isn't it? I mean, when we heard him in the library, it sounded like that's what he wanted."

Then Hunter tells me about the study room in the library. And about Pierce and his friends spying on the faculty room. And telling the school about Mr. D. And Mr. D getting yelled at by Mr. Winslow.

Oh, my God.

"I'm not sure what to do," he says. "I feel awful that Mr. D thinks those other teachers blabbed, when it was Pierce or one of his friends. I told them not to say anything, but they don't give a shit what I think."

He's really struggling. Maybe he just needs a sounding board. He only chose me because we heard Mr. D on his phone.

"What do you think I should do?" Hunter asks.

"Honestly? I think you should let the main office know about the vent in the study room. So it can be fixed."

Oh, my God, I am such a hypocrite! I've never told Pastor Mark that I've overheard his conversations.

"Yeah. I can do that. Even though Pierce and crew are gonna be pissed. And know it was me. Whatever. I can handle them. But should I tell Mr. D about it? To like restore his trust in Ms. Eberhardt and Ms. Scott and Mrs. Laurence?"

"That would be the noble thing to do. But you'd be throwing yourself under the bus. Because you were there too."

"God, it's so messed up. But you're right, I was. And I have to take responsibility for it. Maybe you could come with me?"

We are walking past the back of Ms. Callahan's house when Hunter grabs my arm and freezes. "Do you see that?"

"What?"

Hunter puts his glove to his lips. "Let's go around," he whispers. We creep to the front. In the living room window we can see Ms. Callahan, knitting. Hunter motions toward the woods and takes off, running. I follow him into the woods.

"What did you see?" I whisper.

"It looked like a prowler. Back by that huge pile of wood. Let's stay where we can hide behind the trees but get a little closer."

We plow through the deep snow in silence. Then we see it again. A shadowy figure close to her garage. A burglar? A murderer? A rapist? A voyeur? Hunter stops and I almost run into him. The pounding in my chest sounds as loud as a drum. We hear a steady clunking. Almost rhythmic.

"Up the hill," Hunter whispers. We get to the top and hide behind a cluster of trees. Someone wearing a face mask and a ton of winter clothing is moving from the pile to the garage wall, carrying something in their arms. Clunk. Then they go back to the pile.

"They're stacking wood," I whisper. They're efficient in their movements. It's almost mesmerizing to watch. Mound. Walk five steps. Lay wood. Return five steps. As we watch, the stacked wood grows in a neat wall. The snow is so high next to Ms. Callahan's windows that if she were looking out, she wouldn't see them.

Hunter kind of laughs. "I thought she was in danger! Do you think we should help?"

I remember the story of the elves and the shoemaker. It's a dumb comparison, but when the elves were discovered and thanked, they left. I think this person is working in secret on purpose. Just to help someone who needs it. "No," I say. "That would ruin it."

We sneak back out of the woods and run the rest of the way to Gretchen's house.

Feeling lucky to live in a town where people take care of each other.

54
HUNTER

Luna and I stay after class to talk with Mr. D. He doesn't have another class after ours, and we'll just get late passes to our next one.

"What's up, guys?" His voice is brisk, businesslike.

I have been dreading this all weekend. "Do you mind if I shut the door?"

"Uh, that's fine. I got it." Mr. D. closes it. There is a large glass window in the door; anyone can see in, but at least they won't be able to hear us.

Luna and I sit in desks in front of Mr. D's desk. He waits. My leg is bouncing up and down, keeping crazy time with the smashing beats of my heart. I take a deep breath. "Um, Mr. D, I have to confess something."

Mr. D, like, grimaces. "I think I know what you're going to say. And honestly, I don't blame you. It's human nature to want to share information. It was my fault. I exposed you to something personal, and then I asked you both to keep it a secret."

I jerk my head up. "Wait, you think it was us? Who told on you?"

Mr. D doesn't flinch. "Yes. I told only three colleagues, and they swear they didn't tell."

Luna jumps in. "Mr. D, we didn't tell. But we think we know who did. And that's why we're here."

Mr. D looks confused.

"This is embarrassing," I say, "because I should have come to you right away. But here's what happened. There were a bunch of people in the study room in the library, the one that's next to the faculty room. I didn't know it, but there's a heating vent or something; it's a pipe anyway, that's busted I guess, like the cover is off. And from that room you can hear everything in the faculty room."

"Oh, my."

"Yeah, so the other day, when you told Ms. Eberhardt and Ms. Scott and Mrs. Laurence about your engagement, a bunch of us who were in there heard. I told the guys not to say anything, that it was none of our business, but they ignored me. And then they heard . . . well, I was there too . . . Mr. Winslow getting all mad at you. About this. Mr. D, I am so sorry."

Instead of the anger I expected, there's, like, relief on his face. "Thank you for coming forward, Hunter. I know that can't have been easy. I appreciate knowing that my colleagues are still trustworthy." He straightens a pile of papers on his desk. "It doesn't really matter. I mean, it's out there, but could you tell me who else was in the study room?"

I look down. "I could," I say quietly, "but I won't. I gave my word that I wouldn't tell."

Mr. D nods. "I respect that. We will, however, need to get that vent fixed. I'll let them know at the front office. You may be summoned to show the maintenance staff exactly where it's broken." He scribbles something on a sticky note. "In the meantime, I'll ask Mrs. Moss to keep kids out of that room. Was there . . . was there anything else?"

Luna and I stand. And then we both kind of say at the same time, "We're really happy for you, Mr. D." Or something like that.

He smiles. "Thank you. I am too. I just wish it didn't cause such a ruckus. Just ridiculous. Here, take these late passes. And again, thank you for your honesty."

Luna and I stand in the hall for a minute before heading off to our separate classes. I feel better. Not great, but better. But she looks even more stressed out. "You okay?"

She shakes her head. "Not really. I have to . . . I mean, you had the courage to . . . like I should— "

She's interrupted by the door to the women's restroom swinging open. Emma and Sable come out, laughing. And then they see us.

Luna takes off running down the hall.

55
LUNA

Sitting in Mr. D's room with Hunter was practically unbearable. Not because it was hard watching him confess his guilt. And understanding that his keeping quiet hurt several people. What was hard was knowing that I should have told Pastor Mark a long time ago that I was basically doing the same thing. Eavesdropping on conversations that were none of my business. I'm just as guilty as Hunter, but I've been too scared and weak to admit it.

I ask Mrs. Pugh if I can talk to Pastor Mark today before I dance.

"You most certainly can," she says. "Just have a seat right here in my office. He's with someone now, but he should be out soon."

I sit down. The phone rings. Mrs. Pugh answers it cheerfully. As she listens, she nods her head. "Yes, Marie, yes. Well, I thank you for letting me know. I do keep a sharp eye on that room. And we can only hope that it's bringing a little bit of relief or joy to people in any way it can." She looks at me and winks. "All right. Well, you do the same. And bundle up tonight. It's supposed to go way below zero. I know. Well, at least the light's coming back. Blessings to you and Tom. Bye-bye now."

She hangs up and gives me an amused smile. "Apparently there are rumors floating about that someone, or maybe it's more than one person, is taking stuff from the Free Room and selling it online." She laughs. "Technically, they are getting use out of it. Just indirectly. I'm not too worried about it. Desperate times, right?"

She stands up and walks over to Pastor Mark's door. She puts her ear up next to it. The irony is not lost on me. "It sounds like they're finishing up. He's in there with Sky Patterson. Do you know her?"

I shake my head.

"She's the town manager. Very popular and effective. They meet about once every two months just to discuss town issues and concerns. Oh, I don't envy her. Such a tough year it's been. Straining everyone's resources and patience. I know she's struggling. Budget restraints have cut some vital town services. Everybody's suffering. It's just awful, isn't it?"

I nod. Just then the door opens. Pastor Mark sees me sitting in Mrs. Pugh's office. "Oh, Luna! Sky and I were just talking about the Teo Legacy Project. Sky, Luna here is one of the leaders of the project. She's in Ludovic Deboncoeur's class."

Sky shakes my hand. "You guys are doing great work. Getting our kiddos into a pool is fantastic. But it sounds like it's morphing into something bigger. How can I be of help?"

I am taken off guard. "I . . . I . . . I don't—"

Pastor Mark jumps in. "I just had an idea. Actually, it's an idea I've heard from several people, including Ludovic. How well do you know the mill owners?"

"Well enough to hope they rot in hell," Sky says. "Oh, wait, I'm talking to a pastor. Sorry. I can't believe that popped out of my mouth."

Pastor Mark is unfazed. "I've heard worse. Sky, you've got clout. Do you think you could get them to come to a meeting? Not necessarily in person. We could do it virtually."

"I could try. You'd owe me big time."

"How about I pray for your soul, Sky?" Pastor Mark sounds like he's joking.

She laughs. "Way too late for that!"

"All right." He glances at me. "I know Luna's waiting. Any last items on your agenda?"

She looks at me and holds up one finger. "I'm going to steal two more minutes. Then he's all yours." She turns back to Pastor Mark. "What do you know about the Sunset Samaritan?"

"Who?"

"Someone is going around to people's houses, apparently at night, and doing stuff. Like good stuff. Shoveling driveways. Clearing snow off cars. Even big stuff like fixing fences and clearing and hauling brush."

"Interesting. And you're sure no one has hired her? Or him? You know, to do these projects?"

"Positive."

I think of what Hunter and I saw on Saturday night.

Pastor Mark rubs his hands together. "It sounds like I have a ready-made sermon, eh? Very inspiring. Okay, that's it?"

"Yep." She puts on her jacket and pulls a hat out of the pocket. "Oh, I am so sick of winter!" She reaches the door. "Oh, one last little thing. Always got my ear to the ground. Just wondering if you've thought through the idea of hosting and officiating a . . . a . . . nontraditional wedding?"

"No need for the obfuscation, Sky," Pastor Mark says quietly. "I deserve more respect than that."

"You're right. My apologies. I just wonder if you've heard the rumblings."

"No, I haven't. And frankly, I have little patience for gossip. If people have a problem with my marrying two men, they need to come to me. Otherwise, they're just gutless cowards."

"Don't shoot the messenger, Mark."

"Don't be the fertilizer, Sky."

She leaves without another word.

And I've just heard yet another conversation not meant for me.

Pastor Mark shakes off his frustrated look and beckons me in. He asks, "Door open or closed?"

I shrug. "Open is fine. I just have to tell you something that I should have told you a long time ago."

We hear Mrs. Pugh on the phone again. Murmuring. Laughing.

"I sometimes hear you," I blurt out. "When I'm changing. In that little room next to the sanctuary. And I don't mean to be nosy, but there's a pipe or something that magnifies your voice. And I'm so sorry."

"Thank you for telling me, Luna," he says, seriously. "I will check it out. Was there . . . has any conversation made you feel uncomfortable?"

"No, not really. But they're not my business. And I try to change quickly and put my earbuds in and crank the music, but sometimes I'm not fast enough."

"I trust," Pastor Mark says, "that you are discreet. But I'll get it fixed. And while I have you in here, do you mind giving me an update on this Teo project?"

I do. And he listens, carefully and thoughtfully.

My dancing today is lighter than it's been in a long time.

56
HUNTER

I want Dad to come to the state semifinal game. Like actually be in the gym, not the bar. So ten days ago I summoned up the nerve to ask him. I even made him quesadillas with cheese and ground pork, which he loves. When he was finished, I cleared his plate and brought him a dish of ice cream.

"Dad, I have a favor to ask," I started. "Um, you know the state semifinal is coming up, right?"

"Sure do. You guys are on a winning streak. I think you can go all the way this year."

"Yeah. So like it would be cool to have you there. In the stands." Before he could say no, I barged on. "Would you be able to maybe, um, stop drinking to do that?"

He stopped eating. Put the spoon down. "You sure you want me there? I thought I embarrassed you."

"Yeah, Dad, I do. I really want you there. We've always been a team."

He didn't say anything for a while. My heart sank. I knew it was a risk. And for whatever reason, he's relying on alcohol to get by. Finally, he stood up and shook his head.

"Well, I don't want to break up the team."

"Wait, does that mean that you'll—"

He reached out and put his hand on my shoulder. "Yes. I'll be there. Stone-cold sober. No more booze."

And he's kept his word. I am so stoked.

He's still been going out in the evenings, but when he gets home, he's not wasted. I don't ask anymore. I'm just so glad to have my dad back.

On Friday after school, I race home. Dad's there waiting. He makes me a bacon and lettuce and mayonnaise sandwich, my traditional lucky pregame meal. We talk about the guys we're playing. He knows a lot about their team, I'm not sure how. Especially because they're from southern Maine, near Portland.

"You sound like a scout! How did you get all this info?"

"Aw, it's easy to follow teams online now. I watched them in the quarterfinal match. The game was on that sports affiliate out of Portland. And some outfit livestreamed it. They're impressive, but they have their weaknesses. For example, they have this tall kid at center who's effective down under, but he's slow getting back on defense.

"You guys need to press. They've had trouble breaking it. By the time they've figured it out, their coach will have used up a time-out, and you could probably score six, eight points off it. And they have two guards who can shoot threes. Man-to-man defense is gonna work a lot better on them than zone."

He knows so much about the game. I love listening to his analysis. "You ever think about becoming a commentator? Like for high school or college games?"

"Naw. I don't have the right look. Or smarts. I'm just a mill kind of guy."

"Actually, Dad, you know more than most people. You should look into it. You'd be awesome."

"What time you need to be there?"

"Coach wants us there by six."

"Go get ready. I'll drive you."

Coop was going to pick me up, but I don't want to ruin this. I text Coop. *Got a ride c u there.*

Cars are already filling the parking lot when Dad pulls in. This is a big deal, this game. Especially when there's so little to get excited about in Edgewater.

Dad comes inside with me. He wants to watch warm-ups. A bunch of parents are waiting in the huge foyer, anxious to get in early too. Josh's father calls my dad over. When I go in the locker room, Dad is in the middle of a pack of men whose sons are on the team. And they're shaking hands, talking, laughing. A wave of emotion comes over me. *This is how it used to be.* I am so proud of him.

We hear it during warm-ups. It's subtle, and hard to distinguish over the very large, very loud, very excited crowd. But it's there. A low mooing sound. And it's coming from guys on the other team, who have fancy haircuts and the latest and most expensive Jordans. We look shabby in comparison. Like our skin and teeth aren't perfect, and there's no way we could afford the same shoes. But mooing? Really?

It starts to piss us off. Nate's face is red, like he wants to haul off and hit someone. Coop isn't joking around, like he usually does before a game to get everyone to relax. Coach senses our tension. He calls us off the court early. We hustle into the locker room and gather on the benches.

"Care to tell me what's wrong?" He's too nervous to stand still. He paces.

"They're making, like, barn noises."

"Bunch of preppy assholes."

"Fuckin' Citiots. Think they're better'n us."

Coach stops pacing. "Oh, did they *hurt your feelings*?" He puts one foot on a chair and leans toward us. "Look, I don't care where they're from or how much money they have. Only *you* have the power over you. If you let them get to you, we're going to get blown out. 'Cause they're a damn good team.

"But so are we. I need you out there, 100 percent, focused only on basketball. That's it. Bas-ket-ball. If you hear the sheep or pig or cow or whatever noises, ignore them. Don't react. Because that's what they want. To rattle you. If I hear one of you respond in any way, you're sitting. Got it? The only response you're gonna give? Ball in the hoop and fierce defense. You in?"

It's exactly what we need.

From the tip-off, we are on fire. A tight, coordinated, well-oiled machine. Our passes are sharp, and we're only taking clean shots. And we have like a preternatural ability to anticipate their passes. We steal the ball four times in the first quarter.

Just as Dad predicted, it takes them several tries to break our press. I can tell they are surprised. In their frustration, they get rougher, especially under the basket. And at the foul line, they talk. Like out of the sides of their mouths, so the refs don't hear it. But we do. "What do you do for fun around here? Go cow tipping? Or worse? You stick it in the cows? Can't tell the difference between girls and cows here, huh? They kind of the same?"

It's hard not to answer. Really hard. But we want to win worse.

We force turnovers. Sink threes. Block shots. Our defense shuts them down. Our offense stuns them. It even stuns us. I am in the zone; I make almost every shot I take. After one long three that sinks without touching the rim, I glance into the bleachers. And there's Dad, surrounded by a crowd of parents pounding his back, giving him high fives.

By the fourth quarter, they've stopped taunting. I think they assumed they'd crush us, and they're not sure how we got up by fifteen points. They get desperate, chucking up threes from way too far out, committing stupid fouls, overthrowing passes in their panic.

We blow them out, 76—59. I have twenty-four points, my all-time high, ten rebounds, and twelve assists. After the game, a reporter wants to interview me. I thought he was from the *Portland Press Herald*, but he's from television. Not the little regional channel that they were watching in the bar, but the biggest one in Maine, out of Portland. He sets me up in the middle of the gym floor. A crowd gathers around me, people screaming and cheering. The camera guy shines a bright light on me, and the interview begins. I have trouble hearing because the gym is rocking.

"Hunter Ridley, a junior on Edgewater's team, had the game of his life tonight. A triple-double, a feat rarely achieved at the high school level, especially in tournament play. Hunter, what happened out there?"

"We were really stoked for this game," I say. "Everyone was like in sync. Passing, shooting, defense, everything. We fought hard. Coach did a great job getting us ready for it. But credit goes to their team too. They were tough out there. Made us work to win."

"Your coach told me that this was the best game you've ever had. What inspired that?"

Suddenly I am overcome with emotion. "My dad," I choke out. "He taught me to play when I was about three. He's been my inspiration my whole life."

The reporter eats it up. "Where's Hunter's dad? Get him over here!"

Someone pushes my dad forward. There are tears in his eyes. He holds his arms out, and suddenly they are wrapped tightly around me. The crowd goes insane. The applause is so loud that I can't hear the reporter's next question. He understands and just yells, "Congratulations to Hunter Ridley and the whole Edgewater team! Good luck in the championship! And I wish we all had such great fathers!"

My chest fills with this intense love, for my dad, for our team, for the fans, for the game of basketball.

This was probably the best day of my life.

57
LUNA

"Please tell me you're kidding," Hunter says. "You've seriously never been to Molly's?"

"I . . . I mean, I've had food from Molly's."

"But you've never stepped foot in there?"

"Nope."

"How can you have lived here all your life and never been in Molly's?" I realize he's teasing me, but it's kind of a crappy reminder of how people who look like him have no clue what it's like to look like me. He's not being deliberately mean; he's just oblivious.

"I know you're just joking, Hunter, but this is hard for me. I hate being in public. Where you know, people can see my face."

He stops smiling. "Oh. I am so sorry. I'm an insensitive idiot." He holds the door open for me, but I make him go in first. We sit at a table in the back to wait for Jessica. "I . . . I . . . I forgot about the birthmark. Like I don't see it anymore." His face turns red. "Wait, I don't mean that I don't see you, but it's not the thing that I notice. I mean, I notice—"

He's so tangled up that I have to stop him.

"What's good here? Temmie's brought home soup and bread. And once she got a carrot cake. But that's all I've tasted."

We order lattes and cinnamon rolls. An expensive splurge, one that I'm trying not to feel guilty about. We are still sipping the drinks when Jessica arrives. Hunter introduces me.

"Oh, thanks, but I know Luna from the knitting group. How's Temmie's sweater coming?"

"She's three-quarters of the way finished," I say. "She's taking this really seriously."

"That's fantastic. Those women are so impressive. I finally gave up on learning," Jessica laughs. "My brain isn't wired that way. Do either of you knit?"

We shake our heads. Jessica sits down and pulls out a laptop. "I've never met this guy, but Shep vouches for him. His name is Gustav Olafsson. I promised that I would buy him coffee. He said he only drinks it the Swedish way, black with sugar cubes on the side. I checked with Samantha, and of course they don't have sugar cubes." She pauses dramatically and slowly extracts a box from her bag like a magician pulling a rabbit from a hat. "So I ordered some online. This meeting has to go well."

Samantha comes to our table with coffee and cinnamon rolls. Jessica puts several sugar cubes on the saucer.

A man enters, stamps the snow off his boots, and heads straight for our table. He is tall and lean and Black. Long dreadlocks wrapped in colorful bands give him the aura of a living rainbow. "Hello, Jessica?"

Jessica looks confused. "I'm sorry, I'm afraid we haven't met."

"I'm Gustav! Gustav Olafsson. The wool guy?" He laughs at her expression. "You were expecting Thor, weren't you?"

"Yes! I feel so silly. Please, sit down. Samantha's already brought your order. I took the liberty of adding one of Molly's cinnamon rolls."

"Oh, I don't eat sugar," he says, placing a sugar cube between his teeth and taking a sip of hot coffee. He winks at her. "Well, maybe this once."

"I have two student representatives with me," says Jessica. "They are integral to this project, which we'll tell you about. Hunter Ridley and Luna Lemieux."

He shakes our hands and winks at both of us. "An honor to meet dedicated young people."

Jessica asks me and Hunter to describe the Teo Legacy Project. Mr. Olafsson listens carefully and asks lots of questions, some of which we can't answer yet. Then Jessica asks him to tell us about his work, his background, his goals. He is not daunted by the broad scope of her question. And for the next hour, we are swept up in his world. Not only do we learn about the intricacies of processing wool, but we hear stories about cattle rustling, riding the rodeo circuit, back-country skiing, ice fishing, a hundred-mile snowshoe race, and on and on. He's very matter-of-fact; it never feels like he's bragging. His escapades remind me of a cat with nine lives. It's dark outside when Jessica gives a little start.

"Oh, my heavens, I didn't realize it was so late! I need to leave soon to pick up my son. But back to the wool processing. I'm going to cut right to the chase. Gustav, would you consider serving as a consultant and director of development, implementation, and management for a small operation here?"

"What exactly are you asking?"

"Well, I may be asking a few things. The first is this: Would you be willing to head a wool-to-yarn business in Edgewater? If not, would you consider serving as a consultant?"

"I would be willing to think about it. I'm all for supporting local economies. And I love the idea of sustaining this project beyond a year. Let's meet again in a week, here. You come up with the numbers. And all the details. And another one of those delicious cinnamon rolls."

58
HUNTER

Pierce and his minions are waiting for me at the main entrance when I get to school. "Hey, Ridley! Care to answer a question?"

Oh, God, here it goes. "What do you want, Pierce?"

"Why the hell is our room closed? It's like the Moss Mafia in there. She won't let us near it." They form a circle around me.

"Jesus, Pierce. Get out of my way."

"You told, didn't you? Your word is shit."

"Yeah? What about yours? I told you not to say anything. And now everyone knows about him. You have a frickin' big mouth. Now move."

He shoves me so I stagger back. "Why are you so protective of Mr. D? You got a thing for him? That why you and Emma broke up?"

"Oh, my God! You have no idea what you're talking about. Just move!"

He shoves me again. I can't get in a fight. As much as I'd love to shove him back, I can't. A suspension would mean getting kicked off the team. Just then Mr. D walks up. "There a problem here?"

"No, sir, Mr. D!" says Pierce, brightly. "Speak of the devil! We were just, um, discussing what to get you for a wedding present."

Mr. D doesn't say anything. But he also doesn't move until we've all gone inside.

I'm still pissed as I walk past the office on my way to class. So pissed that I am like mugged into attention when Ms. Cox yells at me down the hall. I turn. She waves me into the office. "My goodness, someone's sleepy this morning. I must have called your name five times!"

I shrug. I am definitely not sleepy. Just the opposite, actually. Like on high alert. "Sorry, Ms. Cox."

"No worries. Look, can you meet Mr. Gateaux here at the beginning of lunch? He's going to fix that pipe and needs you to show him exactly where it is."

Mr. Gateaux is waiting when I go to the office at lunch. His white hair and gaunt frame remind me of my grandfather, who died when I was eight. I offer to carry his tool kit, which he gives to me gladly. We walk to the library. Pierce and his friends are sitting at the table where Luna and I were. *Have they displaced her?* My bad mood only gets worse. Pierce gives me a murderous look.

Mr. Gateaux and I go in the study room and shut the door. I reach up, remove the ceiling tile, and show him the pipe. He's short and can't reach it without standing on the table. "You mind hanging here while I do this? It shouldn't take long. I need you to hand me my tools. And spot me. I don't have the balance I used to."

He pulls out the sweatshirt and immediately the sounds from the faculty room pour in.

"Gimme that wrench. The one with the red handle," Mr. Gateaux orders. He sways. My hands fly up to stop him from teetering off the table.

And then. Mr. Winslow's voice. "Ladies, I need a word with Ludovic. If you don't mind?" It's obvious, from the tone of his voice, that he doesn't give a shit if they mind or not. They'll have to leave. It's like déjà vu. Horrible déjà vu. *Are you kidding me? I do not want to hear this!* But I do. Because I'm stuck. Protecting Mr. Gateaux from falling.

"Got a minute?" Mr. Winslow's voice is tense.

"Again?" Mr. D's voice is subdued. "Why aren't we meeting in your office?"

"There's a water leak. Going on the second week. Anyway, I'll get straight to the point. Look, Ludovic, you're a decent teacher. But this year you've pushed the boundaries too far. First you changed the history curriculum to do some crazy fundraising thing, which technically I never approved."

"I am teaching both history and economics," Mr. D. says. "My students are learning more than ever before. And every single one of them is going to get an 80 or above on the history final. Guaranteed. And what you call 'crazy fundraising' is teaching them economics in a way they will never forget. They're doing something meaningful. And it's far more engaging than dry history lessons."

"Well, Ludovic, that's actually quite revealing. *Dry* history lessons? You admit it, then?"

"Admit what?"

"That your performance is subpar. We're not aiming for 'dry.' We're aiming for excellent. Interesting. Scintillating, even."

Mr. Gateaux bends down. "That sucker is stuck. I need more leverage. Hand me that long-handled wrench. Yeah, that one with the yellow tape on it."

Either our custodian is too focused on the repair to pay attention to the conversation in the faculty room or he's too classy to comment. But he's got to recognize how inappropriate this is. "Uh, Mr. Gateaux, I probably shouldn't be hearing this," I whisper.

He peers down at me. "Try whistling. And I'm working as fast as I can. But I need you to stay."

Mr. Winslow plows on. "There's a second thing, Ludovic. It's your inability to separate your private and professional life."

Oh, my God.

"Here you go." Mr. Gateaux hands me the wrench. "Now gimme that metal plate. And the Phillips screwdriver. And then those six screws." His head disappears into the ceiling again.

Mr. Winslow's voice is steely. "I have a petition, signed by the parents of many of your students, calling for your removal. I didn't instigate this, of course, but I can't ignore it. If your performance is negatively affecting students, parents, and the school community at large, I have no choice but to let you go."

"How many parents signed that?"

"Well, I haven't counted. But it's a significant number. Would you like to see it?"

"No. I wouldn't. I can't stand the idea of harboring unconscious bias against any student based on whose parent signed it."

"Bottom line is that it would be better for everyone if we parted ways," Mr. Winslow says. "I'll let you finish out the year. Obviously that's a probationary situation. If I find further probable cause, I will terminate you immediately. Essentially, you're already at strike two."

"That may be your bottom line," Mr. D says bitterly, "but this is mine: I am being unfairly penalized for (a) adding a meaningful new element to the established curriculum—without, mind you, taking anything away from it—and (b) having the audacity to get engaged."

Mr. Winslow cranks up his voice a notch. "Look, Ludovic, if I have reason not to renew your contract, then I don't renew your contract. Period. If you'd like to file a grievance or lawsuit, fine. Lawyer up. But this petition supports my decision."

"What . . . what am I supposed to do? This is the only high school within fifty miles. And my retirement? And health insurance? Are you offering any severance?"

"You're a year-to-year employee. Of course there's no severance. I'm sorry, Ludovic, but my hands are tied. You'll just have to figure it out. What's next, I mean."

I hear a chair crash to the ground. "Why don't you tell the truth? That I'm being fired for 'Teaching while Gay'? It's kind of like 'Driving while Black.' Or 'Leading while Female.'"

I pray Mr. Gateaux doesn't fall, because right now I am shaking so badly I couldn't catch him. *Mr. D fired? Because he's gay? And the Teo Legacy Project? Oh, my God.*

"That oughta hold," Mr. Gateaux says finally. He hands me the screwdriver. "Thanks for your help." He replaces the ceiling tile, then I help him down. He shakes his head. "That was some conversation, eh? More revealing about our leader than the teacher in question."

59
LUNA

Every day at lunch now, Coop and Hunter have asked me and Kiki to sit at their table with most of the basketball team. The only reason I agree is that I've promised Temmie I would stop hiding. And it's entertaining.

Today Nate holds up a package of Doritos. "Up for grabs," he calls out.

Three guys say, "Mine!" at the same time.

"Okay," says Nate. "Whoever can tell me the first three ingredients gets them. Coop, you start."

"Um, corn. And, um, oil. And salt."

"Close. You got the first two. Josh?"

"Wait, that's not fair! I did their heavy lifting!" Coop protests. "They're just riding my coattails!"

"If you'd gotten it right, you wouldn't think it was unfair, so shut up. Josh, go."

"Corn, oil, and spices."

"Spices? That's way too vague!"

"Am I right?"

"No, you're not right! Justin, you're up."

"I got this. Corn, oil, and cheese."

"Nobody wins. The third ingredient is maltodextrin." Nate rips open the bag and pulls out a chip. He closes his eyes and bites into it, like he's in rapture.

"Who the hell was gonna get that?"

Nate smiles like gleefully. "No one! That's why I did it."

Josh punches him on the arm. "Not cool, bro. Okay, unlike Mr. Maltodextrin, I have a contest that someone can actually win. For one of these cookies that my sisters made." He holds up a plastic baggie with three huge M&M cookies in it. He pulls out his phone. "Okay, I'm gonna play a song from a Broadway musical. Whoever guesses correctly first wins."

"You're kidding, right?"

"No! Come on, we need a little cultcha."

He scrolls through his phone for a minute. "Okay, got it. Here goes." It starts playing.

The guys kind of roll their eyes like they're never going to get it. Then Hunter shouts out, "'Popular'! From *Wicked*!"

Josh hands him a cookie. "Well done, dude."

"How on earth did you know that?"

Hunter is so proud of himself. "There's a lot about me that you don't know."

"Like when you're gonna put Pierce in his place?"

"Yeah, I saw him push you around yesterday. What the hell was that?"

Hunter's eyes darken, but he keeps his voice light. "I think he's jealous of me."

"Jealous of *you*?" Nate shouts. "Of what?"

"Obviously," says Hunter, "my knowledge of Broadway show tunes!"

Everybody laughs. Hunter gets up. "That cookie was awesome. But I need more food. Can I get anyone anything?"

"Naw, we're good."

Hunter weaves his way to the serving line.

School lunches are government subsidized, which means they're free for everyone, but they're not that good. People who can afford it bring their own from home. I've started eating the cafeteria food just to save Temmie a few dollars a day.

Coop picks up Hunter's milk carton. "It's only half gone. Let's spike it. Josh, pour some of your root beer in here. Hurry, before he gets back."

Hunter returns with a full plate of beef and noodles. Everyone watches him in silence, the laughter just an inch away from the surface. He looks around. "What?"

"Nothing, big guy. Just admiring you," smirks Coop.

Hunter turns to me and Kiki. "What did they do?"

Kiki smiles. "I'm sure that if you investigate, you'll get to the root of it."

Josh reaches over to high-five her. "Nice one!"

"I don't get it," says Hunter. He picks up his milk and takes a big gulp. The laughter explodes all around the table. Emma and her minions glare at us from across the cafeteria.

Hunter swallows then cries out like he's in agony, "Oh, my God! That was so gross! You guys know I can't stand root beer!" But he's laughing too. "Luna and Kiki, you gotta protect my stuff from these jerks."

So, yeah, eating with them is fun and funny and safe. I start noticing stuff that I obviously didn't when I spent lunchtime in the library. Like kids pocketing apples, granola bars, packets of nuts, to save for later, when there's not enough food at home. Or the cafeteria workers greeting students by name, wishing them a good day as they ladle slop into their bowls. And kids eating at the same table with the same kids every single day like there's some sort of divine assigned seating. Which I suppose is fun if you have friends. Not so much if you don't. I see those kids, ones like me, hiding behind open notebooks (the homework cover) or phones (the social cover) or books (the literary cover). They are braver than I was; I couldn't even face stepping foot in the cafeteria. I have so much empathy for them.

Which is why I invite Eliot to eat with us. I've noticed him sitting in the back by himself. He looks at the table of rowdy boys and shudders. "N-n-no thanks," he says. "I d-d-d-don't d-d-do well in b-b-b-big crowds."

So Kiki and I leave the team table to sit with Eliot. He seems both baffled by our presence and grateful for it. And the more we sit with him, the less he stutters.

Eliot, we quickly figure out, is brilliant. His knowledge of well, everything, from religion to geography to sports trivia, blows our minds. He must read all the time. And he has some pretty cool ideas of how we can expand the Teo Legacy Project into something more sustainable for the community. He's done tons of research into how to create a website, how to register a trademark, how to market a product, where the best craft fairs in Maine are, stuff like that.

We are mulling over our *Made in Maine* brand, wondering if it's original and catchy enough. "Wouldn't it be cool," Kiki muses, "if someday our brand and logo were recognizable? Like the golden arches? Or the Nike swoosh?" She thinks for a second. "What does 'Nike' even mean, anyhow?"

"D-do you know who Nike was?"

"Uh, no? Wait, wasn't he that guy who ran the first marathon in Greece to deliver a message and then fell over and died?" Kiki looks at Eliot earnestly.

"No, that was Phei-Phei-Pheidippides." Of course Eliot knows that. But he says it in a way that is nice, not snotty. "B-but you are so close.

Be-be-be-because supposedly when Pheidippides arrived in Athens, he said, 'Nike, Nike! Nenikekiam!' which m-m-means, 'Victory, victory! Rejoice! We conquer!' And Nike is the goddess of victory."

Kiki beams. "You are amazing, Eliot. It's really fun hanging out with you."

The tips of Eliot's ears turn red.

I know exactly how he feels.

* * *

Mr. D asked Teo's mom to come to our class today. She's wearing a visitor badge over a green fleece and seems less frail than she did just a couple weeks ago. She listens to Kiki's progress report, Eliot's research, and Gordon's latest count. She gives us an update on the lifeguard training at the clinic, classes in CPR, AED, first aid. Then she tells us about the fashion show.

"It would be really great if the whole class could participate," she says. "I realize that on a Saturday afternoon, some of you may have other commitments, like jobs. But we need as many of you as we can. If you're not actively modeling a particular sweater, you would be skating or sledding in the background."

"Where are we having this again?"

"Dude, she just said it. Wake up!"

Ms. Callahan laughs. "It's okay! I've thrown a lot of information at you. We are going to meet at Mallard Park at noon."

"I can't make it," says Talia. "I have to work."

"Me too," says one of Pierce's friends. "On my beauty sleep."

Ms. Callahan looks at Mr. D, who nods. She continues. "If the pond hasn't been cleared, we'll need you to shovel it. Could a few of you commit to that? Bring some shovels?"

Four hands go up.

"Fantastic. Then I just need to be sure we have enough skates and sleds."

A few kids volunteer theirs.

"The women from the knitting group are going to provide refreshments. Oh, I forgot. Can anyone bring a bunch of firewood? I think we should have a fire going."

Someone whose family has a pickup says she'll do it.

"That's all I have on my agenda. Please know how deeply grateful I am to all of you. Your kindness is extraordinary. I've . . . I've never been part of something like this." Her voice is filled with emotion.

"I have a question," Pierce says.

Oh, no.

Ms. Callahan waits.

Pierce looks at Mr. D. "For those of us who can't make it or don't want to, are we gonna, like, be penalized?"

Mr. D shakes his head. "Of course not, Pierce. This is strictly voluntary."

"Oh," says Pierce, sarcasm dripping from his mouth. "Just like the *economics* part of history class."

A weird chill passes through the room, like a cloud has just blocked the sun for a minute.

Mr. D ignores him. "Okay, that's it, then. Thank you so much for taking the time to visit, Bridget. You'll see a bunch of these students at the pond."

Near me, Pierce mutters under his breath, "Not gonna happen."

Is he going to sabotage this?

Pierce scares me.

60

HUNTER

The championship game, to be played in the neutral location of Northriver, is against Dunlap Junction. When I get home from school on the big day, Dad is waiting with my good-luck sandwich. But something's off. He's too loud, almost manic. "Now listen, you gotta be focused," he says. "They have trouble with man-to-man defense. Stick to 'em like Elmer's."

When he leans over me to pour milk in my glass, I smell it. *No, no, no, no, no! Are you kidding me?*

"*What the hell, Dad?*"

"Don't talk to your father that way."

"You promised!"

"You don't know what it's like. I had the shakes. Felt sick to my stomach. I'm fine. Just had enough to stop the damn shakes. Take the edge off."

What about me? You've always told me that of all the people in the whole world, you love me the most. You can't keep your promise to me?

Fury fills me. "You're not coming to the game like that," I say. "It's an hour to Northriver. No way are you driving."

"Since when have you told me what to do?" He's pissed. "I'll do what I damn well please. If I want to drive to the game, I'll drive to the game. It's the state championship, for God's sake."

Yeah, exactly. Unbelievable.

He lurches to the fridge to put the milk away. That's when I realize he's even worse than I thought. *Shit!* I run upstairs to grab my uniform and gym bag. I text Coop. *Need ride asap.* I hide in the bathroom, my heart trying to blast its way out of my chest and my stomach roiling. I rush to the toilet, and my pregame meal comes spewing out, an acidic geyser of despair. *I am not enough for him.*

"Hunter?" Dad calls from the stairs. "When are we leaving?"

I flush the toilet and brush the foul taste from my mouth. In the mirror I see a scared little boy with a red face and tears pooling in his eyes. I hear Coop pull up. I race downstairs.

"You ready?" Dad struggles to put his coat on. His right arm keeps flailing in the air as he misses the sleeve.

Oh, my God, I hate this. I hate this. It's the frickin' state championship! He and I have played this fantasy scenario over and over in the driveway for years. And he's not even gonna be there. I hate him so much right now.

"I'm going to school to catch the team bus." I yank the door open.

"Get in the truck." His eyes look like they did that night when Luna and I made cookies.

I turn away and swipe at my face. "Coach makes us ride on the bus, Dad. Always has. I . . . I . . . Coop's here. I gotta go."

He moves to block the door. "*I'm* driving you, you son of a bitch!" he yells. "Don't tell me what to do!"

Tears are pouring down my face. I shove him out of the way.

"That's no way to treat your father!" he roars.

I grab his keys from the hook and run to Coop's car. Coop sees the whole thing. He peels out without saying a word.

On the bus he sits next to me. And the whole way, he doesn't talk, which for Coop is highly unusual. He's just there. With me. I stare out the window and see nothing but my dad, fumbling to get his arm in his jacket.

The game is horrible. I play like shit. I miss an easy layup, I throw the ball away twice, and I pick up two stupid fouls. And that's all in the first six minutes. Coach benches me until I can "get my head in the game." My head is so far out of the game. I keep thinking of my dad, sitting alone in the house. Or walking to the bar. Our team does better when I'm not playing, but everyone seems off. We're sloppy, undisciplined, selfish, lazy. Not at all like we played in the semis. I go back in to relieve Justin, who usually subs for me, but I contribute little. It sucks. Dunlap Junction has many opportunities to clinch it, but they can't make their free throws. Probably nerves.

We end up winning, but it isn't pretty. It's almost embarrassing to come away with a win after that performance, especially for the state title. The celebration at the end of the game is subdued. Not as many Edgewater fans are there. And I think everyone in there knew we should have lost.

Josh is hosting a party for the team, but I'm not in the mood. I'm too worried about my dad. Coop drops me off before heading to Josh's. "Text me if you need me," he says.

"Thanks, man. And—" I don't really know what to say. Like how can I thank him for, for like everything? "Uh, just thanks."

"I got you, bro. And hey, we're state champs!"

"Yeah." My voice is flat. "See ya."

Weary and wary, I walk into our dark house. I flick on the lights. "Dad?"

I check his room, the bathroom, all the rooms downstairs. He's not here. I had his keys, so the truck is in the driveway. I call his phone.

No answer. Trying to stem my rising anxiety, I call the bar. *They know him. They'll take care of him.*

The woman who answers is weirdly evasive. She tells me to wait a minute. It's a long time before I hear the bartender's voice. "Hunter?"

I expect congratulations, maybe a reference to the one, maybe two, decent plays I had. But he doesn't even mention the game. "Look, Hunter, I put up with a lot of crap. But your father was out of control tonight. When I asked Finn to bring him home, your dad started hollering and carrying on like crazy. He punched Finn so hard he knocked him out."

"I . . . Jesus. I'm so sorry. Is Finn okay?"

"He has a wicked headache and a black eye. He'll survive. But listen, son, I'm getting tired of running a limo service. We've been a charity long enough."

My face is blazing with shame. "I know. I'm sorry. Um, where's my dad now?

"I had no choice but to call the cops. Before he KO'd a few more people. He's down at the station, cooling off."

I can't ask Coop again. He's at Josh's now, and I already turned his night to shit earlier. The police station is out near the highway, way too far to walk. It's almost midnight. For the hundredth time, I wish I had my license. But Dad has always said there's no need to pay a crapload on insurance for a teenage boy when he can drive me himself. Now what? Gretchen always turns off her ringer before she goes to bed. Who can I call at this hour?

And then I know. I put her number in my phone that first day. I scroll to find it. Hating myself, shaking, praying, I push 'Call.'

She picks up on the second ring. "Hunter?"

"Yeah. Um—"

"How can I help?"

"I am so sorry for bothering you," I say. And then I'm crying. And trying to explain, but my voice is hijacked by these heaving, hiccupping sobs. Like I'm five again.

"Hang on. I'm coming to your house. I'll be there in about seven minutes."

She arrives wearing a sweater and a jacket thrown over her nightgown. I must have gotten her out of bed.

"I'm sorry," I say. "I didn't know what to do."

"I had to get up to stoke the fire anyway. I never sleep more than a couple hours at a time. Now tell me everything."

So I do. And she listens. Without interrupting. Without judging.

"He promised he would stop," I say, still trembling. "And he did. And it was like in the old days before the stupid mill closed. And then, I don't know what happened, but he . . . he . . . I mean, it was the most important game of my life, and he . . . he . . ." I can't even finish because I'm crying again.

She takes me to the station. There's only one little cell. Dad is in it, sitting all alone in the middle of the floor. He looks so small and dejected, like a wounded puppy in one of Shep's cages. There's no more fight left in him. The cop on duty doesn't say much, probably because I'm just a scared kid. Or maybe because he's seen so much of this crap.

She drives us home in silence. I help Dad in. He stinks of beer and sweat and jail, but he's too wasted to stand up in the shower. I just take off his shoes and put him to bed.

She doesn't leave until she's sure I'm okay.

"I don't know how to thank—"

She cuts me off. "Hush," she says. "We take care of each other. I'm glad you called me."

"Thanks, Miz Callahan."

"You're a really special kid, Hunter." She walks back to her car and opens the door. "Call again if you need me."

I'm too shaken to sleep. So I watch an action movie. Stupid. Violent. Predictable. Every time the so-called hero has a fuckin' drink in his hand, I want to throw the remote through the screen.

I feel like an old man.

61
LUNA

Mrs. Pugh calls to me as I head to change into my dancing stuff. "Luna, do you mind helping me with one little thing before you dance?"

This has become a ritual, one I don't mind. I think either Mrs. Pugh is lonely and wants company or she thinks I'm lonely and wants to insert a little joy into my day. Whatever her motive, I usually help her do something every afternoon.

She is sitting at her desk wearing yellow rubber gloves. The cloth in her hand was once white, but now it's covered in black splotches. On the tray in front of her is a set of gleaming silverware. "Someone donated this box of silver," she explains. "It was so dull, almost black, that no one would want it. So I'm polishing it before putting it in the Free Room. Isn't it beautiful?"

The transformation is amazing. "Do you . . . do you want me to polish some?"

"Oh, no. This is therapeutic for me. Mark's at the big hospital in Northriver visiting a parishioner. He asked me to go through the mail that's been piling up. Would you start that for me? There's a letter opener right over there."

I find the mail and the letter opener, which looks like a miniature dagger.

"Most people call or email Mark with their concerns," she explains. "But when it comes to thank-you cards, they usually send them in the mail. That's what I assume most of these are. Just pull them out and open them. I'll put them on his desk before I leave today."

Mrs. Pugh continues to polish while I slit open envelopes and extract cards. She's right; most of them are cards of appreciation for funerals. "He's done three funerals in the past two weeks," says Mrs. Pugh. "All cancer victims. And they all worked at the mill for decades. So sad."

Most of the cards start out, "Dear Pastor Mark, Thank you for a beautiful service last week for my—" I stop reading as soon as I see what it's for and put it in the right pile. I come across one from someone asking about joining the church. Another is a wedding inquiry.

"Mrs. Pugh, I feel a little weird reading someone else's mail," I say.

She laughs. "Oh, you're practically church staff. Mark asks me to do this as part of my job. Anyway, you're not reading much, just the first line or two. Just one more. It's not a card, it's more like a letter. I bet there's a check in there. Probably someone's pledge."

I open it and start to read aloud.

> *Mark,*
>
> *I would have addressed you as "Pastor Mark," but you are no longer my pastor.*

"Whoa, this is not what we thought. Should I stop reading?"

Mrs. Pugh puts down the spoon she's rubbing and pulls off her gloves. "I suppose I'd better read it," she says. She takes it and continues to read it aloud.

I move to leave. She holds up her hand. "Just a minute. One last errand." But she keeps reading.

> *I will never again call you my pastor nor refer to you as such for the rest of my days. You have defiled that name and that calling. May God forgive you, as I cannot.*
>
> *Marriage is the sacred union of a man and a woman. Only a man and a woman. That you are sanctifying a union of two men is blasphemous and a slap in the face of the entire congregation. I do understand that homosexual marriage is legal in this country, but I also understand that there is a separation between church and state.*
>
> *You have not only lost my respect and membership, but you have lost my pledge, which is a significant part of your church budget. I doubt you will recover from this.*
>
> *Your actions have shaken my faith in you and the global church. Shame on you.*

Mrs. Pugh shakes her head and puts it down. "They signed their name," she says. "I'm glad it wasn't anonymous. I won't say who it is, but I know they've been an active member for many years. And they live alone and were very socially involved in the church. Mark will need to pay them a visit. It's a shame, isn't it, this fear?"

I can't help but wonder if this person is talking about Mr. D. "Does Pastor Mark do a lot of gay weddings?"

"No. In fact, this one will be his first. I think that's what's so upsetting to this parishioner. Oh, dear." She shakes her head again. "Let's forget the last errand. You go dance, honey."

I feel as if I'm carrying a backpack that weighs five hundred pounds as I try to dance. I can't shed it. I finally give up and go home.

62
HUNTER

Mr. D asks me, Eliot, Kiki, and Luna to attend a meeting this afternoon after school. "Sorry for the last-minute ask," he apologizes, "but I think the four of you should represent our part of the project."

I don't have anything else to do now that basketball is over, so I'm free. The four of us walk together to Molly's, where a big table in the back serves as our meeting spot. Mr. D waves us over. He makes quick introductions. "Guys, thanks for coming. This is Sky Patterson, Edgewater's town manager. Next to her is Ralls Macintosh, town planner. You obviously know Bridget Callahan. And Jessica Cloud is to her left. Finally, Pastor Mark and his friend Drew Cantor, who's in from Los Angeles, where he is a documentary filmmaker." He turns to the crew. "These are four student representatives from my class: Hunter, Eliot, Kiki, Luna. All four have had a significant role in the development of the Teo Legacy Project."

We sit down.

Sky begins. "I asked everyone to come here today so we could coordinate our information and planning. I've been fielding calls from a variety of people, from the benefits manager of the unemployment office to the regional head of environmental waste management. Essentially, we have two major projects in the works. The first is called the Teo Legacy Project, started by Ludovic's eleventh graders. The second is a longer term, more sustainable, ongoing business that would involve repurposing the mill. Joining us virtually are Ben Schreib and Jay Woodstock, co-owners of the mill. And PJ and Patsy Cutter, who own the Moose and Loon. Thank you all for being here. Ludovic, would you please give us a synopsis of the project?"

Mr. D turns to us. We've decided that Kiki should be our spokesperson. She outlines the purpose, momentum, and goal of the Teo Legacy Project. I would be a basket case talking in front of all these people, but she's focused and earnest. I give her a thumbs-up when she finishes. She smiles and rubs her forehead.

The Cutters confirm their donation to the project, the use of the pool at the Moose and Loon for the express purpose of community swimming. "Once the children learn to swim, we would love for them to be able to use the pool for recreation. So we're looking at an ongoing program for the months when the lodge has usually been closed."

Mr. D pulls out a spreadsheet that Eliot created. "We have the numbers here," he says, "to employ lifeguards, aquatic instructors, and general custodial maintenance for three hours a day, seven days a week, ten months of the year. Our tiny jam operation is barely a drop in that bucket. Unless, of course, we could make it on a much larger scale. But the women's knitting group will contribute tremendously. We also may be able to use some of the money generated by the selling of yarn."

Sky asks Jessica to talk about the wool-to-yarn project. "The expert with whom I am working," Jessica explains, "will lead this entire undertaking. But we need a place—a large, permanent place—for our operation. We want to keep it local and employ people who live in Edgewater. The mill seems the likeliest option."

Sky turns to the computer. "Ben? Jay? Would you please give us the current status of the mill? And what your future plans are for it?"

Ben begins. "As you know, we had to close the mill because of the drastic reduction in demand for the glossy magazine paper we processed. With the dramatic increase in online media, our ability to survive was significantly diminished. Several months ago, we thought we had a buyer, a Japanese company that planned to refurbish the mill. But the process of removing the toxins from the water proved cost-prohibitive. There is a movement afoot, however, of artisans establishing working studios in old mills. We've signed a contract with a ceramics company that will be utilizing the east wing of the building. Edgewater Ware, it's called."

This seems to be news to everybody, even Sky. "What? When did that happen?"

"We signed last week. They're planning to go in soon. In exchange for free rent, they are putting in a new water system. The river, which is still polluted, won't be their water source."

Sky still looks puzzled. "So this pottery company. You give them free rent. They put in a new water system. What else? Who pays utilities?"

Ben and Jay look at each other. Jay takes over. "Look, we want people in the mill. Otherwise, it's an abandoned building that will start to decay. So we've agreed to pay utilities for the first five years. Unless, of course, we sell the building before then. But if we can fill the building with artisans, and it's ultimately profitable and sustainable, then we're not interested in selling. It would serve as a different kind of investment."

I guess a year of not selling the building and having it stand empty has made an impression on their bank accounts. Or stock portfolios.

They seem almost human now. But I wonder if they have any idea how they've screwed up the lives of so many people like my dad. I kind of hate them.

"Have you advertised this space?" asks Jessica.

"Not yet. But we will. In Boston and New York. The words 'rent-free' will have them flocking up here in droves."

Jessica is indignant. "Boston and New York? What about Edgewater? Edgewater, Maine? Have you thought about all the unemployed mill workers right here in this town? Who desperately need work? Whose livelihoods were essentially shut down when you closed the mill? Before you go looking for companies to fill your building and your bank account, it is your moral duty to look right here."

Before Ben or Jay can say anything, she continues. "And first in line are these kids. With their jam. And given the number of blueberries around here, that is a sustainable business. One that could employ a lot of people. As will the yarn operation. I have an investor who will provide the seed money. So there, you have two more wings of your building filled."

If this were a private meeting, I imagine Jay and Ben would not easily acquiesce. But we are all witnesses to their discomfort.

"Uh, we'd need to discuss this further with the actual businesses," says Ben.

Ludovic clears his throat. "You're speaking to the future manager of both enterprises. Right here. Starting on June 20, when my duties at the high school are finished."

Wait, what? Mr. D is going to lead these?

This is all happening so quickly, I can't quite absorb it all.

Sky jumps on the moving train. "Given the awkwardness of a hybrid meeting," she says, "it's impossible to hash out all the details now. But Ludovic can draw up a business plan for both operations and submit them to you in a couple weeks. I think it's clear that all employees will be local hires, with preference given to those who lost mill jobs. Once all costs of the swimming enterprise are met, all profit will go to the employees at a living wage. And certainly, Ben and Jay, you can give a verbal agreement now?"

They nod their heads.

"All right, then," says Sky. "I'll give Ludovic your contact information. He'll be in touch. As will Jessica, once she's finalized plans with her wool guy. The sooner we can get in the mill, the better. And PJ and Patsy, we're hoping to start the swimming lessons in July. We'll be in touch once we've finalized hiring. Thank you all for joining us!" With that, she closes the computer.

Everyone looks slightly stunned. Drew breaks the silence. "Is that . . . is that how big decisions are made around here?"

Pastor Mark looks dazed. "I'm used to the slower pace of church committee meetings, when it takes forty-five minutes to decide which of the two exit doors would best be suited for a wheelchair ramp."

And then everyone is laughing. Like what just happened?

Mr. D leans back in his chair and rubs his eyes. "Oh, my God. I have no idea how to write a business plan, much less run a business! I can't believe I blurted that out, about being the manager. I just got caught up in really wanting these kids and this town to succeed."

Jessica smiles at him. "I'll help. If you can manage several classes of teenagers, this'll be a piece of cake."

"Speaking of cake," declares Drew, "I am so hungry." He jumps up and goes to the counter. By the time he returns, everyone has a drink, a gigantic spice cake is in the center of the table, and Molly is smiling as she cuts huge slices and puts them on plates. I don't think I've ever seen Molly smiling before.

Luna has to get to the church, and Kiki has chores to do at home. Eliot and I hang and talk with the adults, mostly Drew. He and Pastor Mark were college roommates. He's here to be the videographer for the sweater fashion show. An LA filmmaker is going to be shooting in Edgewater, Maine! How cool is that?

63
LUNA

I am reading a text from Kiki as I walk to my locker, so I don't see them until I almost bump into them. They stand in a semicircle blocking my locker. Emma is the first to speak. "What's your deal, Half-moon?"

My heart starts pounding. I don't have any idea what they want. *If I just stand here, maybe they'll go away.*

"Like, I don't get what Hunter sees in you. I mean, you must put out big time."

This feels like a nightmare. Sweat pops out on my forehead. *Just leave me alone!*

When I still don't say anything, Emma turns to her friends, who nod in this like weird silent agreement. "So," she says, "I hear your mother was a druggie. Like major burnout case. And no one knows who your father is. My mother thinks he was probably her dealer. So two addicts make a baby that looks like you. No wonder, am I right?"

If she had smashed my face with the laptop she's holding, it wouldn't have hurt like her words do. They shock me into a state of like paralysis. Emma waits for me to respond or hit her or something, but I can't move. Finally, she tosses her head. "Let's go. She's as stupid as she is butt-ugly."

They giggle and start down the hall. Just as they are turning the corner, Emma spins around. "And stay the fuck away from Hunter! He doesn't need someone who was traded for a night's high!"

This time I don't call Temmie for permission. I run all the way home. She is mopping the kitchen floor when I burst in, sobbing. She sits in the living room rocking chair and holds me as I choke out the story.

"They knew about my mother! The drugs and everything!"

"It's a small town, honey."

"So everybody knows? And I just found out?"

"No one knows the full truth. People like to trade in rumors."

"Temmie, they were so mean! I think they just wanted to see how long it took me to break."

I expect her to tell me that I failed, that I ran away instead of facing my problem, but she just holds me and rubs my back like I'm four years old. Tears are still sliding down my cheeks when I ask her. "Temmie, either she's lying or you are. What really happened? Why did Emma say I was traded for drugs?"

"I don't lie, kiddo. You know that. I already told you the story." She gently pushes me off her and walks out.

Leaving me alone on the rug. Unwanted again.

Her tread is heavy on the stairs. I lie there wondering what would have happened to my mother if I'd never been born. Temmie finally returns, carrying a plastic bin. She grimaces as she rubs her knee before sitting back down. "Here, honey. I was saving these for when you had a baby, but I think you need them now." She pulls out a tiny sweater, some booties, a hat, a onesie, and a blanket. All in a deep blue. "She picked this color because it reminded her of the ocean, which she loved. She made these while she was waiting for you."

I stare at the clothes. And all I can see is the disgust on the faces of the girls. Their knowing smirks. Their mocking jeers. *I am the town laughingstock.* I grab the bin and run upstairs. In my room I pluck out a stitch and start pulling. First the blanket. Then the onesie. The hat and sweater. And finally the tiny booties. When I am finished, I have ripped out every single stitch. This isn't proof of her love. It just shows how much she loved the idea of me, not the real me.

I shove the unraveled yarn to the bottom of my backpack and cry myself to sleep.

64

HUNTER

I look for Luna at lunch, but she's not sitting with Kiki and Eliot. I wolf down a cheeseburger and head to the library. There she is, reading a book and eating grapes. I plunk down next to her. She doesn't look up.

I wait.

She reads.

Finally I can't stand it anymore. "Must be a good book."

She shrugs.

"May I ask what's wrong?"

She shakes her head.

"Um, got any food?"

Without looking up, she points to her backpack.

I unzip it and reach in. My hand gets tangled in a mess of soft wool. I pull it out. "What's this?"

She looks up. Her face turns a shade of angry. She grabs the yarn from my hands and yanks the rest of it from her pack. She stomps over to the wastebasket by Mrs. Moss's desk and throws it in. "That," she declares, picking up her pack and furiously zipping it up, "is garbage." She runs out of the library.

What just happened?

I slowly pick up my own backpack and walk over to the desk. I pull the yarn out of the trash can, stuff it in my pack, and slip out of the library.

Seriously, what was that?

65

LUNA

Temmie wakes me early on Saturday so we can get our work done before the fashion show filming. It's overcast, the clouds "pregnant with snow," as Temmie says. I wonder if we'll have to postpone the show until tomorrow? The forecast is bleak: snow on and off for the next five days.

Temmie tells me I'm eating too slowly, and then she criticizes my sweeping. It makes me mad, but I get it. She's nervous. She likes being on camera about as much as I do. When she complains that my woodpile isn't stacked correctly, I snap. "Geez, Temmie! It's just wood! That's going to be burned!" I shove a thick log in. "Let's just go."

When we arrive at Mallard Park around noon, a bunch of my classmates are already on the ice, either shoveling or playing hockey. I see Drew, the guy from LA, right in the mix with them. He whacks his stick on the ice. "Let's go, you Maineiacs! I'll show you how we play in LA!"

A kid goes flying past him and shoots. Drew laughs. "Yo, you call that a shot? You coulda sent it in the mail and it woulda gotten there faster, big guy!"

Our guys dish their own trash.

"Oh, did that check hurt, California boy? In Maine that's what we call a mosquito bite."

The game heats up as more people join in. The sticks are worn, the skates old, and no one has real hockey gear. They make up in grit what they don't have in flash. And they're clearly having fun. Drew calls time-out, shakes every kid's hand before he gets off the ice, then trades his skates for boots and grabs his camera. He transforms from one of the boys on the ice to consummate professional videographer in about ten seconds.

We make our way over to the group of women, who are clustered around a blazing bonfire. Ms. Callahan asks me to help her match the knitters with the students who will wear their sweaters. I smile as I watch the students put on the sweaters with extraordinary reverence. Polly snorts, "For God's sake, kids, it's just wool. It's not going to break if you move around in it."

A light snow starts falling. Drew begins his choreography. "Go ahead and resume the hockey game. Hunter, you and Austin are showcasing the first two sweaters. I want you on the same team. Just play like we were before."

And it starts. For some reason, my stomach is doing jetés and temps levés. It's exciting and scary and nerve-wracking; this is going to make or break our ability to get kids swimming. And speaking of that, there's a woman in scrubs standing by the fire, signing up my classmates for first aid and lifeguard training. Kiki and I are thinking about taking CPR together.

Drew decides to superimpose the knitters' images and voices over the video after he's filmed it, so now he's just concentrating on getting shots of the sweaters in action. He flips back and forth between still shots and video, juggling two massive cameras on long straps that wind around his back.

When the hockey game is over, the players hang by the fire for hot chocolate and brownies. "These are," says Austin, his mouth full, "the best brownies I've ever had." Ethel beams.

I overhear conversations about sledding, knitting, swimming, Edgewater a long time ago. Two totally different generations in the same place, struggling with a lot of the same challenges.

Drew surreptitiously films some of these conversations, the fire roaring in the background. When the flames die down, one of the sweater models chops more wood and throws it on the fire. Drew catches this, then he hikes to the sledding hill and captures not just kids streaking down but also the long trudge back up the slope. Someone starts a snowball fight, and soon missiles are flying everywhere.

The scene kind of feels like a Hallmark movie, but anxiety and tension bubble under the surface. Is this going to work? Or is it going to be another Edgewater failure?

"Hey, where's Mr. D?" someone calls out. "He should totally be here!"

"He probably has guests in town," Hunter answers. "His wedding is in two days."

Other kids join the conversation. "How do you know that? When he's getting married?"

Hunter shrugs. "I overheard his partner tell someone. I was at the vet with my aunt."

"Oh, yeah, his partner is the vet. Shep, right? He's good. Our cat was so sick we thought he was going to die, but Shep saved him."

"Wait, two days? You mean like on Monday? Who has a wedding on a Monday?"

Hunter has an answer for this too. "Something like doing it on the vernal equinox." I'm impressed. He was definitely paying attention.

"What the hell is the vernal equinox?"

Coop jumps in. "I know this! It's the first day of spring! And when there's the same amount of light in the day and the night. Boom!"

When Drew thinks he has enough material to do justice to each sweater, he interviews each sweater's creator. He quietly and respectfully asks questions about both the sweater design and the knitter. The combination of the women witnessing their sweaters in action and the overwhelming charm of Drew serves as a conversational elixir. I listen, fascinated. There are so many layers to these women who seem so ordinary on the outside. And Temmie, for all her crabbiness this morning, falls under his spell. She is relaxed and articulate as she describes the pine trees she created as her pattern.

Drew wraps up after an hour and a half. The snow is falling harder, and he's obviously sensitive to the comfort of the older women. Ms. Callahan gets us organized in a quick cleanup. Some douse the fire; others bring the table and hot chocolate pot to the cars. Sleds are collected, hockey sticks and skates returned to their owners. Teenagers escort the oldest knitters to their cars.

Ms. Callahan thanks every single person there. By name.

And Drew films her doing so.

66

HUNTER

It's Sunday afternoon and I'm walking to Miz Callahan's when I hear an engine revving behind me. "Dude, you coming?" Nate's head is sticking out of the passenger side door of Josh's truck. They pull over onto the icy shoulder and wait for me to catch up. Loud music is blaring from the jacked-up speakers.

I jog to the truck. "Go ahead. I'll meet you there. Need to run an errand first."

"You're gonna walk all the way to Oak Hill? It'll be dark by the time your slow ass gets there! Just get in."

"I can't. I'm going to Miz Callahan's."

As soon as I say her name, Nate backs off. "Oh, for the project?"

"Um, yeah. A project meeting."

"Got it. Okay, later."

They peel out, sending a spray of ice and dirt all over me. Technically, I didn't lie. It's just not the project they're thinking of.

Miz Callahan is ready. We sit side by side at her large wooden table. I've been studying YouTube videos, but I've never actually tried to do this. She hands me two thick needles. I pull the yarn out of my pack. "Do you think this is going to be enough?"

She rubs the wool between her fingers. "Oh, it's so soft. Yes, this should do. Let's roll it up into balls first. That will make it easier."

Once the yarn is wound in six different-size balls, she teaches me how to cast on. It's slow and tedious, but together we do it. Then the actual knitting begins. And geez, it's way harder than it looks. The yarn is slippery on the needle, and I keep doing what she calls "dropping stitches." She is way more patient than I am. "You're catching on. Just remember to check after every stitch that it's actually on the opposite needle."

"How on earth," I practically pant, "do you do this without looking? Like you can watch TV and knit at the same time!"

Miz Callahan laughs. "Years of practice. Just like I bet you could stand at the free-throw line wearing a blindfold and still sink buckets."

It's a good comparison, and it kind of relaxes me. Stick the needle in one loop, wind the yarn around it, stick it through the other hole, and pull it off. Boom. One completed stitch. About twenty thousand to go.

"If you can finish it," says Miz Callahan, "it'll be gorgeous."

"If? *If?* Ouch!"

She laughs. "Not a dig on your potential knitting prowess. But some people take to it and others don't."

By the end of an hour of painstaking work, I have actually knit five rows of sixty stitches each. It makes a band of about an inch and a half. It's not totally even or anything, but I think it is one of the coolest things I've ever done.

I hold it up to Miz Callahan. "Look! It's like, like really there!"

She smiles at me. "I'm proud of you, Hunter. If you can commit an hour a day to this, you'll have it finished in a couple weeks. I'll show you how to sew up the sides. And how to make the handle."

The guys on Oak Hill have probably quit sledding by now. I'm more exhausted by this than if I had gone with them. I walk home slowly, carrying my bundle of yarn like it's a brand-new baby.

I can't wait to finish it.

67
LUNA

I'm already running late on Monday morning when I realize my laptop isn't in my backpack. I do a panicked search of the house and Temmie's car and come up empty. *Think, think!* The laptop isn't even mine; the school loans them out to people who can't afford them. Temmie's going to kill me if I've lost it. She's out in the car, waiting. I hear the horn blast. *Crap!*

And then I remember. I took it out of my backpack at church. I was trying to learn a new dance from one I saw on YouTube. I must have left it there. *Oh, please, please let it still be there.*

I race out to the car. "I'm so sorry but will you please take me to church first? I left something there."

"Church? We don't have time, Luna. You're already late."

"Temmie, it's important."

"More important than getting to school on time? I doubt it. What did you leave?"

I don't want to tell her. I really, really don't want to tell her. But I have to. "Um, my laptop."

The forehead vein starts pulsating. She doesn't even look at me, just clenches her jaw and heads toward church. She doesn't say a word the whole way there. We round the corner and enter the parking lot. I am putting on my mittens when I hear Temmie gasp. "Oh, my God!"

I jerk my head up. And I see it. Huge red letters spray-painted on the wall next to the entrance.

"GOD HATES FAGS"

And then I remember. It's Monday. Mr. D's wedding day. *Are you kidding me?*

I get out of the car and take two steps when Mrs. Pugh comes flying out the door. "You can't go in there!"

What? "I'm sorry?"

"You can't go in there! Nobody can! It's awful!" She's close to hyperventilating. Temmie steps out of the car. "Carol? What's going on? She just needs to retrieve her laptop. If it's still there."

Mrs. Pugh's eyes are watering and her face is red. "Someone left a stink bomb in the sanctuary. I could barely breathe in there. The whole place is just putrid."

Temmie points to the wall. "Think it's connected?"

Mrs. Pugh gives a startled cry. "I didn't see that! I always park out back and come in from the other side. Oh, my word. Mark's supposed to do a wedding here today."

"Is he here?"

"No, no, he usually comes in at 8:30. I'll call him." She pulls out her phone. "Mark? You won't believe this." She quickly explains what's going on.

Temmie and I get back in the car and sit in stunned silence as Mrs. Pugh talks. She hangs up and climbs in the back. "He's on his way. He thinks maybe if we leave the doors wide open it will help. I don't know; it's pretty bad. What a shame."

The urgency of finding my laptop and getting to school on time is gone. This is way bigger. Temmie gets it. "Honey, do you have a test this morning? Or anything you shouldn't miss? Like a lab or something?"

"Just a vocab quiz. But I can make that up."

"Okay. You know I wouldn't normally let you miss school. But I feel like we should help."

Pastor Mark comes screeching up. He and Drew jump out of the car and run into the church. About ten seconds later, they run out, coughing.

They stand, panting, and stare at the red letters. Temmie and Mrs. Pugh and I join them.

"I guess we'll go to Plan B," Pastor Mark says.

Mrs. Pugh looks confused. "You have a Plan B?"

"Well, I didn't. But we'll make one." He looks at us, as if seeing us for the first time. "Temmie? Luna? What are you doing here?"

We explain. Before I can apologize, Temmie interrupts. "Put us to work. How many hours till the wedding?"

"Four and a half. Even with the doors open, that smell isn't going anywhere for days. The wedding will have to be outside. We'll need to go to the hardware store for paint to cover that filth, though it may not stick in this weather. Then we'll need flowers and an arch. Folding chairs outside. A path shoveled. A sound system set up. Signs to direct the guests." He looks at the four of us. "We can do this."

This is way more exciting than school. Temmie and Mrs. Pugh drive to Hannaford's for ribbon and flowers. Pastor Mark and Drew and I head to the hardware store.

The bell chimes when we open the door. The store owner looks up. "Well, hello, Reverend. What brings you in so early on a Monday morning?"

"Hi, Gary. Paint. We need paint," Pastor Mark says breathlessly. "White paint. Probably four gallons."

Gary nods. "I'll see what we've got." He moves to the back of the store like the sloth from *Zootopia*. Drew wanders the aisles as if he's just looking, but I can tell he's on a mission. He puts some heavy-duty hooks on the counter. And some nails. And several rolls of duct tape. "You got a hammer at the church?"

"Yes."

"And a tall ladder?"

"We do somewhere. What are you doing?" Pastor Mark drums his fingers on the counter.

"Oh, not much. I've just got a feeling."

We wait for what feels like twenty minutes. I grow more and more anxious. Finally, Gary snails back. "You know, it's a funny thing. We're all out of white paint."

"Well, do you have something close to white? Like cream? Ivory? Bone?"

"I checked. Clean out. Must be popular colors nowadays."

"It's still winter! Who's painting in this weather?"

"Well, it looks like you are."

"Could you please check with the store in Landon? Or Northriver? See if they have any in stock?"

"You know, it's a funny thing. I already called them. They're out too." He stands with his hands on both hips, as if daring us to question him. His muscles are huge; his biceps are the size of my quads.

Drew and Pastor Mark look at each other. And then at me. And it dawns on all of us. He's lying. *How could we have been so obtuse?*

Bile reaches the back of my throat. Drew calmly steps forward. "I wonder if there was a run on red spray paint too?"

Gary just stares at him and doesn't smile.

Drew shoves his stuff closer to Gary. "We'll just take these, please."

Gary won't look at Pastor Mark. He rings up Drew's hooks and nails and tape. "You building something?"

Drew smiles. "Nope. Trying to take down a wall." At the door he turns. "You have a beautiful day, sir."

In the car Pastor Mark stares straight ahead. "How do you do that?"

"Do what?"

"Stay so civil. You knew he was lying. I wanted to haul off and punch him in the face!"

Drew bursts out laughing. "Have you ever punched someone in the face? Ever? Especially someone that jacked?"

"Well, no. Of course not. But it doesn't mean I didn't want to."

Drew just smiles. "Mighty Mark the Pugilistic Pastor!"

"I know, I know." Pastor Mark sighs. "I get that it's just homophobia, xenophobia, whatever. But it's so frustrating. When that ignorance and fear hurts others. I wonder how many people were in on it? And how many people have driven past the church this morning and seen that?" He looks out the window at the dark gray sky. "Probably a lot of baggage behind it." He sighs. "We all have a lot of baggage. The grace comes when people help us to unpack it."

He turns to me. "Luna, I'm sorry you were witness to that. I asked you to stay with us because we're going to need your young strength. You up for doing some shoveling and moving chairs?"

Of course I am.

Back at the church we check out the sanctuary. The fresh air pouring in from outside has done little to eliminate the stench. And now it's freezing inside.

Pastor Mark has a new worry. "Do you think I should tell Shep and Ludovic? Or will that freak them out?"

Drew ponders this. "Hmm. Maybe just say you have a surprise. To dress warmly."

Pastor Mark pulls out his phone and calls. "Hey, Ludovic. Mark here. Say, I had an idea to make your wedding more unique. A little surprise. No, I'm not going to tell you what, exactly. Just be sure to bundle up. And bring a scarf. Yes, both of you. And I'll pick you up and escort you to the church. Okay, see you then." He looks at us in wonder. "That was way too easy. Most people are rather intractable about wedding plans." He stares at the ugly letters in blood red. "I also need to call the police. This is a hate crime. But I don't want them crawling around here, putting up yellow crime scene tape, before the wedding."

I feel so bad for Mr. D. I hope he doesn't know about any of this.

Drew advises against it until after the wedding. It's an easy decision. "The minute the grooms and guests are out of here, we'll call. But right now, we've got work to do."

Drew outlines his plan. We raid the Free Room and grab blankets and comforters. I recognize some from Mrs. Orcutt's house. We lay them out in the hall where we can breathe, though it still reeks. We attach them to each other using duct tape. Tons and tons of duct tape. Our patchwork quilt is shoddy and mismatched, but it's bright. And big enough to cover the graffiti.

Pastor Mark gets the ladder from the storeroom. Drew hammers the hooks into the church wall, then we hang our quilt on them. It means we have to puncture holes in the blankets, but we are desperate. We secure the bottom and sides of the quilt with more hooks and call it good. Not quite the picturesque little white New England church the wedding guests are expecting. It looks more like it's wearing a weird sweater.

Drew builds a makeshift arbor while Pastor Mark and I shovel a path to the garden and a large semicircle for the chairs. We lug out thirty folding chairs and set them up.

"It's not a big wedding," Pastor Mark tells me, "but there are going to be a few surprise guests. Three of Ludovic's siblings, who haven't talked to him in years because of his sexuality, are coming. Shep reached out to his whole family. His parents still can't make that leap, but Ludovic's going to be blown away by his siblings' presence."

Temmie and Mrs. Pugh arrive, carrying boxes of flowers. They carefully decorate the arbor that Drew has hammered together. It looks awesome. They also bring cups of steaming hot chocolate and homemade blueberry muffins from Molly's. We take a break to eat and admire our work. Then we make and post huge signs to direct guests to the garden. Hearts with the letters "S" and "L" intertwined.

At 11:45 everything's ready. The five of us look at each other with tears in our eyes. *We did it! We really did it!*

Now we pray that no one ruins the ceremony.

Pastor Mark found my laptop earlier and left it outside. So by the time we are finished, it doesn't smell. Reluctantly, I pack it up, get back in Temmie's car, and go to school.

68

HUNTER

Luna strides into the cafeteria, grabs Eliot and Kiki, and heads directly to my table. I've never seen her so businesslike; usually she's quiet and kind of hangs in the background.

"You look like you're on a mission," I observe.

"Everyone, listen up. We are skipping school this afternoon."

Coop laughs. "Yeah, right. Good one."

Her eyes are blazing. "Not a joke, Coop. I want to get as many kids from Mr. D's class as we can to join us."

"What are you talking about?"

"We're going to his wedding."

I can't believe Luna is leading this charge. But I love it. "Totally! I'm in. But we weren't invited."

She is dead serious. "So we'll crash it."

Coop can't contain his glee. "Luna's become a rebel! I knew we were good influences!"

The guys who aren't on the baseball team are in. The baseball players can't skip classes. If they do, they're not allowed to go to practice, even though it's in the gym because the field is still under a foot of snow.

"What inspired this criminal side?" I ask Luna.

"Long story," she says. "I'll explain later. Right now we have to get the word out to the rest of our class."

Coop offers to help. He goes off with Luna and Kiki and Eliot to recruit wedding crashers. I finish my lunch with the guys, who are discussing Mr. D.

"Is it true or just a rumor that he was fired?"

"I think it's true. Because he's gay."

"Such bullshit. He's a great teacher."

"Did your parents sign that petition?"

"No idea. Wouldn't put it past them."

"Same. Mine are, like, stuck in the 1950s, even though my grandparents weren't even alive then."

"They're gonna be pissed if they find out I went to his wedding."

"So don't tell them."

"Thanks, Captain Obvious."

The four recruiters come rushing back.

"Almost everyone is going to join us," Kiki reports. "A few spring athletes can't. And Pierce and company just laughed in our faces."

"Screw 'em anyway," says Coop. "No surprise there."

"The wedding's at one o'clock," Luna says. "We told people to stagger their sign-out times. We can't all go at 12:45. So the first people are leaving around 12:15."

Coop and I agree to be the last to leave. At 12:45 we go to the office to sign out. The procedure involves writing your name, the day and time, and the reason you're leaving school. The list is already way longer than usual. Ms. Cox winks at us. "Dentist appointment? Or a family emergency? Those seem to be quite popular today."

We both write "Family Emergency" and start to walk out. Just as we are leaving the office, Mr. Winslow enters. "Boys? Headed to class?"

"Uh, no. No, we're not. We, um, have to go somewhere."

He reaches for the sign-out clipboard. "What the devil—?"

Ms. Cox hides her smile behind furious typing on her keyboard. Coop grabs my arm and whispers, "Go!"

But Mr. Winslow senses our movement. "Freeze!" He glares at us. "I find it bizarrely coincidental that so many families are experiencing emergencies today," he growls. "Unless there's been a massive pileup on one of the highways that I haven't heard about. Get back to class. Now!"

There is no way we're going to miss this wedding. But he's kind of caught us in a lie. I look at Coop, who is busy on his phone.

"With all due respect, Mr. Winslow," he says calmly, "this is an emergency. Just wondering if you know the origin of the word?"

Whoa. This is not going to end well. Coop, just shut up.

Mr. Winslow sputters a bit, then says, "Well, I suppose it comes from 'emerge.'"

"Precisely," says Coop.

What kid says "precisely"?

He studies his phone. "Let me read the definition of 'emerge': 'to rise from or out of anything that surrounds, covers, or conceals; come forth, appear, as from concealment.' It is from the Latin word '*emergere*'—not sure how to pronounce that—which means 'bring forth, bring to light, come forth, come up, come out.'" He looks up and grins. "So you've often told us that our school is like a big family, and we should treat each other accordingly. Well, one of our family members has recently come out—*emerged*, if you will—and we are going to celebrate that. Hence, the family emergency."

Mr. Winslow's forehead is all, like, screwed up in concentration, and his mouth is open, but no words are coming out of it. We bolt.

I am laughing so hard I have trouble running. When we get beyond school property, we stop and walk.

I pound Coop on the back. "That was so frickin' brilliant! How on earth did you come up with that?"

Coop is, like, wide-eyed. "I don't know! Honestly! I guess I was channeling Eliot."

"*Precisely*? And *hence*? Seriously, dude, you schooled him!"

"We'll probably get in trouble anyway. But I don't even care."

Snow is falling when we arrive at the church. Several handmade signs point to the garden on one side of the church. Such a cool idea, having an outdoor wedding in the winter. Although, I remember, today is technically spring. A crowd of Mr. D's students stands in the back behind the seated guests. We slip in next to Kiki and Luna.

A woman in a long down jacket and Bean boots sits on a chair in the front. She is playing a guitar and singing John Legend's "All of Me" in this, like, haunting voice. The sound system is impressive, especially for a little church. Two men holding gigantic umbrellas over her join in, like harmonizing, and damn, it's so beautiful that I have chills. The three of them together remind me of that oldies group, Peter, Paul and Mary. Drew, the guy who filmed the fashion show on Saturday, is taking tons of pictures. There's still no sign of Mr. D.

Pastor Mark arrives with Mrs. Pugh. They get out of the car and slowly lead Mr. D and Shep, who both have scarves tied over their eyes, down the path. Everyone is silent; you can only hear the guitar and the three people singing.

Give me all of you, oh.
Cards on the table, we're both showing hearts;
Risking it all, though it's hard,
'Cause all of me
Loves all of you.

They walk up the path and stand next to the lectern under the flower-covered arch. Pastor Mark whispers something to them, and they reach up and pull off their blindfolds.

Mr. D looks around at all the people there in like shock and bursts into tears. The guitarist quietly starts playing "Stand by Me." It's a classic, one everyone knows, but today it has special meaning. People join in, softly at first, then the place swells with the hopeful lyrics.

No, I won't be afraid
Oh, I won't be afraid
Just as long as you stand, stand by me.

All of the students link arms in this like chain of solidarity.

I have one arm attached to Luna and the other to Coop. The snow's falling and our teacher is crying and we're all singing and it's so peaceful and awesome and perfect.

69

LUNA

After the wedding, we decide to bag the rest of school and head to Molly's instead. Samantha is behind the counter when we pile in. "Do you guys have a half day today?"

Josh laughs. "We're all at the dentist right now. Or home dealing with our family emergencies."

Samantha winks. "Ahh. I remember Skip Day."

Hunter needs to clarify. "We did go to school in the morning. But we've just been to church. To our teacher's wedding."

Samantha claps her hands. "That's right! Oh, tell me everything!"

We fill her in as she makes lattes and hot chocolates. She wants to know every detail, like what the grooms were wearing, how they pulled off an outdoor wedding in a snowstorm, who was there, what Pastor Mark said, and what songs were played. "Where's the reception?"

We look at each other. "Uh, we're not sure. Probably at the farm. We weren't invited."

"Actually," Coop declares, "we weren't invited to the wedding, either. That's the first wedding I've crashed!"

We fill two entire round tables, and we're loud. Boisterous, even. We're all so happy for Mr. D and thrilled to be out of school. In a kind of AWOL way. At one point Eliot grins at me. "C-c-can you believe we are sitting here with all these people on a M-Monday afternoon? This is way beyond my com-com-comfort zone, but I'm having a blast!"

We hang out for an hour. When more kids file in, indicating that school's out, Josh stands up. "Let's get going. The party is continuing at my house. We've got plenty of sleds. And we'll make a bonfire. I think between us we can fit everyone in a car. You guys in?"

Amazingly, everyone is. We gather hats and mittens and backpacks, walk back to the school parking lot, and pile into cars.

I'm exhausted after two hours of sledding and a massive Capture the Flag game at Josh's. Our team won, by the way, thanks to a brilliant tactical move by me and Kiki. While Coop distracted their team in a loud ambush to set Eliot and Austin free from jail, Kiki and I ran all the way around the pond to get to their flag from the back. They never saw us coming. Coop and Austin hoisted me and Kiki onto their shoulders after we won, yelling smack at the other team until they were hoarse.

I think it's the most fun I've ever had.

We're all invited to dinner, but we decline. Homework and chores yank us back to reality. We thank Josh and his parents, then Coop drives me home around six o'clock. He's got Eliot, Hunter, Kiki, and Shea still to drop off. I haven't even unbuckled my seat belt when the side door flies open and Temmie runs out.

"Hey, Miz Lemieux!" Coop calls out.

She barely looks at him. Raw anguish covers her face. "*Where have you been?*"

"I . . . I . . . just . . . with them."

"My God, Luna, do you have any idea how worried I was?"

I shut the car door. Coop slowly backs out.

The joy from the day drains away.

"I knew you couldn't dance in that toxic sanctuary. I expected you'd come home after school. And it got later and later, and you didn't answer my texts or calls."

"I'm sorry, Temmie. I'm really sorry. I never have my ringer on. I didn't even think to check my phone."

She storms into the house. "I had you in a ditch somewhere. Dead. Or abducted and sold into a prostitution ring. Or overdosing in someone's basement."

If she weren't so furious, I would laugh at her ridiculous scenarios. But her hands are shaking, and I can see tearstains on her cheeks.

"I'm not my mother, Temmie."

"Yeah, I'm going to do my damnedest to make sure you aren't. I just don't understand why you didn't tell me where you were. That's common courtesy and consideration."

"Temmie, I'm sorry! I really am. I didn't mean . . . I mean, this was the first time in my life I was a regular kid. We went to Mr. D's wedding. Then we hung out at Molly's. Then we went sledding at Josh's. And the whole time, people talked with me. And I didn't hide. At all. I loved it. And I didn't mean to make you worry. It didn't even occur to me. I just . . . I just never had a day like that. Spontaneous. With friends."

She sighs. "I'm happy for you, honey. I really am. But in the future, you need to let me know where you are and who you're with. Got it?"

Just then her phone rings. Temmie fumbles for it. "Yes? Mark. Yes, she's here. Thank God. Sorry for bothering you. I just didn't know who else to ask. Yes, she's fine. Okay. I . . . pardon? For the week? Yes, I'll tell her. Thank you, Mark. Good night."

"You called Pastor Mark?"

"Would you rather I'd called the cops?"

"Is he . . . am I . . . am I in trouble with him too?"

"No. He told me you were at the wedding. But he had no idea of where you'd gone after that. By the way, because of the stink bomb, dancing is out this week. Actually, a lot of the church is cordoned off with yellow crime scene tape. He told me he called the cops after the wedding."

"Oh."

"I want to hear all about the wedding and your afternoon later tonight after I've recovered. Right now you're coming with me to get milk."

Really? Now she's not letting me out of her sight? I roll my eyes. Whatever.

She pulls into the one little market that's open at night. It's attached to a gas station and is way overpriced. You pay for convenience. Temmie gives me her card and sends me in. I grab a gallon of milk and get in line. The man two people in front of me is having a long discussion with the cashier about plowing snow. I assume it's his truck we parked next to, a pickup with a detachable plow.

"Well, you take care now," the cashier bids him. "Eloise will be wondering where you are."

"Oh, she'll stop her complaining when I give her this." He holds up a pint of ice cream. "Moose tracks. Her favorite."

"All right, then. Good night!" The cashier clearly wants him to move along as much as he wants to linger and talk.

"You doing all right tonight?" she asks the person in front of me.

"Yup," he says, putting an energy bar and a bottle of water on the counter. He gives her a twenty and shoves his hands back in his pockets.

She fishes in the drawer for change. "Oh, dear. Do you have anything smaller? I'm low on change tonight."

"I'll check." He digs into both front pockets.

I put the milk jug on the counter. It's heavy and my body is so tired. I'm kind of staring into space when suddenly I am on high alert. *Did I see what I think I saw?*

He's counting out what he owes. And my heart starts pounding. I look at the little bit of his face that isn't covered with his hood.

I gasp. It's Pierce.

He's startled by my reaction. He whirls around and stares. "Oh. It's you."

I am frozen in fear. "Um, hey, Pierce." I look down.

He's still staring. "You okay?"

It's all I can do to look at him. "Yeah. I just . . . I just . . . seeing you reminded me we have a chem test tomorrow. That I . . . I haven't studied for."

"Oh, crap; I haven't either. But relax, there's still time." He hands the money to the cashier.

"Why, look at that!" she sings. "You have exact change. Thanks, honey, that helps me a lot. You have a wonderful evening, okay?"

"No problem. Take care." He turns to me. "Good luck studying." He grabs his stuff and walks out.

I am shaking as I insert Temmie's card. I'm sure the cashier says something, but I don't hear it. *No, no, no, no, no.*

When he counted out the change, I saw it.

His right forefinger.

Stained with red paint.

I flee to the car and fling the milk jug in the back seat. *It's just a coincidence. Maybe he had art class. Or was painting a barn or something. But it is a hate crime. And his dad owns the hardware store and was so weird about the paint. Was he in on it? Do I go to the police? Could I be arrested if I knew something and didn't say anything? But technically I don't* know *anything. I'm just guessing. Should I just confront him? Oh, God, I don't know what to do!*

"You okay?" Temmie peers at me in the light of the lamp above the gas pumps. "You look like you've seen a ghost."

"I . . . I . . . Temmie, I don't know!"

She waits.

"Can we just go home?"

She starts to drive, but I know she's not going to let this go. At home she limps around the kitchen making a late dinner of grilled cheese sandwiches. I sit at the kitchen table, trying to focus on chem, but all I can see is that finger.

"Put your computer away and let's eat. And tell me what's bothering you."

So I tell her what I saw. She mulls it over. "Just one finger? Not all of them, like he was fingerpainting?"

"No, just one."

"Not sure if we should go to the police. We didn't witness him doing anything, and such an accusation is pretty serious. Usually in cases like this, someone tells someone else, and it eventually gets out. I would hate to drag Pierce's name through the mud with no credible evidence."

"But what if he did do it?"

"Then he has to live with that. And chances are, he's going to overhear kids talking about how beautiful and successful the makeshift wedding was, and he's going to realize that despite his best efforts, he couldn't wreck it. Again, that's a hypothetical. His doing it, I mean."

I'm kind of relieved. I didn't want to deal with the police, especially with no solid evidence.

But what if he did it?

70
HUNTER

The first craft fair of the season was near the end of March in a town far south of us. A group of people went, our first official launch of *Made in Maine* blueberry jam. Today Mr. D is letting them share their experience with the rest of the class.

Eliot has created a PowerPoint presentation. Of course he has. I get the feeling that he's going to be like a CEO of some Fortune 500 company someday.

He asks Gordon to narrate. "So we had to leave at four o'clock in the morning to drive down there. Yep, that's me with the coffee mug. And there's Austin with major bed head."

The next picture is from the fairgrounds. "Even though we left so early, by the time we got there, there were already a ton of people buying stuff."

"What kind of stuff?" Shea asks.

"Well, when I took a lap around, it was almost noon, so some booths had already sold out and closed. But I saw crafty stuff like leather belts, quilts, wooden flutes. Oh, and these cool metal drums. And lots of food. Like pies, granola, nut butters, maple syrup. And some that was not, like, to take home but to eat right there. The Mexican food stand was amazing."

"Anyone else selling blueberry jam?"

"I only saw one. And ours had a much cooler label, thanks to Hunter's dad. And Beth's beautiful handwriting. Oh, and Beth also made these awesome posters that she put on this wooden A-frame in front of our booth. Eliot, you have that, right?" Eliot scrolls down two slides. Gordon laughs. "Those are just of us standing in front of the booth. Boring. Oh, here it is. Stop for a sec."

The words "Made in Maine" are large and bold in the middle of the sign. Dad's logo of the trees and mountains and the little boy standing in a pond is like in the background. A picture of Teo is superimposed on it. Directly under Teo's face are the words, "So others may swim." The poster is simple—and striking.

Gordon turns to Beth. "Can you like explain your thinking behind that?"

"Sure! I thought about telling the story of Teo on the board, but I decided not to. Because if there's too much text, no one reads it."

"Just like in that analysis we did," cuts in Coop. "Remember that economics lesson we did on advertising?"

"Yeah," says Beth. "People only look at a sign for about two seconds. I chose to write that one line to like get their attention. So they would maybe ask questions about him. And oh, my God, you guys, it totally worked!"

"Tell them about that one dude!" shouts Austin.

"I'm getting to that. In fact, Eliot has a picture of him. But first, I just wanted to say that people loved the story. I mean, not about Teo drowning, but that we were working toward something in his honor. One woman bought ten jars to give to her friends just because of where the money's going. Okay, Eliot, that guy?"

A face appears on the screen. Bearded. Smiling. Holding up two fingers in a peace sign. "Yeah, so this is the guy that Austin is talking about. Actually, Austin, you tell it."

"Okay, this dude was starting to creep me out." Austin like shudders. "I mean, he was hanging around our booth for like half an hour, watching us. Twice I asked him if we could help him, and both times he just shook his head and held up a peace sign. Gordon's mom was even getting freaked out. And he was wearing clothes that were old and kind of scruffy. We decided that maybe he was homeless, so we offered him a jar of jam for free. Hoping he'd leave if he was a crazy stalker dude or child molester or something."

Austin has us hanging onto every word.

"Finally he reaches into his pocket and takes out his wallet. And he says, 'My little brother had Down syndrome. He died when he was thirty-two. I miss him every day.' He pulls out three one-hundred-dollar bills and gives them to Eliot. 'That's to keep Teo's memory alive. By all those kids you help in the water.' And then he left. We were so stunned we didn't even thank him."

"So then," Beth chimes in, "Eliot ran after him and got him to come back. So we could take his picture. And thank him properly. And just as he was leaving again, Eliot called out to him, 'What was your brother's name?'"

Everyone waits. Eliot's voice comes from the back of the room. "'M-M-Murphy,'" he said. "'It means sea warrior.'"

A hushed pause follows.

Austin breaks it. "Yeah, he was awesome. And honestly, we got a lot of donations from people, beyond the cost of the jam."

"So how many jars did you sell?" Coop asks.

"All of them!" Beth says. "That means, minus the cost of printing the labels, we made a profit of $2,600. That includes the donations.

And Gordon's mom said she would be happy to let us make more jam at their house this weekend. Using the frozen berries people donated."

"What about the seven hundred dollars from Teo's mother?" Shea asks.

"We used some of that to repay Gordon's family. For the jars and sugar and pectin. But I think we have enough of all that left to make another three hundred jars. The rest is going toward setting up our website. And getting our brand officially trademarked."

Eliot ends the PowerPoint with a bunch of silly mug shots. Mr. D turns on the lights. I notice Pierce has his head in his arms on his desk. I doubt he even watched the presentation.

Mr. D updates us on the wool-to-yarn operation that will begin in the mill as soon as Jessica and Gustav get all the equipment installed. "We're hoping that this is an ongoing business, beyond the Teo Legacy Project. But we've committed all the early profits to go to it until we reach our goal."

"Sorry, Mr. D, but I don't get it. What do you mean?"

"No worries. Let me clarify. You guys determined that we need $33,600 to pay for three hours of lessons and pool operation a day for ten months. So the jam money is an awesome start. The sweater auction is in two weeks. All of that will be pure profit. The yarn business is different, because equipment has to be purchased. So we're relying on an investor's seed money for that. Jessica has a rich client who has taken on the role of major investor. But if we don't make our goal between the jam and the sweaters, then all of the profit from the yarn will first go to reaching that goal. Does that help?"

People nod.

"So I have another task for you," continues Mr. D. "We'll continue to use the *Made in Maine* label for the yarn. However, to give it further distinction, we need a name for the dye process. All the ingredients in the dyes are found in nature in Maine. Any ideas?"

People think for a second then start throwing out ideas. "Um, 'Nature Dyed in the Wool.' Get it?"

"Not really. What's the joke or whatever?"

"You know, that expression: 'dyed in the wool'?"

"I've heard it. What does it mean?"

"Actually, I'm not sure. I think it means, like, passionate. Or really committed to a cause."

"How about 'From Maine's Rugged Mountains'?"

"Oh, I know! 'Katahdin Kreated.' But 'created' with a 'k.' You know, get that alliterative thing going."

Coop stands up. "I've got it: 'Dung Dyed.' Hey, that rhymes with 'tongue tied!' I am so clever!"

"Dude, it'd be better if your tongue was tied. Dung, really?"

"Not helping, people!"

Luna raises her hand. "How about using the Maine motto?"

Everyone looks around. "I guess no one else knows it," says Kiki. "What is it?"

"It's *Dirigo*, which means 'I lead.' Dirigo Dyed."

The clapping that echoes around the classroom seals it. Good for Luna. Like really good.

Mr. D smiles. "Thanks, guys. That's perfect. So fitting for this project. Lead on, eh?" And he dismisses us with a giant wave of his arm.

71

LUNA

I can finally dance again at church. The sanctuary smells like fresh paint. The walls are gleaming now, making the space look not just brighter but also bigger. Mrs. Pugh was so excited to tell me about it. "When I got word out that we were going to have a painting party," she says, her eyes sparkling, "which, between you and me, is just a way to get free labor, I thought we'd maybe have fourteen people. At most. Some to paint, some to clean up, some to provide advice and refreshments. And that would be enough to cover that awful graffiti."

I wait. She's enjoying keeping me in suspense. "Oh, my word. Do you know how many people showed up? Seventy-eight! And not all of them were church members, just people who heard about the project and wanted to help. They painted the entire church, inside and out. Paint and brushes and rollers and ladders just kept appearing.

I couldn't believe it! They even did the Free Room. Oh, it's all so gorgeous, isn't it?"

It is. It's awesome, all those people helping.

I cut my dancing short today—honestly, because even though the paint looks good, it makes it a little hard to take deep breaths without inhaling a lot of intense fumes. I bundle up and open the door to the hall. And that's when I see them.

Two cops.

"Who's that?" One of them jerks her finger at me.

"That's Luna Lemieux," says Pastor Mark. "She spends her afternoons here."

"We need to talk to her."

"I hardly think that—"

The other cop cuts him off. "Anyone who was here may have seen something. We need to interview everyone."

They march up to me. "Officer Wang, Officer Justice. Just here to ask a few questions. We understand you spend your afternoons here."

I nod.

"Did you see anything unusual in the days before March 20? Someone lingering in the parking lot, maybe? Or people in the church who usually aren't there?"

I shake my head.

Officer Justice gives me his card. "If you remember anything, call me. Okay then, thank you all for your time. We're headed to the hardware store now. It's the only place in Edgewater that sells paint. Hoping they know something."

Just then Officer Wang's beeper goes off. She walks away from us to talk. Her voice gets louder. "On our way. In fact, we were headed there anyway."

She strides back and nods to Officer Justice. "Let's go. The safe at the hardware store was broken into. Thief didn't touch the money, just took the gun."

They take off. Leaving me and Mrs. Pugh and Pastor Mark looking at each other, kind of blankly.

"Oh, dear," says Mrs. Pugh. "Trouble all over. Well, I'm off. I'll see you both tomorrow."

Pastor Mark heads back to his office, and I leave for home. With every step I ask myself if I did the right thing. *Should I have told them about Pierce's finger*? A false accusation could ruin his life. I need to talk with Temmie. She's the only person I told about his finger. I wish I could tell Hunter and Coop and Kiki and Eliot, but I promised Temmie I wouldn't.

I'm about halfway home when a car stops beside me. Unbelievably, it's Pierce. "Hop in," he calls. "I'll give you a ride."

No way am I getting in a car with him. "Thanks, I'm good."

He doesn't move. I pick up my pace. He drives ahead a little and pulls over, blocking my way. "Luna, I'm not kidding. Get in."

The casual tone of his first greeting has been replaced by something far more insistent. Even a little sinister. "I'd rather walk," I say. "Thanks anyway." *I've got to get out of here.*

And then I see it. He picks it up and aims it with one shaking hand. "Luna, dammit, I'll use this if I have to. Get in the fucking car."

Is this a nightmare? He's seriously pointing a gun at me? What can I possibly have that he wants? The shock that I fall into makes me more curious than scared. At first.

Like a zombie, I open the door and get in. I know I shouldn't; my God, I've seen enough true crime shows to know. That you don't get in the car. You run, you scream, you fight. *You don't get in the car.*

But I do.

"Gimme your phone." He grabs it and turns it off. Then he takes off, still holding the gun. And drives wildly way out of town, past Oak Hill. We pass no one. Sometimes cops hang out to catch speeders, but I know where the cops are. Investigating a burglary at the hardware store. No cop is going to be out here. Pierce is driving way too fast for me to open the door and jump out. I have never been so terrified in my life.

It's freezing in the car, but I am drenched in sweat. And then I feel another wetness, pooling out of me. *Oh, my God!* The stink of urine fills the car.

He careens down a muddy road, already riddled with potholes. *I'm gonna die. He's probably going to rape me then kill me. I am so stupid!* I think of Temmie. Hunter. Coop. Kiki. Eliot. Pastor Mark. Mrs. Pugh. Mr. D. The knitting women. The kids in Mr. D's class. The littles at Sunday school. The Teo Legacy Project. *I'm not ready to die!*

I have to make him talk. "Where are we—"

"Shut up!" he yells. "Just please shut up!"

His voice sounds weird. I look over and see tears streaming down his face. And then he's sobbing—huge, guttural howls of despair. I am so surprised that I just stare. "Pierce, what's wrong?"

He shakes his head. And keeps driving. Finally he pulls off into a tiny parking lot. I recognize it from Gretchen's taking us here. The Chateau de Glace. The perfect place to kill me because it's so remote.

He turns off the engine. "Luna, I am so sorry. I didn't mean to scare you. I just . . . I just needed to tell someone. Before I'm gone. Why."

"You didn't mean to scare me? *You have a gun!*"

"I know. I'm sorry. I have some clean sweats in the back. For you to . . . you know, if you want something dry. Although they're gonna be way too big. But you know, it's so cold out, and—"

"Pierce, what the hell is going on? What do you want? Why'd you kidnap me and take me out here?"

He gets out of the car and fumbles in the trunk. He comes around to my side of the car with a pair of black sweatpants. "Here. Put these on. I won't look. And here's a bag for your clothes."

I should run, but we're so far out in the boonies that I wouldn't be able to get help for miles. So I take off my soaked pants and underwear and put on the sweats. It's hard to do because my hands are shaking and I'm so cold. I ball up my clothes and put them in the plastic bag. *Now what?*

"You good?" he asks. He's standing on the other side of the car.

"No! What is going on?"

He reaches into the car and grabs the gun. Leaning against the hood, he twirls it in his fingers. I'm terrified that it's going to go off. He starts crying again. "God, Luna. I . . . I . . . I chose you because I trust you. And I think you get it. You know, what it's like to be different."

I nod. I am way too scared and confused to say anything.

"But everyone can see why you're different. So in a way it's easier. Like you can't hide it."

Hah! If only he knew how hard it was to look like me. "Are you . . . are you hiding something?"

"Yes. And I hate it. I've never told anyone. But it doesn't matter now, since it's almost over."

"Since what's almost over?"

"Me."

"Pierce, what are you talking about?"

"That gun wasn't meant to scare you. I got it for me. I'm going to do it at the castle, a place I love. You can drive my car back and explain."

Whoa. Is he for real? He's planning to kill himself? I am so far beyond understanding any of this. But I do know that I can't let him.

There is so much pain in his face that I can't help but walk closer to him. I've honestly never seen someone in such deep anguish.

"What is it, Pierce? That you're hiding?"

"I like . . . God! I can't even . . . fuck! I like . . . I like guys."

He's gay? But . . . but . . . this makes no sense.

"But it's okay to—"

He interrupts with a cry of agony. "*No, it's not okay!* All my life I've been raised by a Navy SEAL to be tough, to disparage sissies, to hate faggots. And I am what he hates!"

"Don't you think that if your father knew, he would like change? About you, I mean?"

"No. He'd disown me. Or kill me. Before anyone else found out."

"Oh, wow. Um, what about your mother? Maybe you could tell her first."

"It wouldn't matter. She's terrified of him. Probably from all the years of him using her as his punching bag."

Oh, God. "Whoa. That's awful. I'm so sorry."

We stand in silence. Then I summon up the nerve to ask. "Was it you who vandalized the church?"

He stops twirling the gun and stares at me. "How on earth did you figure that out?"

"I saw your finger. At the minimart."

"Wow. You're observant. Yeah, Dad thought it would serve them right. And I went along with it. To please him."

"Serve who right?"

"The minister. Mr. D. And his partner. And I guess everyone in town who had anything to do with the wedding."

"You know they still got married, right? And lots of us were there to support them. Like we would for you if you got married."

"Hah! Not gonna happen. Ever."

"It could, Pierce. And you don't always have to live where your parents do. You could move to a city where you'd have more freedom. And privacy."

"Whatever. It's just easier for everyone this way."

He's serious. I need to get the gun from him. But if I try to yank it away, it could go off. Killing him or me. *Think!*

"Not for everyone who loves you."

He just shrugs his shoulders. "Conditional love is too hard."

I need to keep him talking. "Why do you hate the Teo Legacy Project so much?"

To my surprise, the tears pour out even faster. He wails, "Phoebe!"

"Who's Phoebe?"

He's crying so hard he can barely talk. "Phoebe was . . . was . . . my baby sister. So beauti-beauti-ful and per-per-fect. She was only three."

"What happened?"

"She fell off the tractor. Dad didn't see her. And backed over her. And no one did anything to honor *her* memory. There was no Phoebe Legacy Project. Nothing. And my parents are so fucking broken by it, they won't even mention her. Oh, my God, I miss her so much!"

I've never heard this story. "How old were you?"

"Twelve. We lived in Virginia then. That's why we moved to Maine. To escape. But it like haunts me all the time."

"Oh, Pierce, I am so sorry."

He's hunched over in grief, and I just want to hug him. But he's still holding the gun.

"My life is so fucked up. Our family has never been good again. Since Phoebe died. And I'm a jerk to everyone because it feels like there's a volcano in me just waiting to explode."

"People can help you."

"That just shows I'm weak."

"You don't think your dad is grieving inside? But he has this like macho exterior, and he takes out his anger and frustration and sadness on you and your mom. Is that who you want to be?"

He wipes his whole face on the sleeve of his hoodie. And looks me straight in the eyes. "No. But it's too late. That's who I am."

"Yeah, on the outside. But that's not really you. If you'd let people know the inside, you'd be a lot happier. I mean, God, look at me. You may not know this 'cause you moved here later, but my mother was a druggie. And gave me up so she could keep using. I spent my whole life hiding, hating myself, blaming myself. And only now am I finally starting to make friends and get out of that darkness. Let my inside show. And you've got to, too. You could talk to Mr. D, for one. He has family members who won't have anything to do with him because he's gay. So he could totally relate to your experience. And I bet Teo's mother would appreciate someone talking to her about losing a young child, 'cause you actually know what it's like."

He twirls the gun slowly. And it looks like he's thinking about what I said. "It's way too late to start over."

Is he considering it? "No, it's not, Pierce. I am. And yeah, it's really hard. And there are so many times that I just want to give up. But I'm trying not to quit, not be like my mother. And you don't have to be like your father. Please, will you just talk to Mr. D and Teo's mom? They're really good people. And they would totally get you."

"Shit. I've screwed up big-time. Hate crime. Defacing church property. Armed abduction. I could go to jail for this. I would seriously rather be dead."

"No one has to know. Just let me text my aunt so she doesn't freak out. I'll tell her where I am and not to worry."

"That's all? You promise not to tell her I forced you at gunpoint?"

"Not if you promise to get help."

"What about the gun? I stole it from my father's safe at the store."

"Yeah, I think he called the cops. Did you, like, break into the safe or use the combination? 'Cause I assume he'll know it's you if it's not busted, right?"

"I used the combination. But then I bashed it to make it look like a break-in. Shit."

"Maybe if you told him why, he'd be more concerned about you than about the stupid gun."

"I can't. I just can't. He's . . . he's . . . I just can't. I don't even know why he keeps a gun at the store. It's not like he's ever needed to use it."

I'm not sure how many laws I'm breaking, but I really don't want him to have access to a gun. "Let's just get rid of it. Again, no one has to know. I'm good at keeping secrets."

He lets me get my phone. I send a quick text to Temmie. "Let's hike to the castle," I suggest.

It's the weirdest walk of my life. I don't know how intent on suicide he was, or still is, but it seems like he just needed to tell someone about this poison that's slowly eating him up from the inside.

I take lots of pictures of the frozen waterfall and send two to Temmie. We climb up to the top of the castle. The perfect place to get rid of a gun. When the ice melts, there will be so much water gushing through here, no one could ever find it. "How about throwing it off right here?"

"He'll kill me if he finds out."

"He won't find out. I already promised."

Pierce winds up and throws it, hard. It flies way out over the ice and lands in a part of the river that is already starting to thaw. It falls through a hole and disappears.

And then he turns to me, sobbing again. I wrap my arms around him. We stand there, both of us crying, for a long time.

72
HUNTER

Ever since Luna got in trouble with Temmie the day of Mr. D's wedding, we've been hanging out at her house in the evenings. It's warm and fun, and there's always food. We play cards and Rummikub and Catchphrase. Sometimes we pool our ingredients and bake dessert. Usually it's me, Coop, Kiki, and Eliot. Often Nate and Josh and Shea join us. Twice Austin and Gordon and Beth have come. And, weirdly, Pierce. Who is way more chill now. I still don't know what his problem was all year, but he's changed. Temmie makes us finish our homework before we listen to music or play games or watch a movie. Then, at ten o'clock sharp, she shoos us all out.

Yeah, so life at Luna's is calm and predictable. Dad is still drinking, which means life at my house is exactly the opposite. Tense. Chaotic. Unpredictable. When Coop drops me at home tonight, the house is dark and cold. Dad is definitely not home, though he must have been sometime today, 'cause the kitchen is a mess. The counters are littered with empty beer cans, and the remains of scrambled eggs are stuck in a frying pan. Garbage spills out of the kitchen wastebasket, and bananas are rotting on a shelf. I swear the place was neat this morning when I went to school. *How did it get this bad?*

I set right in, scrubbing and mopping and throwing crap away. Under a greasy paper towel, I find Dad's phone. Dead. I wipe it off and plug it in.

I keep listening for Dad's truck as I clean. The later it gets, the more worried I am, and the more frenzied is my cleaning. I dust and polish furniture and Windex the windows. At midnight the house is spotless. Still no Dad. Reluctantly, I call the bar. The bartender says he wasn't in tonight. I sit on the couch, wrap myself in a quilt, and wait. And I guess I fall asleep.

In my dream, we are playing in the Final Four. Someone keeps pounding on the bleachers and screaming, "Open! Open up!" I think they're yelling for me to move, get open for a pass, so I do. And then I crash into Josh and fall down. The pounding continues.

It takes me a long time to pull myself out of the gym and into my living room. Someone is knocking on our front door. Like really loud. I stumble to the door and open it. Two cops are standing there. I recognize one from the night we were at the station.

"Hunter Ridley?"

It feels like someone is smashing a board on my chest. I squint at them. *Why are they here*? "Yeah. Yes, I'm Hunter."

"Can we come in?"

"Um, yeah."

They sit at the kitchen table and motion for me to sit. "Officer Justice, Officer Wang. It's about your father, son," one of them says softly.

Oh, no, oh, no, oh, no.

"Is he all right?"

They look at each other. "Do you . . . do you know where he was headed last night?"

"Um, no. I mean, I was at a friend's house until ten o'clock. He was gone when I came home. What time is it?"

The one from the station, Officer Justice, nods. "It's 6:40 in the morning. Do you know if your dad was drinking?"

"I . . . I assume so. I mean, there were empty beer cans on the counter. But he didn't go to the bar. I checked. So where is he?"

Officer Wang gives me a sad look. "Do you have family in town?"

"Uh, my aunt. Why?"

"Could we have her number?"

Why won't they answer my questions?

I grab my phone and find Gretchen's number. "Here."

Officer Justice copies it.

"Why? Where's my dad?"

Officer Wang reaches out and puts her hand on my arm. "We are so sorry, Hunter, but your father was found in a field about three miles from here. By someone walking her dog."

"Found? What do you mean, found? Like he was passed out? Where is he now?"

Officer Justice clears his throat. "He's dead, son."

Dead? My father? Dad? Dad's not dead! He'll be home any minute!

"We think he died of hypothermia," says Officer Wang. "Exacerbated by excessive intake of alcohol."

I hear a scream that sounds like it's coming from a wounded wolf. It won't stop. It gets louder and louder and then everything turns black.

I wake up on the couch. Gretchen is sitting in a chair next to me, gently stroking the top of my head. The cops are still in the kitchen.

And then I am sobbing. "Daddy*! Daddy! I need you, Daddy!*"

73
LUNA

After the funeral, Hunter asks me, Coop, Nate, Josh, and Kiki if we can spend the night with him at his aunt's house. Temmie lets me. She is really broken up about his dad, what it means for Hunter to be an orphan. Ever since that trip to the Chateau de Glace, she and Gretchen have become good friends. Thank God Gretchen can lean on Temmie now.

Temmie and a bunch of women are upstairs with Gretchen while we hang in the basement. We're just chilling, listening to music and talking about his dad. The guys knew him well from years of being on the same basketball team. They have funny stories, mostly about getting in trouble. I learn a lot about his dad. Like how he was recruited by some powerhouse basketball colleges but had to get a job in the mill to help support his family instead. How he proposed to Hunter's mother at the top of Mount Katahdin in a snowstorm in

June. How he won Employee of the Year four times at the mill. How he loved to draw and would include a little sketch on a sticky note in Hunter's lunchbox every single day of elementary school.

Hunter looks at me and Kiki. "I wish you had known my dad a long time ago. When he wasn't the town drunk."

"I love hearing these stories," I say. "It's like I only knew him in black and white, and now the movie has totally transformed into color. Three-dimensional. With music."

"Yeah."

"I didn't know him well," says Kiki, "but my family never called him the town drunk. They knew him as the man who did an amazing job as a single dad. And the guy who knew so much about basketball. But he was a lot more than that. It honestly sounds like he was an awesome, talented, multidimensional man. Who loved you so much."

"I hate what alcohol did to him," says Coop. "He was such a good guy."

"And geez, he was devoted to you," says Nate. "He used to be at every single one of your games, no matter how far he had to drive to get there."

Tears start running down Hunter's cheeks. "Until he started drinking. And what the fuck was he doing out in that field? Passed out next to a bunch of logs and a falling-down fence? With his truck only one hundred yards away?"

"It was a massive fuckup," says Josh finally, "that never should have happened. Just a horrible accident."

We are silent for a while.

"One of my favorite memories," says Nate, "is winning the state semifinals this year. Your dad was frickin' ecstatic. Remember that interview? My dad has it on video. I'll send it to you."

Hunter wipes his face. "Yeah. That was awesome. He wasn't drinking then. I just don't get why he started again."

"It's an illness," I say quietly, "that some people can recover from and others can't. Like your dad. And my mom."

The others look at me in surprise. Because I never talk about her. And definitely not this openly. "I used to think that she chose drugs over me. But now, I'm beginning to understand that there's not always a choice. Like my mom and your dad wouldn't have chosen drugs and alcohol over us if they weren't already addicted. It makes me sadder than ever for them. And for us."

Hunter reaches over and takes my hand. Kiki puts hers on top of Hunter's. Then Coop covers Kiki's with his. And Josh and Nate reach in their hands to cover Coop's. And we just sit there like that. Holding on. Holding on. Holding on.

74
HUNTER

I didn't think I could survive. The first three days were unbearable, like I was stuck in this bizarre nightmare and couldn't get out of it. And then, when I finally understood that this reality wasn't going anywhere, that I wasn't waking up from it, an overwhelming sadness just engulfed me. There were days when I hurt so bad I could barely function. Those days still happen, but slowly I am able to edge past the wall of grief that envelops me.

I live with Gretchen now, in her house that's close to town. She keeps me super busy, which is her way of trying to deal with both her mourning and mine. She says we'll fix up Dad's house and sell it this summer. She insists that I go to college in a year; we'll use the money from the house sale to pay for it. Or at least part of it. Several coaches from Division 3 schools have already sent recruiting letters for basketball. I used to just throw them away because I didn't think

I could ever afford college. Now I know that's a possibility. It's kind of surreal.

I wish my dad had had the same opportunity. And I wish he could see me play in college.

Today Gretchen greets me at breakfast with a wrapped box. "I know it's not your birthday, but I thought you'd appreciate these now."

She must have heard me crying last night. I just miss him so much.

I tear off the paper. First I come to an envelope. Inside is a brief note: *You are registered for driver's education lessons. They start next week.*

"Really? Hah! Wait till I tell Coop!"

"Oh, believe me, he already knows. It was his idea."

I reach down in the box and pull out four books. Each is labeled "HUNTER, MY HUNTER." I open the first. It is filled with photos of me and my dad when I was a baby. And between the pictures are sketches and little stories, written in his hand. I am speechless. I swear, I've never seen these pictures. I turn the pages slowly. There's me in a pirate costume, complete with an eye patch and a hook for a hand. *Four years old. Your first time trick-or-treating at the town's trunk-and-treat event. You were far more fascinated by a little girl named Shea, dressed as a ladybug, than in getting candy. At the end of the night, you gave Shea your hook as a token of your admiration. She gave you three pieces of candy corn.*

There's one of me in Dad's arms. My face is beet red, one eye swollen shut, and I'm screaming. *Your Aunt Gretchen took this of us. We were picking raspberries when you were stung by a bee, right on your eyelid. You refused to eat raspberries for a long time after that.*

My hands tremble as I leaf through the pages. I'm sort of like gobbling up all of these memories. The books are organized by age. When I reach the last page of the first one, I give a little cry. Gretchen leans over to look. It's me in little blue swim shorts, my back to the camera, wading in a pond. In front of me are pine trees, beyond them are mountains.

Gretchen laughs. "I was there when he took that! Oh, that water was frigid! But you loved it."

"This is . . . this is . . . the *Made in Maine* logo! That he drew!"

And then I am a mess again. And Gretchen's there to hold me.

When I finally calm down, she tells me, "He worked for years on these. For your eighteenth birthday."

We sit for a solid hour going through the four volumes. Me with a fishing pole. Me with my new firefighter backpack. Me and Dad in front of a tent. Me sitting in the driver's seat of Dad's new pickup, barely tall enough to see out the window. Me and Josh and Nate and Coop, sitting on sleds in snow pants, gathered around the kitchen table with a birthday cake in the center, in basketball uniforms with medals around our necks. And so many notes of silly little things I did and said, things that would be long forgotten if he hadn't documented them.

There are even, to my complete surprise, several pictures of Mom.

At the end of the most recent one are several blank pages.

I will fill them, starting with a photo of me and Dad at the end of the semifinal basketball game.

I put the books on the shelf right next to my bed. Where I can look at them. And where, even though it sounds kind of weird, I feel like Dad and Mom are there with me when I sleep.

75
LUNA

Hunter asks me if I'll go with him to visit Teo's mom after school.

"What, are you hungry?" I tease.

"Well, she invited me . . . us . . . over to talk about my dad and the project. So I do expect there will be cookies." He winks at me. "It would be terribly rude not to eat them, right?"

I channel Jane Austen. "Oh, inexcusably so. Unthinkably boorish."

It's warm enough on the walk over to go without a hat and mittens. Puddles and mud mark the disappearing snow. Our feet are soaked by the time we arrive at Ms. Callahan's.

She envelops us both in a warm hug.

Nobody says anything.

Nobody needs to.

We gather around the kitchen table. Ms. Callahan places a plate towering with butterscotch oatmeal cookies in the center. Hunter devours three before lifting his head. "Today is the first time I've actually felt hungry," he says. "Ever since Dad died, I've had zero appetite."

Ms. Callahan pours another glass of milk and puts it in front of him. "I know what you mean. It feels like you can't breathe, much less eat. Tell me about him."

Hunter starts with the drawings that covered his bedroom wall. Then he segues into the photo books his dad made. And camping trips. Basketball. Sunday-morning blueberry pancakes. Chores always accompanied by soundtracks to Broadway musicals blasting through the house. Learning how to chop and stack wood. Making Christmas sugar cookies for the neighbors. And then some of the bad stuff. The drinking days. The abuse.

"It's a small town, but I didn't know your father. How I wish I had! But you know, knowing who you are helps me to know who he was. I love that most of your memories are such happy ones, honey. Because it's those that are going to sustain you."

We sit in peaceful silence. Finally Ms. Callahan gets up to put another log in the stove.

"The fashion show starts tomorrow in New York," Ms. Callahan says. "We're having an official premiere of the video at the library on Thursday at one o'clock. In the community room. You guys are coming, yes? Ludovic said he's already gotten permission for an educational field trip to the library for your whole class."

We nod. I'm a little nervous to see what Drew did with it. Nervous and excited.

"I can't wait for people in New York to see your sweater," I say. "It's stunning."

"Thanks, Luna. All of those sweaters are. Such a wonderful project."

I know Temmie is really pleased with how her sweater turned out. What's wild is to think of the trade, that every stitch meant another splash in the pool.

Ms. Callahan clears her throat. Twice. Then gives Hunter a funny look. "What are you waiting for?"

Hunter stands up and gets his backpack. He takes a deep breath and looks at me. "Okay. Promise you won't laugh."

"Um, what? Laugh at what?"

He reaches into his pack and pulls out a wrapped package. "This is from Miz Callahan and me," he says.

For me? No one except for Temmie has ever given me a present. Ever. I slide my fingers under the tape and pull back the paper. Lying there is a soft bag made of ocean blue wool. *What on earth?*

Hunter looks like he is hyperventilating. "Do you . . . do you like it? Miz Callahan and I made it! It's a bag for your lunches!" He's talking so quickly I can barely understand him. "Or I guess you could use it for, like, books or maybe your dance shoes or, um. You know, like, I'm not the best knitter, but Miz Callahan taught me and helped a lot, and I now I'm really into it and I don't know, I just thought, um—"

"I love it," I say, wiping a tear from my cheek. My throat feels so swollen it's hard to get the words out. "It's beautiful. I can't believe you made this!"

The relief on his face is so obvious that Ms. Callahan bursts out laughing. And then I'm laughing too, while tears keep streaming down my face. I'm not sure he'll ever know how much this means to me. It's my mother's wool. He knew. In a way that no one except maybe Temmie and Ms. Callahan can ever understand. *Who does that? For me?*

The sun is low in the sky when we finally stand up to leave. Ms. Callahan insists that we take the leftover cookies with us. "I'll make more for the premiere," she assures us. "Hunter, will you grab some Ziploc bags from the pantry? They're on the second shelf from the top. On your right."

Hunter disappears into the pantry.

After a minute, Ms. Callahan calls, "Hunter? You find them?"

He slowly reappears, holding a green baseball hat. His face is white. "Where did you . . . why is this in your pantry?"

She sees how shaken he is. "Why, what's wrong? I found that a while ago. Lying behind my woodpile. That someone stacked for me."

Hunter can barely speak. "This . . . this was my dad's." He swallows, hard. "From a basketball tournament in Massachusetts when I was in middle school."

Ms. Callahan falls heavily into her chair. She has turned as pale as Hunter. "Oh, my sweet boy. Have you heard about the Sunset Samaritan?"

76
HUNTER

I haven't been on a field trip in years. It feels like we're in second grade, marching in partners to visit our local dentist. There's the same air of festive anticipation, only the stakes are way higher than learning about the importance of flossing.

We crowd into the library and realize that there are so many people already assembled, there's no way we'll fit into the Community Room. Mr. D sends us all back outside to wait while the librarian finds a better meeting space. In five minutes, Mr. D comes back out and leads us over to the church. "Pastor Mark said the sanctuary is available. Good thing too. I never dreamed this many people would show up!"

People stream into the church. They hang their jackets in the coatroom and swarm into the sanctuary. By 1:20 the pews are packed. Mr. D asks us to wait to sit until everyone else has a seat. We help

Pastor Mark set up folding chairs along the sides and in the back of the sanctuary. And people keep coming in. When we run out of chairs, people just stand. The buzz and the crowd make it feel like Christmas Eve.

I spy Officer Wang, who also serves as the town fire marshal, approach Pastor Mark. "Normally, I'd never allow this," she says. "But I'll make an exception this once. Could you say a little prayer for safety? I assume you got a direct line to the Omnipotent One."

A very old woman stands up at the front, and the sanctuary quiets down. Pastor Mark hands her a microphone, which she holds kind of gingerly. "Oh, my. Welcome to everybody. Thank you, Mark, for letting what we thought would be just our knitting group and Mr. Deboncoeur's class and maybe a few friends invade your space.

"My name is Barbara, and I represent the women's knitting group. This is a celebration of one part of the Teo Legacy Project, which began with Mr. Deboncoeur's history class and grew to include lots more people."

She asks Mr. D and another knitter and Gustav and Jessica to speak. To a person, they are humble and brief. Then a woman who Jessica introduces as Cheri Reina steps to the microphone. "I just flew in from New York," she says, "where I was marketing a line of women's winter jackets at a fashion show. I wanted to let you know that the video you made was amazing. People loved it. Not only did your sweaters sell at auction—I won't tell you for how much now, but I will say that you'll easily be able to have that pool open for lessons—but several companies asked if you would do it again next year."

The wild applause takes several minutes to die down. I look down the row of kids standing next to me—Coop, Josh, Eliot, Kiki, Pierce, Nate, Luna, Shea, Austin, Beth, and Gordon—and I'm overcome with emotion. We all look at each other in like wonder. Coop is cruising up and down the row, high-fiving everyone. "We did it! We frickin' did it!"

Pastor Mark and Mr. D pull a large screen to the middle of the chancel. Then Mark runs back and cues the video.

And we wait.

77
MADE IN MAINE

Soft music plays. Scene opens with a bull moose standing in the snow. It turns and lumbers into the forest. The camera follows, as if going into the woods, then slowly fades back out to reveal a pond in front of the pine trees with mountains in the background. A small boy in blue swim shorts stands knee-deep in the water. The words "MADE IN MAINE" appear, superimposed over the image. Music and picture fade.

A picture pops up of Teo, a little boy with a huge smile, with his arms wrapped around his mother's neck. Strains of "You are My Sunshine" accompany the text, which explains the Teo Legacy Project.

The action begins with a snowy hockey game on a frozen pond. The sound of skate blades scraping the ice and players calling to each other fades when an older woman's voice takes over.

"I'm Barbara. I remember skating here when I was a girl, oh, my, more than eighty years ago. I met my husband here, actually. He couldn't

afford skates, so he borrowed my brother's. My brother always took credit for our getting married."

The game stops while a player digs in a snowbank for the lost puck. The camera zooms in on Hunter, a tall young man whose cheeks are red with cold. He is wearing a gray sweater that features streaks of orange and yellow on the front. He turns on his skates. The back of his sweater is a darker gray, almost black. It is streaked with dark tangerine, reds, purples.

"This sweater is called Ecclesiastes 3. That's the passage that reminds us there is a time to be born and a time to die. Oh, dear, I hope that's not too morbid. Do you think that's too morbid? At my age you think a lot about dying. But I watch that young lad whipping around on the ice, and it reminds me of my youth. There's hope in the sunrise and peace in the sunset."

Just then Hunter receives a pass and races to the goal. Another boy checks him, and he falls. Sitting on the ice, he throws his head back and laughs. Barbara's voice returns. "Oh, to be young! Their energy. It's something, isn't it?"

The next scene features Beth standing next to Ruth, who huddles under a blanket in a wheelchair. They are talking about theater. Beth throws two logs onto the nearby fire. She wears a sweater that is a study in blues and whites. She picks up another log then slowly twirls before throwing it onto the blaze. "Tell me about this sweater," she says.

Ruth wraps her scarf more tightly around her neck. "I named it the Chateau de Glace," she says. "It was inspired by a natural ice castle in our town. Winters are hard in Maine, as they are in many places all over the world. But there is beauty in the bleakness. Nature's way of making the long, cold, dark season more bearable."

Subsequent scenes are shot of the knitters and the students—drinking cocoa, sledding, engaging in a snowball fight, or chopping wood—each one featuring another sweater and the knitter's story.

The videographer's voice returns. "The final sweater in the show was knitted by Bridget Callahan, mother to Teo and friend to everyone, it seems, in the entire town of Edgewater."

Bridget's sweater is on the slight figure of Eliot, who is pulling a red sled up the hill. The camera zooms in on his back. The background of the sweater is black. Rising up from the waist are white tree trunks, flecked with black. Eliot climbs steadily up in the falling snow. There is no sound until Bridget's voice quietly emerges. "My sweater is titled 'Birch Trees in Moonlight,' she says. "I chose to create this scene as a way to heal from the loss of my beloved son. There is a bird feeder in the birch tree outside my bedroom window. And every day in those dark, horrible weeks after Teo drowned, a cardinal at the feeder was my reason for living.

"In the Celtic tradition, the birch tree is sacred and believed to have protective powers. It is a symbol of rebirth. Birch trees thrive in harsh conditions, and they are the first to regrow after a forest fire. I am forever grateful to—" She is too choked up to finish. "Sorry. It's just that . . . people have been so—" She stops again. A few moments later, she resumes, her voice raw with emotion. "I have that one beautiful birch tree in my yard," she says. "I just never realized that I was surrounded by birch trees."

The camera slowly pans away from the group around the fire. The hills and mountains in the background grow smaller and smaller, and finally there is simply a dot on the screen. The dot disappears.

And then appear the three words: "MADE IN MAINE."

EPILOGUE

LUNA

Hunter and I go like once a week to the cemetery, just to hang out and talk to his dad. Hunter always fills him in on the latest news, like getting his license and talking to college coaches. And about getting certified to teach swimming lessons. And about Mr. D hiring Ms. Callahan to work with him at the converted mill. And having Pierce join our friend group.

It sounds weird, I know, but talking to his dad is actually kind of peaceful. The grave is on a hill with an amazing view of the mountains. Sometimes we just sit there in silence, listening to the birds and feeling the breeze. Once we went in a pouring rainstorm and ran around, getting soaked, screaming and crying and laughing and letting our tears mix with the rain.

Today we listen to a country music station on the way home. And I have a bizarre idea. "Let's write one."

"One what?"

"A country music song. About this year. Our town."

He grins at me. "Uh, why?"

I don't know where this comes from, but I blurt it out. "So we can perform it in the talent show at next year's Lodge Party. Coop on drums, Kiki on ukulele, you and me harmonizing."

I wait for him to say I'm crazy. 'Cause that's what I'm thinking.

Sing?

In front of a crowd?

Me?

"You're crazy," he says. "But I'll do it. Don't tell Josh and Nate. They're gonna be blown away."

He pulls his aunt's ancient Volkswagen over and turns off the engine. I dig into my blue bag for a notebook. We sit on the shoulder of the dirt road, enjoying the breeze blowing through the windows, and try to compose a song. We scribble and cross out and rewrite and argue. "Technically, it wasn't a holiday ball," he says.

"Well, yeah, but can you come up with a rhyme for Lodge Party?"

"Uh, no. Fine, call it a ball."

"Find a rhyming dictionary on your phone," I say. "We need a rhyme for volleyball," I say.

"Okay, just a sec." He studies the screen. "Um... got it! Cholesterol!"

"Really? *Cholesterol?*"

"Okay, then, Crabby Pants, how 'bout 'conference call'?"

"Oh. My. God. Have you ever even listened to country music?"

He starts laughing and I whack him with my notebook. Eventually, we finish the song.

Gotta Give a Damn

The holiday ball was free for all, but the actual cost like Eden's fall.
You mix volleyball and alcohol, cannonballs, they hurt us all.

Chorus:
Ask a bunch of guys, how do you rise? When the mill closes, it's your demise.
When your lives capsize and there ain't no prize, that little thing called hope, it dies.
A town can't be resuscitated, so it just stays intoxicated.
The river is contaminated, all hope, it's done evacuated.

Hard to keep your pride and be dignified when you feel like you been cast aside.
Ain't nothin' in the classifieds, so you start thinkin' suicide.
(Chorus)

Well, life it must be fair out there somewhere, but here it's just a damn nightmare.
The dark despair ain't goin' nowhere, no solace in the good Lord's Prayer.
(Chorus)

Been scarred and scared, your bodies bared, some damage just can't be repaired.
So unprepared for those who dared to give a rip, to say they cared.
(Chorus)

Bridge: I'm wonderin' if anybody gives a damn?
. . . 'Bout who I am? . . . 'Bout who I am?

Then wool from a lamb and blueberry jam means you're not just a battering ram.
The depression was a traffic jam, but now somebody gives a damn.
(Chorus)

When times are tough, the goin's rough, you gotta call the devil's bluff.
Your hands ain't cuffed, reach in your stuff to give a damn, 'cause that's enough.

DISCUSSION QUESTIONS/ THOUGHTS TO PONDER

1. The issue of abandonment is prevalent in the novel. How does this color Luna's view of herself? How does it affect Ludovic Deboncoeur? What does it mean for the town after the mill closes?

2. Some might argue that Luna and Teo are abandoned or rejected by their biological parents; others see them being placed with adoptive mothers as a gift. What do you think? Temmie Lemieux, Bridget Callahan and Gretchen Ridley all become adoptive mothers without ever seeking the position. What does this say about their characters?

3. Discuss the impact of addiction in the plot of the novel. How do social or sport drinking and drug use become debilitating and destructive?

4. What role does social media play in the novel? How does it affect Hunter, Mr. D, Emma and others? What role does it have in your life?

5. How does place become a character in this novel?

6. Does the place where you live have an annual communal gathering such as the Lodge Party? What is its purpose? Does it survive simply because of tradition?

7. What do you think of the 4-3-2-1 Challenge? Does the element of danger contribute to the fun? Would you participate in this one?

8. Pierce is a complex character, driven by shame and failure to live up to his father's expectations. Once you know his backstory, does your view of him and his father change?

9. Pastor Mark's decision to conduct a gay wedding is not universally embraced by his parishioners. Knowing he is losing a longtime parishioner and financial contributor because of this decision, why does he proceed with it?

10. Emma and her minions are present in many schools, workplaces, and other social gatherings. What motivates them? What gives them power?

11. With which character do you most identify? Why?

12. There lies a fine line between hope and despair. Several characters rebound back and forth between these emotions throughout the novel. How does the Teo Legacy Project contribute to providing hope? Whom does it help?

ACKNOWLEDGEMENTS

Bring me all of your dreams,
You dreamers,
Bring me all of your
Heart melodies
That I may wrap them
In a blue cloud-cloth
Away from the too-rough fingers
Of the world.

Langston Hughes, The Dream Keeper

I am deeply grateful to those who believed in this dream and helped to wrap it in our own blue cloud-cloth.

To the visionaries at When Words Count, thank you. Steve Eisner, your kindness and interest began this journey. Your team of Barb Newman, Amber Griffith, Athen Desautels, Asha Hossain and Peggy Moran supported me in ways far beyond my expectations. From accompanying me as I sang in public (me!) and creating covers on the fly, to finding knitting venues and really listening to me, you were amazing.

Ben Tanzer, Colin Hosten and Marilyn Atlas, you saw a novel hiding in my first draft that I didn't. You were right, you were right, you were right. How much I appreciate your wisdom and enthusiasm!

To my WWC mates, Alison McBain, Rebecca Lowry Warchut, Amy Bleu and Julie Cadman, shine on and on. I was blown away by both your talent and the generosity of your spirit.

To David LeGere and the entire team at Woodhall Press, thank you for welcoming the heart melodies. Dreams live on because of you.

Sincere gratitude to the Grosse Pointe Public Library and Grosse Pointe Theatre for supporting and encouraging writers. I am well aware of the hundreds of volunteer hours that went into those contests. Karen Pratt, Joan Hall and Victoria Hill, your writing never ceased to impress and entertain me. How I miss our group!

Cyndy Lambert, a kindred spirit and fellow writer, thank you for reading my first draft. I hope Quinn will star in this movie.

To my colleagues at the Davidson College Office of Alumni and Family Engagement, your exuberance makes me smile every day.

Growing up in a home filled with books and love (and no television) was a gift for which I shall forever be grateful. My apologies to my genteel parents for the oft profane language in this novel, but I know they are cheering me on from heaven, as they always did on Earth.

Thank you, Jan, Scott, Thor and Nord, for your remarkable and constant support as siblings and fellow lovers of literature. Some of my fondest memories of childhood are those we spent reading together.

The encouragement I've received from dear friends is overwhelming. From the WFS and Pink House crew to the LLC and DCPC, you have buoyed my spirits and warmed my heart.

A Knightly shout-out to my University Liggett School students, whose enthusiasm for my "starter novel," *Shooting for Gold: Mystery at the Winter Olympics*, kept me writing.

To librarians and teachers of writing everywhere, know that your work is extremely important. You are making a difference, one book and one student at a time.

Finally, to my husband, Peter, and our children: Atticus, Haven and Whittier, you are forever wrapped in my own cloud-cloth, which is bursting with love. Your support through this journey has meant more than perhaps you'll ever know.

ABOUT THE AUTHOR

Shawn Samuelson Henry grew up in Hanover, New Hampshire, where trips to the library were as exciting as those to the Dartmouth Skiway. After earning degrees from Bucknell University, Harvard University and the University of Wyoming, Shawn taught English to teenagers for more than a decade. In the summers she led young adults on backpacking and bicycling trips in New England, Colorado and the Pacific Northwest. As a children's librarian, she wrote her first middle-grade novel about a blood-doping scandal at the winter Olympics solely for the purpose of entertaining her students. Having lived in small towns and big cities in eleven states and three countries abroad, she has a keen awareness of the universal humanity that binds people across the globe. Shawn is an avid playwright whose plays have won competitions and been produced across the United States and Canada. Shawn currently lives in Davidson, North Carolina, with her husband and three children.